FUSED

LEGACY OF MAGIC
BOOK 6

LINDSAY BUROKER

ACKNOWLEDGMENTS

Thank you, elf, dragon, and half-dwarf fans for following along with my Legacy of Magic books. You're about to dive into the longest novel of the series, and I hope you'll find it a satisfying adventure.

Before you get started, let me thank my beta readers, Sarah Engelke and Cindy Wilkinson, for their help throughout. Also, thanks to my editor, Shelley Holloway, who's been with me for more than ten years now. Thank you, also, to my audiobook narrator, Vivienne Leheny, the voice of Matti, Val, Zavryd, Sarrlevi, and —of course—the goblins. Lastly, thank you to Gene Mollica Studio for the cover art for this series. Happy reading!

1

"OH, I KNOW." VAL GRINNED BACK AT ME, HER BLONDE BRAID whipping in the wind. "It could be shaped like a *sword*."

"Your new mailbox?" I did my best to focus on her instead of the lush temperate rainforest below—the rainforest filled with millions of tall, pointy trees that would impale a foolish half-dwarf who fell on them. Even though our ride, the dragon Zavryd, flapped his wings sedately as we zigzagged back and forth over the northern end of the Olympic Peninsula, thoughts of falling were never far from my mind. Dwarves, even *half*-dwarves, were not meant for heights.

"Yes," Val said. "You haven't started it yet, right? Is there still time for design modifications?"

I *had* started the mailbox project, but the post and container were made from metal, which I could alter easily enough with my enchanting magic. Even if it *hadn't* been easy, I would have agreed to as many design modifications as Val wished. After all the favors she and her black-scaled mate had done for me, I owed her as many home improvements as she wished.

"Sure."

"The post could look like a sword blade, and there could be a big cross hilt that holds the mailbox. Or maybe the cross could even *be* the mailbox. Hm, that might not look balanced though."

"I know how important aesthetics are to you," I said, thinking of the garish mushrooms forming a working fairy ring in Val's front yard, not to mention the dragon-shaped topiaries guarding the perimeter. Those weren't garish, but the glowing eyes and smoking nostrils terrified innocent moms with strollers who had to walk past the property on their neighborhood loop.

"Hey, my house looks good. Zav is an excellent remodeler." Val patted his scaled back.

Zavryd, who was focused on searching the wilds below for signs of the dragon magic that he and Xilneth had sensed a few days earlier, hadn't been participating in our mailbox conversation. It was possible his focus wasn't the *only* reason he hadn't been participating.

Dragons do not usually deign to employ their powerful magic for the purpose of crafting abodes, Zavryd told us telepathically, *especially since my kind prefer natural caves to fussy dwellings, but I did wish my mate to be happy in our lair.*

"And your mate appreciates that very much." Val patted him again.

"I'm surprised you don't have a cave on your property," I said.

Maybe there wasn't room. A large chunk of the backyard was taken up by the combination hot-tub/sauna/steam-room that a clan of goblins had given the couple as a wedding present.

Val held a finger to her lips. "Trust me, we've discussed it. For the moment, I've convinced Zav that the *man cave* in the attic is sufficient for his needs."

I hadn't seen their attic, but it was hard to imagine theater seating, a giant TV, and a beer tap. Instead, I envisioned faux rock walls, a burbling pool, and meat smokers lined up along the wall.

"For my mailbox," Val said, "I'm picturing it thrusting into the grass between the sidewalk and the curb like the *Sword in the Stone*."

"The *Mailbox in the Median*?"

"Exactly. And I'm sure you know it needs to be sturdy."

On Earth, the grassy strip between the carriageway and the sidewalk is called the road verge, Zavryd informed us.

I raised my eyebrows, surprised someone who referred to meat loaves as *meat cubes* would know that.

"He's re-read the dictionary recently," Val explained. "He said our words change meanings with alarming frequency to a long-lived individual."

"That's probably true."

"His dictionary interest was prompted by a conversation with Amber, which he followed very little of." Val lowered her voice. "I didn't have the heart to tell him that he would be better off consulting the Urban Dictionary than Merriam-Webster."

"*I* need to consult the Urban Dictionary when I talk with your daughter." I made myself lean to the side to peer down at Crescent Lake with Highway 101 meandering along one side. A handful of cars drove along it, their passengers probably on their way to Forks to look for vampire paraphernalia. Little did they know that the Washington State vampires congregated in Val's basement in Green Lake.

"Does that mean you'll have trouble communicating with her if I succeed in getting her to take that job with you?"

"Nope. I'll hand her things and point to where she can carry them. No words need be exchanged."

"It's strange that she's balking at this job."

"I think so." I pointed toward the snowy peaks of the Olympic Mountains, the atypically sunny day highlighting their stark contrast to the green forest. "Don't you think we should search more in that direction? If the organization that's kidnapped my parents has been hanging out with a dragon, they've probably got their hideout in a cave, right?"

Even though the Olympic Peninsula wasn't anywhere near as populated as the east side of Puget Sound, I couldn't imagine a secret base nestled in the trees near the highway. Wouldn't they have set it deep in the national forest that took up more than six hundred thousand acres of the interior and included the mountains? That sounded like the perfect place for the lair of a dastardly organization of nefarious kidnappers embroiled in schemes to take over the world—or whatever they planned. I was still fuzzy on the details.

Xilnethgarish and his dwarven assistants said they sensed the magic of the dragon Varlatastiva near the coast along the northwest of this land mass, Zavryd informed us. *I will admit that he is a suspect source.* He *did not even know that Varlatastiva was his uncle. Such ignorance is unfathomable.*

"Because he wasn't born yet when his uncle disappeared," Val said. "Or so he claims. I believe him. Given that the Starsingers all rushed to Seattle to retrieve a stolen egg for their queen last year, I figured they're fairly close-knit."

I have also heard that the uncle has been gone for a century, Zavryd said, *though few from other clans noticed his departure. All those who care what Starsinger dragons do—which is not many, since they are pleasure-seeking hippies who do not involve themselves in politics or policing the Cosmic Realms—believed him dead.*

Something about the idea of dragon *hippies* made my mind boggle, but from what I'd seen of Xilneth, he was definitely the lover-not-a-fighter type. Not that I'd seen anyone show interest in his romantic advances.

"The organization could have put their hideout anywhere on the peninsula really," Val said. "None of the cities are very big. Besides, between the dragon's magic and whatever your mother could have enchanted—" she waved back at me, "—they could probably hide a humongous base in Central Park in New York City."

I grimaced at the reminder that my dwarven mother, with powerful enchanting magic that was beyond anything I would ever be able to master, was essentially working against us. Or, as I believed, she was being *forced* to work against us.

Before, I'd wondered how our enemies had been convincing her to build things for them for decades, and had assumed they might be using my and my father's lives to ensure her cooperation, but now that we knew a dragon was in the picture, it made more sense. Even though dwarves were supposed to have good mental defenses capable of resisting compulsion magic, I had no doubt a dragon could find a way to coerce someone to work for him. With talons and fangs if not magic.

This is the area where I sensed the other dragon's magic before, Xilneth spoke telepathically to us from the coast miles ahead, where his green-scaled body was barely visible in the sky, my dwarven allies, Hennehok and Artie, riding on his back. *I do not understand why I do not sense his magic now.*

He must have realized a need to hide his base more thoroughly after we encountered him at the lair of the enemy, Zavryd replied. *He is good at hiding himself.*

Yes, it is unfortunate that you were too slow to catch him, but we both know how poor you are at races.

I am not poor at anything, Zavryd replied. *Had you not been cowed by his magic and forced to sit on that bridge, with your tail clenched around the supports, we could have caught him.*

I was not cowed; I simply did not believe the supposedly mighty Zavryd'nokquetal could not catch a single dragon and deal with him.

He used compulsion magic to try to keep both of us from giving chase. Only I was strong enough to shake it off.

Little good it did you. He escaped.

If we encounter him here, he will not escape again. I reported to the

Dragon Council that he has been on this wild world, possibly for decades, and is up to schemes that could affect dragon-kind. The queen and the other elders are doing research.

Perhaps we should hear his side of the tale, Xilneth suggested.

He can tell it while my talons are around his throat. Once that is accomplished, you may ask him questions if you are not clenched to a bridge again.

I was not clenched to it before. I knew of the need to assist your mate and her companion against the enemy and the crazy elf, so I voluntarily stayed behind.

A tale that nobody believes.

I winced at the description of Sarrlevi as the *crazy elf* but reminded myself that he was not that any longer. Once Barothla's cure had been injected in his veins, he'd healed remarkably quickly. When last I'd heard from him, he'd sounded like his old self.

Unfortunately, with the dragon queen wanting him brought in for punishment and rehabilitation, and Zondia hunting him down, Sarrlevi was still in trouble. Would there ever be a day when we could spend time together without either of us being in danger? I longed for a weekend away at his secret chalet on another world, but he was, understandably, off looking for his ill mother. Since Barothla had kidnapped Meyleera but then died without revealing her location, we worried there was nobody caring for her. In her weakened state, she might not survive long like that.

I refused to contemplate that it might already be too late. For Sarrlevi's sake, and all he had sacrificed for me, I dearly wanted him to have a happy ending. Or at least to accomplish what he'd been fighting to do all along, see his mother cured of that horrible disease. Even though I didn't want to lose him, I knew he would accept the fate the dragons had in mind for him if he first knew she was out of danger.

Do you sense anything, Sorka? I touched the haft of the hammer wedged under my leg.

I doubted even a powerful magical weapon could sense something a dragon couldn't, but one never knew. Since she'd been forged by my mother, she might have a link to her.

I believe I may, Sorka replied. *A couple of times, as we've flown over this area, I caught the barest hint of your mother's aura. I do not sense it* exactly *but almost a ghost or memory of it. I believe she was here in the past.*

Hope stirred in my breast at this confirmation, however slight, that we were in the right place. Or at least in the vague general area.

After months of searching and years—no, *decades*—of missing her, I longed to finally find my mother and get a chance to hug her for the first time since I'd been four years old. And was my father being held prisoner in the same place? I wanted so badly to reunite my family and get to know my parents.

I am certain he was right here. Xilneth issued the telepathic equivalent of a frustrated huff.

Now, both dragons were flying along the coast, the waves growing more turbulent as we traveled from the Strait of Juan de Fuca toward the Pacific Ocean. Below, rocky cliffs and jumbles of boulders, occasionally with a lone tree growing from them, were more frequent than beaches, and we spotted few people. I suspected a lot of the coves were inaccessible except by boat. And any boat would risk being battered against the rocks if the waves grew turbulent.

The cliffs might be a good location for a secret base, or at least the entrance to one.

"Maybe the flag could be designed to look like a sword tassel. Not that *I* would ever put a tassel on Storm, mind you—" Val tapped the magical sword in the scabbard on her back, "—but one should stick with the theme, don't you think?"

"Are you still musing about your mailbox?" I asked.

"We've been out here for three hours. I've got to muse about something. Also, Zav?" Val touched his back. "I need to pee."

In the human way or the elf way? Zavryd asked.

I raised my eyebrows. Though the bathroom facilities in Sarrlevi's houses weren't what I was accustomed to, I didn't think there was much biological difference in the way such needs were taken care of.

"The elf way is fine." Val looked back, as if she'd anticipated my raised eyebrows. "That's his way of asking if I'll go behind a tree or if he needs to take me to a gas station."

I imagined Zavryd landing on the roof of a Chevron while knocking a few pumps over with his tail.

"Though elves do have indoor facilities," she continued, "it's common for them to squat in the forest if they're on a long trip riding their flying birds."

"Information I didn't need to know."

"I hear dwarves have a lot of interesting sanitation systems built into their tunnels in case they need to squat while mining." Val smirked at me. "Hennehok was telling me about it. When you said he was an engineer, I didn't imagine a *sanitation* engineer."

"Me either." Originally, I'd assumed he'd helped my mother build that power reactor, but unless he'd studied in numerous fields of engineering, that might not be the case.

As Zavryd adjusted his wings to take us toward a cliff, I wondered when Sarrlevi and I would get to the point in our relationship where we would casually discuss toilet preferences. Sometime after we finally got to have sex, I supposed. For now, it was hard for me to imagine putting a hand on my handsome and haughty elf's shoulder and announcing the urge to urinate, preferably not in the elf way.

Zavryd banked to head toward a point. As he arrowed toward the very edge of it, I flattened my hands to his scales, wishing for handholds. And seat belts. Since trees filled the point, there wasn't a lot of room for landing, and the water was far, *far* below.

I clenched my eyes shut.

Your comrade once again attempts to enchant my scales, Zavryd informed Val as he spread his wings to slow down. *As I informed her before, this is not possible.*

"She's subconsciously trying to affix herself to your back so she won't fall," Val said.

My efforts weren't *that* subconscious.

Zavryd landed lightly, facing the trees while his back end hung off the cliff. Behind us was a drop of hundreds of feet to waves crashing against black rocks. It was all I could do not to wrap both my arms around Zavryd and clench every muscle in my body.

Like the agile and fearless-about-heights half-elf that she was, Val hopped lightly off and trotted into the trees.

Perhaps you should also attend to biological needs, friend of my mate, Zavryd told me, doubtless worried that I would, in my fear, lose control of at least *some* of my clenched muscles.

"Good idea," I said but couldn't bring myself to let go, not with the drop-off and the churning waves in view from my position. I turned my head but had the same view on the other side of the dragon. "Could you scoot—"

Magic swirled under me and hefted me into the air.

I squawked in alarm, almost losing my hammer. Fortunately, as Zavryd levitated me toward the trees, I kept my grip on Sorka. She, I had no doubt, would survive being dropped off a cliff and into the ocean, but she would have scathing commentary for me.

That is correct, Sorka told me. *Your mother carried me in a beautiful custom-made leather sling with ancient Dwarven runes embossed in the leather that proclaimed my greatness.*

Really? I had a hard time imagining my mother, who everyone said was a kind and gentle soul, being boastful enough to declare that something she'd made was great.

The runes may have translated literally to large hammer, Sorka said, *but there were flourishes. They implied greatness.*

As I landed among the fallen needles of the evergreens, there was little time to do more than admire the great beards of moss dangling from the branches before Val stepped back into view with her phone in hand.

"I got a call from Zoltan. There's not much reception out here, and he said he's been trying to get in touch for hours." Val held my gaze, her eyes grim with significance.

Because whatever Zoltan had been calling about would be important to me? I glanced at the sky and then the time on my own phone. It was almost noon, an extremely late hour for a vampire to be awake.

"What was it about?" I asked warily.

"The call broke up before I got everything, but he asked if you were with me and said he has news about the formula he used to cure Sarrlevi."

My stomach tried to pitch off the cliff.

"What kind of news?" Dread filled me as I added, "That its effects are only temporary? Or something else bad?"

I hadn't seen Sarrlevi since the day after Zoltan had given the formula to him. What if he wasn't off looking for his mother? What if he was descending once again into madness?

"I don't know, and there's not enough reception to get him back. Zav, can you take us home? It might be important."

I didn't squawk again when Zavryd levitated me onto his back. I was too busy worrying.

2

I OPENED MY FRONT DOOR, EXPECTING SARRLEVI, BUT THE ELF WHO stood on my threshold wasn't anyone I'd met before. With his blond hair streaked with gray and back in a clasp, he was handsome, as so many elves were, but his green eyes gazed at me with cold aloofness.

With thoughts of assassins leaping to mind, I lunged and grabbed Sorka. Why hadn't I sensed this guy approaching?

Wait, I couldn't detect his aura. Even now, it was as if he wasn't truly in front of me.

That didn't mean he wasn't a threat. How had he gotten past my wards?

"Matti Puletasi," he stated.

"That's right. Who the hell are you?" I gripped my hammer in both hands. "Didn't you see the no soliciting sign?"

He looked over his shoulder, but I'd been sarcastic. The only sign in the yard, which was stapled onto a carport post at goblin level, said that donations for all useful materials, including computer housings, springs, metal of all types, and old appliances could be left in the driveway.

"I did not come to solicit but to warn," the elf said, looking back, calm and indifferent to my hammer. "I am the Caretaker."

He didn't appear to have any weapons, but that didn't mean much. The three-piece suit he wore had deep pockets that could have hidden a lot.

I blinked at the realization that he was wearing a suit, one that looked like it had come from My Haberdasher in Seattle. He also spoke in English and didn't have much of an accent. If not for the pointed ears and elegant features, I might have doubted that he was an elf.

"What do you care for?" I asked. "I'm not in need of a house sitter right now. All my plants are already dead."

"As I said, I come to deliver a warning."

"About the need to be home often enough to water indoor plants? I've already gotten it."

His eyes closed to slits. "If you don't stop your search, your family will not make it."

My family? My parents? Or my grandparents, sister, and niece and nephew? Or everyone?

"Those you seek to protect," he added. "Cease your search if you wish them to live."

He could only be referring to my search for my parents. Had the organization sent him to threaten me? His sleeves hid his wrists, so I couldn't see if he wore one of those control bracelets.

"They'll be all right." I tried to sound tough, not rattled, and reminded myself that wards now protected my sister's and grandparents' houses. Though this guy had waltzed past my wards... "They can take care of themselves," I added, even though I didn't believe that. Penina and my grandparents weren't warriors, and Josh and Jessie were kids.

An image of my young niece and nephew playing in my sister's backyard came to mind.

The Caretaker smiled, a chilly knowing smile. "Can they?"

A new image came to me, this one inserted from the outside. From him. It was of Penina on the roof of her house, an orc assassin behind her with a dagger to her throat. That event had happened, exactly like that, but how could this strange elf know the details?

"Those with mundane blood are so vulnerable to the magical, aren't they? Especially those who are elderly." This time, he showed my grandparents in their home with dark hooded figures breaking in, blades in their hands and blood already on the floor.

Ice flowed through my veins.

"End your search," he whispered, then stepped back and faded from view. As if he'd camouflaged himself. Or as if he'd never been there at all.

I woke with a lurch, blinking and looking around, alarm filling me as I took in the empty sky to either side.

It took me a moment to realize I was still on Zavryd's back with Val, heading back to her home in Green Lake.

"You okay back there?" Val asked over her shoulder. "You jerked so hard I thought you would pitch off."

I will not allow my mate or her comrade to fall, Zavryd informed us.

"I know." Val rested a hand on his scales. "You're a good dragon."

Yes. You will reward me later.

Of course.

"What's it called when you fall asleep in the middle of the day while doing things?" I rubbed the back of my neck, uneasy about the dream and finding it odd that I'd nodded off for it. "Narcolepsy?"

"I think so."

"I've never had that before."

"Maybe you find flying on a dragon's back soothing."

I peered over Zavryd's side at the trees and houses alarmingly far below and tried to weld myself to his scales. "No, that's not it."

I thought about sharing the dream with her but decided against it. With all that was going on, it wasn't surprising that my subconscious mind was stirring things up. Besides, Zavryd had already placed wards at Penina's and my grandparents' houses. What more could he and Val do?

"If Xilneth and the dwarves don't find anything today," Val said as Zavryd banked and we flew over Green Lake toward her house, "I may see if my mom can help."

"Uhm. Your mom?" I'd heard Val mention her mother a couple of times, and knew she lived outside of Duvall and was *not* dating a werewolf, but nothing had implied she could help locate things that dragons couldn't find. "She's not magical in any way, is she?"

"Nope, but she volunteers with Washington State Search and Rescue and helps track down people lost in the woods. More specifically, *Rocket* tracks down people. That's her golden retriever."

"My parents aren't hikers who wandered off a trail during a storm."

"I know, but she was working in that area this summer." Val tilted her thumb back toward the Olympic Mountains. "She tried to get Amber and me to come visit her at some hot springs over there. Originally, I thought she meant the Sol Doc Resort, and might have been down for that, but she had camping in mind, and these were remote trailside hot springs—more like mud holes with warm water seeping up out of the ground—where clothing is optional. *Very* optional. I decided not to expose Amber to that."

"I was in your yard with Amber when your naked mate wandered out of his steam room," I pointed out. "She's probably used to seeing weird things with you. Naked weird things."

"Fine. I decided not to expose *myself* to a bunch of nude, hairy mountain men."

"Fair."

There is nothing weird *about nudity,* Zavryd informed us as he glided into their neighborhood. *What is odd is the human preoccupation with clothing.*

"Dwarves and elves like clothes too," I pointed out.

Not in a hot box.

"Possibly true." I didn't know if elves and dwarves enjoyed saunas or not. Could one build a sauna in a tree?

"Anyway," Val continued, as Zavryd landed not in the yard, where we could have easily climbed off his back, but on the roof of their Victorian house, "I'll reach out to my mom. She has a lot of contacts, and I wouldn't be surprised if she knows someone who's an expert on the national forest. Maybe someone who's even seen some odd goings-on over there."

"Okay. Thanks." I was skeptical that mundane humans could find what dragons couldn't, but if someone lived in the area, they might have seen something. Like magical cargo helicopters bringing loads of stolen artifacts and kidnap victims to a remote base.

Thankfully, Zavryd levitated Val and me down into the backyard, so I didn't have to test my ability to clamber off her roof without a ladder.

During the trip back, Val had texted Zoltan a couple of times, hoping for an update. Once we'd had good reception again, she had even called. Zoltan hadn't answered. That had done nothing to alleviate my worries. I hoped he was simply taking a nap.

A text popped up on my phone as I trotted toward the basement door with her. It was my friend and real-estate agent Zadie, not Zoltan.

I would have waited for later to answer, but her message asked, *Any chance you're in Green Lake?*

I am. What's up? I opened the basement door, stepped into the "light lock," and impatiently waited for Val to slip in behind me so I could open the second door.

Price reduction on the house across the street from your quirky friend. The agent said I could show it anytime you're available. Apparently, it's vacant. Very vacant.

"Am I the quirky friend?" Val asked over my shoulder. In the tiny dark room, with my phone screen the only source of light, it was probably hard for her not to read it. "Or is that Zav?"

"I believe you're collectively quirky." *I'm here but busy with something right now,* I texted back.

"Hm."

We pushed open the door and stepped into Zoltan's laboratory, infrared lights bathing the counters, cabinets of curiosities, and equipment in a glow that didn't disturb vampire eyes the way sunlight and normal lamps did. I sensed Zoltan, not hard at work at one of the stations but in the back corner, the area sectioned off by a black curtain and the brick foundation for the upstairs fireplace. Maybe he *had* gone to sleep. How much would he complain if we knocked on his coffin to wake him?

How about in an hour? Zadie asked.

Fine, I texted back before stuffing my phone into my pocket. At the moment, house hunting was low on my list of priorities. Besides, I doubted that place would be snapped up quickly, even with a fat price reduction.

"Zoltan?" Val called. "Are you awake?"

"Certainly, dear robber," came Zoltan's voice, though it sounded weary. "I have slept little of late. As you know, my mind has been vastly stimulated by experimenting on, researching, and deducing the purposes of the various formulas that your muscle-bound half-dwarf acquaintance acquired for me."

"My muscles are well-proportioned to the rest of my body." I pulled aside the curtain, since it didn't sound like he was in his coffin, and found him sitting in one of the velvet wingback chairs.

"For a body brimming with dwarven blood, yes, of course." His eyebrows climbed toward his widow's peak as he watched his curtain shift aside. "You may be aware that this is my *private* abode. Do I barge in upon you when you're reading?"

"Reading?" I eyed the book in his hands. Was that one of the ones Freysha had lent me? A notepad of translations rested on the side table, and a pencil perched between his fingers.

"Yes, reading is the activity one pursues in order to absorb information located in paper-filled objects known as books." Zoltan looked past me to Val. "Do you not have any academically inclined friends?"

"Willard loves books," she said, as I scowled at Zoltan, "but you don't love her."

"That awful woman has almost as many muscles as the half-dwarf and has threatened to hurl me against the walls. An inebriated orc would be less brutish."

"It's possible you don't inspire congeniality in the people you interact with." Val looked at me. "Willard doesn't care for the rates he charges for his formulas."

"I was surprised *because* he's reading, not because I don't know what books are." I folded my arms over my chest.

"I assumed."

"Zoltan, is Sarrlevi okay?" I eyed the book again.

"I'm certain I do not know. Are there not dragons seeking to slay him?"

"Just torture him for two years before wiping his memory, I believe," Val said.

"So much better," I muttered, then raised my voice. "I mean, is everything okay with his brain? I thought you called Val about the potion you gave him."

"The *formula*, yes." Zoltan set aside his book and stepped into the laboratory with us. "When I applied it to the elf assassin, I knew nothing of it beyond that it destroyed the magical chemical compound in my Petri dishes that had been feasting on the brain matter within. I was not positive it would do more than destroy the foreign substance inside him. Even that was not a certainty since nobody listened when I requested the elf be sent for brain scans."

I nodded, remembering that Zoltan hadn't been entirely positive Sarrlevi would recover. "You gave him a second formula to help with the healing, right? In addition to Barothla's cure."

"I did, and I'd read that elven and dwarven brains are more capable of regenerating than human brains, but even among their species, it is not uncommon for people who suffer traumatic injury to never fully recover all of their cognitive abilities."

Impatient, I shifted from foot to foot, wanting to know if Sarrlevi was safe or not. Had Zoltan explained that yet?

"As it turns out, I needn't have given an extra formula, as the original has *vast* restorative properties. I suspected that was the case when I saw how quickly the assassin recovered from what had to have been substantial brain damage. It was rude of him to leave so quickly the next day. He didn't allow me to run experiments on him. I so badly would have liked to study some of his brain."

"He didn't want you drilling holes in his skull to extract samples?" Val asked. "Rude."

"Indeed, *and* ungrateful. Also, a sample could have been obtained without *drilling*. I could have extracted the brain matter through an orifice. Have you not read about lobotomies, dear robber?"

"Oddly, that's not my choice of subject matter when relaxing before bed."

I clinked my hammer against the brick fireplace foundation. "Zoltan, what's the problem? It sounded like something was wrong."

"Wrong? No, I believe something may be very *right*, at least when it comes to elves." Zoltan walked to a counter and patted an empty spot next to a rack of vials, the contents of some glowing, the contents of *all* magical. He pointed to one in particular. "This is the formula I used on the assassin without knowing its name. But I believe it *has* a name and has been written about in a journal." He opened another of the books that Freysha had given me, the words inside in Elven. "It is called *dyunda lukobar*. It's actually a dwarven name, but it's written about in here."

Why did that sound familiar? "Oh, *lukobar*. Barothla demanded to know where that was when she was cussing me out for having stolen her belt."

Zoltan lowered the book and gave me a disgusted expression. "You had the *name* of this formula and did not relay the information to me? That would have made my research vastly simpler."

"She didn't explain what *lukobar* was. At the time, she was busy trying to knock my head off with her hammers."

"Dwarves." Zoltan sighed. "It is a wonder they stand erect and have language skills."

"What does the *lukobar* do? Besides curing elves afflicted with that chemical compound?" Val glanced at my tight knuckles around my hammer haft. "Matti looks like she's on the verge of bashing things if you hold her in suspense any longer."

Zoltan eyed me and my hammer. "I would hope you wouldn't let any of your houseguests unleash their weapons in our domicile."

"She's a visitor, not a houseguest. And an occasional handywoman." Val beamed a smile at me. "Have you seen her improvements to the gutters and roof?"

"Visitor? Handywoman? Please. She's here more than I am."

I growled. I wouldn't bash anything, but I *might* be tempted to grab Zoltan and shake him a little.

"Be still, my muscled mongrel." Zoltan held up a hand. "The *dyunda lukobar* was written about in this journal because it is what the alchemist dwarf princess used on the elves afflicted with *Shiserathi* Disease. It is what cured them."

I rocked back. Did that mean we had the formula that could fix Sarrlevi's mother?

The last I'd heard from Freysha, the elven alchemist Hyslara Broadleaf had used Sarrlevi's ingredients to make some of that formula for use on her ill people. But since Sarrlevi's mother had been kidnapped, she hadn't received the treatment. And there was the question of whether the elves would agree to treat Sarrlevi's mother regardless.

"In hindsight," Zoltan continued, "it makes sense that a formula designed to reverse a degenerative brain disease would also work on the magical chemical compound that afflicted the assassin's brain, but, I'll admit, it took me a while to realize there might have been multiple reasons the princess was carrying that particular vial around."

"Can we call him Sarrlevi instead of *the assassin?*" I asked.

"I don't even call *you* by name, my pugilistic half-dwarf."

"You say that as if it's a defense rather than a character flaw."

"Hm." Zoltan looked at Val. "She may not be as dim as I originally believed."

"The hammer confuses people." Val thumped me on the shoulder, then pointed at the vial. "So, does Matti just need to carry that around until Sarrlevi finds his mother and then have her swig it?"

"*Swig?*" Zoltan clasped a hand to his un-beating heart while gripping the counter. "Certainly, you would not want this formula to pass through the digestive system and be broken down. According to the literature, several doses should be applied, injected into the bloodstream once a week for several weeks or until all signs of the disease are gone and the damage has been reversed. A trained medical professional with magical blood should be able to ascertain that."

Val plucked clean syringes from a drawer, then the vial from the rack, and handed the items to me. "No swigging."

"Got it." Even as I accepted them, Zoltan's fingers twitched toward the vial.

"I had hoped to do more research," he admitted.

"Matti hopes to cure someone," Val said.

"It's possible it could be the answer to human degenerative brain diseases as well as elven ones," Zoltan said.

"That would be amazing. You've got the formula, right?" Val waved at his notebooks.

"Indeed, but Earth lacks many of the ingredients."

"I suppose the pharmaceutical companies would balk at formulations that call for manticore tail," she said.

"That is an ingredient for a different formula," Zoltan said. "Several, actually."

"Earth should become more open-minded and accept that other worlds with intelligent beings exist. Then maybe they could send ambassadors to those worlds, open up trade, and get ingredients—and medicines—from elsewhere."

While they spoke, I looked for a kerchief or something I could use to wrap the vial and syringes in so they wouldn't break before I met up with Sarrlevi again. My gaze landed on Barothla's belt of pouches.

Zoltan followed my eyes. "Earth could also simply wait for half-dwarves to brutalize intelligent beings from other worlds and steal ingredients and medicines."

"I only brutalize the ones who start the fight," I said. "And I'm noticing that you're studying the contents of those stolen pouches, not giving me the belt back and insisting it be returned to the next of kin."

Who *was* Barothla's legal next of kin? My dwarven grandfather? Her sister? I laughed shortly, imagining finding my mother and handing the belt to her.

"Naturally, I couldn't trust such a brute as yourself to do that." Zoltan yawned, though he looked longingly toward his wingback chair and books instead of his coffin. "The belt is better off in my hands."

"Naturally."

"We'll leave you to sleep," Val said.

"Thanks for the help," I added.

However obnoxious Zoltan was, he *was* useful.

"Do you have a way to get in touch with Sarrlevi?" Val asked as we headed for the door.

"I wish. I don't even know what world he's on." I paused in the light lock, envisioned his face, and attempted to telepathically project words to him. *Sarrlevi, I have the cure for your mother. Come find me, please.*

If he was on another world, it wouldn't work. And if he was more than a few miles away on Earth, it also wouldn't work. The odds were against him looking for his mother in Green Lake, but I couldn't help but feel we had a link and maybe he would somehow sense from afar that I needed him.

When I reached the front yard, I eyed the fairy ring and was half-tempted to ask Val if she knew how to use it for travel, but even if I could have left Earth, I wouldn't know where to look for Sarrlevi.

"Over here, Matti," came a familiar call.

Zadie stood on the sidewalk across the street with her *Star Trek* messenger bag over her shoulder and her electric car parked along the curb. That was daringly close to the dragon landing pad that was Val's yard.

"That's not who I was telepathically calling out to," I murmured.

"Oh, are you going to look at the house?" Val asked.

Zadie pointed meaningfully at one of several for-sale signs staked around the property.

"Looks like," I said.

"If you buy it, I promise I'll keep Zav from smashing any of your vehicles with his tail."

"I only have *one* vehicle now." I grimaced at the reminder that my truck had burned to pieces along with Kurt Hart's mansion.

The police had come by to question me shortly after I'd filed the insurance claim, a claim that nothing had come of yet, and I'd had a mild panic attack on my front stoop. I'd told them I'd been there the night of the party because I'd been called in for a plumbing incident. They'd taken some notes and left, but I couldn't help but worry I might end up being blamed for the carnage, despite Xilneth destroying all the security cameras in the fire he'd started. With the way things were going, I might find my mother only to have to flee Earth forever. If that happened, I hoped she and my dwarven grandfather would be willing to give me a room in their city.

Sadly, that was doubtful. General Grantik, my grandfather's right-hand man, had witnessed me battling Barothla and Sarrlevi killing her. If I showed up on Dun Kroth, the dwarven guards might arrest me on the spot. Or shoot me for guilt by association. I wasn't welcome on the elven home world either.

I shook my head bleakly, feeling the walls closing in around me.

"Oh, yeah," Val said absently as she frowned toward the west. "Sorry about that, but the old Harley is cool, especially with all the mods you've done. You'll definitely want to keep it from being smashed. I bet if you put in an offer for that house, it'll be accepted, pronto. A couple was interested last week, but they wandered over here for some reason—maybe drawn by our beautiful dragon door knocker—and they set off Zav's topiaries. Smoke flowed from the nostrils, and the eyes glowed and everything. Not only did the couple sprint to their car and take off, but a priest showed up that afternoon."

"To pray for your soul?"

"That may have been involved, but he mostly waved some beads around and threw holy water at the topiaries. They smoked and glowed at him, and he took off, muttering about the Devil's work."

"Little did he know that they were the work of an elven princess."

Val, still gazing to the west, lowered her voice to a mutter. "Speaking of dragons..."

At first, I only sensed Zavryd, who'd transformed into a human, shucked his elven robe, and ambled into the sauna in the back. But then I detected a second dragon, one flying in our direction, and I groaned.

What did she want, now?

Zondia'qareshi soared slowly over the neighborhood, not coming in for a landing to join her brother in human recreational activities, but she looked pointedly down at us. Or... at *me*?

Val waved up at her, but Zondia didn't flutter a wingtip or anything in acknowledgment. If she said anything telepathically, I didn't hear it.

"Is she checking on me because she thinks Sarrlevi will show up in my wake?" I asked.

Val turned to watch Zondia fly out of view to the east. "That might be exactly right. Her mother tasked her with finding him, remember. And from what I've seen, neither she nor Zav does anything but what their mother wishes."

Great. And I'd shouted out to the cosmos, calling Sarrlevi to me. Wherever he was, I now hoped he hadn't heard me.

3

ZADIE LED ME UP THE WALKWAY TO THE EARLY 1900S VICTORIAN house across the street from Val's. It had a similar look, a turret rising up on one side with second-story windows looking toward the lake, but it hadn't been renovated. Curls of faded purple paint stuck out from the sagging siding, a thick carpet of moss grew atop the roof—or maybe *was* the roof—and the worn front-porch boards creaked ominously as we walked on them. An alarmed rat scurried out from underneath and disappeared into overgrown bushes under the windows.

"You're lucky," Zadie said. "Thanks to its quirks, and its lack of a remodel, it's still on the market."

"I figured it wouldn't go quickly." I glanced skyward, sensing Zondia flying around at the edge of my range.

Val had gone back to talk to Zavryd and hopefully convince him to tell his sister to leave, but I didn't know if Zavryd had the power to make that happen. He might be a strong dragon and powerful warrior, with Zondia being his *younger* sister, but I'd heard that females called the shots in dragon society.

"It's got good bones." Zadie waved her phone and unlocked the electronic key box hanging from the door latch. "Someone was on the verge of making an offer last week, but I guess the bushes over there started smoking and glowing."

"I heard that prompted a visit from a priest."

"I don't know about that, but your friend's Halloween antics are going to get you a good price if you're interested. Just hope the homeowner doesn't figure out that you two are connected, or he might get a lawyer and accuse you of teaming up to drive away other clients and force down the price."

"If I decide to buy, I'll offer a fair price. Is there a workshop? Or room to add a garage?"

I wasn't sure I wanted to move, but my neighbors in Lynnwood would be delighted if I disappeared. Oh, Mrs. Ming might miss me, but the others no longer found me restful. It had to do with the numerous battles that had taken place at my house recently, not to mention the magical elven vines and leaves patching my siding, roof, and front door. For-sale signs had been popping up around the neighborhood like mushrooms after a rain.

"It's a big lot, so you could easily add a workshop. Even a DADU, if you wish." Zadie opened the door but paused on the threshold and looked toward the street.

A clattering coming from somewhere out of sight sounded like it was heading this way. Someone's jalopy in major need of a tune-up?

I snorted as I sensed a familiar goblin approaching. As well as a number of *un*familiar goblins.

As the clattering grew louder, plumes of smoke rose from that direction. A steam-powered truck that might have been built at the turn of the century—the turn of the *last* century—came into view. It wobbled and swerved from side to side, the open bed full of junk and goblins. I decided jalopy was an apt word. A hubcap fell off—not from one of the tires but out of the bed—and rolled between two parked cars.

A white-haired green goblin head was visible over the wheel, and Tinja sat on the open bench seat next to the driver.

"Oh, good," Zadie said.

"What about the approach of that vehicle could be deemed *good*?" I asked, though I waved at Tinja. She'd been scarce at the worksite the last couple of days. Now that her demo tiny house was complete, and she'd filmed numerous videos, she was on the internet day and night, editing them and building her social media channels while waiting for tiny-house-plan orders to flood in.

"Nothing," Zadie said, "but I asked Tinja to come to the showing. Your roommate is an important person to consult when considering the purchase of a new home."

"My roommate who doesn't pay any rent?"

"Doesn't she compensate you in other ways?"

"You make it sound like she's doing sexual favors for me."

"I assume the hunky elf guy with pointy ears handles those."

I wished. But as Zondia floated through my senses again, I was glad Sarrlevi wasn't around.

"Tinja draws blueprints for the homes you remodel, right?" Zadie asked.

"Whether Abbas and I ask for them or not, yes."

"And didn't you say she made a flier for you?"

"She did, though I think we're even on that since my business account purchased the trailer, most of the wood, and a slab of granite for her tiny home."

The driver of the jalopy started to park it in front of Val's house, but several goblins in the bed shouted *no* as they waved their arms and pointed at the topiaries.

Even though the guardian shrubs only threatened people who crossed onto the property, the driver nodded and adjusted his route to park in front of the for-sale house. Another hub cap fell off. That one *did* come from one of the tires.

"It's such a mystery as to why this house isn't getting offers," Zadie murmured, leading me inside.

"Yeah." I glanced toward the sky, not the goblins, before following her in. For now, Zondia had flown out of my range, but I couldn't help but feel like the bait in a trap. A trap meant to capture the man—the elf—I'd fallen in love with. If, after all we'd been through together, I lost Sarrlevi to the dragons...

No. That wouldn't be acceptable.

"Don't look so glum. Exploring houses is a joy." Zadie gestured expansively at the foyer and living area, the rooms dim even after she turned on the lights.

The 1970s ceiling fixtures were relatively recent but far too sparse and diffused for the oft-cloudy Pacific Northwest. Installing adjustable can lighting in all the rooms would be one of my first actions if I bought the place.

I wandered through the house, walking across stained carpets nailed to hardwood floors and checking out a white-and-black tile kitchen adorned with appliances that might be considered antiques. In the back of the house, I found the stairs leading up to the bedrooms and the turret.

A desk left behind suggested the turret had been someone's office. A closet would have to be added—and maybe there was room for an attached bath?—to make it a bedroom.

It wasn't until I walked inside to look through the dirty windows toward the lake that I sensed Sarrlevi in the room. He stepped close, wrapping his arms around me from behind, and rested his chin on the top of my head.

Maybe his abrupt appearance should have startled me, but it was as if my body had been waiting for him. I automatically leaned back against his chest and lifted a hand to grip his arm, hoping to keep him close, even though I felt compelled to warn him that he was being hunted.

"There's a dragon looking for you."

"I'm aware." Sarrlevi kissed the top of my head. "I've kept my camouflaging magic close about me. It is easier now that my brain is once more cooperating with my wishes."

"I'm glad." I didn't want to step out of his embrace, but I twisted and looked up to check his face. The last time I'd seen him, he'd been recovering and improved but still haggard. His color, inasmuch as pale elves had color, had improved, but a weariness lingered, and I half-expected a droop to his pointed ears, but they weren't as flexible as goblin ears and didn't do that. "Have you been sleeping much? You still look wrecked."

His eyebrows arched at the term. Maybe he hadn't been reading Earth dictionaries, urban or otherwise, lately. "Does that mean my masculine allure hasn't returned?"

"No, it's fine."

"Fine?" His lips pressed together at this anemic description of his beauty.

Even tired, he remained achingly handsome, and maybe I should have said so, but he'd always been so haughty and certain of his appeal that it hardly seemed necessary. After all, he could read my mind, enough to get the gist anyway, and he knew I fantasized about him when he was holding me—and when he wasn't.

Though I doubted his ego needed bolstering, I said, "*Very* fine. As we speak, it's taking all my willpower not to tear your clothes off and pounce on you like a puma."

"Here?" Sarrlevi looked around the room, his gaze lingering on an ancient stain on the equally ancient threadbare carpet, and his lip curled.

"Yeah, here. Right on that dirty spot over there. Would the entropy make you underperform?"

"Are you mocking me, Mataalii?"

"Every chance I get." Maybe I wasn't the best at ego bolstering. "It's fair play for all the times you've called me a plumber." I rose on tiptoes to kiss him before turning back toward the dirty window, movement outside catching my eye.

Tinja and three other goblins scurried about in the yard, looking under tarps and peeking in a children's playhouse so overgrown with weeds that I assumed the kids had gone off to college decades ago. It had started raining, but that didn't deter them from their scavenging.

"Did you not *plumb* during the scheme to get into your enemy's lair?" Sarrlevi's hands roamed as he spoke, and I leaned back into him.

"Yes, I did. With aplomb." I closed my eyes, ignoring the goblins and enjoying his touch. My nerves tingled, especially as I imagined where else his hands might go. Hell, maybe I *would* pounce on him. Turret doors had locks, didn't they? "How long have you been here?"

"Since you returned on Zavryd'nokquetal's back. I first sought you at your domicile to the north, but only your roommate was there until that dubious conveyance clunked up to the home, and she climbed in." His tone turned dry. "Had I known it was coming to you, I needn't have made a portal to another world and back only to arrive at the same destination."

Maybe I would tell him about the public bus system someday. "Even if you *had* known, would you really have caught a ride in a goblin jalopy?"

"Perhaps not. It is burning wood for fuel, and the scent is almost as off-putting to an elven nose as that of your petroleum-igniting vehicles." Sarrlevi kept letting his hands roam as he spoke, and I melted deeper into his embrace, thoughts of romantic weekends at his chalet returning. Had a clunk from downstairs not reminded me that we weren't alone, I would have turned around and kissed him again. Less briefly this time.

"Not everybody has giant magical birds to ride around on," I murmured.

"This is a backward and deprived world."

"I won't argue with that, but I've got some good news for you." I gripped his hand and guided it to the pocket that held the vial and syringes. "Have you found your mother yet?"

Sarrlevi sighed. "I have not. That is the reason I've slept little and my appeal may only be *fine* currently. I came to request your help, though I will understand if you don't feel you can give it."

"If I can, I will." I was still aggrieved that the one previous time he'd asked for help, I'd been trapped inside Broadleaf's laboratory and unable to escape and assist him. "Check this out." I pulled out the vial. "This is the formula that healed your brain."

Sarrlevi eyed it more like venom dripping from a rattlesnake's fangs than a miraculous cure.

"Does the vampire believe you'll need to apply it to me again?" A hint of uncertainty flashed in his blue eyes.

Though there was some appeal to Sarrlevi's uncharacteristic vulnerability, I didn't want him to worry and hurried to say, "No. But he learned that it's also—or maybe *originally*—the cure to your mother's condition."

Sarrlevi froze, not breathing as his eyes sharpened and locked on the vial.

"Little did we know, you didn't need to stalk the realms looking for ingredients. We only needed to yank Barothla's belt off." I grimaced, since saying her name reminded me that she was dead and that the elf with his arms wrapped around me had killed her.

Sarrlevi hadn't been himself, and she'd *deserved* that fate after what she'd done to him and his mother, but it was still chilling to remember. And I feared the ramifications, not only from the dragons but the dwarves. I didn't think the dragons blamed *me* for what had happened, but would my dwarven grandfather? I believed General Grantik and the dwarf with him had recovered Barothla's body and taken it with them when they'd left Earth. I shuddered to think what my grandfather now thought of me.

Before, he'd been open and friendly, believing I had to be a decent person because his daughter was. But now?

By now, he might have ordered his troops to hunt me down.

"I don't usually attempt to remove belts or otherwise disrobe my enemies in battle," Sarrlevi said.

"Maybe that's a tactic you should add to your repertoire. People don't fight well with their pants around their ankles."

"I strive to employ *honorable* tactics against my enemies."

"Does that mean if someone's pants fell down, you would wait for them to find a safety pin before resuming the battle?"

"I might repair the garments myself if they were incapable of doing so in an expedient manner."

"With magical vines?"

"Perhaps."

"You're still an odd elf."

"Yes." Sarrlevi smiled and reached for the vial but paused, his brows rising again.

I gave it to him, figuring he would be the one to find his mother, then pulled out the syringes for him and relayed Zoltan's instructions.

After accepting the items and tucking them away, Sarrlevi wrapped his arms around me again and let out a pleased sigh. From him, it was as good as a thank-you, and I leaned back against his chest once more.

A part of me missed how open with his emotions he'd been when he'd been affected by the chemical compound, admitting in a letter and also in words that he loved me, but I wouldn't wish him back in that state for anything. Besides, I now knew how he felt, and it touched me, especially when I'd never thought I would be good enough—pretty enough and appealing enough—for him.

Sarrlevi lifted a hand to my head, sliding his fingers through my hair and massaging my scalp. I might have melted to the floor if not for his body supporting me. Perhaps he'd caught my thoughts, for he kissed the side of my neck so tenderly it almost brought tears to my eyes.

Distracted by his touch, I almost didn't notice the hint of magic that flowed from Sarrlevi toward the window. Other tendrils of his power wafted behind us toward the floor. It took me a moment to figure out what he was doing. The goblins had come into sharp view in the yard below, the glass sparkling clear now.

"Really, dude? You're snuggling me in the most tender way while also cleaning?"

"This domicile is begrimed."

"I know. That's why, if I decide to buy it, I would be able to get a good deal." Well, that wasn't the *only* reason. "Don't fix anything until I've had an offer accepted. We don't want other people seeing the potential and bidding against me." Besides, there were probably rules about cleaning someone else's house without their permission.

"Hm."

I leaned around him to check out what he was doing to the floor. No, the carpet. The stain must have been too set for even his amazing elven cleaning magic to thwart, for he'd cut a hole in it— or maybe incinerated a hole?—and, as I watched, slender elven vines wove themselves to the fibers, creating a patch.

A car honked in the street. It probably had nothing to do with us, but it reminded me that dangers were about, including a giant dragon.

"What's your plan to find your mother?" I asked. "And how can I help?"

"Even though I agree with you that it is unlikely Barothla would have been brazen enough to take an elf noble captive and keep her in the dwarven royal quarters, that is a place that is inaccessible to me. My mother *may* be in the capital city somewhere. If I create a portal to Dun Kroth, will you go see the dwarves and attempt to find out?"

I stared bleakly out the window, my trepidation about what kind of greeting I would get returning. Even though I hadn't been the one to kill Barothla—and she'd tried to kill *me*—General Grantik had watched me work with Sarrlevi before and knew we were linked. I'd also once promised him that we wouldn't kill Barothla. That had been back in the dwarven tunnels, not here on Earth, but he might consider it a broken promise regardless. If I showed up at the steps to the city, his people might arrest me on the spot. Or *shoot* me on the spot.

"I do not think the dwarves will attack you," Sarrlevi said, no doubt catching the gist of my thoughts. "I would not ask this favor if I believed it would endanger you."

I took a deep breath. Even if he was wrong and it *would* endanger me, I had to do this for him. We had to find her. "Okay."

His arms tightened, and he kissed me on the neck again. "Thank you," he said, surprising me by voicing the words.

"You're welcome. But you can't come with me, or they *will* shoot on sight."

He hesitated. "I know, but I should wait outside the city in case something goes awry and you *do* need help."

"You think I would be able to flee out to reach you again?" Somehow, I doubted Grantik would look the other way if I tried to escape their city a second time.

"You've proven resourceful at evading enemies."

"All right. Let me tell Zadie and Tinja that I need to head out." Despite the words, I was reluctant to step out of his embrace.

"You are able to go now?" Sarrlevi lowered his arms. "I'd hoped that would be the case, as this is an urgent matter, but I know you have your own quest."

"It's on pause, since the dragons can't find what they detected before. Val is going to bring in a special, high-powered tracker."

Sarrlevi cocked his head.

"Her mother and her dog."

"*I* would be a more effective tracker than a mundane human and canine."

"Are you sure? Dogs can smell a few million scents on a dandelion."

"I employ magic when I track, but elven noses are exquisite."

"Must be why you were so sensitive to the botanical-rain-scented laundry detergent."

"An *orax* with its snout cut off would have found that offensive."

I leaned in and sniffed his tunic. Wherever he'd been the last few days, the detergent scent had worn off. Now, he smelled pleasantly of nature. As befitting an elf, I supposed. It was a clean and appealing scent, but I couldn't help but smirk as I imagined him standing naked under a tree and bathing his armpits with clumps of moss.

"When you think of me naked, should not your focus be on my appealing musculature rather than my armpits?" Sarrlevi asked.

"Nope." My smirk broadened. "I get excited by the whole package."

"The allure you've mentioned emanates equally from all portions of my body?"

"Yup."

"You are an odder mongrel than I am an elf."

"Possibly true."

Sarrlevi couldn't have been deeply offended, for he bent to kiss me, not on the neck but on the lips.

A happy surge of pleasure ran along my nerves, and I wriggled about to wrap my arms around his shoulders and return the kiss. If more vines grew over the carpet while we embraced, I didn't notice. I was too busy longing for the moment when we could spend more time together, especially in a horizontal capacity.

When my mother is safe, Sarrlevi spoke into my mind, his lips busy caressing mine, *I will return and help you with your quest. I will show you that I am a superior tracker.*

I look forward to it.

Elves are superior in many *ways.* He either put thoughts of us writhing naked on a bed of moss into my mind, or maybe my stimulated brain conjured them on its own.

Either way, as I ran my hands over the hard planes of his back, thinking of shoving his tunic over his head, I wondered if we might explore each other in a *horizontal capacity* right there. His hands slipped under my shirt, tendrils of magic flowing not toward the carpet but into my body, making my every nerve spring to attention.

Titillated by his touch, physical and magical, I willed my magic to flow into *his* body, to excite him the way his did me. Though all I knew how to do was enchant objects, he'd implied it had felt good when I'd rubbed his ears and willed my power to give him pleasure.

A growl emanated from his throat, and he backed me against the wall by the window, his kisses deepening. They ignited desire within me, desire that left me breathless and craving this—craving him. I arched against him, feeling *his* desire, knowing he wanted me, maybe even as much as I wanted him. Maybe he even dreamed of *me* naked.

Often, he whispered into my mind, the buttons of my shirt opening with a whisper of his magic. His hand slid past the defenses of my bra and cupped my breast, hot zings of pleasure ricocheting through me as his thumb brushed my sensitive skin.

My shirt drooped off my shoulders. I reached up and wriggled against Sarrlevi, wanting to turn him on as much as he did me, and smiled when I elicited another growl from him. A hungry, animalistic growl.

After all we'd been through, we deserved to satisfy the longing that had been building within each of us. I checked, and the door *did* have a lock.

No sooner had the thought crossed my mind than Sarrlevi pulled back. I murmured a protest, my fingers tightening involuntarily on his shoulders, but he released a sigh of frustration as he looked skyward.

"My huntress returns," he said, his voice husky.

"I'm starting to hate dragons," I whispered, a hitch in my own voice.

"You see why so many plot against them." Sarrlevi brushed a lock of my hair behind my ears, then stepped back, disappearing from my view and my senses. *I will return when she's gone, and I will take you to Dun Kroth.*

It took a noble effort not to request that we stop at his chalet along the way to finish what we'd started. His mother and mine had to be our priorities.

The cheese cellar there is well stocked, Sarrlevi spoke into my mind, his voice already growing more distant. He probably didn't want to test his camouflaging magic too much by standing right under Zondia when she landed on the roof. *We will visit it soon.*

It's your bedroom I was thinking we'd spend time in, I replied.

Oh? Have you decided you would prefer to romance me instead of my cheese?

Well, you first.

I'm pleased to have earned a place of preeminence in your heart.

You have. But if there was a tray of exotic cheeses next to the bed, I wouldn't complain.

I assumed, he said, smiling into my mind before disappearing completely from my awareness.

4

ZONDIA FLEW OVER THE HOUSE BUT DIDN'T LAND ON THE ROOF. Certain she could read my mind as easily as Sarrlevi could, I attempted to keep it empty, not letting thoughts of his face—or his naked body—linger. Since I was still a little breathless—and extremely turned on—from our kisses, it was hard.

Fortunately, Zadie came upstairs, offering a needed distraction. "Are you still up here, Matti?"

"Yeah." I rubbed my face and attempted to compose myself, only remembering as her footsteps sounded in the hall that my shirt was half-off. Shit.

As I hurried to button it, the door opened at the same time as I realized my bra lay crumpled on the floor at my feet. How the hell had he gotten that off without my noticing?

Zadie stepped in as I snatched it up, but, in the empty room, there was nowhere to hide it. I shoved it behind my back and leaned against the wall.

"Hi," I blurted as her eyebrows climbed.

She looked around, no doubt searching for a lover. "If the

turret is getting you that excited, that's a good sign. Did you want to put in an offer today?"

"Uhm, maybe after I see the rest of the house."

"Did you want me to leave you alone so you can finish?" Zadie smirked and waved at my rumpled, half-buttoned shirt.

"Not alone, no."

Her smirk widened. "I'll assume that's not an invitation since we have a strictly professional relationship."

"And since I'm not into girls, yeah."

Her gaze caught on the vine patch—hell, there were *three* of them now—on the carpet. "What are those?"

"The work of the person I *am* into," I said.

"Your elf lover? Is he under the desk?"

"No. He had to leave."

"Huh. I was going to warn you that if your roommate steals anything else from the toolshed, you'll *have* to buy the house, but maybe the window cleaning makes up for petty theft. Did you do that? I was up here before, and you couldn't see the lake through the grime."

"Sarrlevi did. With magic."

"Your elf lover cleans windows? No wonder you're into him."

"Windows, trucks, carpets... He's the whole package." Remembering that I'd told him I appreciated the *whole package* scant minutes before brought him to mind again—naked—and I waved my bra and pointed down the hall toward the bathroom. "I'll be right back."

As I dressed and straightened my clothes in a mirror that was also in need of elven cleaning magic, Zondia alighted on the roof of the house next door. I groaned and glanced out the window, certain she would pester me.

From the bathroom, I couldn't see her, but I *could* see several goblins ambling down the street and pointing at a Craftsman listed for sale a few houses down. That one was less my style and didn't have a view of the lake, but it amused me that as many properties were popping up for sale in Val's neighborhood as in mine. We truly were a menace to the Seattle housing market.

"Goblins don't have enough money to buy property, right?" I asked Zadie when I joined her in the hall so she could give me the tour of the rest of the house.

"You're the one with a goblin entrepreneur for a roommate, so you'd be more likely to know than me. That said, they don't exist, as far as the government is concerned, so I'm sure they can't get mortgages."

"If the government doesn't acknowledge their existence, they may not have to pay taxes."

"Meaning they're able to hoard more money for house purchases?" Zadie asked.

"Possibly."

Val had sounded excited by the prospect of having me for a neighbor—at the least, she'd liked the idea that I wouldn't be fazed by any of her magical guests. Would she be equally excited to find goblins living on her street?

As we reached the kitchen, the back door banged open. Tinja ambled in with her arms full of rusty corrugated metal, lawnmower blades, and long iron nails that looked like they'd been forged by hand in the 1800s.

"I found ammunition for my goblinator," she announced. "This house is wonderful, Matti. When will you purchase it?"

"I haven't decided if I'm going to put in an offer or not. Which means you can't take anything from it."

"But it is clear from the lack of furnishings, other than the strange hammock in the basement, that the homeowner has moved out. He must not wish to continue owning these items. I am being polite and removing them for him."

"Hammock? Who strings a hammock in an unfinished basement?" I looked at Zadie, certain the listing had described it thus.

Hadn't there been a photo of knob-and-tube wiring strung between the ceiling joists down there?

"It's not a hammock," Zadie told me. "It's a sex swing, and there are a bunch of mirrors and poles down there too. You and your elf should have been groping each other in the basement instead of the turret. Though there are broken windows down there. He might have tried to repair them with vines."

I wrinkled my nose, thinking *Val* might not be the only quirky person living on the street. Maybe a passel of goblins would be a welcome change from the usual.

"Did you know that my new friend Mugrot has a junk-hauling service?" Tinja pointed toward the steam truck parked out front, and the goblin in the driver's seat waved through the window at us —at *her*. "It is a wonderful business for a goblin. He has invited me to visit and scavenge in his junkyard any time I wish."

The driver waved again and winked, making me wonder if Gondo might not be the only goblin interested in my roommate. Though it was possible Zadie's description of the basement had put my mind in a dirty place. Or Sarrlevi's visit had. The goblin might only be interested in all the junk Tinja had found.

"I approve of this dwelling for us, Matti," Tinja said. "With the help of blueprints that I would sketch for you at an affordable rate, you would make it magnificent. It is very large, and there is so much potential. Much more so than in the little rectangle house in Lynnwood. This home would be befitting our stations in life."

"Our stations?"

"Yes, me as an up-and-coming, soon-to-be-vastly-wealthy entrepreneur, and you as the famous half-dwarven enchanter who sells her projects for great sums of money. Before long, we will be swimming in gold coins and able to establish the urban goblin sanctuary for those like me who have no interest in living in the forests. I will invite all of my impoverished kin to the sanctuary where they can find respite while they learn the ways of the city and how to contribute to the society of this world." Tinja nodded firmly as she trundled toward the front door with her stash. A nail and a refrigerator coil clunked to the ripped vinyl floor. She glanced down but couldn't pick them up with her arms full. "I will send Mugrot to collect those."

Zadie watched her go.

"You're not going to keep her from taking stuff?" I asked, though Tinja was probably right that the homeowner didn't care about what he'd left behind. Maybe he'd fled the state in fear for his life after witnessing one of the battles in Val's yard.

"Nah. You're going to buy the place, which will mean she's simply stealing—*scavenging*—from you." Zadie smirked. "Like usual."

"You're that certain? I haven't even seen the basement yet." Though, after her description of what the homeowner had left behind, I wasn't that eager to run down there.

"When a woman makes out with her boyfriend in one of the bedrooms, it's a sure sign that she's excited by a house and an offer will be forthcoming." Zadie glanced at my chest, though my buttons and bra were back in the proper places now.

"It's an office, not a bedroom, and I need to think about it. Even with the bad-neighborhood discount, it's a lot of money, and I—"

The elf assassin was here, Zondia boomed into my mind from her rooftop perch. *His aura lingers, and I see in your mind that you were with him.*

Damn.

Yes, I was briefly with him. Greetings, uhm, Lady Zondia'qareshi. Was that the correct address for a dragon? Zavryd called himself a lord, but his sister seemed more uptight. She was the daughter of a queen. Did that make her a princess? *Or is it Your Highness? Are you seeking a romantic partner for yourself, by chance? I recently worked with the dragon Xilneth, and he was hoping to run into you. I understand he wishes to sing to you.*

Do you seek to distract me from my task by switching to the topic of that feckless, tone-deaf, showboat of a dragon?

Of course not, but is he really tone-deaf? I wished Xilneth would show up now to distract her with singing. *He was quite confident that you would enjoy his crooning.*

He is not tone-deaf, Zondia surprised me by admitting, *but he is feckless. And far too young to appeal to a mature female such as myself. A powerful mature female who could choose from* many *mates.*

I have no doubt. But, sometimes, young men apply themselves to romance more assiduously and earnestly than older males.

The elf assassin is not younger than you.

No. He's ancient. But he was assiduous and earnest in the cheeses he hunted down for me. I wished he were still here, with his arms wrapped around me, not forced into hiding by Zondia's approach.

Not for an elf. Certainly not for a dragon. Zondia, still perched on the roof, lowered her long lilac neck so that she could look through a window at me. The rain had picked up, making her scales gleam with dampness, but it didn't appear to bother her. I supposed it was too much to hope for a thunderstorm—and that dragon scales attracted lightning.

"Remind me to plant some trees around the yard here if I buy this house," I muttered.

Zadie, with her mundane human blood, didn't see the dragon and was frowning at me, no doubt wondering why I'd broken off in the middle of our conversation.

"For privacy purposes," I added.

"Maybe your handy elf can grow some foliage for you. Make sure to recommend he do it *outdoors* instead of indoors. Vine carpets aren't any trendier than moss rugs, which we've discussed."

"We have. I'm still not convinced you can't buy those on Etsy."

Listen to me, mongrel, Zondia said, her compelling gaze holding mine. *I heard the words of the dwarven princess and yours as well, and I have seen into your mind.*

I remember. I winced at the memory of her mind scour, her magical mental talons feeling like they'd been shredding my brain. And that had been the *kind* version, or so she'd assured me. She hadn't been trying to do damage.

I know Barothla sought to enact a show to rile me and ensure I wished to capture or kill the assassin.

Oh? I asked warily. Though I wanted Zondia to be reasonable and see the truth, I didn't know if she would.

Had he not attacked me, I might not have assisted Barothla.

You were assisting her before we got there. Before *he attacked you. And that wasn't his fault. If you can read my mind, you know all about the chemical compound Barothla infested him with.* I doubted *infested* was the right word for chemicals, but it had acted like a parasite. An awful brain-eating parasite that had almost killed Sarrlevi.

I do. She used it to defend herself from him when the two of you captured her.

We briefly held Barothla to question her because she used her power to make Sarrlevi's mother sick. And then she kidnapped her. She's still missing. None of that was about her defending herself. She was just pissed at Sarrlevi because he didn't want to assassinate her sister for her. Barothla was evil. My grandmother would have chastised me for speaking poorly of the dead, but I couldn't bring myself to amend the words.

I was aware of her ambitions, though I only learned later that she was responsible for her sister going missing. That was disappointing.

Because you knew my moth—Princess Rodarska and liked her? Was it too much to hope for that?

I did not know her well. It was only in recent decades that I came to know Princess Barothla. She brought formulas and magical tinctures to the dragons that our kind find useful. One of Zondia's lilac wings came into view as she flexed it. *She was the person responsible for my current coloring. I had an... issue that caused an itch and discolored my scales, and our own healers were uncertain of how to fix it, as it resisted even dragon magic. Barothla also could not cure it fully, but she came up with a balm that healed the itch, and she also had the idea to use a coloring on my scales.*

I stared at her. Barothla had bought Zondia's loyalty with hair dye? *Scale* dye?

I'm sorry. I know what it's like to feel, uhm, flawed and not entirely attractive and appealing in one's body. I didn't know if a *dragon* would feel that way, but, hey, if she appreciated someone commiserating with her, I would be happy to. If there was even a slight chance that I could win her over, or at least make her not want to capture Sarrlevi, I would take it. *I tweeze my eyebrows because they're like furry caterpillars if I don't.*

Not exactly the same as having a skin—scale—issue, but...

Furry eyebrows are not appealing to mongrels?

Nope. Nor to humans or elves. I wasn't sure about dwarves, since their males *and* females had little trouble growing copious amounts of facial hair. *Eyebrows are supposed to be arched, even, and not trying to grow together in the middle.*

Hm.

Zadie lifted a hand, as if to snap her fingers in front of my eyes, but she ended up leaning close so she could follow my gaze through the window. "Are you communicating with the porch over there?"

"The dragon hanging down from above it, actually."

"Ah, about what?"

"Eyebrows and scale rot at the moment."

"You're such a weird client."

"But you love me anyway because I do so many deals with you."

"This is true. I don't even complain when I catch you half-naked while on a house tour."

"I was hardly naked." Though things might have gone in that direction if Zondia hadn't shown up.

I seek the elf because my mother has ordered it, Zondia told me. *Perhaps I could have forgiven that he struck at me, since his mind was altered, but he has killed many, and, as an assassin, he is dangerous to those our kind have placed in power throughout the Cosmic Realms. He has proven that he can get through a dragon's defenses, which makes him dangerous to our kind as well. If someone paid him to attack a dragon—*

He wouldn't take that gig. I can make sure of it.

You? Zondia scoffed into my mind. *A mongrel?*

A mongrel that he has feelings for. Surely, you agree that women are capable of influencing men who care for them. Wouldn't Xilneth leap off a bridge for you if you asked it? I supposed that wasn't a great example since dragons regularly perched on bridges and would fly, not fall, after leaping from them. *Or fling himself into danger?*

He is a foolish dragon who does not know me well. Listen, mongrel. Tell the assassin to reveal himself to me. I will take him to see the queen, and she will read his mind and determine his guilt or innocence.

While he's pinned under her talons and can't escape?

She is fair, not cruel.

But she would probably decide he needs your punishment and rehabilitation, regardless of his innocence or guilt, right?

It would be better for him—and you—if dragons were not seeking him forevermore. Tell him to reveal himself to me. If, as you say, you have the power to influence him, he will do so.

Maybe, but I sure as hell wasn't going to make that request of Sarrlevi.

I will wait for him at the spire in your city. Zondia put an image of the Space Needle in my mind, promptly making me wonder how often diners were enjoying their lobster and salmon in the revolving restaurant while an invisible-to-them dragon perched above. *We need not be enemies, mongrel.*

I watched bleakly as she lifted her head, sprang into the air, and flew toward downtown. Hadn't Barothla said something similar to me when she'd been trying to convince me to help her find my mother?

We need not be enemies.

"Yeah, right."

5

Sarrlevi didn't show up after Zondia left, making me believe he'd decided to follow a lead or check another source for information about his mother. Hopefully, he hadn't gotten into trouble. I tried not to worry.

After finishing the house tour and helping Zadie chase off the scavenging goblins, I thought about heading to the job site to get some work done on the homes Abbas and I were building, but he texted to let me know he was calling it a day because of the rain. It had picked up, with the thunderclouds I'd been fantasizing about earlier rolling in. With a longing sigh for my lost truck, I rode my Harley home in the rain, a few flashes of lightning in the distance convincing me not to dawdle.

Before leaving, I'd let Val know to direct Sarrlevi to my place if he showed up back at her house. After telling me Zavryd had forbidden her from speaking with Sarrlevi, she had promised she would announce my whereabouts into the ether if she believed he was in the area.

When I arrived, Tinja wasn't home yet, and I wondered if one of the jalopy goblins had talked her into going on a date. More likely, she was caressing her new finds in that junkyard while making plans for improving them.

Rain pounded on the overhang as I let myself in the front door. It might have been my imagination, but the elven repair vines seemed to turn their leaves toward the downpour, eagerly taking in the water. Given enough time, would the plants grow larger and take over the house?

"Maybe another reason to move," I murmured before remembering the vine patches Sarrlevi had given the carpet in the turret room. Hopefully, *they* wouldn't grow larger.

After changing into dry clothes and eating leftovers for dinner, I headed back to my room and lay on the bed to twiddle my thumbs. Though the heavy cloud cover made it seem like nightfall had come, there were three hours of daylight left. I had any number of projects that I could do indoors, but I kept expecting Sarrlevi. When he arrived, he would want to head to Dun Kroth. The sooner we found and helped his mother, the sooner he could help me find mine.

Curious about whether Xilneth, Artie, and Hennehok had chanced across anything after we'd left, I tried to send a telepathic message to Artie. Doubtful that I could reach her if they were still on the Olympic Peninsula, I didn't expect a response.

Your skills are improving, girl, Artie replied without hesitation, her voice faint in my mind.

My skills at telepathy? Or have you seen my enchanted drainpipes?

I speak of the former, but I've heard about your drainpipes.

Oh? I'd been joking. From Val?

Yes.

I hadn't realized their ability to shoot water and trespassing squirrels all the way to the street was prompting her to speak of them to others.

I think she brought them up to change the subject since Xilneth was informing her how pompous and odious her mate is while explaining that Starsinger dragons are superior lovers.

You must be enjoying your time with him.

If we find Princess Rodarska, it will be worth enduring his wit.

Wit, right. Any news? I assumed not since Artie hadn't brought it up yet.

I fear not. The storm has forced us to seek shelter.

Understandable. Lightning flashed outside my window, and I hoped Sarrlevi was somewhere dry. He could use his magic to keep the rain from drenching him, but I had a feeling he would set up his camping cot and moss rug and stay in the wilds instead of attempting to rent a hotel room. Even with magic, that didn't sound appealing in a storm. *You're not holed up in a cave, are you? You can come stay at my house if you want.*

We have rented a cabin at the 3 Rivers Resort and Guide Service in Forks, Artie said.

Do they guide you to dragons?

To vampires, I believe. There is a sign indicating the current vampire threat level in the area.

If their guides don't take you straight to Val's basement, they can't be very good.

Probably not. We will update you if we find anything.

Thanks.

As I waited, the rain pelting my window every time the wind gusted, I grew drowsy. Maybe that wasn't surprising since I was lying on my bed, but it was only evening, so I didn't expect to nod off. Nonetheless, sleep came, and, once again, I dreamed.

The Caretaker stood before me, not at my front door this time but in a vast underground chamber. Though again clad in a three-piece suit, he carried a rifle now. A magical rifle. I still couldn't sense him or get a feel for his power, but I detected its magic. He pointed it toward a shadowy wall in the chamber.

"If your family means nothing to you, perhaps his passing will disturb you."

I stared. Sarrlevi was chained spread-eagle to the wall by his wrists and ankles, hanging like a human target in an axe-throwing show. He was barefoot and bare-chested, gashes marring his exposed flesh, his face twisted in rage. Or maybe pain. Was that a bullet hole in his abdomen?

I shook my head in disbelief. "There's no way you have the power to capture him. This isn't real."

The Caretaker smiled and rubbed his rifle. "It could be. We have artifacts of great power and have captured many elves. If you don't abandon your quest for us and return to your mediocre existence, the assassin will die. Search for us no more."

"You have my parents, you asshole." There was no way I would give up on them.

"But they live. And the rest of your friends and family could live too. It's your choice. If you press us, we'll get rid of everyone you care about."

"Why are you working for a bunch of humans? You're an elf."

"It is the dragon I am allied with, a dragon who has promised the safety of my friends and family." A hint of bitterness or maybe resentment flashed in the Caretaker's eyes, but that didn't keep him from smiling and waving toward the high ceiling of the underground chamber.

A strange wind kicked up, stirring his hair. Underground wind?

Then lights appeared, the running lights for one of the enchanted helicopters. Though the Caretaker kept his rifle pointed toward Sarrlevi, he waved for the pilot to take care of him, to end his life. The enchanted aircraft descended toward where he was chained, magical guns flaring with power as they launched their rounds.

I jerked awake from the dream, my hands tangled in my comforter and sweat sticking my shirt to my body. Full darkness had fallen, and the rain still pounded at the roof.

A thud came from the front of the house. That wasn't the rain.

Swearing, I rolled out of bed, grabbed my hammer, and sprinted down the dark hallway.

Tinja screamed as I sprang into the living room with Sorka raised over my head. Only then did I realize I sensed my roommate's aura, and only her aura, in the house.

Do you intend to use me to brain a goblin? Sorka asked dryly.

No. I lowered the hammer. "Sorry, Tinja."

Good, Sorka said, *because goblins are not worthy opponents. I seek to go into battle against serious and dangerous foes who threaten those without the power to defend themselves.*

I might have a new elf that we can whack together. If the Caretaker was real, I would.

Hands raised over her head as she gaped at me, Tinja found her voice. "I was not camouflaging my aura, Matti."

"I know." I apologized again. Then, haunted by the dream—the nightmare—I added, "I'm on edge."

"I am also on edge. And then I came in and was scared in my own home."

"Why are you on edge?" I made myself ask, though I was preoccupied with my own problems. Were these dreams being conjured by my own mind? Or was something else going on? "I didn't think goblins ever got tense or irritable."

"It is not that kind of edge, Matti. I am on the edge of despair." Tinja draped herself on the sofa and flung her arm over her eyes.

"House-plan sales not going well?"

"They trickle in one at a time here and there, but I do not charge much for the plans, so these monies are not significant. What little I have made I have already spent on my website and marketing. I need so much more. Do you know what it costs to build an urban goblin sanctuary?"

"I don't, but if you need to buy a house or even land as a starting point, Seattle isn't the cheapest metro area to invest in."

"It is very expensive, yes. I need many thousands of human

dollars. *Hundreds* of thousands. When I started my social-media channels and put my videos online, I thought *millions* of people would watch them and be led to purchase my house plans."

"How many *have* watched them?"

"My flagship and most popular video has thirty-seven views, and I believe half of those are from Gondo. He shows my videos to the other goblins at the coffee shop."

"That's nice of him."

"Yes, but *goblins* do not purchase house plans to build tiny homes. They spend all their money on coffee and gaming accessories."

"I've seen their dice."

"I must have *human* viewers."

I scraped my fingers through my damp hair, tempted to grunt in commiseration and leave Tinja to solve her problem on her own, but I still didn't sense Sarrlevi, so it wasn't like I was in a hurry. "What do your videos do?"

"Do? They show the beauty of our demo tiny home. You know this. You helped me record the one where I highlighted the dazzling granite countertop and cleverly concealed storage space."

"Are all of them like that? Video sales brochures, essentially?"

"Yes. As I said, I wanted to show off the great beauty of the work that we did together."

I didn't point out that her drawing plans and me assembling everything from scratch didn't fit my definition of *working together*. "It's good to have some videos like that, but I think you have to put up things that are helpful or entertaining to get a lot of views. What does Zoltan say? He's the expert at this stuff."

Tinja lowered her arm from her eyes and scratched her jaw. "He teaches people how to make alchemical formulas."

"See? Teaching is helpful. Teach people how to solve their problems, and you should get lots of views."

"I asked him what his most popular video is, and it gives

instructions on creating a formula to cause one's ex-lover, odious professor, or other mortal enemy to sprout warts all over their body."

"I guess that solves some kind of problem."

"Yes…" Tinja's eyes brightened with calculation. "I know. You could help me put together instructional videos that teach people how to build all the components that go into a tiny home. Then they would know what to do once they purchase my house plans." She sat up with a smile, her despair wafting away. "Oh, this is a good idea, Matti."

"All except the part where *I'm* doing the instruction. You've been my intern for almost a year, and you build lots of things from scratch. I'm sure you can show people how to install a toilet."

"Not as well as you, Matti. You are an expert!"

"Abbas is an expert too. Maybe he'd like to help you."

"He does not fit inside the tiny home."

"A design flaw in the plans that I overlooked."

Tinja waved dismissively. "Trolls and half-trolls are not my target demographic."

"I'll help you record a *couple* of videos. Then you have to do the rest yourself. You're cuter than I am anyway."

The doorbell rang. I swept out with my senses, again hoping for Sarrlevi, but he didn't usually ring the doorbell.

I didn't sense him or anyone else with a magical aura. After checking my phone to see if someone had said they were coming over, I grabbed my hammer again and headed for the door. The memory of my first dream popped into my mind, of finding the Caretaker on my doorstep.

Before opening the door, I peeked through the peephole. Nobody was out there.

"What now?" I muttered.

"Is it a cheese delivery?" Tinja asked hopefully.

"I wish."

"I hope it is not a delivery of poisoned elven soda."

"Me too."

Though I was tempted not to open the door at all, my instincts told me that I'd better.

On the doormat rested a ceramic souvenir spoon rest from Hawaii. Dread flooded into me. I recognized it. I recognized it because it had hung in my grandparents' kitchen since I'd been a kid. It should have *still* been hanging there.

A wrecking ball of certainty crashed into me. The Caretaker was real, and this was a message from him.

6

"THIS IS THE OFFICE OF COLONEL WILLARD," CAME GONDO'S VOICE over the phone.

Something *thwacked* off the desk or maybe a wall in the background. Another goblin project gone awry?

"It's Matti. Can you put me through to her, please?"

"Good morning, Plumber Puletasi. Yes, I can transfer your call, but I must warn you that Colonel Willard has consumed only two cups of coffee today and is thus in a grumpy mood."

"She's always in a grumpy mood, isn't she?"

"Sometimes, she is only slightly surly."

"It's fine. Put me through."

Morning sun beamed on the puddles all around the worksite and gleamed off the metal of my Harley. No more dreams had plagued me the night before, but I hadn't slept well, so I'd come out here early to take out my frustrations by doing manual labor. I'd already texted Val about my dreams of the Caretaker and the stolen spoon rest, and I'd talked to my grandparents to make sure they were okay. When I'd asked Grandma if her souvenir was missing, she'd been startled to realize it was but had assured me that nothing weird had happened. Neither she nor Grandpa had seen anyone strange around the neighborhood, and nobody had been in the house.

I'd almost pointed out that *somebody* had been in the house, or the spoon rest would still be there, but I didn't want to scare her. I was scared enough for my entire family. Unfortunately, Grandma had shot down my suggestion that she and Grandpa pack suit-cases and go to stay at Val's house again.

While I *hoped* someone had used levitation to float the spoon rest out through a window, and hadn't been skulking in the house, I didn't think the wards should have allowed that, not any more than they permitted strangers to set foot on the premises. More likely, as a full-blooded elf, the Caretaker was someone powerful enough to get around magical defenses.

A thought that made me glad there was work to be done here and things I could pound with my tools. I *wanted* to pound this Caretaker, but I had no idea where to find him. Worse, Sarrlevi hadn't yet shown up, so my worry for him was growing. The memory of the dream of him chained to that wall floated through my mind. It wasn't possible that he had been captured and was in that exact position, was it?

"This is Colonel Willard," she drawled.

"It's Matti. Val said you might be able to send some soldiers to keep an eye on my sister's and grandparents' houses." I'd asked Val if *Zavryd* could keep an eye on them, but he couldn't be in multiple places at once, and he was already helping with the hunt to find my parents, regardless. There was no way I would be deterred from that quest. I'd almost driven back out to the Olympic Peninsula that morning instead of to the job site, but until Val brought in her mother and what I hoped would be a cadre of trackers, I didn't know where to look. "I think they're in danger," I added, realizing I would have to fill Willard in if I expected her help.

"Yes, Val told me. I love it when she volunteers my troops for missions."

"I can pay. Or fix your house up. Whatever you want. It's important."

"The Army pays for me to lease a modest apartment in the area."

"I can fix that up too. Or build you things. I'm getting better at enchanting. Val said you have a home gym. What if I enchanted your punching bag so that it punches back, and you get a better workout?" I had no idea if I could do such a thing, but I'd try to do whatever Willard wanted.

"All right, quit trying to bribe me. I'll send people to keep an eye on them."

"People with magical blood. And powerful artifacts and weapons. In case they need to deal with a badass elf."

"Better than a dragon, I suppose. You'd better find your parents soon, Puletasi."

"I'm planning on it. Thank you, ma'am."

Relieved that there would be more than wards to watch over my family, I hung up and went to work.

Despite all the distractions in my life of late, the new houses were coming along. Abbas, who arrived mid-morning and joined in, wanted to hire a couple of guys to help with the siding and roofing. It wouldn't have been a bad idea, but I didn't know how to adjust the wards to let new people on the property, so we had been making do with our own labor.

While he worked on roofing for one of the houses, I ran electrical cables inside. Often, I paused to search the area with my senses, hoping to detect Sarrlevi. I also glanced outside and toward the sky, reminded that I had to worry about dragons too, not only my new Caretaker problem.

Even though Zondia had turned semifriendly and said she would wait for me to send Sarrlevi to the *spire* to her—as if—I thought it more likely she was trying to lull me into believing she wasn't still using me as bait in a trap. As I well remembered, she could camouflage herself. For all I knew, she was on the roof of Tinja's tiny home, watching intently as she waited for Sarrlevi to show up.

Daughter of Rodarska, a familiar dwarven voice spoke softly into my mind. Hennehok. It sounded like he was still over on the Olympic Peninsula.

Hi, Hennehok, I replied. *It's Matti, remember?*

That is not a Dwarven name.

I rolled my eyes. *When we find my mom, we can ask her to give me a Dwarven name, and you can call me that, okay?*

Very well. I wished to let you know that we have convinced the dragon to continue looking for Rodarska today instead of flying off to sing to the lilac-scaled ishnaka *who seeks to seduce him.*

Uh, if that's Zondia, I'm positive she's not seducing him. I had no idea what an *ishnaka* was, but my mind plugged in *siren*. My mind, however, refused to place Zondia in that role. *She thinks he's a pest.*

Because he is *a pest.* Hennehok issued the telepathic equivalent of a *harrumph. But the Starsinger queen promised us his aid, and we reminded him of that. We continue to look.*

Thank you. I felt guilty that *I* wasn't over there looking. Even if I doubted I could find what dragons couldn't, I ought to be there, tracker or not. If Sarrlevi didn't come soon, I would head back over.

A black sedan slowed to a stop in front of the property, not pulling into the driveway. Would the elven Caretaker ride in a car?

After grabbing my hammer, I strode outside. Unless an enemy had arrived, I needed to keep whoever it was from stepping across the wards and being zapped. I would welcome the zapping of enemies.

"You expecting someone?" Abbas called down from the roof.

"Only trouble."

"Can't you stop giving *trouble* our address?"

"I wish."

One of the back doors opened, and a young blonde woman in a skirt and sandals stepped out. She bent, waving her phone at the driver and pulling out a cute blue purse before standing, so I didn't see her face right away. It was my senses that first identified her.

"Amber?" I held up a hand to keep her from coming up the driveway and hurried to meet her so I could explain the wards, though I had no idea why she'd come.

"Hey, Matti." Her nose wrinkled as she peered around the property. The wheelbarrows, tarp-covered materials, and partially constructed houses might not have impressed her.

"Did Val send you?"

Though I had said I would find work for Amber, if she decided she *wanted* to work for me, we had agreed that it should wait until after assassins stopped targeting me. Fear made my heart kick into double-time at the thought of Val's kid being killed because she happened to be standing next to me when snipers opened fire. Though Amber was as tall as her mother, her six feet towering over my five-foot-one, and had a quarter-elven blood and a year's worth of sword practice with her mom, that didn't mean she could repel bullets. Unfortunately, I couldn't either.

"No, but she's been telling me I could work here after school if I want to make some extra money. It's hard to get a job in retail clothing right now. The economy is depressed."

"So I've heard."

"The allowance Dad gives me for doing chores around the house isn't keeping up with inflation. Have you *seen* the CPI lately? At the rate things are going, my twenty dollars a week won't buy me TicTacs next year."

I blinked at this unexpected awareness of the economic state of the world from a kid. "Try buying lumber."

"You're a grownup, and you own your own business, so it's different."

"Right. Abbas and I don't worry about inflation. Due to our vast wealth, we place our orders for materials from the decks of our private yachts."

Amber looked toward the roof as Abbas paused in his banging to scratch his armpit. Then she considered my mud-spattered overalls. "Your wardrobe doesn't suggest you're slaying it *that* much." Her green eyes glinted with speculation. "I could help you with that, you know. Your wardrobe. What if, instead of hitting nails with hammers, I became your personal fashion advisor? Or even your personal shopper. I could take your measurements and go pick out clothes for you. You wouldn't even have to leave your —" Amber looked around the property, groping for an appropriate term, "—office," she decided on.

"We call it the worksite, and I was planning to have you carry things. Do you have gloves? Sturdy pants?" I considered her legs, which were bare from the knees down. "Closed-toed shoes? Boots would be better."

"Boots?" she mouthed, nose wrinkling again. "As your fashion advisor, I would have some more attractive footwear recommendations. Aren't you trying to hook up with that savage blond guy?" She pointed at her ears.

I was fairly certain she meant *savage* as a compliment, but since Sarrlevi had recently been literally savage, my expression was grim. "We're already—" I caught myself before saying *hooked up*, since that wasn't quite true yet, "—seeing each other."

"The low-key thing worked? Huh. I would have figured you'd have to glam up for him."

"He's an elf of substance who sees past muddy boots and overalls." I thought about mentioning that he'd also seen me nude, swinging my hammer at his laundry device early on, but that might traumatize the kid.

"You should definitely keep him then."

"I'm going to try. He's a pretty amazing guy. There are wards around the property, or I'd invite you to look around." I gazed toward the two on either side of the driveway, able to sense them easily, and wondered if I could use my growing enchanting skills to modify them. Sarrlevi had set them, and I was coming to know his magic well. It might even respond to me.

"You're *sure* you don't want to hire me as your personal shopper? I could have you looking Gucci in no time. Actually, in six to eight hours a week."

"That's how much your dad is allowing you to work?"

"Yeah."

I hadn't spent six to eight hours clothes shopping in the last *year,* and my mind boggled at the thought of spending that much time in a mall. I had too many projects calling to me for that. Admittedly, I'd been known to spend hours selecting just the right wood for those projects.

"As long as my grades don't slip," Amber added. "I get A's. I don't know what he's stressing about. They're both giving me a hard time since I quit swim team, but I didn't want to do sports for the rest of my life."

As she continued on, expounding on the woes of being a teenager, I examined the nearby wards, sending out tendrils of my magic and attempting to adjust them the way I might a drainpipe. Their power accepted mine, almost doing the magical equivalent of opening arms wide, and I wondered if Sarrlevi had intentionally created them so that I could easily alter them.

With Amber's face firmly in my mind, I attempted to imprint it on the wards, letting them know she should be allowed to pass. They buzzed faintly in what seemed like agreement.

"I think you can come onto the property," I said.

"You think?"

I stepped back, waving for her to join me, though I eyed the wards, hoping that hadn't been too easy. If the property's magical defenses zapped Amber, that might dull her interest in working here. She already looked like she might turn her nose up at the idea. Which would be fine. I liked helpers who found this kind of work satisfying and didn't care about getting dirty—or wearing boots.

She also eyed the wards as she stepped onto the driveway, having enough elven blood to sense their magic. They didn't react, and I let out a relieved breath and pointed toward the house we'd already finished remodeling.

"Check that one out if you want to see a finished project," I said. "What all the carrying of lumber can be turned into."

"You're really selling this job."

"Did you want me to talk about salaries and benefits?"

"*Salaries,* for sure. I don't need a 401K."

"I pay minimum wage for hours worked."

That earned me another nose wrinkle before Amber walked toward the house.

"I *am* an elf of substance," came Sarrlevi's familiar voice from the empty air a few feet away.

"I know this," I said, turning and smiling in relief. "Where have you been?"

Sarrlevi stepped into view and wrapped me in a hug and bent to give me a kiss. Maybe my assessment of him had pleased him. This time, he didn't push me up against any walls—only the mailbox would have been available nearby for that—and only held the embrace for a moment before capturing my hands in his and radiating his approval at me.

"A number of dragons arrived in the city yesterday," he said, "and one had the power to knock out my camouflaging magic. He was casting his spell over miles-wide swaths of territory, so I had to leave the area, and eventually this world completely, to avoid them. They were Stormforge dragons sent, I believe, by the queen."

"To look for you?" I winced.

"They did not say. It is possible, though the human term *overkill* comes to mind."

"I'm glad they didn't find you." I squeezed his hands and kissed him on the cheek.

Amber had paused to look back at us. I expected some teenage eye-rolling at our public display of affection, but she smirked and gave me a thumbs-up before stepping into the house.

"Zavryd did say something about other dragons *researching* what Varlat is doing," I remembered. "Maybe it had to do with that instead of you."

"I shall hope but avoid them nonetheless."

"A good plan." I summed up what Zondia had told me the day before, making sure to emphasize that I thought it was a trap.

Sarrlevi nodded. "Likely so. It is surprising that she would admit to having a flaw to you, a near stranger."

"Only to lull me into thinking she's not a bitch, I'm sure."

His mouth twisted wryly. "For a dragon, she is somewhat reasonable. But I doubt she'll disobey her mother in this matter."

"So we have to kiss the queen's ass if we want all dragons to leave you alone?"

Sarrlevi blinked a couple of times and glanced toward my lower half. "That... idiom is unique to your culture."

"Not its intent though. I'm sure people suck up in all cultures. Especially all cultures dealing with dragons." I debated if *suck up* was as odd an *idiom* to a non-native speaker as references to ass kissing.

"Do you want to head to Dun Kroth now?" I almost started to tell him about my dreams and the threat to my family, but he might think I should stay here if he learned of my new problem. Maybe I *should*, but since Willard had agreed to have people watch my family and all I was doing at the moment was installing electrical, I could get away for a few hours to help him. I wanted so badly to help him, to find his mother and fix *his* problems.

Before Sarrlevi could answer, Amber jogged out of the house and toward us. Was she done looking around already? Maybe I should have offered her a tour and suggested a few things I could teach her instead of simply saying she would carry loads around the worksite. I could give her a few skills she might find useful in life even if she got as many degrees as my sister and became a desk jockey.

"Hi." Amber waved at Sarrlevi as she approached, smiling a little shyly, and I wondered if he would fluster her the way he had me when we'd first met. But after the greeting, she turned to me, thrusting her hand out, a few items that hadn't yet been hung in the house on her palm. "These are amazing. Did you make them? Val said you do crafts."

"Crafts, yes." I managed to keep my tone from turning dry, though that term made me think of the macaroni hammer glued on construction paper that my nephew had made for me.

"What do these do?" Amber held up one of three pewter squirrels, the tails curved to be hooks. They'd been inspired by the real deal chattering at me from a nearby tree.

"Hold up the shower curtain." I waved at the trio of squirrels—the rest of the set rested on the vanity in the bathroom. Tinja and Zadie had both told me that home sellers didn't have to provide shower rods and curtains, but I believed in delivering a complete package.

"Oh, I see it." Amber held one up in the proper position.

"You enchanted gewgaws for holding up a curtain?" Sarrlevi's eyes twinkled with amusement.

"Yes, I did. If I did it right, they'll help keep water from getting out on the floor too. Don't tell me that's weird. You had enchanted stuff all over your house."

"True." His eyes continued to twinkle, and I knew *exactly* what he was thinking about.

"Before you bring it up with your typical aggrieved expression, I'm planning on making you a new soap dispenser."

"I look forward to it."

"I just need to figure out how to make items float and assail innocent houseguests with their contents." I eyed Amber, suspecting the conversation would have her pointing out how weird we were.

But she was considering the hooks with surprising admiration. She lowered them and held up a book-shaped charm. "Did you make this too? I *love* books. *Real* books, not ebooks. I want to be able to hold them and put them on my shelves." She squinted at me. "Do you read? You seem like someone who might not..." She glanced at my hammer but didn't finish the sentence.

As I'd noted before, she wasn't as quick to take digs at me as at Val. Mothers and daughters had special relationships.

"I do read," I said, though I doubted she would be impressed by my largely nonfiction collection on real estate, business, and motorcycle and car repair. "But that is actually my attempt at making a translation charm. I'm not sure yet if it works. I need someone to whisper sweet nothings to me in the Elven tongue."

Sarrlevi smirked and said something. It was probably about his maligned soap dispenser.

"I haven't activated it yet," I told him.

"Wow, a translator?" Amber rotated the trinket. "I thought it might just be a bookmark, which would be dope."

"I suppose you could use it for that too, though I would want to add a long flat part to go in the book, not a chain."

"I did not know you were learning to make charms," Sarrlevi said.

"During my last lesson with Santiago, he started teaching me. I've been asking to learn to make something useful since the day we met. He instructed me on how to craft a charm that measures one's heart rate—apparently, that's simple and a common first project. We have watches for that, so, after a few half-hearted attempts, I switched to this. He didn't know how to make translation charms, so I kind of, uhm, willed it to do what I wanted while I was molding the metal." Realizing how silly that sounded—and like it would never work—I added, "I've accidentally enchanted things I was crafting without understanding the magic, so I was hopeful."

"Can you make jewelry?" Amber asked. "Like necklaces? Or a tiara?"

"A tiara?" I supposed Amber did have that princess look, but I couldn't imagine crafting something so delicate. And feminine.

"Or earrings. Of books!" Amber smiled at me and held the charm to her chest.

"Book earrings? Are those trendy?" I couldn't imagine the girl who had a Prada and Gucci purse collection walking the high-school halls with books dangling from her ears.

"They will be if *I* wear them. And if they're silver instead of pewter. My English teacher would love them. I bet I could even *sell* her a pair." Amber's eyes took on the same calculation that had been in Tinja's when she'd been plotting her marketing plans. "Can you show *me* how to make jewelry? Like instead of forcing me to work outside in the mud, carrying things?"

"If you carry my lumber, I'll pay you minimum wage *and* show you how to make jewelry."

That resulted in more nose wrinkling as Amber peered around the worksite, her gaze lingering on Abbas on the roof, his butt toward us as he hammered. Sarrlevi had once remarked that he found *me* intriguing in that position, but he didn't appear inclined to ogle my business partner's posterior.

"I guess," Amber said. "Do I have to buy the jewelry materials?"

"I'll get them as long as your tastes don't run toward gold."

"No, silver is good. Gold is soft, and you have to be really careful with it." Speculation entered her eyes again. "My dad would love it if I learned to make him silver Dungeons and Dragons dice. He's a total geek."

"I'm sure he would. Handmade gifts make great Christmas presents."

"He might be so tickled that he would let me go on the holiday ski trip with my friends this year instead of with him."

I scratched my jaw at this calculation, though I'd been making gifts lately as bribes to elves—and half-elves with access to a dragon—so maybe I couldn't judge her.

Amber returned the trinkets to me. "Is there any chance you can give me a ride home so I don't have to pay for another Uber?"

"My truck blew up recently." I waved toward my Harley. "All I've got is—"

"Can you give me a ride on your *motorcycle*?" Amber blurted, her eyes widening with appreciation. "I've never been on one."

"Uhm." I'd planned to go off with Sarrlevi, and would rather spend time with him than ferrying a teenager around, but I supposed one should be good to one's future employees. "Does your mom care if you get a ride on a motorcycle?"

I'd never thought it was particularly dangerous—nothing like having assassins gunning for me—but my sister disagreed. Vehemently.

"Nope," Amber said with certainty.

I squinted at her, decided Val might measure danger levels similarly to me, and added, "Does your dad?"

"Uhm, maybe you could drop me off a block away from the house."

"Perhaps a portal," Sarrlevi murmured, "on the way to Dun Kroth."

"Okay," I said, though Amber's dubious expression suggested

she would want that to open up *more* than a block from her house. "Wouldn't we have to go somewhere else before landing in Edmonds? To another world?"

I couldn't imagine taking Val's kid to another planet without asking for permission. Judging from Amber's slight eyebrow raise, she didn't know if that was something she desired or not.

"Briefly, yes. As you know, I am aware of places where there would be no danger, and it would be only a brief stop before—" Sarrlevi paused and looked toward the street.

At first, I worried Zondia would appear there, that she'd been skulking around camouflaged the whole time, but I sensed the magic of a portal forming.

The Caretaker? A dragon? Someone new?

"You might want to hide, Varlesh." I checked the wards to make sure I hadn't altered them in a way that would prevent them from keeping out strangers. Not that it would matter if a dragon showed up.

"It is elven magic," Sarrlevi said.

"You should *definitely* hide then."

Sarrlevi sighed but didn't disagree. After releasing my hands, he stepped back and camouflaged himself from my senses again. I braced myself to deal with another visitor.

7

As a portal formed in the air, I grabbed my hammer and told Amber to go back into the house. An elf could be the Caretaker, and it could also be an assassin. Those half-orc–half-elf guys had used elven magic, after all.

A cloaked figure leaped out, landing lightly in the street with a magical sword in hand. *She* was magical as well, and I tensed, sensing elven blood as well as... dwarven blood?

When she turned to face me, I recognized her. I couldn't remember her name, but she was the Assassins' Guild leader. She'd been at Val's house the night several assassins had attacked, wanting to kill me. They'd tried to destroy Val and her property in the process.

Though the leader hadn't attacked us, instead standing back and observing, she'd chewed out Sarrlevi after the battle and kicked him out of the guild. That left me predisposed to dislike her for reasons that had nothing to do with the fact that he'd admitted they'd had a relationship once—or that he'd at least had sex with her.

She asked me something in Dwarven. Though I only recognized the word *where* and Sarrlevi's name, I got the gist.

"He's not here," I answered in English, then responded telepathically as well, to skirt the language issue, though it occurred to me that I could test my translation charm on her.

Her eyes narrowed. *Are you certain? The female goblin believed he might be in this place with you.*

I gritted my teeth. *Did you interrogate my friend?*

I asked her where Sarrlevi was, and her green lips said she didn't know but her mind formed an image of you, and him with you. It took a few more questions to learn where this place was so that I could form a portal here. Meanwhile, I had to endure her attempts to sell me house plans. Goblins are strange creatures, are they not?

Not trusting her in the least, I dug out my phone to text Tinja to make sure she was all right. As I typed my message, I didn't take my eyes from the assassin.

Sarrlevi spoke in Elven, startling me, then appeared a few feet away. With his swords in hand, he faced the assassin leader.

She hadn't drawn her weapons yet and arched her eyebrows as she replied to him, also in Elven.

While I waited for a response from Tinja, I tapped my charm to see if it would work.

"You have a female now?" I was in time to hear.

The assassin looked at me, her expression difficult to read.

Even though she was half-dwarven, and maybe I should have felt some kinship toward her, her elven half meant she had six inches in height over me. Not to mention a handsome, haughty face with eyebrows that probably sorted themselves out without need for tweezing.

I lifted my chin, deciding I hated running into Sarrlevi's old lovers, but refusing to feel inadequate. Or at least refusing to *admit* I felt inadequate. That was the first step in building self-confidence, wasn't it?

Sarrlevi considered me before answering. Debating if he wanted to admit to *having* me?

I squinted at him.

He snorted softly. *Debating if you would mind if I told her I have you. As I recall, you objected to me claiming you were mine when we faced the orc hammer hunter.*

Because you were possessively gripping my shoulder and waving your sword at him in a penis-comparison contest.

Penises did not come up when we were discussing your worth.

They were implied. Trust me.

Really.

Yes. I nodded firmly at him. Realizing I hadn't responded to his question about whether he could claim me, I started to nod again, but the assassin snorted and spoke first.

"You have a female," she decided, then stepped forward, ignoring Sarrlevi's drawn swords, and punched him in the shoulder. "Good. You need someone to sand your prickly edges. Your *many* prickly edges."

"*Your* edges are not without prickle," Sarrlevi said stiffly. He'd looked like he'd wanted to block that punch and had decided at the last second to let it fall.

"They are not," she agreed, then told me, apparently realizing I now understood her, "It's an assassin thing."

"I've observed that they're not as warm and cuddly as half-dwarves."

As I've noted before, Sarrlevi told me silently, *your assessment of yourself as cuddly may be groundless.*

Wait until you see me after you've sated all my desires and you're hand-feeding me cubes of cheese from the bedside tray.

Oh? Will you nuzzle me like a fawn?

I'll let you rub my head, and I might rub something back.

Intriguing.

"I'm glad from the expressions on your faces that I cannot hear your words," the assassin said. "Does your female have a name? Or do you call her *mongrel* because you're certain you're superior to her?"

Her wry expression and tone made me think he'd once called *her* that. Maybe it hadn't entirely been the fact that Sarrlevi had killed his father that had kept her from letting him into the guild immediately.

"This is Mataalii Puletasi." Sarrlevi nodded toward me without looking away from the assassin. Despite the friendly punch, he didn't appear inclined to relax around her. "She is a crafter and enchanter."

I smiled at him for not mentioning plumbing or modifying enchanter to indicate I was a student. I wouldn't have minded the latter though since it was true.

"An enchanter who pounds assassins with a giant hammer?" She smirked. Were most enchanters nonviolent pacifists?

"She is half-dwarven," Sarrlevi stated, as if that explained aggressive tendencies.

"Indeed." The assassin's smirk widened.

Sarrlevi sheathed his swords. "What do you want, Nesheeva? Not to reinstate me in the guild, I trust."

"With dragons asking where you are because they either want to slay you or punish and rehabilitate you? No, I would not wish to draw their ire to the guild or for its members to be considered guilty by association."

"Its fine, upstanding members, none of whom are ever targeted by dragons or other vengeful, powerful entities because of their own actions."

She—Nesheeva—gave him an edged smile. "None have collected powerful, vengeful enemies so quickly as you have this month. In addition to the dragons, the dwarven and elven royals would like to see you pounded to slag or strung up from trees, respectively. Did you know?"

"I'm aware. What do *you* want?" Sarrlevi watched her through slitted eyes. "Have I not also irritated *you* of late?"

"Tremendously so, yes, though if the target of the prestige hunt is your new mate, it's somewhat understandable. I thought you were simply defending her to vex me."

"You factored not in the least in my decision to defend her."

Maybe you should be polite to her, I suggested silently to Sarrlevi. *It sounds like she knows a lot about what's going on in the Realms. At least when it came to him. Maybe she could be a source of information. Haven't you mentioned before that she sometimes tells you things?*

Not without requiring payment.

Maybe she knows where your mother is. That would be worth payment.

"How little I mean to you these days," Nesheeva said. "Even so, I am pleased with one thing you did of late and came to tell you that if you find a way to resolve your dragon problem, I may be willing to take you back into the guild. You know I miss our witty repartee."

"You miss my dues."

"I miss the dues of the assassins you've killed. Should I invite you back in, expect a steep fine and to pay extra for a few years."

"I'd be a fool not to grovel at your feet for permission to rejoin."

"Clearly." Nesheeva winked at me.

"What favor?" I wondered. A few weeks ago, she'd been pissed at him, as she'd admitted. Belatedly, I realized she wouldn't understand English unless she also had a translation charm.

But Nesheeva nodded as if she understood, and since I sensed magic on her from more than her weapons, maybe she did. "Princess Barothla was a manipulative bitch who would have made a nettlesome dwarven ruler. While assassins can earn steady work during unrestful times, and I wouldn't have objected to her irking leaders of other nations, I wouldn't have cared to have to tiptoe around someone so vengeful and volatile. Besides, King Ironhelm is a relative of mine. I wouldn't like to watch someone in the guild kill him after being hired by his overly ambitious daughter."

Did that mean Nesheeva was a relative of *mine*? When Sarrlevi had tested my heritage, his magical blood analyzer had only popped up my dwarven mother, aunt, and grandfather, so it hadn't occurred to me that there might be cousins and such.

"I hadn't realized you disliked her," Sarrlevi said.

"Many did. Those she wasn't actively currying favor with—and some she was. Dwarves aren't the best at charming people."

"Indeed." Sarrlevi slanted a look at me.

Please. I was more charming than *he* was. And more cuddly. I put an image of him feeding me cheese cubes into his mind.

Sarrlevi smiled faintly before facing Nesheeva again. "I don't suppose you had any encounters with Barothla before her death? Or know where she likes to stash kidnap victims?"

Nesheeva tilted her head. "Kidnap victims?"

I slumped. Given all that she knew, I'd thought she might have an idea where Barothla had hidden Sarrlevi's mother, but I supposed it would have been odd if a random assassin had that information.

"Yes," was all Sarrlevi said.

In case Nesheeva was reading my mind, I wiped away thoughts of his mother. He might not want that information getting out.

"She was known to take *captives* to a volcano research station on Dun Kroth," Nesheeva said. "Is that what you mean?"

"The dwarven princess regularly took captives?" Sarrlevi asked.

"Beings she experimented on is what I heard they were. For her various potions and concoctions. One of our guild members got caught up in that, imprisoned because he was half-troll and half-elf, and she wanted to see the effects of some draft on mongrels." Nesheeva curled her upper lip.

"She had cages full of animals in her laboratory in the dwarven capital." I found Sarrlevi looking at me and met his gaze and nodded, probably thinking the same thing he was, that his mother might have been taken to this hidden facility. If Barothla already had such a place established, why not use it?

"Yes, for her experiments." Nesheeva nodded. "That's what I've heard. But animals can't be enough to test potions on, not potions that will ultimately be given to intelligent beings."

"She had goblins in her lab too." I scowled at the memory, still wishing I could free them somehow. Maybe some of the other dwarves who lived in the royal quarters, being less vile than she, had already done so. I hoped that was the case.

"Few care about goblins," Nesheeva said, "but I doubt King Ironhelm would have allowed her to keep dwarves, elves, gnomes, and the like in cages in his city."

The thought that he might not have cared about goblins disturbed me, and I hoped he'd been more oblivious to what his daughter had been doing in that laboratory than approving of her experiments.

A response to my text came in. Tinja said she was fine but that she didn't like the rude, mind-reading half-dwarf who'd visited.

Did she buy a set of your tiny-home plans? I replied, relieved that *rude* was all Nesheeva had been.

No.

Would you have felt more warmly toward her if she had?

Obviously.

"Do you know where this volcano facility is?" Sarrlevi asked Nesheeva.

"Yes, but only because of Jugnoth, the one I mentioned who was captured. After he escaped, he came to a guild meeting, trying to gather allies to go back and destroy the place as payback for

Barothla keeping him there. But it's well-protected by magic. He didn't think he could tear it down on his own."

"Did he find allies?"

"At a guild meeting? People who would risk themselves for no financial gain? Don't be foolish, Sarrlevi."

If she'd offended him, he didn't show it. His eyes were still slitted, this time in speculation, his focus probably wholly on finding his mother. "Then this facility likely still stands."

"Likely."

"Where on Dun Kroth is it located? There are *many* volcanoes there."

"Indeed." Nesheeva smirked at him—it seemed to be her favorite expression. "This information is of value to you? Because someone you know has been kidnapped?"

Sarrlevi eyed her without responding. Because he feared she would demand a high price if she knew who Barothla had taken? Gold, I was certain, he would pay, but might she want some more onerous favor?

"It's of value to me," I said, not caring if Nesheeva wanted an onerous favor from *me*. "Will you trade the information? I don't have a lot of gold, but I can make some mean shower-curtain hooks." I exchanged my phone for the hooks, showing them off, though I was certain they wouldn't interest her. "Do assassins have problems with water escaping the cubicle and getting all over the floor?"

"Cubicle?" Nesheeva mouthed.

Maybe other worlds didn't have showers. If she was half-elven, she might bathe herself in the forest with dewy clumps of moss.

Nesheeva waved away the question—and the offering. "Sarrlevi, since I feel minutely bad that your female is the prestige hunt, and you did, as I said, brutally slay someone I found despicable, I will give you this information for free." She smiled. "As a favor."

His sigh promised he expected her to one day request that he return her favor—and he would have rather paid for the information.

Nesheeva only smiled more broadly. "Jugnoth said the cave, once hollowed out by lava, has an entrance high on the side of Mount Karbrek. Or perhaps low on the side of it. Something like that. As you say, the dwarves have many volcanoes. I barely paid attention to his story and only remember the location because of half-forgotten geography lessons from my youth. My father insisted I learn about Dun Kroth even though I grew up on Veleshna Var."

"Did your parents live in a house on the ground?" I asked.

"They did. Mother took me often to visit family in the trees, but my father preferred to keep his feet on the ground. Or even under it. He excavated tunnels under our living room, to the bemusement of the elves." Nesheeva pointed at Sarrlevi. "That volcano is supposed to be a place where prisoners of war were once sacrificed by being thrown into the caldera. According to legend, their souls haunt the volcano, and bad things happen to those who travel to the area."

"It sounds like a good place for a secret research laboratory." The words *off the beaten path* came to my mind.

"Or at least to stash things one doesn't want tourists to find." Nesheeva bowed to Sarrlevi and, surprisingly, to me as well, then stepped back and lifted a hand to form a portal. "I'll contact you in the future if I need a favor, Sarrlevi."

"I have no doubt," he said.

Nesheeva started to turn toward the portal but paused, considering me for a moment, then looking at my hand. She plucked one of the squirrel hooks from my grip, bowed again, then sprang through her portal.

"Maybe water seeping onto the floor *is* a problem in other realms." I made a mental note to craft another hook for the set.

Sarrlevi only sighed again.

Surprised he wasn't more enthused, I said, "It looks like we might not need to visit the dwarven capital."

I did wonder if I should ask him to send me there, regardless. Even though I hadn't killed Barothla, I felt compelled to apologize, or at least explain my side of things, and give my condolences to my grandfather, if he would accept them.

"Perhaps. Nesheeva may also have come to set a trap for me."

"You don't think you can trust her?"

"Certainly not." Sarrlevi glanced at me, as if surprised I would suggest such a thing.

"I suppose I could see her angling to get you, especially if dwarves, elves, or dragons hired her to do so."

"Yes. It's also possible she was under a magical compulsion placed by a dragon. Zondia may be seeking other ways to reach me."

"I don't think Zondia has tried to magically compel me." Not unless she was more subtle than I thought. Thus far, my experiences with dragons suggested they had the subtlety of a pile driver.

"No? You may not have been aware of it." Sarrlevi considered me. "In your last meeting, while distracting you with talk of other things, she might have implanted in your mind a compulsion to smash me in the back of the head with your hammer as soon as we go into a battle and I'm distracted." One of his eyebrows twitched. "Perhaps after you destroy my belt so that my trousers descend."

"If I pull down your pants, it's not going to be to smash you."

"No?" His eyelids drooped, and a smile turned up the corners of his mouth. "What would it be for?"

My cheeks warmed, and I looked away, remembering that we weren't alone on the property. Changing the subject, I said, "I hope your assassin leader *was* being straight and not setting a trap. She seemed kind of decent, way more so than any other female you've slept with that I've met."

"She punched me and called me prickly," Sarrlevi said.

"That's *decent* compared to the elven bitches. And she's not inaccurate with her assessment."

"Really." He stepped closer and slid his fingers through my hair. "Should not someone who wants her every sexual desire satisfied, not to mention being hand-fed cheese cubes, be more flattering to her inamorato?"

Ina-what? Was that a lover? Zavryd might not have been the only one reading dictionaries.

"Nah." I leaned into his touch, hoping he would rub the back of my neck—and maybe other things. "You like honesty, not flattery. And you know you're prickly. I am too. It's okay."

His strong fingers stroked the tight muscles in my neck, and I melted into him. Damn, that felt good. I reached for his chest, thinking of rubbing something of his and sharing some of my magic with him.

The front door of the house opened.

"Did you make these too?" Amber called, holding up a bronze drawer pull in the shape of a leaf.

"Yes." I forced myself to step back from Sarrlevi, not wanting Amber to tell her mom that we'd spent all our time in her presence groping each other.

"Return her to her domicile," Sarrlevi said. "If this doesn't turn out to be a trap, and we must traverse through lava tubes, I should pick up a few supplies."

"Food, water, fire-resistant shoes, and charms to protect against toxic underground gases?"

"That last *would* be useful." His eyes glinted. "In case I fall unconscious in your presence again and you presume to launder my clothing in Earth chemicals."

"I was doing you a favor, dude. Your clothes were filthy."

"Perhaps you could also make a chemical-free-laundry-cleaning trinket with your burgeoning enchanting skills."

"*Perhaps* I could make a trinket that delivers an ass-kicking to elves who aren't appreciative of their inamoratos."

"You would be an inamorata." Unperturbed by threats of ass-kicking, he kissed me before forming a portal, promising he would return soon, and leaped through.

"I wonder what supplies he'll get in case this *is* a trap," I muttered.

8

SHORTLY AFTER I DROPPED OFF AMBER AND PARKED MY HARLEY AT Val's house, Sarrlevi found me, his pack not appearing any more stuffed with items than usual, but I trusted its magical alternate-dimensional nooks were filled with fireproof ropes, grappling hooks, and whatever else one needed to tramp around inside an active volcano. Despite my dwarven blood, spelunking had never called to me, so I lacked experience in that area.

It concerned me that we were heading to Dun Kroth without permission from the king. I'd thought about writing a letter to my grandfather, and maybe tucking a gift of an enchanted shower-curtain hook into the envelope, but the handful of Dwarven words I knew weren't sufficient for the task. I didn't want to delay Sarrlevi's quest, regardless. As soon as he arrived, I nodded my readiness.

"Do you still wish to go?" he asked. "It occurred to me that the research outpost won't likely be as well-defended as the city, and, if my mother is there, I won't need you to speak with your grandfather."

"If she's *not* there, you'll want to try the capital next, right?"

"Yes."

I nodded. "I'll go. What kind of inamorata would I be if I didn't walk through molten lava with you?"

"I plan to levitate us *over* the molten lava."

"While being exposed to noxious sulfuric fumes, though, right? Your delicate elven senses might be overwhelmed. If you pass out, you'll need me to carry you out of the volcano." Sarrlevi opened his mouth, but I held up a finger. "Don't make me remind you that you almost passed out from the laundry-detergent fumes."

He squinted at me. "I believe you're teasing me more often of late."

"Because I've gotten comfortable around you, and you've admitted you care about me and are unlikely to lop off my head when we're done working together."

"Confessing my feelings to you in that letter might have been a mistake."

"It wasn't. I loved it. And I love you." I'd kept his letter in my pocket until it had grown grimy and crinkled. Then I'd found a tin box to protect it, and it now resided in the drawer in my night-stand. Smiling, I rose on tiptoes to kiss him on the cheek—though it would have been the jaw if he hadn't bent his head. Elves were so damn tall. Lovable but tall.

"In that case, I will allow periodic teasing."

"Generous of you."

"As assassins are known to be."

"Someday, I'm going to get you to retire from that work and join me in my business. It's clear from all the things you repair with vines that you crave a career in home renovations."

"I merely seek to bring order to chaotic environments."

"*Exactly.* That's what renovations are all about. You'll be perfect." I smiled dreamily as I envisioned him with a broom in one hand and his kerchief in the other, magically cleaning up sawdust as I cut lumber.

"Perhaps I should employ ass kissing to convince Nesheeva to take me back into the guild."

"I don't know why you're denying your natural calling."

Sarrlevi unbuttoned a pocket and fished out two identical charms. They looked like triangles. Or maybe mountains. Or... volcanoes?

I raised my eyebrows as he pressed one into my hand, then hooked the other on his belt.

"These are to ensure you *won't* need to carry me out of the volcano. I assumed you wouldn't have time to make charms to protect the wearer against noxious gases, which are indeed likely in lava tubes, so I purchased them."

"Were they expensive?" I wished I *had* had time to try to make some. My success with the translation trinket delighted me.

"Yes."

"Can you return them if I succeed in copying them and making charms for free?" I hooked the triangle on my keychain next to the translation and camouflaging trinkets and resolved to study it later.

"As long as you don't let your roommate provide the materials."

That didn't quite answer my question. "Thank you for getting one for me."

Sarrlevi must have been fairly certain I would come along. That knowledge pleased me. I wanted him to believe he could count on me.

"Of course," he said. "Your lungs will need to be hale in the event you *do* need to carry me out of a lava tube."

"It won't be a problem. If I can manage a ramp, I can handle a tube." As long as molten lava wasn't flowing along the bottom. He hadn't brought me a levitation trinket, and I doubted any enchanting magic taught one how to float.

Sarrlevi tilted his head curiously.

I smirked, realizing he'd been unconscious and didn't know. "I've carried you before. After Broadleaf knocked you out on her ramp."

An expression of distaste replaced his curiosity. More because he didn't like that he'd been helpless, I was sure, than because he objected to my assistance.

"Don't worry," I said. "You liked it. I had my hand on your ass."

He managed a smile. "As long as I enjoyed myself."

I texted Val to let her know where I was going and that I'd be back to continue the search for my parents once she'd rounded up her trackers. A message had come in from Willard, letting me know she had operatives in place at my sister's and grandparents' houses. Good.

After I put my phone away, Sarrlevi formed a portal. Only as we leaped through did it occur to me to wonder how he knew where to take us. He hadn't touched Nesheeva's head to extract the location from her thoughts.

I only had a second to pray that we wouldn't end up in the middle of a volcano before the usual out-of-body, dream-like state swept over me.

We came out of the portal under an angry red sky dominated by storm clouds with jags of lightning shooting between them. A hot humid wind blew across the plateau where we landed, ash wafting in the breeze and immediately coating my nostrils. We weren't in a lava tube, not yet, but the air smelled as sulfuric as I'd imagined. Not one but three volcanoes were visible through the hazy air, one right behind us. Our plateau rose up from its base.

Glad Sarrlevi had arrived beside me, I was half-tempted to clasp his hand. Usually, I wasn't the type of girl to get scared at movies or worry about haunted houses, but this place had a desolate and eerie quality that set me on edge. Beyond that, the lightning branching among the clouds above was a legitimate concern. Not convinced we were safe, especially when I held a big metal hammer, I looked around for cover.

On the other side of the plateau, monolithic stone—no, iron—pillars formed a circle reminiscent of Stonehenge. A *magical* Stonehenge. Twin beams of yellow light ran between the tops of the pillars, then flowed into an R2-D2-shaped cylinder squatting on a stone slab in the center. Whatever it was, it hummed with power.

Lightning flashed overhead, and a streak zapped one of the pillars. I jumped, half expecting it to explode, but it absorbed the electricity. Momentarily, the beams flared brighter before settling back to their previous state.

"Hopefully, that thing is like a big lightning rod that'll keep us from being struck," I said.

"It may be."

Sarrlevi pointed past the pillars to a one- or two-room structure that reminded me of a log cabin, but the stacked "logs" were made from cement instead of wood. It had a doorway with no door and windows with no glass or shutters. Though it didn't look like much of a shelter, we headed toward it.

"Is all of Dun Kroth like this? On the surface?" As I waved toward the angry red sky, another branch of lightning escaped the clouds, sizzling through the air to strike one of the pillars. When we'd visited the world before, I'd only seen the subterranean capital city and equally subterranean area around it.

"My understanding of Dun Kroth's history is that it used to be like this everywhere, at least for a time, and that's what drove dwarves to take shelter underground and use their magic to adapt themselves to survive without much exposure to sunlight. These days, I believe it's contained to this continent, which is filled with volcanoes and unbalanced magic."

"Ring of Fire, huh? There must be earthquakes too then. I'm surprised anyone would want to live underground here."

"I believe the effects of earthquakes are more extreme at the surface and the natural arches of the Dwarven stone passageways offer strong support."

"But you'd still rather be in a tree, right?"

"Of course."

The structure, with the windows looking out to the pillars as well as each volcano, appeared to be for observation. Counters ran along the inside walls, and a few pieces of magical equipment rested on them, all collecting dust. I didn't say anything, not wanting to dash Sarrlevi's hopes, but it didn't look like Barothla or anyone else had been here for a long time.

He knelt beside a rectangular trapdoor that blended with the stone floor, making me think of crawlspace access panels. Before opening it, he formed protective magic around us.

As soon as the door rose, a faint beeping started up, and we tensed. It came not from below but from outside. One of the pillars pulsed, emanating waves of power as well as sound. They didn't hurt us or disturb the structure, but it was hard not to find it ominous.

"Is that happening because we opened the trapdoor?" I asked. "Or did enough lightning hit the pillars to trigger something?"

Maybe the beeping simply started up every hour, like Big Ben announcing the time.

"I know little of the research that dwarves are doing on their world," Sarrlevi said. "It would be a remarkable coincidence, however, if the beeping had nothing to do with me opening the door."

He frowned into the darkness below.

"Meaning we'd better hurry in case that's an alarm going off?" I asked.

"If it is, I suspect it will take time for someone to arrive, but there are many reasons to expedite our adventure."

Sarrlevi conjured a globe of light to send below, and I peered over his shoulder. A metal ladder ran down to what might once have been living quarters—bunk beds remained attached to one wall—but what should have been the floor had crumbled away, as if a sinkhole had opened up. Far below, a river of orange magma glowed as it meandered through what might have been a freshly hollowed-out lava tube.

"Do we... levitate down there and follow that tunnel into the volcano?" I couldn't say the idea excited me. With intense heat wafting up from below, we would have to worry about more than fumes.

"I don't think there's enough space for that." Sarrlevi pointed. "The magma flow is high, still forming that tube."

Outside, the beeping continued.

Sarrlevi closed the door. The noise didn't stop. He walked to one of the windows and pointed out. "I believe that is Mount Karbrek. Nesheeva put an image of it and this location in my mind."

Ah. So that was how he'd known where to open his portal.

"She hadn't been and didn't know much about the area," Sarrlevi added. "She was basing her directions off a map and memories of geology studies. I was prepared to pop into the air above lava flows and have to summon a levitation spell very quickly."

"You still might need to if the rest of this plateau drops into that sinkhole."

"Indeed." Sarrlevi gripped his chin as he gazed at the volcano and then over at me. "My memory of your plumbing scheme is fuzzy, since my mind was compromised, but I remember you speaking of using your power to follow pipes under the magical barrier of the enemy's stronghold."

"Hart's mansion? Yeah."

"Were you able to sense the pipes and manipulate them from afar?"

"Yes."

"Hm."

We hadn't seen so much as a sink in the structure, so I didn't know what he was angling toward. There couldn't be any pipes in the volcano. "I torqued the heck out of a toilet from up the street in a neighbor's driveway. My hammer wasn't sure if my mother would have approved of me using my power in such a way or not."

Realizing I had a resource who'd spent more time on Dun Kroth than either of us, I squeezed the hammer's haft. *Sorka? Have you been to this area before?*

I have. Not this precise location, but your mother once came to this continent with a research party to study volcano magic and geothermal energy as a natural power source.

Do you have any thoughts about where prisoners—hapless victims —might be kept around here?

I do not. The continent spans thousands of square miles.

The Assassins' Guild leader mentioned this specific volcano.

And she is a reliable source?

We don't know.

I do not sense anyone magical in the area, but, of course, such entities could be hidden with camouflaging or insulating magic.

"Do you think," Sarrlevi said slowly, back to studying the volcano, "you could sense the various lava tubes inside and tell if there are any large hollowed-out areas or anything anomalous?"

"Uhm, lava tubes aren't much like pipes."

"No? A liquid flows through them."

"But they're not made of metal. It's the metal I was sensing."

"Dwarves are very attuned to dirt, ore, *and* rock. You may have the power to sense caves and lava tubes. Alternatively, we can levitate all around the outside and hope to float across an opening."

"We should have brought a dragon."

"I am not inclined to ask any dragons for help."

"Understandable. Let me see if I can sense anything."

A volcano was a lot bigger than a house, even Hart's pretentious mansion, and I felt daunted as I rested my hands on a counter and gazed out the window at Mount Karbrek.

Sarrlevi gripped my shoulder and nodded encouragement.

"If I ever need anything sensed in a forest, you better be there for me," I told him.

"I will help you track down your parents after this," he said, though I hadn't been thinking specifically of that. "I *can* sense many things in forests."

"Good." I closed my eyes and reached out toward the volcano with my mind.

At first, I worried I would have to get much closer to have a shot at detecting anything, but, as when I'd been on Dun Kroth before, magic came easily to me. My senses seemed to flow—almost *fly*—out of me, skimming over the contours of the volcano. They followed its slopes of jumbled black lava rock and soared up to the caldera. Even from miles away, I could almost see the pockets of magma inside of it, emitting steam.

There didn't appear to be anything unnatural in there—which was good, because I didn't want to tell Sarrlevi we had to hop into the caldera—and I focused on the exterior again, seeking the entrances to old lava tubes, ones that had cooled and might allow access to some interior cave or base.

A headache burgeoned behind my eyes as I kept searching, and weariness crept into my limbs. It was strange that using one's mind—one's *magic*—was as tiring as running on a treadmill, but it drained me rapidly.

Sarrlevi must have sensed my growing fatigue, for he slipped an arm around me, and some of his power flowed into me. It mingled with and somehow recharged mine, making it easier for me to keep searching. I longed to find sign of his mother, sign of anything. He'd helped me so many times. I wanted to help him.

Even as I slumped against him, letting him support my body, I kept searching for something besides rock and natural lava tubes inside the volcano. With my senses stretched to the far side, I was about to give up, or at least take a moment to regroup, when something unusual stuck out. Metal.

Not ore but forged metal. A door?

Sarrlevi, maybe sensing what I saw through me, stirred.

"That may be something," I whispered.

"Yes."

I opened my eyes. "I'm not sure how volcanoes work on Dun Kroth, but on Earth, they don't come with doors."

"Dwarves like to install things underground."

"Let's check it out." I shifted to step toward the exit, but my weak muscles almost gave out.

Sarrlevi hadn't released me, and his grip tightened to keep me upright.

"Sorry," I said. "That was a little taxing."

"You did well." Magic flowed from him and lifted us both into the air.

My stomach flipped sideways at the sensation of my feet dangling without support. I'd been levitated before but not across distances—and lava fields.

"Thanks," I said, more to his compliment than his magic. I might have preferred riding a dragon to this.

"Really," he responded dryly.

"Are you reading my mind again, Varlesh? Is that polite?"

"I merely seek to see through your eyes so I can guide us to the door."

"Uh huh."

Sarrlevi kept his arm around me and also erected a protective barrier as we flowed out of the abandoned research laboratory. The beeping and pulses of power hadn't stopped, and, as we sailed off the plateau, I hoped again that it wasn't an alarm system alerting someone to our arrival.

9

WE SOARED QUICKLY OVER BARE BLACK SLOPES DOTTED WITH POOLS of lava, rivulets running down from them. A part of me wanted a more sedate pace but another part wanted the trip to be over as soon as possible. Heat and sulfuric fumes bathed us, making me glad for Sarrlevi's barrier, though it didn't fully keep out scents.

I dipped a hand in my pocket and rubbed the charm he'd given me.

Sarrlevi glanced at me. "You didn't do that as soon as we arrived?"

"I was enjoying the pungent tang in the air," I said instead of admitting I'd forgotten about it. The odor also hadn't been as noticeable on the windswept plateau.

"Your dwarven blood sometimes prompts strange words to come out of your mouth."

"Says the elf who's admitted to bathing himself with moss."

"That's not strange. Moss is dewy and clean."

As Sarrlevi swept us halfway up the backside of the volcano, we passed several openings that might have been shallow caves or tubes, some actively dripping lava and others hardened into black rock. Hopefully, my door wouldn't have lava flowing past the threshold.

"That one," I said with certainty, pointing at an entrance.

Lava *did* drip from the mouth of the tube but only a trickle. With luck, that wouldn't turn into a river once we were inside.

"There *is* a door in there." Excitement infused Sarrlevi's voice, making me realize how rarely I'd heard him exuberant or even calmly happy about anything.

"Of course. Finding pipes and doors is my specialty. As long as they're made from metal."

He smiled at me as he levitated us into the tunnel. "I believe you will end up having many specialties."

"I am pretty wicked with hooks and drainpipes."

"Yes."

As we floated farther back and upward through an impressively straight tunnel, the lava flow remained a trickle, heat emanating from the sluggish orange liquid. I tried to pick up the auras of magical beings, but my senses thought we were the only people crazy enough to be in the area. Not even the door, which soon came into view, emanated magic. If anything, it was the *opposite* of magic, feeling almost dead to my senses.

Set into the side of the lava tube, which continued deeper into the volcano beyond it, the riveted door looked to be thick, making me think of bank vaults. *Large* bank vaults. It would have been wide enough and tall enough to drive a semi-truck through.

Interesting. Maybe that meant someone had designed the entrance to be able to accept deliveries. Though I couldn't imagine the dwarven equivalent of FedEx dropping off freight inside a volcano.

"No doorknob or latch." Sarrlevi set us down on the black rock in front of the door, the lava oozing past scant feet behind us.

I expected the ground to scorch me through the soles of my shoes, and it *was* warm but not as much as I'd feared. As long as I didn't inadvertently take a step back, such as when some booby trap sprung, I would be fine.

Even though I didn't sense magic, that didn't mean there wasn't a security system. I eyed the ground for cracks, wires, or other signs that might indicate a trap.

Sarrlevi rested his hand and cheek on the door. "It's designed to deaden senses—to keep people from detecting magic beyond it —but I can detect a hint of something. Artifacts, I believe." That excitement had crept into his voice again. "Maybe this *is* the place."

"You'll owe Nesheeva a favor if she sent you the right way," I said before remembering they'd been lovers once. I didn't want him owing *that* kind of favor.

"Unlike Slehvyra, she accepts gold," Sarrlevi said, "though I suspect she'll ask me for something more difficult to deliver. It will be worth it if my mother is here."

"If need be, I'll make a whole set of curtain hooks for your guild leader."

As Sarrlevi continued to inspect the door with his senses, I tried not to think about all the things that could go wrong. Though traps had been on my mind, the most concerning notion to me was that his mother might be in there but might have already died. It had been several days since he'd killed Barothla. If she'd expected to return soon, she might not have arranged for anyone to care for his mother. How would one even get a nurse to come out here?

Sarrlevi probed the door with a strand of his magic, but nothing happened. He stepped back. "It also absorbs the power I use on it. I could blast out the rock to either side, but I'm wary of setting off traps, especially when we're standing in a lava tube." He eyed the ceiling warily, though it appeared sturdy.

The *lava* was of more concern to me than the ceiling. It did, however, amuse me to realize that being in tunnels might bother

Sarrlevi as much as walking across rickety rope bridges in elven cities disturbed me.

"Will you try?" Sarrlevi extended his hand toward the door. "Dwarven magic may be better suited for this."

"As long as you keep telling me I'm doing a good job. A girl likes to get praise." I smiled at him and pressed my palm against the warm metal, using my senses to search for a locking mechanism.

"I will." He rested his hand on my back, ready to lend magical support again.

As he'd suggested, the door was difficult to probe, seeming to absorb the magic I sent into it. I couldn't feel whatever he'd detected on the other side and worried I wouldn't be able to do anything, but then I sensed what had to be the locking mechanism. It was near the floor, and I realized the door slid up instead of opening outward on hinges. A giant hook attached it to a bar underneath. I might have corroded it, as I'd once used my enchanting magic to do on a cage lock, but I first tried to nudge the hook aside.

A faint *clunk* emanated from the ground. After strengthening the protective barrier around us, Sarrlevi used an abrupt surge of power to heft open the door. It creaked as it lifted, then thudded into the hollowed space in the rock above. He might not be a master of metal and locks, but he had no problem moving something heavy.

With his swords out, he peered through the doorway. I lifted my hammer, ready for something to spring out and attack us. Hadn't Nesheeva said this place was well-defended? Or maybe she'd said it was haunted by sacrificed prisoners of war. That wasn't appealing either.

A tunnel stretched ahead of us, curving slightly as it led into a large chamber that hadn't been excavated by flowing magma but by chisel or, more likely, magic. Either someone had left the lights on, or they'd come on when we'd opened the door. Whether they were electrical or magical, I couldn't tell from the entrance, but I could now sense the magic Sarrlevi had promised. A lot of it. Not people but devices.

Be careful, Sorka warned. *As your elf said, there is a magic-dampening quality in the walls. Our power might not be as effective inside.*

I'm sure I can still use you to wallop things.

I have little doubt. Sorka shared an image of rows of old cabinets in the chamber ahead and me tearing into them.

I'm sure there's not a kitchen to demolish in there.

We shall see.

A faint *clink-clank* came from the depths of the chamber or perhaps from another one beyond it. From the doorway, our view was limited.

"I sense... people?" Sarrlevi rarely sounded uncertain, but he did now. "Orcs and trolls and... more than one elf. But something is off about them. Their auras are very muted."

I nodded, though I struggled to pick living beings out from all the magic that emanated from artifacts. Swords still in hand, Sarrlevi strode into the tunnel. A premonition made me glance back after we'd gone a few steps. The door slammed down behind us.

"Uh." I paused as the clink of the lock reengaging brought back thoughts of traps.

"I can form a portal if we need to leave." Barely glancing back, Sarrlevi kept walking. More than that. He broke into a run.

Maybe one of the auras he sensed belonged to his mom.

As I followed him into the chamber, it turned out to be more of a cavern with magical machinery and pipes along one stone wall. The opposite wall held what I could only think of as jail cells, dozens of hollowed-out alcoves with invisible barriers across the fronts.

Faint green light emanated from the alcoves, and most were

occupied, one person in each. They were the sources of the weak auras, but they lay unmoving on the ground. In a couple of cases, they were floating in the air, as if suspended in Jell-O. None of the prisoners appeared to be awake. If not for their weak auras, I would have feared them dead. Or frozen in something like cryonic suspension, as if we'd walked into a sci-fi movie.

The people were all fully dressed, and many wore armor as well, their scarred faces and muscled arms suggesting they had been—or still were?—warriors. Even those flat on their backs appeared formidable. What strange test subjects. Why wouldn't Barothla have picked up street urchins or downtrodden homeless people? Those would have been easier marks, and they might not have been missed by many.

Sarrlevi jogged past most of the cells, then paused to peer into the last alcove. Beyond him, the cavern continued, but it was too dark for me to tell how far it went. Worried about the continuing *clink-clanks* coming from somewhere in that darkness, I walked slowly past the alcoves on my way to join Sarrlevi.

Bronze plaques written in Dwarven were bolted to the stone wall beside each cell. Though I could only pick out a few words, they looked like names and information on each occupant. That was surprising. Would Barothla have cared that much about the lives of those she'd captured? Maybe the plaques simply said something like *Subject 1A* and listed physical traits. Still, the permanence of the bronze seemed an odd choice for that. Unless she'd expected them to live long enough for her to run a lot of experiments over the years, wouldn't she have opted for something more temporary?

Inside the cells, the occupants ranged from full-blooded trolls, ogres, and orcs to half-bloods with elven or dwarven heritage to a full-blooded dwarf and two elves. It chilled me to think that Barothla had been experimenting on her own people, but little would surprise me about her at this point.

One of the figures made me pause, a handsome but fearsome-looking male who'd been frozen in a crouch, with his arms raised, his fingers curled into fists, and his eyes open. Wearing armor, with an empty sword scabbard at his hip, he looked like he could spring out of the chamber to fight at any second. His aura was as dim as the others, but something about it made me stare.

With pointed ears and lean, angular features, he appeared fully elven, but I also got a dragon vibe from him. Was that possible? I hadn't thought dragons could produce offspring with anybody but other dragons. That was more because I'd never *encountered* a half-dragon than because I'd asked one of them for the details.

"Who are these people?" I wondered, glancing at his plaque, but I couldn't read anything on it. My hand drifted into my pocket, and I rubbed my translation charm, but I'd only been thinking of interpreting spoken languages when I'd made it, not reading text. Even though it tingled, a sign of the magic activating, the plaque didn't grow legible to me.

"That one is surprising," Sarrlevi said, though his tone was distracted, and he kept facing the alcove he'd stopped in front of.

"Yeah. Can dragons and elves hook up and make babies?" After using my phone to snap a photo of the plaque, I left the mystery man and continued toward Sarrlevi.

"Not naturally."

"Can they do it *un*naturally?"

"I'm aware of some experiments that were done nearly a thousand years ago that resulted in half-dragon offspring but nothing recent. I believe there were only a couple dozen of them. It was someone's idea to make super powerful warriors that would feel allegiance to their people—the people of their non-dragon halves." Sarrlevi reached out to touch a glowing panel on the wall.

"So that guy is either really old or has been frozen in here for a really long time?" I tilted my thumb over my shoulder, but Sarrlevi didn't look. "Just how long was my aunt running experiments?"

"I believe *these* are the captives Nesheeva spoke of." Sarrlevi flicked his finger toward the alcoves closest to him and looked grimly at me, his gaze haunted. "It's gnomish magic that's keeping them in stasis, but this is dwarven magic on the barrier and locking mechanism. Will you take a look? It's repelling my attempts to use elven magic to remove the barrier, and I'm hesitant to use too much brute force when..." Sarrlevi extended his hand toward the occupant in front of him, though the solid walls between the alcoves kept me from seeing inside until I got closer.

The last few chambers before I reached him held more what I would expect of captives in a science experiment. People barefoot and bare-chested or in medical gowns, appearing wan as they lay frozen on the ground under the green light. That color lighting could have made anyone appear wan, but these people were definitely less hale than the armored warriors, and I could barely make out their auras. In one chamber, I couldn't, and I feared the half-elf female might have died, even with the stasis thing running. Or... as a result of some concoction Barothla had injected her with?

Reminded of Sarrlevi waiting for me, I hurried to his side. His mother was lying on the stone floor inside the alcove he faced, her eyes closed. There was no sign of the magical elven IV that had been medicating her—or keeping her alive?—in the capital. Barefoot, like the others, she wore only a dirty and rumpled gown.

Unlike with the other female, I could sense her aura, but it was so weak that fear shot through me. What if she died as soon as we figured out how to turn off whatever device was keeping her in stasis? Before the formula could start to work?

"She'll need to go to a doctor right away, I think," I whispered.

"Yes. A healer."

"If Zavryd is at the house, he could help."

Sarrlevi grimaced but didn't reject the idea outright. Maybe he didn't have anyone better that he could trust.

"And Zoltan has potions," I added, "in case she needs more than the formula can provide."

"We must free her first." Sarrlevi pointed at the panel and the barrier. "As I said, these are dwarven and I believe a result of Barothla's magic. The gnomish magic is much older. It is what was used to create the stasis chambers. This place likely existed long before Barothla took it over for—" his mouth twisted in disgust, "—victim storage."

I nodded and focused on the panel, hoping I could help again and seeing right away why he was hesitant to smash it with a sword or incinerate it with less subtle magic. It was sophisticated, and the gnomish magic was even more so. It all seemed to tie together.

As I probed the panel with my senses and a trickle of magic, trying to understand how the barrier worked at the base level, the *clink-clanks* grew louder. Whatever was making them was now heading our way. Magic in that direction that I'd scarcely noticed before flared and grew stronger, as if something that had been hibernating had woken.

Sarrlevi spun toward the darkness and drew his swords.

"Keep working," he said as he strode forward to face the threat.

The clinks turned to straight clanks, like heavy metal footsteps on the rock floor, and a familiarity to them twanged at my senses. Now that the magic was stronger, it was also more familiar. It was similar to...

"The furnace guardian under the park," I blurted with abrupt realization, then grimaced. When I'd battled the guardian, I'd hit it with my hammer but hadn't been able to defeat it or even stop it for long. Only ducking behind the magical pedestal had protected me until the construct had realized I was a friend and not someone it needed to kill. Somehow, I doubted that one my aunt had left behind to guard her lab would feel similarly about me.

"Two of them," Sarrlevi said without looking back. He wasn't surprised. He'd already known.

"Oh, good. Because one wasn't bad enough."

10

"I'LL HANDLE THEM." SARRLEVI GLANCED BACK AS THE CLANKS GREW louder and shadows stirred in the darkness, the pair of furnace guardians approaching. They might have been around a bend in the shadowy cavern before, but their crimson eyes were visible now, at least fifteen feet above the ground and drawing closer every second. "Help free my mother. Please."

"I will, but—"

Sarrlevi sprinted toward the barely visible magical and metal creations, hurling a wave of his power ahead of him. I kept quiet, since I didn't want to distract him, but was tempted to point out that we could free his mother *after* we made sure we would both survive the furnace guardians.

Then a muffled bonging sounded, emanating from the stone walls. It wasn't the same as the beeping at the observation outpost, but it reminded me of it, giving me that same sense of an alarm going off. Of someone being alerted to our presence.

What if the furnace guardians had been unleashed to distract us? To keep us from getting away with Sarrlevi's mother before someone—or *something*—even more powerful and dangerous showed up?

Hand planted on the panel next to the stasis chamber, I explored it with my senses as quickly and thoroughly as possible. I had no idea how the thing worked—especially the part built by gnomish magic—but I sensed a conduit of power that flowed from the back of the panel to the front of the cell, providing energy for the barrier. If I could cut the flow of that, the protective field might drop. But would I also be blown across the chamber?

Fire blasted in the cavern, highlighting Sarrlevi as he leaped and slashed toward the head of one of the guardians—and highlighting it and its mate as well. They *were* the same metal dragon-like creatures that I'd faced before.

More magic flared, and clangs rang out as Sarrlevi defied gravity to leap twenty feet into the air, somersaulting to avoid snapping jaws, and landed on the head of the guardian. The construct beside it lunged toward him as the one he rode reared up like a stallion. Neither move kept him from driving his swords through the metal skull under him, but the other guardian caught his cloak, tearing a chunk free.

"Damn it." Though I wanted to do what he wished, I left the panel to throw my hammer at the snout of his attacker.

Metal screeched as Sarrlevi ducked another bite from the construct while pulling his swords free. What would have been a fatal blow against a flesh-and-blood opponent didn't stop the furnace guardian. It swiveled its battered head and fire spewed toward Sarrlevi.

Sensing my hammer approaching, the other guardian spun toward it, and I feared some barrier would deflect my attack. But Sorka smashed into the construct's face, metal denting. Unfortunately, the powerful blow didn't knock the head clear off as I'd unrealistically wished. It *did* prompt the guardian to focus on me.

That, I told myself as Sarrlevi deflected fire with magic and drove his blades once again into his foe, was what I wanted.

"*Vishgronik,*" I barked, though my hammer was already flying back toward my hand.

Again, again, Sorka crooned into my mind as she landed, the guardian stomping toward us. This *is what I was crafted for.*

And I'm glad to use you this way. Since we were pressed, I didn't point out that hitting a hunk of metal wasn't *that* much different from demolishing a cabinet.

Wishing I knew what a debilitating target might be, I threw the hammer again, aiming for the chest. Since Sarrlevi had sheared off the side of the head of his construct, and it continued to attempt to reach him with its flames, it was clear *that* wasn't a vulnerable spot.

My guardian surprised me by swiveling its head to the right, rotating like the hands of a clock, and catching my hammer in its jaws. Sorka took out a few metal teeth when she landed, but that didn't keep the construct from clamping down. And leaving me without a weapon.

Sorka, I blurted, backing away as the guardian rushed toward me, *any chance you can escape that?*

Magic flared, and the hammer flashed silver-blue. *I am trying.*

The construct's own magic grew in power to thwart her efforts, and its jaws remained shut.

"Sarrlevi," I called, though I hated to interrupt him in his own battle—and I hated even more to *need* help, "when you're done there, I could use a hand."

Or a *shield.* With my hammer in its mouth, the construct wasn't breathing fire at me and presumably couldn't bite me, but as it caught up, its legs longer than I was tall, it tried to stomp me into pieces.

I backed farther, leaving behind Sarrlevi's mother and Baroth-la's other victims, and scurried past alcoves holding prisoners. The furnace guardian sprang, metal talons slashing toward my face. I threw myself to the side, rolling to get away from the attack as it smashed its heavy paws down, trying to pin me to the ground.

I sprang up and faced it, but without my weapon, I had no way to attack, no way to keep it from attacking *me*.

Silver light flashed as Sorka did her best to escape. *This machine's magic is too powerful for me to overcome.*

Any chance you can extend your barrier over me? I asked as it lunged at me again.

This time, I dove forward and between the construct's legs. A risky maneuver, but I somersaulted rapidly through, hoping Sorka could extend her protection around me if I was closer.

You must be holding me for that to work. Oozing frustration, Sorka shot out branches of lightning. They hit the ceiling, the floor, and one curved to strike the guardian in the side, but the construct didn't slow down.

Damn.

Barely missing being trampled by a back leg, its metal talons scant inches from my eyes, I rolled out on the far side of the construct. Striking the rock wall between two of the alcoves halted my roll and jarred me. As the guardian turned around, flames leaking through its mouth around the hammer—fortunately, Sorka was able to deflect them—I glanced over my shoulder.

The frozen half-dragon warrior was in the alcove beside me. Poised in a fighting position, he appeared ready to spring into battle, if he were simply removed from the stasis chamber. Could that work?

Clangs and wrenching metal kept ringing out from Sarrlevi's battle, and something heavy clunked to the ground—one of his construct's limbs. Another moment, and he would be victorious—I was certain of it—but I didn't have a moment.

I flattened my palm against the half-dragon's panel, my senses telling me it was identical to the other one I'd studied. With a quick snip from my power, I severed the magical conduit leading to the barrier.

The protective field went down instantly, but it didn't have anything to do with the stasis magic. It only kept people out—and maybe the prisoners in before they were frozen. The stasis magic was gnomish, not dwarven, and I had no idea how it worked, nor did I have time to figure it out.

Like a charging ox, the construct rushed forward, trying to pin me against the wall and trample me. Though I leaped to the side, its talons slashed so close that they tore chunks of my hair free. I barely avoided being crushed.

A beam of orange power shot above me, and I swore, startled. It struck the guardian in the side. The magic of Sarrlevi's sword, I realized.

The beam bored a hole in the shoulder of the construct, perhaps striking some mechanical joint, for its forelimb crumpled. Its metal shoulder pitched into the wall, and its huge head thrust into the stasis chamber, almost smashing the frozen occupant.

Sorka flared again, trying to use the moment to free herself. Lightning shot out as the guardian's own magic flared.

A clatter sounded—my hammer dropping?—and an inferno of fire filled the alcove.

I winced, afraid the guy who'd been imprisoned for however many years would be toast and never wake up to see his end. While the guardian staggered back, the limb that Sarrlevi had struck dangling, Sorka escaped the alcove and flew toward me.

She landed with a firm smack in my palm.

I'm going to need to be more careful about throwing you, I admitted.

Into the mouths of magical constructs? Yes.

I was aiming for the eye.

Whatever reply she'd thought to make was drowned out when an explosion came from inside the stasis chamber. The ground rocked, and I stumbled back. Hell, that guy was *definitely* going to be toast.

Or so I thought. What had been his very faint aura swelled in power to my senses.

Though limping now, the guardian had no trouble swinging toward me on its other three legs. Its great metal maw opened as smoke wafted out ahead of its attack.

"*Hygorotho,*" I barked, relieved to have the hammer back in my hand.

Sorka's barrier wrapped around me before the flames arrived. They struck, turning the world around me fiery orange, but they didn't break through her protection.

Fighting the urge to back away—or *run*—away—I darted toward the rear of the guardian. Maybe I could take out another of its legs.

I sensed Sarrlevi, now done with his battle, running toward me to help. Before he reached me, the furnace guardian's gout of flame stopped abruptly. The construct's head turned back toward the alcove in time for it to receive a blast of magic. Metal wrenched, and the great power ripped the guardian's head off.

Happy to pile on, I slammed my hammer into a knee joint—unfortunately, I couldn't reach the shoulder joint that Sarrlevi had proved was vulnerable. Sorka flared, adding her power to my strike, and the metal dented, but the leg didn't break or budge.

Sarrlevi sprang into the air, somersaulting onto the guardian's back. Someone else landed up there with him—the half-dragon. At first, I stared, amazed he'd survived and revived. Then I worried the guy I had helped free would attack Sarrlevi.

But they barely seemed to notice each other, instead tearing into the guardian.

I pounded at the knee again, wanting to do my small part, but Sorka reminded me why we'd come.

The assassin's mother?

Right. In the chaos of the battle, I'd stopped noticing the gonging of what I feared was an alarm, but it got through my thick skull now. If the alarm had been unhappy because we'd trespassed, it might be *really* unhappy that one of the prisoners had escaped.

Leaving those with elven blood to finish demolishing the guardian, I sprinted back toward the chamber holding Sarrlevi's mother. The construct he'd battled lay unmoving farther down the cavern, its head and two legs torn off.

Dwarves are heading this way, Sarrlevi spoke into my mind as the clangs of his battle continued sounding, his and the half-dragon's magic swirling around the guardian. With its head ripped off, it couldn't spew gouts of fire from its maw anymore, but it also wasn't defeated. It kept trying to buck off the attackers on its back as it stomped around on its damaged legs, seeking ways to harm them. *Many dwarves. An army.*

Are they in the tunnels yet? I didn't sense them, not through the magic-dampening walls.

Trusting Sarrlevi to keep me apprised, I flattened my palm to the panel of his mother's stasis chamber. As I'd done at the other one, I funneled my energy in to snip the magical cord that powered the barrier.

They are flying this way, and they have— Sarrlevi sighed into my mind. *Zondia'qareshi.*

Shit.

The cord snapped, and the barrier dropped. But, as with the half-dragon, the stasis chamber continued to work, its green glow emanating from the walls and bathing Sarrlevi's mother. I didn't know what the construct had inadvertently done to make the other chamber stop working. Crash into it, as far as I'd seen, but that seemed a bad way to turn the thing off. If another explosion went off, it would surely kill Meyleera Sarrlevi. She wasn't a half-dragon who had been imprisoned at the prime of his life.

A bead of sweat ran down the side of my face as I examined the gnomish magic that powered the stasis chamber. Its complexity daunted me. Not one but dozens and dozens of tendrils of magic flowed into the rock and into Meyleera, each one subtly different, a great combination of effects at work.

"I have no idea." Frustrated, I barely resisted the urge to start bashing things with my hammer.

A final thunderous clatter came from the battle. The guardian toppled to the ground, its warped body landing beside its detached head.

Sarrlevi and the half-dragon sprang free of it and landed facing each other. Only Sarrlevi was armed, his two swords raised as he squinted at our new possible threat.

Great magic wrapped around the half-dragon, and he squinted right back at Sarrlevi, his fists raised, no fear in his eyes as he faced the swords.

Thanks for the help! I called telepathically to the half-dragon, attempting to sound cheerful and friendly. The last thing we needed was another enemy. *Any chance you know how to turn off these stasis thingies? Without blowing anyone up?*

Not glancing at me, the half-dragon asked Sarrlevi something in Elven. Sarrlevi arched his eyebrows and answered. Only then did the half-dragon look at me.

He'd been imposing when he'd been frozen. Awake, with immense power emanating from him, he was terrifying, even without weapons in hand. His eyes were violet, like Zavryd's, and when they met mine, they flared with inner light.

I swallowed and resisted the urge to say that was creepy.

A crawling sensation started up under my skull. Mind reading. From him? Fortunately, it was brief and not painful.

For the first time, I sensed Zondia and the approaching dwarves. A *lot* of dwarves. I didn't know if they had flown here on her back, but they seemed to be coming from the sky and were heading down for a landing. Within minutes, they could be here.

Sarrlevi cursed and must have decided he didn't have time for a stare-down with the half-dragon. He ran to join me at his mother's alcove, then started to step inside.

"No." I grabbed his arm. "It's still on; it might freeze you too."

Though I didn't know if the power worked that way, Sarrlevi must not have known either, for he paused.

"How do we turn it off?" he asked.

"Crash a furnace guardian into it," I said.

"There has to be a switch. One that doesn't result in an *explosion*." His face twisted with anguish as he looked at his unconscious mother. She was so close and yet untouchable.

A distant clank sounded, and I sensed dwarves and Zondia heading into the lava tube. They knew exactly where we were.

A whoosh of power swept between Sarrlevi and me. He jumped back, spinning toward the half-dragon again. But it wasn't an attack. The green light in the chamber went out, and the stasis magic turned off, as if someone had flipped a switch.

The faintest sigh came from Meyleera. Sarrlevi rushed into the alcove to pick her up.

Still facing me, the half-dragon nodded curtly. Without speaking out loud or telepathically, he stepped back and disappeared, magical camouflage cloaking him from my senses as well as my eyes.

"What did he say to you?" I wondered, though I didn't know if Sarrlevi would answer.

He'd gathered his mother gently in his arms and was murmuring softly to her in Elven.

"He asked who freed him, and I said you." Sarrlevi stepped out of the alcove with Meyleera, and magic swelled as he attempted to form a portal.

"I wish I'd thanked him a little more thoroughly for the help."

I thought about broadcasting an unfocused expression of gratitude in case the half-dragon remained close enough to hear, but the dwarves and Zondia would also hear. My senses told me they'd reached the metal door. Any hope I might have had that they wouldn't be able to get in was quashed when it clanked upward. "I thought this was a secret place the dwarves had all forgotten about." I'd *hoped* that.

Sarrlevi swore. I'd sensed him conjuring portal magic, but nothing had happened.

"The dampening magic in here is keeping me from making a portal. Camouflage yourself." Sarrlevi did so himself as he spoke.

Clanks sounded, dwarven plate boots thudding on the lava-rock floor.

I shook my head. "Take your mother and sneak away. Get her the help she needs. I'll distract the dwarves."

"No. We'll *both* sneak away."

"They're standing in front of the door, dude." My senses told me that only some of them were coming in. The rest—*and* Zondia—were waiting at the door, blocking the way out. "You won't be able to get by them even camouflaged. Not as long as they're there. And if enough come in and search, they'll find you." I glanced into the darkness the furnace guardians had come from. Though I didn't know how far back the cavern went, I doubted it was that far.

There's not another way out back there, Sarrlevi admitted as the first troops came into view, led by General Grantik.

Scowling, the dwarves pointed at me and the mess we'd made. That their *guardians* had made.

Sarrlevi growled.

Sssh, I murmured telepathically to him. *I'll try to get them away from the door so you can slip out. Take your mother, and get help for her. I'll be fine. I wanted to talk to my grandfather, anyway.* A true statement. Too bad I wasn't sure the dwarves would take me anywhere but to a dungeon cell.

Several of Grantik's troops pointed crossbows at me. Maybe believing they would even take me to a dungeon had been optimistic.

Grantik said something to them in Dwarven. They hesitated.

"Do it," he snapped, words I recognized.

They lowered the crossbows.

After she's safe, you can come back to— I broke off before saying, "to rescue me." *To check on me,* I said instead. If Sarrlevi believed I was in danger, he might not go at all, but Meyleera couldn't have that long to live. I had to make sure he prioritized her. *Find a way out, Varlesh. I'll be fine until you get back.*

One of the dwarves pointed at the dark alcove where the half-dragon had been and shouted in alarm. All the other dwarves looked too. Grantik frowned and clanked toward the plaque.

Go, Varlesh. They're distracted. Now's your chance.

Zondia and other dwarves remained at the entrance, so I didn't know if that was true, but maybe there would be an opportunity for him to slip away. If not, I would have to *make* an opportunity.

All right. Sarrlevi sounded defeated and torn. *Cooperate with them, and I'll come back to get you as soon as possible.*

I know you will.

After a hesitation, he added, *I love you.*

I love you too and look forward to the day when you can say that without being beaten down, bloody, and half-afraid you're going to die.

I'm more concerned that you will die right now.

That won't happen. Dwarves love my charm.

And dragons? His voice came from farther away. He was moving toward the exit. Good.

An irritated roar came from the lava tube. Zondia.

The jury is still out on that.

I am not familiar with that expression.

In that case, yes, dragons love *me. It's my bluntness. They find it endearing.*

Hm.

Grantik flicked a finger and said something. Several of his troops strode forward, fingering their weapons and looking like they intended to take me prisoner.

I didn't drop Sorka, but I did spread my arms and attempt to appear unthreatening. Cooperate with them, Sarrlevi had said. It didn't look like I would have a choice.

11

THIS ISN'T NECESSARY, I TOLD GENERAL GRANTIK AS ONE OF HIS MEN snapped cuffs—no, make that *shackles*—around my wrists to trap my hands behind my back. *I wasn't going to run.*

You have a charm with camouflaging magic, Grantik replied, though he didn't look at me. His troops surrounded me, but he was still standing in front of the empty alcove that had held the half-dragon. He didn't so much as glance at the one that had held Sarrlevi's mother.

Yes, everyone has them these days. They're very trendy.

One of the dwarves grabbed Sorka. Though I wanted to cooperate, my hand tightened around the haft of its own accord.

The dwarf snarled at me and yanked again. With my arm tucked back in an awkward position, it almost pulled my shoulder out of the socket.

I was tempted to pull away and order Sorka to raise a barrier. I was a little surprised she hadn't done it herself when the warriors had first approached, but maybe she didn't want to fight her own people. Maybe she *wouldn't* fight her own people.

Let go, daughter of Princess Rodarska, Grantik spoke into my mind. He knew my name, but maybe it was better that he called to mind my mother, for the warriors surrounding me lowered their crossbows further. *You will not be permitted to walk into the capital armed. Especially not when you came to free the ancient enemies of our people.* Grantik gave me a puzzled look as he gestured to the empty stasis chamber.

I was so surprised that I didn't tighten my fingers when the dwarf pulled on Sorka again, and he succeeded in taking the weapon from me. "Uh, that's *not* why we came."

Reminded that they couldn't likely understand much English, I repeated the sentence telepathically, changing *we* to *I*. I had little doubt they knew Sarrlevi had been with me, but I didn't need to remind them of that.

That was an accident. With my arms bound, I couldn't point a finger, so I jerked my chin toward the empty alcove. *Your furnace guardian crashed into the workings, and it broke whatever is freezing those people. I came to free the elf noble, Meyleera. That's it. You know Barothla was keeping prisoners here and* experimenting *on them, right?*

I turned to face the alcoves holding the recently added victims, glad that most remained to back up my story. If Grantik didn't know anything about Barothla's use of this place, he might not be quick to believe that Meyleera had been here.

Indeed, the general's brow furrowed as he walked along the row of alcoves, past those with plaques and to the end, where Barothla's victims remained frozen.

Will you free them? I asked. *I don't know anything about those other prisoners, but these people can't deserve to be here. They're like the caged animals—and* goblins—*in Barothla's lab. Here only for her to experiment on.*

Something she is no longer doing. Grantik turned his frown on me. *You promised me you wouldn't attack her, but your assassin killed* her.

Because she used one of her potions to turn him into a monster. You were there. You know he was crazy. I didn't actually know that. Yes, Grantik had been there for the battle at Hart's mansion, but he'd been under Barothla's magical compulsion. It was possible he didn't remember much of that night.

High Priest Lankobar stepped out of the tunnel and into view. At a nod from Grantik, he went to the alcove that had held the half-dragon. When he rested his hand on the panel, the same panel I'd tinkered with, unease crept into me. I had a feeling the dwarves were about to find out that the furnace guardian hadn't *solely* been responsible for freeing the prisoner.

Look, I'm sorry the princess died, I told them. *That wasn't my intention. I just wanted to learn where she was holding Sarrlevi's mother so we could find her and heal her.*

You were correct, Sarrlevi whispered into my mind, probably being careful not to let his telepathy give away his presence. *With Zondia'qareshi standing precisely in front of the doorway, I can't slip past. Even my camouflage is not strong enough to keep me invisible to a dragon at such close quarters.*

Damn. And his mother didn't have much time.

Lady Zondia, I called to her. *I have information for you.*

Information on where the elf went? came her cool reply.

Where he'd gone was ten feet in front of her in that tunnel.

Yes.

You did not send him to the spire to me, as I requested.

He wasn't open to that, not while his mother still needed his help. But he's freed her now. Come see, if you don't believe me. She was a prisoner right here. I wasn't foolish enough to try to compel her to come in, but I shared an image of the empty cell and also my memory of Meyleera crumpled unconscious in it. Hopefully, Zondia would be curious and come take a look.

But it was the priest's words that brought her in. *We could use your opinion, Lady Zondia'qareshi,* Lankobar said. *A powerful prisoner was freed, and we are not certain if our people will now be in danger from him. If our history is correct, Azerdash Starblade not only slew hundreds of dwarven warriors when we battled against the elves, but he was also a threat to your kind, wasn't he?*

Zondia left the doorway and headed into the chamber.

I held my breath, hoping Sarrlevi could avoid her notice. The tunnel hadn't been that wide, and with his mother in his arms, maneuvering about would be more difficult than usual.

Fortunately, no cries of *Ah ha!* or whatever dragons said when they found someone came from Zondia's lips. She strode straight toward Lankobar, Grantik, and the empty stasis chamber. Her gaze skimmed over the remaining prisoners but not for long.

I have heard that name. Zondia wasn't in her dragon or human form but appeared today as a stout female dwarf with lilac hair. *However, the unauthorized—and deeply forbidden—half-dragon experiments were before my time. I would have to research that particular being in order to advise effectively.*

It may be wise to do so, Lankobar said, *as will we. If the half-dragon does not soon learn that the war between the dwarves and the elves is long over, he may attempt to resume doing what he was doing when he was captured. Killing our people.* Lankobar frowned at me.

The thought that I'd inadvertently freed a heinous and extremely powerful criminal made me squirm. All I'd been trying to do was save my ass from the furnace guardian.

Zondia considered the half-dragon's empty alcove for a moment, glanced at a few of the stasis chambers that continued to operate, then walked toward the empty one I'd shared telepathically with her, what had been Meyleera's prison. Along the way, she paused at each of the alcoves occupied not by war criminals but by victims of Barothla's experiments. I hoped that, whatever happened to me, they would be freed.

Rodarska's daughter used magic on this panel to disable it, Lankobar said from the half-dragon's alcove.

That prompted Grantik, the rest of the dwarves, *and* Zondia to frown at me again.

I tried to lift my hands in innocence before remembering they were bound. *It was an accident. I mean, I did it intentionally but only because the furnace guardian was trying to kill me. It had my hammer in its maw and backed me up against that alcove. I didn't have many options. I thought that maybe if I could get the guy inside out, he would help fight it.*

Grantik stared at me. *Girl, you have unleashed one of the greatest war criminals of the past millennium.*

I resisted the urge to blurt, *He didn't seem that bad.*

Just because he'd helped us get Meyleera out didn't mean he was a good guy. If he'd been working for the elves, he might have deemed Sarrlevi an ally, and he might not have known *what* I was. How aware had the rest of the Cosmic Realms been of Earth and humans a thousand years ago? I didn't know.

I'm sorry, I told them. *I didn't know. I only came to help the wrongfully imprisoned Meyleera escape before she died of a horrible disease.*

I've slipped out, Sarrlevi whispered into my mind, his voice now distant and muted. *And I'm almost out of the lava tube. I should be able to make a portal once I'm outside. Are you all right? My mother is... I don't think she has long.*

With more than a dozen dwarves and a dragon glowering at me, I didn't feel *all right*, but I would never forgive myself if Sarrlevi came back for me, and his mother died because of it. *I'm fine. Get her to help.*

I will. Thank you.

His presence disappeared from my mind.

As Grantik and Lankobar conferred, I wondered what the punishment was for freeing a war criminal. Maybe Sarrlevi and I would end up side-by-side in the canyon where the dragons meted out justice, where they tortured people for two years before wiping their memories and destroying everything they had been.

I think I'm in trouble, Sorka, I told the hammer, though she was in the hands of one of my captors now.

I believe they will not kill you.

I didn't point out that there were plenty of other unpleasant things they could do to me. *Maybe your next handler won't demolish cabinets with you.*

Sorka sighed into my mind. *I still wish to find Rodarska.*

I know. Me too.

But as Grantik ordered me to be searched for other weapons and taken to their ship, I worried I wouldn't get that opportunity.

The dwarves took me aboard a dirigible, the spacious enclosed cabin large enough for a platoon of troops, the entire craft wreathed in magic. We flew northward, as General Grantik had informed me, toward the continent that held the major dwarven population centers.

The stormy red sky continued to produce lightning, and more than a few bolts struck the metal dirigible cabin, but its magic protected it, and we felt only faint jolts inside. It was unsettling but not worse than air turbulence, at least so far.

With no ability to read the instrumentation on the panels, I had no idea what our speed was, but the ground blurred past below, making me believe we were zipping along far faster than typical for a dirigible. Of course, I had only the Goodyear blimps to use as a comparison.

Grantik and High Priest Lankobar were with me in what my mind wanted to call the cockpit, but that was spacious for that designation. A pilot stood in front of us, operating the craft by resting his hands on a glowing blue orb that jutted up on a pedestal in front of a large window.

What had prompted Zondia to come to Dun Kroth and join

the dwarves, I didn't know, but she'd formed a portal and left instead of accompanying us. That worried me. If she knew Sarrlevi had been with me, she'd have left to continue her hunt for him. If he'd taken his mother to a healer that only he knew, she might not have any luck, but what if he'd done what I suggested and taken her to Zavryd and Zoltan? That might be the first place Zondia looked.

I flexed my arms, wishing I hadn't let myself be shackled and Sorka taken from me. If I cried *vishgronik* and tried to get her to fly to me, would she? Or, like the dwarves, did she condemn me for having inadvertently let that criminal go? Since my mother had made Sorka, she had to identify with dwarves and would doubtless hate someone who'd killed her people.

At my stirring, Grantik looked at me.

I'll volunteer for mind scouring or the dwarven equivalent, I told him, my meandering musings making me wish I'd camouflaged myself and tried to sneak away with Sarrlevi. Maybe we both could have gotten away eventually. Not that his mother had had enough time for *eventually. So you can see I've been telling the truth about everything.*

Dwarves do not forcibly read the thoughts of others, Grantik replied.

Not even if it could determine someone's innocence? And they're volunteering for it?

No. Since dwarves are good at resisting mind magic, it isn't considered a reliable method of learning the truth. Only if someone with extreme power and aptitude employs the technique would we give the findings great weight in our justice court.

Maybe you shouldn't have sent the dragon away. Zondia likes *mind-scouring me.*

She is on her own quest.

"Tell me about it," I muttered.

Grantik raised his bushy eyebrows.

I'm sorry about the princess and *the prisoner. Will you let me see my grandfather and tell him what happened? I wanted to explain things to him anyway.*

Then you should have come to the dwarven capital, not skulked about on our world uninvited with the assassin.

There wasn't time. You didn't see his mother. She was almost dead. Because Barothla kidnapped her from her sickbed. I know you're mad about her death, but you can't believe that what she was doing was right. I turned my most imploring gaze on him.

Before, Grantik had been something of an ally to me. He hadn't seemed to approve of Barothla's methods—or of her. Aside from my grandfather, Grantik was the most likely one to speak up for me, but his face was hard to read. I did have a sense that he was more pissed about the half-dragon guy getting away than Barothla's death. Too bad because the prison break really *had* been my fault.

It is likely your grandfather will wish to speak with you at some point, Grantik said. *I must first report to him that an ancient enemy has been released and may even now be in our world, killing our people.*

I didn't roll my eyes, not when that could be a real danger for the dwarves, but it was hard for me not to react with frustration.

Outside, the sky faded from red to what my Seattle-raised mind considered a normal color: gray. The volcanoes had faded from view behind us, and we flew from the lava-rock-filled continent out over an ocean.

If he was that horrible, I asked Grantik, *why did your people capture him instead of killing him?*

In addition to being half-dragon, he was an elven prince, the eldest son of the king of the time. Had we killed him, the war might have continued to escalate. Elves and dwarves might never have come to peaceful terms and ceased hostilities. At the time of Starblade's capture, the elves had some of our most important people as prisoners, just as we had others of theirs. It was part of the treaty that the prisoners be given back to their respective sides, all save for Starblade. He'd killed too many, and he hated dwarves, so we couldn't trust that he wouldn't go rogue or perhaps join the Assassins' Guild so he could continue to kill us. Though the elves were reluctant to do so, they, somewhat coerced by the dragons, agreed to what was, until a couple of hours ago, Starblade's current fate. Alive but in stasis and held on our world.

Until when?

Until always.

That time, I did roll my eyes. From the point of view of Starblade's family, how was that better than killing him? *Were you there? Is his father still alive? He can't be, right? Or Eireth wouldn't be king now.*

This was before my time and two elven kings ago, but all dwarves are familiar with this history. Grantik gave me a judging look, as if it was my fault that I didn't know anything about Dun Kroth's past.

Sorry, dude. We only had Earth history in school. Why did the elves and dwarves have a war anyway? I remembered Sarrlevi implying that their peoples hadn't always gotten along, but someone had also said that dwarves and elves coveted different resources so they were natural allies, not natural enemies. *Dwarves can't possibly want anything elves have. You like rocks; they like trees.*

Grantik arched his eyebrows. *There are other reasons people go to war. It was a complicated time. Of late, things have been far more peaceful.* He grimaced. *I hope that by releasing him, you have not ushered in a new period of chaos.*

Buddy— General, your furnace guardian chasing me is what released him. I wouldn't have known how to turn off the stasis chamber on my own. It was gnomish and complicated as hell.*

Had you not gone to the volcano, Starblade would not now be free.

Had your princess not kidnapped Sarrlevi's mother and done her best to screw up his life, I wouldn't have had go to there.

The pilot said something, and Grantik didn't respond to me, instead walking to a panel and resting a hand on it. A hologram of a gray-haired dwarf's head appeared above it, and they conversed. I caught my mother's name several times but couldn't get the gist from the scattered words I recognized. Thinking of my translation charm, I tried to get a hand in my pocket, but the shackles thwarted me.

When the conversation ended, the dwarf head disappearing, Grantik didn't enlighten me. Lankobar left the cabin and headed into the back, and a couple of warriors came up to stand guard. Nobody offered me a seat, so I sat cross-legged on the deck. Since the dwarves could make portals, I wondered why they were bothering with the airship. Even if they had to make a portal to another world before returning to a different location on theirs, wouldn't that have been faster than this?

Admittedly, the dirigible sailed over the ocean quickly. I'd barely had time to convince my escort to take me to pee—and to decide the in-flight snacks, being mostly mushroom- and algae-based, were deplorable—before we reached land.

The new continent was almost as rock-dominated as the last, but the snow-capped mountains not far ahead didn't appear on the verge of erupting. That was a plus. Further, some trees and grass dotted slopes that looked like they'd been carved by receding glaciers. The sky remained gray and spat drizzle at the dirigible, with rivulets running down the windows, but it was free of lightning.

When we sailed straight toward a mountain, I clambered to my feet for a better view. My shackle chain rattled, but nobody seemed worried that I would make an escape attempt. Why *would* they worry? I had given up my only weapon, and it wasn't as if my magic could threaten them in a major way.

As we approached, giant doors that appeared no different from the rocky slope around them slid open to reveal a hangar. At least, I thought it was a hangar. There was no floor, and as soon as we entered the cavernous space, the walls glowing with faint magical light, we stopped moving forward, switching instead to descending.

How far we dropped, I didn't know, but it had to be the equivalent of floating down to the bottom of the Grand Canyon. Veins of what might have been silver streaked through the gray and brown rock surrounding us, and the running lights of the dirigible almost made it sparkle. A hint of magic also came from those rocks, and when I reached out with my senses, I realized there was a lot *more* magic below us. I detected the auras of people as well. *Lots* of people.

My first thought was that we were dropping into a large military base where I would be questioned. But as the walls opened up and it grew brighter, I could see below and recognized the city that sprawled from side to side in the wide cavern. The capital.

Even as I sensed the magical barrier that protected the city, the pilot touched something on the side of the pedestal, and an opening formed in it. We descended through it and toward a landing pad in a part of the capital that I hadn't seen on my way to the royal quarters. Two other dirigibles rested on the cement, and there was room for several more.

"Welcome to the dwarven airport," I murmured, wondering if dragons were invited to come that way into the city when they visited. Though I again wondered why the dwarves wouldn't simply use portals.

Maybe big craft were more practical when cargo had to be transported. As I'd seen before, the dwarves had an underground rail network too.

As soon as we landed, Lankobar returned, and I expected him and Grantik to grab me and take me for questioning. But Grantik didn't stir. Nobody in the pilot's cabin did, though a few voices and the clunk of a hatch shutting came from the larger cabin behind us. I sensed my hammer on the move and whirled toward the door.

"Where are they taking her?" I blurted aloud and tele-pathically.

Grantik looked at me but didn't answer, only opening the door and heading out. The guards and pilot remained. So did Lanko-bar. He smiled tightly at my question.

What did *that* mean? That Lankobar was pleased they'd had the opportunity to take the hammer back from me? I grimaced, remembering that most, if not all, of the dwarves I'd met had wanted that from the beginning. Only my grandfather had been willing to let me keep Sorka, wanting me to use her to help find my mother. But Ironhelm had warned me that if I *didn't* find her, the dwarves might take the weapon back. Whether they meant to give Sorka to some more fitting wielder—I winced—or stick her in a museum I didn't know, but the thought of either of those things made me sick. I would have willingly returned the weapon to my mother, but, after thirty years, I hated to lose Sorka to a random dwarf.

Unfortunately, I doubted Sorka felt that strongly about me. She hadn't wanted to end up in Barothla's hands, but that didn't mean she felt any loyalty toward me.

Are we going to disembark? I asked, trying to sound calm, not like someone panicking over the thought of being parted from her weapon of so many years. *Or do I get to hang around to see if the in-flight dinner is better than the in-flight snacks?*

What food would your Earth-half prefer? Lankobar's sneer promised he was certain my Earth bits liked inferior food.

Cheese and salami are good. I know you have cheese. Sarr— Someone told me the capital has cheese caves.

Lankobar squinted, no doubt catching my slip.

Barothla rudely did not give me a tour and show them to me the last time I was here.

It is unlikely you'll receive a tour this time either.

Except of the dungeon, right?

We shall see. Lankobar looked through the window, though there wasn't a lot of activity on the landing pad.

The distant pounding of metal on metal reached us, making me think of the smithies we'd passed the last time I'd been to the city, and of how I'd longed to visit them, to interact with and learn from the people. The odds of that happening were lower than ever, and sadness sank into me. If only I could have found my parents before heading off to help Sarrlevi with his quest. I didn't regret assisting him and prayed we had been in time for his mother to be saved, but it would have been so much better if I could have returned to Dun Kroth with *my* mother at my side.

As time dragged on, I asked, *How much longer?* and tried not to feel like a kid in the back seat of a car on a road trip.

We shall see, Lankobar said again.

I wanted to strangle him.

The hammer is being questioned, he added.

I blinked. It hadn't occurred to me that they could do that or would think to do that. Until a few weeks ago, I hadn't known Sorka was sapient and that she could converse with me. Of course, it made sense that the dwarves, some of whom would have been around when my mother crafted the weapon, knew. Would they consider her a reliable witness to what I'd done? A good judge of character?

I stared bleakly out the window, not sure Sorka's rendition of me would be flattering. I didn't think she detested me, but she hadn't been shy about sharing her disapproval that I was seeing Sarrlevi, the assassin who'd been hired to take out her maker, and she hadn't stopped bringing up all the times I'd used her for home renovations.

Feeling despondent, I sank to the deck again. If my fate was in her hands, I truly could end up in the Dragon Justice Court.

12

WHEN GRANTIK RETURNED, HE, LANKOBAR, AND SEVERAL WARRIORS escorted me out of the dirigible and to one of the open-air train cars for a ride to the royal quarters. I didn't know whether to feel hopeful or not that the sprawling complex was our destination instead of a dungeon filled with interrogation cells. My *last* visit to the royal quarters hadn't gone well for me.

"Guess I'm still not going to get a tour of the city's cheese caves," I murmured.

Lankobar looked over at me and said something.

"Sorry, it's been a while since I rubbed my translation charm, and I can't reach it." I shrugged to rattle my shackles and started to repeat the words telepathically, but he responded first.

You should have learned our language by now. Apparently *he* had a translation charm he'd recently rubbed.

"When I find my mother, you can lecture her on her woeful choice to teach me the language of the country we were living in instead of Dwarven." I felt compelled to add, "She did teach me some rhymes and songs," since it was possible Mom had *tried* to get me to learn Dwarven, and my four-year-old mind hadn't been swift enough for it. More likely, she'd thought we would have more time for it later.

We *should* have had more time. That familiar pang of loss and longing filled me, and I looked forward, toward the wide steps we were climbing, instead of at Lankobar's judgmental face.

Cheese is valued and treasured among dwarves, he said. *We do not show strangers our secret caves.*

Secret cheese caves? Hell, now I *really* wanted to visit them. I imagined hidden doors leading to tunnels with exotic wheels and bricks of cheese around every bend. I salivated at the thought, or maybe it was because I hadn't eaten anything for a long time. The mushroom and algae cubes didn't count.

"I feel the same way," I told him. "If I didn't have a roommate, *nobody* would know about the vegetable crisper where I keep my stash."

Lankobar squinted at me. Maybe *vegetable crisper* didn't translate.

My escort took me through wide halls I'd seen before, then turned me into a huge audience chamber that I hadn't. No, not an audience chamber. The *throne* room.

Though the dais and throne at the end were empty, I let myself hope they were taking me to see my grandfather. He might be more lenient than these guys. Though... he might also be disappointed in me. Disappointed that I'd let his daughter die, that I'd failed to find his other daughter, and that I'd also freed a half-dragon criminal.

My gut knotted with dread. I barely knew King Ironhelm, but I didn't want to disappoint him. Why couldn't anything have worked out?

A door behind the dais opened, and two armed guards stepped out, taking positions to either side of it. The king's bodyguards. The knots in my gut tightened.

My grandfather walked out, clad not in armor and with a

horned helmet, as I'd last seen him, but in somber gray clothing the color of rock. Dwarven funeral clothing? I didn't know if they preferred gray to black, but his glum expression suggested he was in mourning. His curly red-gray hair that had stuck out from under his helmet before seemed to droop now. Even his beard lacked its earlier luster.

Surprisingly, Ironhelm carried Sorka. He pointed the hammer at Grantik and said something.

Grantik bowed and stepped behind me. I tensed, not sure what to expect. Metal scraped softly, and my shackles loosened.

As soon as I was free, I wanted to jam my hand in my pocket to rub my charm, but I hesitated. Even though Grantik had searched me before loading me on the dirigible, the bodyguards wouldn't know that and might think I was reaching for a weapon.

May I activate my translation charm? I asked as King Ironhelm came around the throne and stopped in front of me.

My grandfather's bushy eyebrows raised. *You have not done so already?*

I couldn't get my hands in my pockets when they were bound, and I'm not flexible enough to kick my shoes off and use my toes to grab things.

His eyebrows drifted higher as he looked down at my feet. Lankobar frowned at me. Maybe irreverent humor wasn't permitted with a king.

Most dwarves have that problem, was all Ironhelm said. *We lack elven flexibility.*

The thought brought Sarrlevi to mind, and I imagined him saying something smug about the things he could do with his toes, before wondering where he'd taken his mother and if she was receiving the treatment she needed.

Most species do, I think, I said.

Ironhelm smiled. It was a faint and fleeting smile, but it gave me hope. Maybe he wasn't *entirely* pissed at me.

His fingers flicked toward my pocket, the one with the charms. Of course, he would be able to sense them. Though I hadn't heard anything about him being a great magic user, he had a powerful aura.

I pulled out the keychain, rubbed the translation charm and looked wistfully at but didn't touch the camouflage charm.

Ironhelm raised a hand to stop me from returning the keychain to my pocket. "You made the translation charm? It has a magical signature similar to..." He didn't say my mother's work, but I was sure that was what he was thinking.

"Yeah. I'm learning enchanting from a half-dwarf who was born on Earth like me."

"A half-dwarf not from this world knew how to teach translation magic?" Ironhelm looked at Grantik and Lankobar, as if they might know all about it.

"Well, he's been teaching me some foundational stuff, like how to keep nails from rusting, which is probably not much of a problem down here. And then I'm kind of able to teach myself other things. Or, I don't know, *will* them to happen while I'm crafting." Suggesting I could teach myself sophisticated dwarven magic might have been cocky, but I hated to admit I'd accidentally been enchanting stuff I worked on without knowing what I was doing. That sounded like the kind of thing masters would roll their eyes at.

"You have Rodarska's gift then." Ironhelm smiled again and waved for me to put the keychain away, then pointed the hammer toward a seating area in an alcove at the back of the room. The blocky furniture was carved from the same salt as the walls and floor, but cushions added a hint of softness. "I have been speaking to Sorka. Let us talk."

I grimaced, wanting to say that whatever Sorka had been telling him wasn't true. Or it at least wasn't *fair*. I hadn't known she was anything more than a tool when I'd demoed cabinets with her, and I'd only lost my temper and thumped her into the ground a *couple* of times since learning about her intelligence.

"She's not my biggest fan," I admitted as the guards shifted to allow me to walk with Ironhelm toward the seating area.

"No?"

"She doesn't think I've been properly reverent with her, she critiques me a lot, and, uh, she doesn't like who I'm dating." I doubted I could get through our conversation without mentioning Sarrlevi—Ironhelm would surely want to know what happened when Barothla died—but I wouldn't start out bringing him up. So far, my grandfather didn't seem that angry with me. I would prefer to keep it that way as long as possible.

"She critiqued my daughter too." Before sitting, Ironhelm asked a servant to bring food and *uglarth*, which my translation charm didn't have a word for. A drink? "She also has few qualms about critiquing *me*."

How might dwarves improve and become the greatest their blood will allow if there is nobody to guide them and recommend superior behavior? Sorka asked.

Ironhelm's lips twisted wryly. Had her words been meant for both of us?

"Suggesting one's monarch needs beard-combing and a haircut isn't going to help him achieve greatness," Ironhelm said.

If you believe that, you have much *work yet to do in the area of self-improvement.*

Sorka, I said, *I'm trying not to get thrown in a dungeon cell. Maybe you could be circumspect with the king.*

Dwarven hammers are not circumspect. They are blunt.

"Literally." Ironhelm sighed, rested the hammer on an end table, and sat on a long couch. "She has told me what has been happening since you were here last and... about the death of my daughter."

"Barothla," I said, hoping he knew my mother should still be alive. I *hoped* she was still alive and tried not to think about the most recent threats to my family. "I regret that and wish it hadn't happened. I just wanted her to leave me alone and stop messing with, uhm, my ally."

Ironhelm's lips pressed together. He knew who I meant, so I supposed there wasn't any point in avoiding using Sarrlevi's name.

"I'm still hopeful that I'll find my mother," I added, in case it helped. "I'm closer than I was. I just need to be permitted to return to Seattle." I raised my eyebrows. Would I be?

"You are not a prisoner here."

"No?" I sat across from him, with a coffee table—did dwarves have coffee?—between us. "The shackles suggested otherwise."

Ironhelm slanted a look toward the other dwarves. Grantik and Lankobar hadn't joined us in the alcove but remained within earshot. "There was some confusion about your role in releasing an ancient enemy. Sorka explained it, and while I'm aggrieved that you chose that particular cell to open—"

"It was the one the furnace guardian mashed me up against," I blurted.

"—I understand that you did not know who he was or have much choice."

"Yeah." I told myself not to interrupt further. It sounded like Sorka had told him what had happened. I hadn't expected her to be my advocate, but even if she had simply told the truth, that ought to somewhat clear my name. Or at least explain that I hadn't intended to mess things up for the dwarves. "I'm sorry and hope he won't be a problem for your people."

"For *our* people." Ironhelm held my gaze. "Whether you wish it or not, you are half-dwarven and, as my daughter's daughter, have a place here if you desire it."

That sense of longing returned for an all-new reason. "I *do* wish it. I'd like to know more about my mother's people. I just didn't know if I could hope for that." I eyed Lankobar warily.

"It would perhaps be difficult right now," Ironhelm said, "as the truth has been spoken about my daughter's death, and many people are angry about the assassin and..."

"The half-dwarf who hangs out with him?"

"Yes, but my daughter was not..." Ironhelm inhaled a long slow breath, looked up at the arched ceiling, and exhaled even more slowly. "This was not the first time Barothla created a monster that turned on her."

I barely kept from saying that Sarrlevi wasn't a monster, especially now. I didn't want to argue when Ironhelm was being reasonable.

"One does not work in the smithy and expect never to be burned," he continued. "Barothla was like her mother. Our marriage was arranged. Did you know?"

I shook my head. "I haven't heard anything about your wife."

"She passed some time ago, also as a result of her ambitions. The elves were not the only ones who experimented with producing hybrid dragon offspring, hoping to create great warriors that could protect their people."

So, Grandma had been another mad scientist?

"Rodarska, I believe, is more like me. More accepting, less ambitious, but she—both of our daughters—inherited their mother's power. *You* have some of it too, however tempered by your human blood. Power tends to make one feel superior to others and to long for more."

"I'm positive I'm not superior to anyone, and I only long for cheese and good tools." I was still grumpy that I'd lost my toolbox in the fire in Hart's mansion.

"I heard you're interested in our cheese caves." Ironhelm waved to the returning servant.

With impeccable timing, he'd arrived carrying a platter large enough to require two hands. He came in and set it on the table. A jug and ceramic mugs wobbled but remained upright, perched in the center and surrounded by numerous types of salamis, ballotines, terrines, cheeses, and a plate of what might have been desserts, little red and yellow rectangles crusted with sugar crystals.

"You really *are* my people," I whispered in approval, finding only the bowl of dried mushrooms a little sketchy. They looked rubbery.

"As I told you." Ironhelm picked up several slices of salami and gestured for me to try the food. "You said you still seek Rodarska and believe she's alive?"

After tidying a stack of napkins, the servant stepped back to the wall, standing within Ironhelm's view in case he needed anything else.

"Yes. When I left, my friend Val was arranging for a tracker to help us find the lair of her captors. We found out there's a dragon in the mix, so things got more complicated."

"Such is often true when dragons are involved."

"Do you, ah, resent that they rule over the Cosmic Realms and... influence your people?"

"They influence *everybody's* people," Ironhelm said dryly. "It is unwise to resent that."

"That sounds like a yes." I picked up a cube of cheese dotted with glowing algae. Thanks to Sarrlevi, I'd sampled something similar and knew it was delicious.

"Given my position, I cannot complain about the injustice of the system, and there is perhaps more peace than there would be if they did not rule. The war between the elves and the dwarves occurred during a time when the dragons were busy with their own politics and paying little attention to the rest of the races. Perhaps it could have been avoided if they'd ordered us to leave each other alone. That was a costly war for both sides, and, as we later learned, orc spies, under assignment from their leaders, were the ones who instigated it. A coalition of their people hoped we would destroy, or at least seriously weaken, each other and that their kind might charge in and claim both worlds as their own."

"Huh." I noshed on more cheese—and that salami was *amazing*—as he spoke, and attempted to look polite and attentive, but, now that I'd apologized for Barothla's death, my mind was turning back to my missing parents. I also longed to check on Sarrlevi and his mother. After our talk, would Ironhelm agree to send me home?

"It is wise, when tensions are high and all occurrences seem to be driving your people toward war, to step back and figure out who stands to gain from the possible outcomes of such an event. It is rarely the citizens of the respective powers and never those who are sent to do the fighting." Ironhelm poured a brown liquid from the jug into two mugs, offering me one and taking the other for himself.

"That seems true on Earth too." I sniffed the liquid, wrinkling my nose for it smelled musty and fermented. Perhaps fermented in must. "This isn't made from mushrooms, is it?"

"Fungus, honey, and spices. It's strong enough to grow your beard to your toes."

"My hair growth is more than sufficient already. Trust me."

Ironhelm looked dubiously at my bare chin. Would he be offended if I mentioned that I tweezed anything wayward that grew where I didn't want it?

To be polite, I took a sip from the mug. It was as musty going down as it smelled, and I imagined spores being left behind to inoculate fungi all down my esophagus. I took more bites of cheese to get the taste out of my mouth. And a few bites of salami. And more cheese.

"It's an acquired taste." Ironhelm took a long swig from his mug, and I watched his beard to see if the effects were instantaneous. They were not. "I'm tempted to offer to go with you to seek my daughter," he said quietly. "My advisors don't think it would be wise for me to risk endangering myself—or being captured and ransomed. I could ignore their counsel, as I'm sometimes wont to do, but I must reluctantly agree that their concerns are legitimate. Especially if dragons are involved."

"There are assassins after me too. After this is all resolved, I would be happy to show you around Earth if you want to visit. My part of it anyway. Though I have to warn you that my house is covered in elven repair vines right now, and there's a goblin living in my guest room. You could stay in my room, but it's usually full of entropy."

Ironhelm blinked slowly, either at the vines or the entropy—or all of it.

"I'd find a place for you. Uhm, you and your bodyguards." I imagined his whole entourage piling into my one-thousand-square-foot house. Maybe some of them would agree to stay in the tool shed.

"Elven repair vines, unless they're grown by a master, are meant to be temporary. Your abode should have something more substantial. Something worthy of one with dwarven blood."

"It used to be substantial before trolls, assassins, and an angry aunt started beating up on my house."

"Ah. If I visited, perhaps I could help you with repairs. I *do* have an engineering background, you know."

"I didn't know."

"I was the one who taught your mother to craft." Ironhelm smiled. "The enchanting she learned from others, but the rest..." He held up his calloused palm. "Do you need help against those who have captured my daughter? I could send a few legions back with you. My dwarves are well-trained warriors, and I would happily unleash them against the foes who presumed to kidnap my daughter and hold her for decades."

Legions would *definitely* be hard to house in the tool shed.

"Unless some of them are good at tracking people in rain-forests," I said, "I may not be ready for legions yet."

Ironhelm took another drink of the musty liquid while he pondered that. "Are there *tunnels* under the rainforest?"

"I can let you know if I find any."

"Very well." His expression was contemplative behind beard and mustache.

I wondered if dwarven legions would show up on Earth whether I wanted them or not. Once we found the entrance to the enemy lair, more help might not be a bad idea, but... what if the leaders of the organization did something like holding a knife to my mother's throat to keep the dwarves from advancing into their compound? Or what if they were powerful enough to simply take the legions prisoner, the same as they had my parents and all those elves and dwarves with glazed eyes that I'd seen?

I couldn't help but think it would be better to sneak in, if that was possible at this juncture, and get my parents without starting a war. As Ironhelm had mentioned when talking about war, his legions would likely end up being victims in such a conflict.

"Your warriors might be needed here if that half-dragon guy becomes a problem," I pointed out, "but I really hope he doesn't. I feel bad about that."

"Do not concern yourself, daughter of my daughter. We will do our best to recapture Starblade, or we will call the elves and request that they come get him. Elves commanded him and the other half-dragon warriors during their time, so he should see them as allies. Hopefully, he will obey King Eireth."

I nodded, glad that might be a possibility. "If you don't need me for anything, I'd like to resume the hunt for my parents. I appreciate you sharing your food and talking to me." I picked up a couple of pieces of the sugar-crusted dessert to try. I was a little tempted to ask if I could take some of the leftovers with me. If I had to trek through a rainforest, I would need snacks, after all. "Is there someone who can send me home?"

Ironhelm rose. "*I* can send you home. You're certain you don't wish my legions to accompany you?"

"I'm certain." I popped one of the desserts into my mouth.

Oh, those were good. They reminded me of Aplets and Cotlets from Eastern Washington. I took two more, then—after making sure neither Ironhelm nor the nearby dwarves were looking judgmentally at me for being a pig—two more. Too bad they would get smooshed if I stuffed them in my pocket. I eyed the napkins on the tray, but they were made from linen or something similar and looked nice. I couldn't swipe one to wrap food in.

"Perhaps," Ironhelm said, "in a couple of days, I will send General Grantik to check in to see if you've reached a point where my troops could be of use."

"I'm not sure your general loves Earth—" I thought of the *last* time he'd been, magically compelled by Barothla to do her bidding, "—but that would be fine."

"He minds it less than my priest, who is disgruntled that Sorka wouldn't deign to talk to him."

"What does that have to do with Earth?"

"Nothing, but it's causing him to feel peeved today."

I had a feeling Lankobar was peeved a lot but didn't say so. Instead, I balanced two more dessert rectangles on my palm. Then, deciding there was room for a few pieces of cheese and salami, I added to the pile.

Ironhelm watched more with amusement than judgment. He took one of the napkins and held it open, nodding for me to deposit the food in it.

Still by the wall, the servant lifted a finger, probably to suggest that he could get some Tupperware, or the dwarven equivalent, but Ironhelm waved in dismissal.

I eyed Sorka, wanting to pick up the hammer as well and tuck her under my arm. But would Ironhelm and the other dwarves allow it? Grantik and Lankobar were watching us again—watching *me* again—and something told me they would prefer I now be taken to a nice cell rather than released into the wild to make more trouble for them.

"I gather you're not interested in the *uglarth*." Ironhelm hefted the jug, as if he might give that to me too.

"No, thank you. Though there are a lot of bald guys on Earth who might be interested in the recipe if it grows hair on heads too." Somehow, all I could imagine sprouting from a layer of the thick liquid was fungi. Even those struggling with baldness might not want mushrooms growing on their pates.

"Despite the legends, I believe the scientific studies on its effects on hair growth are somewhat limited." Ironhelm picked up Sorka, and the knots returned to my gut. "I am unfamiliar with your world, but if you allow me to see in your mind where you wish to go, I can open a portal there."

"Sure." I hesitantly reached for the hammer. "Will you let me keep her? At least until I find Mom?" And forever after, if Sorka would allow it, I thought but didn't say.

"I was wondering if you wanted her or only the snacks." Ironhelm smiled and rested the haft in my hand.

As if mediocre food substances could be anywhere near as desirable as an enchanted hammer, Sorka said.

"I want her *and* the snacks," I said.

"Equally?"

Certainly not, Sorka said.

"She may be a little more important to me. Though the dessert is really good."

"A dwarven king must have the best chefs."

"Perks of the job."

"Indeed." Ironhelm lifted a hand to my temple and brushed my mind lightly.

I started to imagine my house but realized Sarrlevi wouldn't have gone there. I wasn't sure if he'd gone to Earth at all, despite my suggestion that Zavryd and Zoltan would be able to help heal his mother, but I had to make sure Zondia wasn't there harassing him. Or worse. I imagined Val's house in my mind.

Ironhelm nodded, and a portal formed in the middle of the throne room.

"She will find Princess Rodarska and the half-dragon?" Lankobar asked.

"The *half-dragon* is not our main concern now," Ironhelm said, escorting me to the portal.

Even with the napkin, I had to walk carefully to make sure cheese cubes didn't tumble free. Maybe I shouldn't have taken so much, but after the week—the *months*—I'd been having, I deserved a stash of good snacks, damn it.

Lankobar wrinkled his lips in silent disagreement, but he didn't object aloud.

Grantik nodded gravely at me. "Good luck, daughter of Rodarska."

"Matti."

I didn't expect him to use my name, but he managed a faint smile. "Matti, daughter of Rodarska."

That was a mouthful, but I would take it.

"We all hope you find her," Grantik added. "If you need help..."

"I know. Legions are available. I'll ask Artie and Hennehok to get in touch if we need them. Thanks."

"Be careful, daughter of my daughter," Ironhelm said, holding his hand out toward the portal. Then, softly, he added, "Matti."

"Thanks." I kissed him on the cheek and hopped through, hoping I wouldn't return to utter chaos.

13

THE HOPE THAT I WOULDN'T RETURN TO CHAOS WAS DASHED WHEN I came out of the portal in Val's backyard and heard cursing and swords clashing in the front. Or maybe in the street?

Sensing Zavryd and Sarrlevi, I groaned. Was Zavryd denying Sarrlevi access to the house—and Zoltan's healing formulas?—again? When Meyleera dearly needed the vampire's help?

No, I realized, as I ran for the gate in the fence. I sensed Meyleera inside the house, not in the basement laboratory but up in a guest room. Zavryd had at least let *her* in. So what was this about?

Everything okay, Matti? Val asked as I hurried toward the front yard.

My senses told me she was in the house, also upstairs. Freysha was there too. That alleviated some of my concerns. That meant someone was keeping an eye on Meyleera, and did her aura seem a touch stronger than it had been in the volcano prison?

You tell me. It sounds like Sarrlevi and Zavryd are trying to kill each other in the street. When the sword-wielding combatants came into view, I confirmed that it *looked* like that too.

They're dueling. Val didn't sound concerned.

Is that different from trying to kill each other?

I think they'll stop short of manslaughter. Or dragon-slaughter.

Comforting.

Zavryd was in human form, wielding a fiery blade made purely of magic and slashing and parrying as Sarrlevi came at him with his twin longswords, eager silver glows emanating from them. The duelists cast magic as well as swinging and slashing with their weapons.

As I'd noticed before when they sparred, human Zavryd wasn't quite as fast as elven Sarrlevi, but with his dragon power, he could keep enemy blades away with magic as well as his sword. He was the one pressing Sarrlevi back, battering him from all sides with blasts of that power. The last time they'd battled, his yellow Crocs had apparently made things a little difficult for him. Today, he wore the elven slippers that went with his silver-trimmed black robe.

"You odious, arrogant fool of a serpent," Sarrlevi spat as he defended against the magical assaults, sweat dripping from his jaw. "I do not wish to spend time within your domicile and care nothing about whether you lower your wards or not."

"Then why did you challenge me to a duel, sniveling criminal who cowers from the Dragon Justice Court like an orc caught thieving in the night?"

With my hammer in one hand and my napkin stuffed with goodies in the other, I passed the topiaries and stopped on the sidewalk, not going farther. Thanks to all the magic being hurled about, the street would be dangerous to bystanders. Judging by the broken branches, shattered glass from car windows, and a bent hubcap lying in the intersection, it was dangerous to *everything*.

"Because you insulted my mother, you slit-eyed reptile." Sarrlevi glanced at me, jerked his chin in a quick nod of acknowledgment, then sprang at Zavryd, slicing through a magical barrier to slash his swords at his foe.

"I insulted *you*, you pointy-eared hollow tree of an elf. Are you so eager to cut into dragons that your mulish brain cannot tell the difference? As you cut into my *sister*?" Snarling, Zavryd deflected the sword strikes and lunged in, swiping his fiery blade toward Sarrlevi's head.

It cut through his barrier, popping it like a balloon, but Sarrlevi was too quick to be in danger. He rolled away, sprang up, then rushed at Zavryd's side.

"Sarrlevi," I blurted, afraid I would have to step in—it looked like his blow would land.

But Zavryd spun in time to deflect the barrage of strikes that threatened him. Even though his sword appeared to be made of magical fire, it sounded like metal when their blades came together. The clangs rang out so loudly that every pedestrian at Green Lake must have heard the battle.

"You *know* I was the victim of a dwarf manipulating me and making me crazy," Sarrlevi said.

"Because you have a *weak* mind and deep down did not wish to disobey the order. You resent dragons."

"*Everyone* resents dragons."

By some silent agreement, they paused to wipe sweat from their brows. Chests heaving from their exertions, Zavryd and Sarrlevi both looked around the front yard before their gazes settled on me.

"Where did my mate go?" Zavryd asked, though he had to be able to sense Val in the house. Maybe he hadn't noticed when she'd left? "She was supposed to keep track of how many times we each drew blood so we would know who the victor is."

"You can't count your own cuts?" I asked.

Zavryd huffed and lowered his arm, the fiery blade extinguishing and disappearing. He prodded a hole in the side of his elven robe, then pushed a sleeve up to reveal a gash in his elbow. "Two."

Sarrlevi sheathed his own swords, touched a cut on the side of his head, then lifted the back of his hand to show a burn mark. "Two."

"It is a tie then?" Zavryd asked. "This battle has decided little."

"Do you wish to resume?" Sarrlevi squinted at him.

They both looked a little weary, and I wondered how long their *duel* had been going on.

Zavryd sighed. "Not at this time."

"Just to be clear, you did not insult my mother?"

"I said she must have been disappointed when she hatched you. Clearly, that is an insult to *you*, not to her."

"I thought when you implied I'd been *hatched* that you believed she was a bird or reptile." Sarrlevi curled his lip.

Zavryd propped a fist on his hip. "The greatest beings of all are hatched, you ignorant elf."

"Elven babies are born."

"Thus their inferiority."

Their eyes narrowed, and Sarrlevi's hands twitched toward his sword hilts again.

"How's Meyleera doing?" I asked brightly, attempting a cheerful smile. Anything that would head off Round Two.

"She is improving rapidly," Zavryd said, "because I, despite how deplorable and unpleasant her offspring is, funneled my healing energy into her, that she might be bolstered for the application of the vampire's formula."

"She is in a slightly improved state." Sarrlevi lowered his hands again. "Or so I'm told. Even though the dragon took her into his abode so the vampire could treat her, he forbade me from passing through his wards."

"Again?" I asked Zavryd.

"The elf is lucky I did not open a portal and punt him directly to the Dragon Justice Court. My mother and sister seek him. They will be furious with me for not immediately placing him in magical chains."

"You could *try* to chain me," Sarrlevi said.

"No, no." I hurried to Sarrlevi's side while smiling again at Zavryd. "No trying necessary. Salami?" I held open the napkin to offer some of my stash.

Zavryd eyed the only slightly smooshed contents. "I should not allow the friend of my mate to bring me food. A dragon should only be fed by his mate."

"Dude, I've brought you food like ten times."

"Yes. Val has said it is acceptable to her."

"I'm so glad." I knew nothing about dragon culture but had a feeling dragon mates were even more challenging than elf mates. Not that Sarrlevi and I were *mates*. Not yet. I might have smiled a little wistfully at him as I hefted the napkin toward Zavryd again. "Salami?"

This time, he investigated. He pushed aside the cheese cubes as if they were poisonous—fine by me—and selected a few slices of meat. He popped one in his mouth, made a contented noise, then waved his hand. The rest of the pieces of meat floated out of the pile and into his palm before he headed for the front door.

"Why can't you just bring him food to settle disagreements?" I asked Sarrlevi. "It's a lot less dangerous than dueling with him."

"I enjoy the challenge." Sarrlevi came up to my shoulder and looked down at the now-meatless mountain of snacks. "Did you raid the cheese caves in the dwarven capital?"

"Of course not. I'm not a criminal." My chin went up. "I raided my grandfather's charcuterie tray."

"It must have been a substantial tray."

"He's the *king*. Who would dare give him anything but an amazing assortment of goodies?"

"He is the king and a *dwarf*, yes," Sarrlevi said, as if the latter were the main reason for the prodigious spread.

"Don't tell me the elven king gets meager appetizer plates from his kitchen staff."

"Elves are known for sampling small portions of exquisitely prepared foods, not slurping down huge logs of meat and cheese."

"That must be why they're all so snobby. Their constant hunger makes them uptight."

"All?" His eyebrows rose.

"*All*," I said firmly.

"Some elves are a touch elitist," Sarrlevi admitted.

"It's no wonder you came looking for me." I popped a little triangle of cheese into my mouth.

Sarrlevi's eyes crinkled as he wrapped his arm around my shoulders. "Yes."

I offered him a piece of cheese, a well-proportioned cube, not a *log*. He accepted it and ate without hesitation—or saying anything snobby about it. Even if he didn't usually consume massive quantities of cheese, I knew he liked it. He wouldn't have a cheese cellar of his own, otherwise. And this stuff was good. *Very* good. I had to make myself share.

"The vampire has injected the first dose of the formula." Sarrlevi touched one of his pockets. "I have further doses. Once my mother is stronger, I will take her somewhere safe to recover in peace."

"A peace free of nearby street duels?" I was certain *Val* and *Freysha* weren't doing anything that would disturb a recovering elf.

"Yes. And dragons."

I thought he meant Zavryd, but Sarrlevi added, "Zondi-a'qareshi arrived shortly after I did. I'd just asked Zavryd'nok-quetal for permission to bring my mother to the vampire when I sensed her portal forming. I barely had time to camouflage myself."

"Zavryd didn't tell his sister you were here?"

"He did not. Before he could, Xilnethgarish showed up—you must contact him, as I believe he and the dwarves have an update for you on the organization's lair. He started... Well, *he* called it singing. An elf would describe it as caterwauling. It was sufficient to convince Zondia'qareshi to flee the area."

"Was that... Xilneth's intent?"

Was it possible Xilneth had known Sarrlevi needed someone to distract Zondia and had made his singing less pleasant than usual? Or maybe, despite his claims otherwise, all dragon singing was caterwauling.

"I am uncertain. He spoke of romancing her. She did not appear romanced. Regardless, once she left the area, I dissolved my camouflaging magic, and Zavryd levitated my mother inside. I have remained in the area in case I am needed."

"So Zavryd helped you. He seems like a decent guy. For a dragon. Maybe you should stop squabbling with him."

"He helped in a haughty and arrogant manner."

"Imagine that."

"I would not, however, have challenged him if not for the insult."

"About hatching."

"Yes."

I patted Sarrlevi on the chest.

"I would like to go in and see her," he admitted softly, looking toward the second-story windows, though the guest rooms were at the back of the house, so he could only see inside with his senses.

"Maybe if you asked Zavryd politely, without stabbing him or challenging him, he would allow it."

"Doubtful. Earlier, there were threats of incinerating. *Before* we began insulting each other." Sarrlevi eyed the topiaries. "I am powerful enough that I could disable his wards, but with him inside..."

I pulled out my phone and opened the food-delivery app to find a suitable dragon bribe.

"For a smart guy, you can be a little obtuse, Varlesh." I patted his chest again and leaned on him to take the sting out of the insult—I didn't want him to challenge *me* to a duel.

"I refuse to pander or be obsequious to him."

"Yeah, that's the obtuse part." *Val,* I said, switching to telepathy, *Sarrlevi would like to see his mother. How many pounds of meat do I need to have delivered to make that happen?*

Zav is up here saying how good the dwarven salami you gave him was, she replied.

I don't think the king's kitchen on Dun Kroth is on DoorDash. The delivery fees were bad enough for *Earth*-based restaurants.

Give me a second.

"I think Val is schmoozing him," I reported to Sarrlevi.

"As his mate, she likely finds that less odious than I do."

"Let's hope."

The elf may enter the premises for ten minutes to see his mother but must at once depart if another dragon arrives in the area, Zavryd boomed into our minds. *No bribes of meat are required at this time.*

"See?" I told Sarrlevi as Zavryd's magic wafted out of the house, altering the wards—and the topiaries—at the front of the property. "He's a decent guy."

If the elf is still on the premises at minute eleven, he will be incinerated promptly and without warning.

"Yes, *decent,*" Sarrlevi said. "I believe he volunteers at orphanages when he isn't busy devouring herds of herbivores."

After stuffing the remains of my snack stash in my pocket, I grabbed Sarrlevi's hand and led him to the front door. We didn't want to waste our ten minutes, especially when Zondia could return at any time.

14

On the way up to the guest room, we encountered Zavryd on the stairs. His face stiffened, and he lifted his chin as Sarrlevi brushed past him, but he didn't make any further comments about incineration.

"Thank you for this, Lord Zavryd." I had less of a problem being obsequious than Sarrlevi. Especially in this case. Zavryd was helping out, and it didn't seem wrong to call him *lord* and thank him. "It means a lot to me, to both of us."

Since Sarrlevi had already continued on to the guest room, he couldn't deny that. I doubted he would regardless.

"Especially since your mother is looking for him," I added quietly.

"Hm. It is possible she is wrong about the assassin."

"Yes," I said promptly, though I also blinked in surprise at the admission. Since Zavryd and Sarrlevi had more or less declared themselves mortal enemies, or at least forever dueling partners, I hadn't expected a concession from either that the other person might be okay. "Can you tell your mom that? And your sister."

"Family does not always listen to family," Zavryd said. "*Female* family especially does not always listen to male family. Besides, the way to change a dragon's mind is through action, not words."

"I thought it was through meat." I waved my phone, the food-delivery app still on the screen.

Though Val had said bribes weren't required, Zavryd noticed and prodded a picture of brisket. "Suitable tributes *can* soften a dragon's feelings toward a member of a lesser species, but we also admire honor, bravery, and battle ability."

"Sarrlevi has all those things."

"Then he must show it to the queen." Zavryd continued down the stairs but called back, "Two pounds of slow-roasted meat is a suitable tribute."

Val and Freysha were in Freysha's room, Val using her magic to practice poofing elven vines into existence. She paused and leaned out as I passed. "You *don't* have to order him meat."

"Okay," I said but put in the order anyway. Maybe Zavryd would give Sarrlevi twenty minutes with his mother if he was busy gorging himself in the kitchen.

"My mom said she'll be here later today with a tracker acquaintance," Val said. "Someone who can find anything and anyone, apparently. She's even better than Rocket."

"If she's willing to help, I'll gladly accept. I've also received an offer of legions of dwarf warriors to assist us."

"You declined it?"

"Well, I put it on pause. I thought sneaking in would be better if at all possible." The image of my mother with a knife to her throat came to mind again. Or the Caretaker with that rifle—or helicopter guns—pointed at her. "I'd like to free my parents without starting a war where innocent people might be hurt." This time, I thought of my father, my poor father who had only been kidnapped because I'd started snooping around. The memory of the prison and him calling my name returned often. I'd been so close that night and yet hadn't even gotten to see him.

"I suppose a legion of armed dwarves marching down Highway 101 might also concern the locals."

I nodded, though I wasn't that worried about the locals. "Does your friend Nin make anything that might help with an incursion? In case the sneaking isn't entirely effective?"

"She's mostly retired from the magical-weapons-crafting business, but she still supplies me with ammo and grenades when I need them. *Magical* grenades that can get through the armor and barriers of lots of my opponents."

"Like dragons?"

"Lots of my *lesser* opponents."

Thinking of the elf, dwarf, troll, and orc minions I'd come up against, I decided many of them might qualify. "Do you think she would unretire long enough to make me a batch of grenades?"

Was *batch* the right term? Like with baked goods? My mind conjured a dozen grenades sprouting up from a muffin tin.

"Probably so," Val said. "Especially if you come by regularly to buy lunch at her food truck."

"Text me the location, and I'll gladly do that."

"Good. I'll let you know when Mom and the tracker get here." Val waved for me to continue to the guest room.

As I started toward it, my phone buzzed with a text. Penina.

Josh has his first tennis tournament next weekend and wants to know if you can come.

I closed my eyes and pressed my phone to my forehead. Could I? I felt guilty about how little I'd seen my niece and nephew of late, and I hated to miss their big events. Until my life had gotten crazy, I rarely had. But with assassins continuing to be a threat, I worried about drawing attention to them.

Not that it mattered when it came to this Caretaker. He already knew all about my family.

I grimaced at the realization that Willard's soldiers wouldn't likely leave their stations at the houses to follow the kids to tennis tournaments or anywhere else, so they would be vulnerable. The urge to tell Penina to hunker down and never leave the house came over me, but that wasn't realistic.

I'll try to make it, I texted instead, resolving to find my parents before the tournament, before anything else bad could happen to my family. *Send me the time and place.*

After putting my phone away, I peeked through the open guest-room door, not certain if Sarrlevi would want me inside with him and his mother. Even though I'd met Meyleera briefly, it wasn't as if she knew me well.

Inside, he was kneeling beside the bed and clasping her hand. Meyleera lay on her back, much as Tinja had a month earlier when she'd been sick. Her eyes were closed, her long silver-and-blonde-streaked hair loose about her shoulders, but she seemed to be sleeping rather than unconscious. She wasn't as pale as she had been in the volcano, though I didn't know how much of a health improvement that indicated. The green light in the stasis chamber hadn't exactly been good to show off one's color.

Not certain if Meyleera would stir while we visited, I stepped inside and rested a hand on Sarrlevi's shoulder.

"I am resisting the urge to say *Mother* over and over to her while repeatedly poking her in the shoulder." He smiled slightly. "As I did when I was a boy."

"Elven kids do that too, huh?" I asked.

"When she was paying attention to my sister instead of me."

"How rude of her."

"Yes. I was the eldest so clearly the most important." The smile faded as a mixture of emotions crossed his face. Even though his sister had passed long ago, he probably regretted ever trying to steal his mother's attention from her.

"Your arrogance kicked in young, I see."

Meyleera's eyelids flickered, and Sarrlevi leaned forward.

"Mother?" he asked softly in Elven without poking her, simply holding her hand.

Her eyes opened, unfocused at first, but they soon tracked his face. "Varlesh?"

"Yes." He said more, but I couldn't understand it. Most likely, he was explaining that we'd found a cure.

I thought about activating my translation charm, but I didn't even know if I should be there, intruding on their privacy.

"Do you want me to wait outside?" I whispered when Sarrlevi paused for her to digest his information.

"No. She will want to see you." His smile returned as he looked up at me, but it was a little wry and lopsided. "I am less certain she wants to see me."

"She does." I squeezed his shoulder and glanced at the bedside table, empty save for an old alarm clock. "I'll get some water. Being frozen in stasis is probably dehydrating."

"I am not certain that is true, but water would be appreciated." His eyes narrowed. "Water without an abysmal taste and chemicals in it."

I snorted and ruffled his hair, remembering that he'd wanted me to put a whole-house water filter into the Bridle Trails home, for *his* sake, not that of the future buyers. "I'll see if there's any Perrier," I said, though I didn't know if Val was the type to buy bottles of fancy mineral water. She had to spend all her money on keeping her dragon fed.

Meyleera was watching us, and I gave her a shy wave before going downstairs to root in the refrigerator, where I found not one but two types of bottled mineral water. Maybe Zavryd also found Earth tap water to be substandard.

Not certain a wan woman recovering from a horrible illness was up for something as adventurous as carbonation, I selected the spring water and took it and a glass upstairs.

Sarrlevi and his mother were speaking softly. Despite his

certainty that she would want to see me, I hesitated before stepping inside. But he waved me in and pointed to my pocket. I activated my translation charm before pouring water and offering it to her. He had to help her sit up to drink, but she had the strength to reach over and pat my arm.

"I am pleased to see you, Matti," she said in Elven.

I'm very *pleased to see you awake and on the mend,* I told her telepathically before eyeing Sarrlevi. "*She* uses my name."

"I use your name."

"*Now.*"

"Mataalii objected to being called a *mongrel* when we met," Sarrlevi informed his mother in Elven, "though she is indeed of mixed blood."

"Women like to be called by name rather than referred to by generic and especially derogatory labels," Meyleera told him.

"I had not yet realized her value at that point." Sarrlevi lifted his chin. "She called *me* haughty and arrogant."

"So she assessed you accurately as soon as you met?" Her eyebrows rose. "She must be a good judge of character." She clasped his arm, smiling at him as she patted it.

I grinned. "I like her."

Sarrlevi snorted softly and brushed his fingers through my hair. "Excellent."

Meyleera beamed pleasure at us—or maybe at seeing us together. The last time I'd spoken to her, she'd been surprised—if not shocked—to learn that Sarrlevi and I were friends. More than friends. Apparently, she'd heard about the various beautiful and manipulative elven women—and who knew what else—he'd slept with over the years. It warmed my heart to think someone might find me, with my mongrel blood and lack of striking beauty, more appealing than they.

After helping her to drink more water, Sarrlevi explained that she would need more injections of the formula and that he had them. He tapped his pocket. He didn't mention Barothla, probably wanting to forget all about her and move forward, but Meyleera asked if she would be a further problem.

"She is dead," Sarrlevi said in a flat tone.

Meyleera's mouth parted in an *oh*, and she looked at me. Even though she couldn't have had any love for the dwarf princess who'd first caused her to develop Shiserathi Disease and later kidnapped her, her visage grew disturbed.

Though Meyleera knew Sarrlevi was an assassin and could probably guess that he'd been responsible for Barothla's death, I didn't want her to think he'd been running around in a fit, slaying people left and right. Sticking to telepathy, since *she* didn't have a translation charm, I explained everything from the fingernail slash as we'd tried to get the formula out of Barothla to his descent into madness.

Sarrlevi's face grew grim as I relayed the story, but he didn't interrupt or deny anything. After all, he'd been there. He knew the truth.

"That must have been hard for you," she whispered not to him but to me, though she also patted his arm again.

It was hard to see him... Even though I was speaking telepathically, my throat tightened with emotion, making me pause. Sarrlevi was better now, but it had happened so recently that the memories weren't far removed. It *had* been hard. *Yes,* I finished.

Meyleera touched my cheek, then focused on Sarrlevi. *My son, I am pleased you are with someone who cares about you.*

He inclined his head but didn't say anything. Maybe a little emotion was tightening *his* throat too?

And I am pleased that you are... someone a woman can care about. Meyleera still seemed a touch surprised by that, making me wonder how many awful stories of his work various elves had shared with her over the years. But she recovered and smiled, adding, *A woman besides your mother. I have always cared, even after... after they drove you out.*

After he'd killed his father, she'd almost said. I was sure of it.

I know, Sarrlevi said. *I have followed your work over the years. I regret that my actions—that the past—made you less happy.*

Her smile turned bleak, though she didn't drop it completely. *I have been lonely,* she said. *Even among our people, I did not feel that I had any close family remaining, anyone who understood.*

He swallowed. His throat was *definitely* tight. *I wish I could have visited you.*

As do I. Perhaps I should have left Veleshna Var and sought you out, but I did not think... based on what I heard about you... I did not think you would wish to see your mother.

Another swallow, and Sarrlevi wiped his eyes, the slight moisture clinging to his lashes. I was tempted to hug him, but I didn't move, barely breathing. I didn't want to disturb their moment.

I know, he said instead of claiming that he *would* have wanted to see her. Maybe that was the best answer. The other would have made her feel guilty for not having gone to check on him.

Sarrlevi dropped his head, and, for a moment, neither spoke.

Meyleera stirred, looking at me again. *Perhaps I will now be moved to paint something more cheerful. Will there be a wedding?*

Sarrlevi's head came up, but he didn't look as shocked by the question as I thought he might. I was especially touched that he didn't look *appalled.*

"We have not discussed such things." Sarrlevi paused. "She has not seen my cheese cellar yet."

Meyleera's mouth opened, but it took her a moment to come up with a response for that. "Is that a euphemism for sex?"

He started to shake his head but paused and looked at me. *Maybe thinking it could apply to that?*

He's told me it's amazing, I said instead of clarifying, *but we haven't had time for him to show me his, uhm, fromage.*

I trust from all I've heard that it's adequate. Meyleera looked wryly at him.

Sarrlevi blinked a few times, and was that a hint of chagrin in his eyes? *That is not the gossip I would have expected to find its way to you on Veleshna Var.*

Some of your paramours have been vocal.

Sarrlevi rubbed his face.

Do you need anything else, Meyleera? I asked to change the subject. Though I didn't mind seeing Sarrlevi mortified in front of his mother, it seemed polite. *Something to eat?*

"Not yet, but thank you. Varlesh, when I am stronger, I will ask you to make a portal and send me back to Veleshna Var with the remaining doses of the formula."

Sarrlevi lowered his hand. "You wish to leave our company?"

"I hope to see much more of you—both of you—in the future, but I must speak to the king and queen about Barothla. I must tell them that she kidnapped me."

"You need not concern yourself about her ever again. As I said, she is dead."

"But the elven king and queen are not. What they believe to be the truth is important if you ever wish to visit our home world again."

"They won't allow that." Sarrlevi lowered his voice. "I've killed elves. Not only he who sired me."

That disturbed look returned to Meyleera's eyes, making me certain she would like it if I one day succeeded at convincing Sarrlevi to give up being an assassin and come work with me, but she only nodded firmly. "I will speak the truth to them regardless. *All* the truths. After your sister passed and you... *he* was gone, I was too distraught to speak up for you to those determining your fate. Also, I'd let myself become such a small person then, someone of no importance, that I didn't know if they would listen. I regret that deeply. I regret not trying."

"It's all right, Mother."

"It is not." Meyleera took a deep breath, weariness replacing the other emotions in her eyes. "I will speak to the king and queen."

Sarrlevi didn't appear to want that, maybe afraid she would end up getting herself ostracized too if she tried to defend him, but all he said was, "For now, you will rest."

"Yes." Meyleera managed another smile as she took my hand, then his, then rested them atop each other. "Matti, I hope you find Varlesh's cheese collection adequate."

My cheeks warmed though I had no idea if she was using that as a euphemism or not. At the least, since she'd brought it up, she was aware of the double entendre.

"I'm sure I will," I said.

Still smiling, her eyes closed, and she drifted off.

15

—————

AFTER STEPPING INTO THE HALL AND CLOSING THE DOOR TO THE guest room, Sarrlevi slumped against the wall. I could almost *see* the tension seep out of his muscles. Part of it might have been weariness, after all he'd been through these past few weeks, but part of it had to be relief. His mother was alive and recovering, and *he* was alive and sane. For a time, he must have doubted if either of those things would come to pass.

"Are you all right?" I asked quietly. "Do you need a minute?"

Sarrlevi studied me, the weariness in his blue eyes fading and some of their usual intensity returning. He lifted a hand to the side of my face, knuckles brushing my cheek and sending a tingle through me before he pushed his fingers though my hair to cup the back of my head. "I need *you*."

"Oh?" Though this wasn't the ideal place for him to show me his *cheese collection*, my body had no desire to object to being needed by him, and I stepped closer.

He rubbed my scalp as he gazed down at me through his lashes. I melted against him, the heat of his muscled torso warm through my shirt.

"You have been at my side, like nobody else ever has," Sarrlevi murmured. "Even when we should have been enemies, even when I didn't *want* to feel anything for you, you were there. Loyal. You shouldn't have been. I knew you were attracted to me, and I used that to my advantage. I was a smug ass."

"Yeah." Maybe I should have said something more articulate and agreed that he *had* been intolerable at first, but his fingernails scraped over my scalp, sending intense shivers of pleasure through me, and words fell out of my mind. Trickles of his magic followed, zinging along my nerves and arousing every part of my body.

He bent his mouth toward mine, and I rose up on tiptoes, eager for the kiss—for him. After our lips met, teasing and caressing, he switched to telepathy.

I did not deserve your loyalty, but you gave it. His free hand slipped under my shirt, stroking my side on its way up to trace the curve of my breast. *Now you will have* my *loyalty.*

After all the times he'd sprung into battle to protect me, I knew I'd had it for a while, but I was way too turned on by his physical and magical touches to explain that. All I managed were a few eager murmurs as I wrapped my arms around his shoulders and kissed him back, such intense desire and longing building in me that I almost forgot we were in someone else's house and his mother was only a wall away.

Val and Freysha had gone downstairs, and I didn't sense Zavryd at all, but we were in the middle of the hall. We couldn't—

His finger brushed my nipple through my bra, and I gasped, arching into him. I needed him too. Anywhere he wanted.

For so long, I'd dreamed of this, woken hot and horny and alone in bed, wishing he were there with me. Maybe we could find a place and finally be together. After all, there wasn't anything more important we could do until the tracker arrived, right?

Sarrlevi's arm shifted, and he picked me up. Reflexively, I tightened my grip and wrapped my legs around his waist.

With a pleased growl at my response, he headed across the hall, using his foot to nudge open the door to the other guest room. Anticipation thrummed through me as we entered, Sarrlevi shutting the door behind us, using his magic to lock it, to ensure we wouldn't be disturbed. I pushed my fingers through his hair, willing my own magic to trickle into him and arouse *his* every nerve.

His next growl was more heated, and he swept my shirt over my head, letting it fall to the floor. Too distracted to worry about tidiness this time? That delighted me, and I let my kisses deepen, hungrily wanting to keep all of his attention on me.

Sarrlevi might have meant to carry me to the bed, but he pushed me against the wall instead. Well, that was better than a tree. I smirked against his mouth, though he might have disagreed.

I'll have you in the forest yet, he promised, reading my thoughts, tightening his grip on me.

Will there be a bed?

A bed of moss.

Romantic.

It will be. He shared an image of us naked and entwined on the forest floor, dew dripping from branches and onto our sweaty bodies.

Never had I imagined such a thing would turn me on, but his expert touches ensured I could think of nothing except how much I wanted him. In forests, on beds, against walls... anywhere. But especially here. Now.

A zing of his magic coursed through me, and I gasped and dug my fingers into his muscled shoulders, wanting to tear off the rest of my clothing so there would be nothing between us.

Maybe I should have asked him about condoms—did elves have such things?—but I'd started birth control again as soon as I'd believed our relationship might turn into something physical, and I trusted he could use his healing magic to take care of any diseases. If not, maybe Zoltan had a formula...

The thought of asking a vampire alchemist about such things made me smirk again, and I wondered if Sarrlevi was still following my thoughts.

I am clean and without disease, was all he said, sending more magical pleasure charging through me, bringing my mind fully back to him.

I slid a hand up to stroke his ear, brushing the point with my thumb as I willed my own magic into his body. I imagined it zipping along his nerves, arousing great pleasure and intensifying as it reached his cock.

He broke our kiss, gasping as his head tilted back. "*Mataalii,*" he growled my name.

Hearing it like that, his longing and desire wrapped around the syllables, filled me with such emotion that tears almost came to my eyes.

I whispered, "Varlesh," my voice also full of longing, in case it moved him similarly.

He groaned and tilted his head toward my touch, and I knew without a doubt that his pointed ears were sensitive. Maybe even erogenous. I sent more magic into him, wanting to excite him in ways his beautiful elven lovers never had.

Pure raw need stamped his face as he met my gaze, his breath quick, his eyes savage. I glimpsed his thoughts, him tearing off my clothing and pounding into me, and I tightened my legs around him, wanting nothing more than that.

But he caught my hand, pulling it from his ear. "I wish to reward you for your loyalty."

"Trust me," I whispered, my voice hoarse—I was panting too. "You in my bed—or against this wall—is the reward I want."

"You'll have that," he said, his eyes never leaving mine. "*Many* times."

Once more, he kissed me, my back pressed against the hard wall, my chest against the hard *him*.

My shoes and jeans loosened. Thanks to his magic? Or mine?

As they fell free, I thrust against him, wanting *his* clothes off as well. But it was my bra that slipped to the floor next, joining my shirt. His mouth lowered from my lips, and I might have protested, but his tongue traced its way to my breast, rousing me with magic as well as his teasing touch.

Pleasure charged to my core, and I groaned, already throbbing in anticipation of more. I gripped his head as I shifted my chest toward him, wanting him to have all the access to me that he wished. He teased me, sucking and nipping, stealing my breath, making me writhe. My fingers dug into his scalp as my body pulsed with need.

"Varlesh," I groaned. "It's not necessary... to take things... slow."

It is, he disagreed, teasing me further, though thankfully his tongue soon traveled lower.

His hands held me against the wall, his magic peeling away the rest of my clothing until I was naked before him. I squirmed against the wall, against him, deliciously pinned, my body responding to everything he did, even his soft breaths on my flushed skin.

He hooked my legs over his shoulders as he knelt and inhaled deeply before stroking me eagerly, *hungrily*, with his tongue. I hoped he was as aroused as I. His hands—or was that his magic? —soon had me bucking with desire. His tongue explored deeper, finding my clit, and I almost climaxed at his first touch. The magical and the physical combined as he evoked ever more intense sensations. Again, I bucked against him, and I couldn't keep from crying his name aloud.

I didn't want to make noise when there were others in the house, but I couldn't help it, couldn't keep from pleading for him to take me over the edge. In another state, I might have been embarrassed by my thrashing need, might have hated to beg, but I was so far beyond any arousal I'd ever experienced. I could barely think of anything but him taking me to heights I hadn't believed possible.

Make all the noise you wish, Sarrlevi whispered into my mind, holding me up, pinned against the wall as he licked and sucked. *None will hear. Except for me. And I enjoy the sounds of your pleasure.*

He smiled against me, that smug, knowing smile that I'd once hated with all my heart. Now, I could only find it erotic. He looked up at me with heated lust in his eyes, our gazes meeting past my breasts, my whole body quivering with need. Seeing that he wanted me only made me hotter, and I thrust toward him.

"Please, Varlesh. I need—"

With a perfectly placed touch from his tongue and zing of his magic, he took me to my climax with such an intense blast of ecstasy that I threw my head back and cried out. Waves of pure pleasure rolled over me, and I would have collapsed, every muscle going limp, if he hadn't held me up.

Skin slick with sweat, I lowered my legs and rested my hands on his shoulders, wondering why he was still clothed, wanting him to take *his* pleasure as well. Even sated, my body throbbing in the aftermath, I longed to see ecstasy on his face as he took me, wanting him to enjoy it as much as I enjoyed him, as much as he'd enjoyed others. *More* than he'd enjoyed others. I selfishly wanted to be special for him and willed my love and magic into him.

"Mataalii," Sarrlevi groaned softly, nuzzling me. "You make it difficult to be a gentleman." His voice was raspy, and I could feel the tension in his body. Again, he inhaled deeply, as if the scent of my arousal was the most glorious thing in the world.

"I want you to be satisfied, *more* than satisfied," I whispered, lifting a hand to his head again, brushing my fingers along his ear.

"You've had such a hard life, never gotten what you deserved. I want you to enjoy this. I want you to—"

His tongue slid into my core again, and I lost my words, my body growing greedy in anticipation of more. After a few precise strokes, fully awaking the need within me again, he rose lithely to his feet, lifting me with him. This time, he carried me to the bed, laying me gently on it, though there was a wild tension barely restrained in him, and I suspected he wanted to thrust me down and spring atop me like a panther.

I wouldn't have minded in the least and pushed his shirt and trousers off as he lowered himself onto me. He kissed me, hard and hungry, as his fingers trailed down my body, his thumb rubbing me exquisitely and almost making me forget about pleasuring him. But no. I ran my hands over his muscular chest, breaking our kiss so I could taste him, slide my tongue over his nipple just as he'd done for me. After so many erotic dreams of him, getting the chance to explore him in reality excited me almost as much as his touches, especially when I caught those glimpses of lust in his eyes. The knowledge that he wanted me badly made me feel beautiful and desirable.

You are extremely desirable, Sarrlevi spoke into my mind, *and beautiful. Even when you're furious.* He smiled and held my gaze as his hands roamed. *Especially* when you're furious.

Later, I might ask him for examples of when I'd been furiously beautiful, but all I could reply with was, *You're beautiful too.* That wasn't the right word, but with his fingers stroking my sensitive flesh, my mind was on the fritz again.

Loyal, he said. A correction? The quality that meant more to him than his looks?

Amazingly loyal, I agreed, even as I shifted under his touch. *I never thought I'd have someone like you in my life.*

Someone who can satisfy your every need?

Yeah. Let me satisfy yours. I curled my fingers around his shaft, guiding him toward me, willing my touch to excite him more than ever before.

Whether I succeeded at *that* or not, I didn't know, but he came to me without hesitation. After his delicious ministrations, I was more than ready for him and might have put thoughts of pounding into *his* mind. Despite that, he was slow and gentle, not wanting to hurt me, I knew, but I was tough, tough and aching for him all over again.

I urged a quicker pace, willing more of my magic into him, and his restraint burst like a dam. He growled and thrust into me, filling me, his magic enticing and erotic as his powerful presence wrapped around me.

As we rocked together again and again, animal instincts taking over, he looked at me with love as well as lust in his eyes, and I hoped he understood how much he meant to me. I might have been attracted to him and longed for this from the beginning, but I hadn't *wanted* to want him. Not back then. Now, with all my heart, I couldn't imagine ever wanting another.

We both cried out as we came, and I flung my arms around him, basking in the knowledge that he'd enjoyed it—he'd enjoyed me.

He shifted, as if to move off me, but I pulled him down on top of me and kissed his neck, wanting him to stay, not wanting this to end.

Sarrlevi seemed disinclined to plop his body down and smash me, and I almost laughed, because I'd been smashed by spent boyfriends in the past, men who hadn't been nearly as appealing, nearly as *caring*.

Seeming to understand that I wanted him to stay close, at least for a time, he settled for resting his weight on his elbows. His fingers came up to brush my hair out of my eyes as he gazed at me.

"You're amazing," I said, though I knew he already believed that, even before his smug smile confirmed it.

"*You* are amazing." The smile shifted from smug to gentle. Serious. "I love you, Mataalii."

"I love you too," I whispered, touched that he'd said it. Not only in a letter, not only when we might die, but here in my embrace. Just because.

He kissed me tenderly, but a hint of humor turned his gaze less serious. "I had no idea you'd learned so much in your magic lessons."

I hoped I hadn't tried to put an enchantment on his penis. I'd only wanted to share the same pleasure with him that his magic had evoked in me. He might be disturbed if his favorite appendage started glowing in the dark or resisting rust.

He smirked, doubtless following my thoughts.

"I've found my second gift in life," was all I said.

"After plumbing?" His eyes crinkled as his amusement deepened.

"That's right."

He stroked the side of my face, and we kissed for a time, making me contemplate challenging his vaunted elven stamina to another round, but he paused to gaze down at me, seeming to remember something.

"Another threat has found you," he said.

I frowned. I'd been enjoying *not* thinking about that.

"Thorvald told me that you believe an elf who is not an assassin is threatening you," he said.

"Yes, isn't it a welcome change? A non-assassin?" I tried to smile, but it wasn't very funny.

"Why did you not tell me? I can protect you better when I'm aware of all that threatens you."

I sighed. "I didn't want to delay *your* mission, and... I'm not even certain yet how much is a real threat and how much this guy is just messing with me. I've only met him, uhm." I hesitated, realizing how stupid it would sound to finish that sentence with *in my dreams.* If not for the stolen spoon rest, I wouldn't be certain the Caretaker was real. Technically, I didn't know if he had been responsible for that.

"I am not always reading your mind," Sarrlevi said, watching my face, "but I believe I am following you now. You were threatened through dream magic?"

"Dream magic? That's a thing?"

"Not all mages can do it, but some are experts at mind manipulation and can indeed send visions through dreams. They can even manipulate your body from afar to make you sleep so you are more susceptible to them."

"That's exactly what happened and why I wondered if it was real. He could have just spoken to me telepathically, right?"

"Then you might have more easily pinpointed the mage's location. Also, our minds are less well protected when we slumber. As one with dwarven blood, you are aware that you have some natural resistance to mind magic. You may have been able to thrust him out of your thoughts if you'd been awake."

"I'd like to thrust him off my entire planet, assuming he's here."

"He must be on this world to use his magic on you."

"I don't suppose you know him and know why he might be messing with me? He implied he's working with Varlat, but I couldn't tell if he had control bracelets and was being forced to do so." I shared my memory of the suit-wearing elf from my dreams.

"I do not recognize him, no, but since I've been on the elven home world so little these past centuries, that is not surprising. As to the rest..." Sarrlevi grimaced. "If a dragon wishes you to ally with him or her, it is not wise to say no."

"So we should deal with the dragon, and maybe the Caretaker problem will go away too."

"Yes. I will help you deal with this issue." He brushed his fingers through my hair again. "I am enjoying lying here with you, and I can tell from the way that your leg is wrapped around my backside, as if to claim me, that you feel the same way, but if you are ready to seek the dragon and your parents, I am ready to help you find them."

"Val's mom and a tracker friend are supposed to come here, and then we can go." I supposed we could have gone ahead, but it seemed I should wait to answer any questions they might have that could help them find the enemy lair. And maybe I *was* claiming Sarrlevi, reluctant to release him and return to the real world. I wished we could linger all day and spend the night together as well.

Sarrlevi smiled and kissed me. *I am certain the dragon of the house will return to threaten my incineration before then.*

I'm surprised he hasn't already. Though I was grateful that he hadn't.

Perhaps your bribes sufficiently appeased him.

More likely, the queen or his sister had called him away.

I'm glad we had this time together. I glanced toward the door, half-surprised that someone else hadn't disturbed us.

Sarrlevi's magic lingered about it, including the lock. I hoped he'd meant it when he'd said he would keep the sounds of our gasps and cries from escaping the room. I wanted to be able to look Val in the eyes again. And Sarrlevi's mother too.

As am I. As Sarrlevi returned my kiss, his fingers slid up to cup my breast, his nails grazing my sensitive flesh.

The heat of anticipation flushed my body, and I couldn't help but hope the world would stay away for another hour. Maybe two.

If we must wait until this tracker arrives, Sarrlevi said, *I suggest we make good use of the time.*

I'm good with that.

His eyelids drooped for a sultry and smug smile. *I can tell.*

16

It was almost sunset when a text came in from Val, the beep faint since my phone had somehow ended up under the bed. Sarrlevi watched in bemusement as I hunted for it, my bare butt toward the ceiling, his hand stealing a caress before he levitated it into my grip. Earlier, he'd levitated bottles of water from the kitchen to us so that we could quench our thirst without getting up. Dating a powerful elf mage had its perks. A *lot* of perks.

I smiled slyly at him, suspecting Sarrlevi would be reading my mind, but he was looking toward the window now.

"I sense a number of goblins approaching the area," he said.

"Maybe that's what Val texted about." I pushed my hair out of my eyes to read the message. "No, she says the tracker is on the way."

Now, I could also sense goblins approaching. My roommate was among them, but there were several other auras with hers. Had she come back with the junk-collection wagon? I hadn't put an offer in on that house or even thought more about it since I'd visited, so she *shouldn't* think she could raid the belongings left in the backyard.

"That is good. It is time to finish your quest." Sarrlevi kissed me. "We will finish our sexual encounter later."

"Finish? We've been in bed all afternoon, and I, uhm, finished a number of times." I grinned at him, and it might have been a little smug since I knew he'd enjoyed himself multiple times as well.

"Does not the human expression of *clear your calendar* that you shared with me convey that many days are required for an adequate encounter?"

"I am amenable to the idea of spending days with you when we have time, but this was very adequate. I hope you agree."

"Yes, but too brief. We will join again later. Often."

"I look forward to it."

"Yes." He smiled, still cocky, then gently brushed my cheek with his fingers before slipping out of bed. The simple gesture touched me, the *comfort* of it. Of him. "I will check on my mother while you dress and determine if the goblins represent a problem."

"I suppose that's a good idea. Are you going to tell her I liked your cheese collection?" I smirked at him as he tugged on his trousers.

"This is the first day I've spoken to my mother in more than two hundred years. Do you truly think I will speak of my sexual activities with her?"

"Are you going to smile smugly if she *asks* if I liked your cheese collection?"

"Of course." Sarrlevi smiled smugly at *me* before slipping out.

After watching in bemusement as his magic trickled through the wall to tidy the bed, I washed up, dressed, and trotted downstairs, pausing when I spotted Dimitri playing video games in a giant beanbag chair in the living room. He glanced back at me, and my cheeks heated as I wondered if Sarrlevi had *truly* used his magic to dampen sounds coming from the guest room.

"Your drainpipes are dope," Dimitri told me, waving a hand. "The last time it rained, a wad of leaves shot all the way to the mailbox."

"Thanks. It's the kind of elite enchanting I dreamed of doing as a little girl."

"Val said a chipmunk trying to stash nuts in there went flying one morning too." Dimitri grinned.

"I've heard. Do you know where she went?" Her text hadn't said. "And Zavryd? I kept expecting him to kick out Sarrlevi."

"I'm not sure about him, but Val got called to Willard's office a few hours ago. She asked me to let her mom in when she gets here." Dimitri frowned toward the front window, though he couldn't have seen out from his horizontal position in the beanbag. "She didn't say anything about goblins coming to visit. I hope they don't try to get past the wards. Goblins are flammable, you know."

"I think we all are." Before stepping outside, I pushed aside a curtain to peer out. Then rocked back and groaned. Tinja and the other goblins had not only brought their steam-powered wagon, but it was hooked up to the tiny home that had previously been out at the worksite. "Why did she bring that *here*? You can't park a tiny home on a random city street. There's not even a license plate on the trailer. It's not legal to tow it."

"You need a license plate to tow something?"

"Yeah, look at the next trailer you see being hauled off to a campsite. It'll have a plate."

"I'm not really a campsite guy."

"Well, look at the next trailer full of junk you see being hauled to your shop for parts."

"I've never had a trailer full of junk delivered." Dimitri looked wistful. "Maybe someone will get me one for my birthday."

"Are you sure you're not part goblin instead of part dwarf?"

"Yup." He grinned.

As I stepped out onto the porch, hoping to tell Tinja she couldn't park her tiny home here *before* they unhooked it, a Subaru SUV drove up, the driver and a passenger peering curiously at the goblin vehicle. My senses said the driver was a mundane human, but the passenger was not. She was a halfblood, like me, but I couldn't tell what her other half was. It felt vaguely elven, but something about her was different from Val.

Was this the tracker? And Val's mom?

Tinja hopped out of the truck and waved, calling what sounded like directions to the goblin driver. The magic of my translation charm had long since worn off, but, judging by her hand gestures, Tinja was planning to direct him to back up the tiny home to park it squarely in front of Val's house.

The Subaru stopped alongside the curb around the corner from the goblin activities. One of the back windows rolled down, and a golden retriever stuck his head out. He woofed at the goblins, though it sounded more like he was barking encouragement than objecting to their activities.

"Tinja," I called from the porch. "What are you doing?"

She smiled brightly as she waved at me. "Placing my demo tiny home in a more publicly accessible location. One with foot traffic. It will be much easier to get people to see its magnificence and desire to purchase my plans if they can come to Green Lake instead of far out into that rural area."

"I thought you were going to try some new marketing videos."

"We will also do that. As soon as you have time to record instructional footage."

"Right." I pointed at the tiny home. "Did you get permission from Val for this? From Val and *Zavryd,* Zavryd the extremely powerful and frequently testy dragon who calls this his lair?"

"I did ask the Ruin Bringer if I could store something here, yes."

"*Something*? Like a giant house on wheels?"

"It is not giant; it is tiny. And I did not specify precisely what I would store. Besides, is this not a public street? Any may park here, yes? As long as my goblin comrades and I—and our visitors —do not cross the sidewalk onto the dragon's property, he should not object."

"Oh, I'm pretty sure he'll object."

Sensing Sarrlevi coming down the stairs, I waited on the porch for him. Tinja kept directing the goblin parking the tiny home. As someone who well knew the challenges of backing up a large trailer, I wasn't surprised when the driver ran it up on the curb. Several feet away, the eyes of the dragon topiaries glowed, and smoke wafted from their foliage nostrils.

Val's mom and the tracker hadn't gotten out of the Subaru. Though the front windows were still up and I couldn't hear whatever conversation they were having, I had no trouble imagining it.

Is this neighborhood safe?

I thought it was, but I may have been mistaken.

I might have changed my mind about helping this friend of your daughter's.

I wouldn't blame you. I hope my car isn't in danger.

Meanwhile, the dog barked more encouragement.

Behind me, the door opened, and Sarrlevi stepped out. Torn between going to introduce myself to the tracker and making another attempt to shoo Tinja and her buddies away, I looked back at him.

"Will Zavryd'nokquetal allow that?" Sarrlevi pointed at the tiny home.

"I don't know, but I would be distraught if he, in his anger, used his magic to hurl it into the water." I waved in the direction of Green Lake, where walkers on the path were oblivious to the strange goings-on a block away. "I did most of the work on it."

"Didn't you do *all* of the work on it? It emanates your magic." Sarrlevi smiled at me. Proudly?

Even though I was in the middle of feeling distraught, I allowed myself a moment to appreciate his approval. "Tinja drew the blueprints, which, as she'll be quick to point out, is the most important and arduous part of the building process."

"The drawing is arduous?"

"Immensely so." I leaned against him as the chaos unfolded. A part of me wished we'd stayed in the bedroom.

Sarrlevi noticed the Subaru and frowned in that direction. Meanwhile, two more cars arrived, the occupants mundane humans. Who now? I didn't know if the goblins were camouflaging themselves so normal people wouldn't see their short greenness, but the tiny home was definitely *not* camouflaged. The drivers of both vehicles gaped at it. One of the cars had a real-estate sign on the door.

Hell, was someone trying to show the home across the street?

"Now is not a good time," I muttered.

The real-estate agent must not have agreed, for he parked by one of the many for-sale signs and waved for the other car to do the same. As he jogged for the front door, he glanced warily at the truck and trailer, the latter up on the grass strip for the third time as the driver, who was barely tall enough to see over the steering wheel, struggled to line it up parallel to the curb.

Broken glass from the earlier duel crunched under the wheels. Once again, the real-estate agent waved to the people in the car, but they were looking at the tiny home, the goblin steam wagon, and the dragon-shaped topiaries. They hadn't parked their vehicle yet, much less gotten out.

"Do you think the glowing eyes on the shrubs are visible to people without magical blood?" I wondered.

Sarrlevi wasn't paying attention to them and didn't seem to hear my question. Though he remained close, his arm still around my waist, he pointed at the Subaru with his free hand.

"Who is riding in that conveyance?"

"I think it's Val's mom and her tracker friend. If she's part elf, the tracker might be really good, right? Because she can use magic, not only her nose and eyes and knowledge of trackery stuff?"

Sarrlevi slanted me a look, and I thought he would object to *trackery stuff* as a sufficient term. "She is part *dark* elf, a heritage that would make her more adept at finding sacrifices for her people's demon gods than locating forest bases."

"Are you sure?" I'd never seen a dark elf and wasn't sure how all they differed from regular elves, except that they were supposed to be albino and preferred tunnels to daylight. The stories said they, like Zoltan and his vampire brethren, couldn't endure sunlight or even be outside on a bright moonlit night. I had no idea if any of that was true. If any dark elves lived underground in the Seattle area, they'd always left me alone.

"I am certain. The auras of elves and dark elves, even *half*-dark elves, are distinctly different." Sarrlevi didn't *say* he believed dark elves were far inferior, but his tone conveyed it without trouble. "My people carry the sun, the wind, the forest, and all of nature with them, melded into their auras."

"What's melded into your people's auras is haughtiness."

"Should you insult the elf you hope will one day hand-feed you cheese from his cellar?"

"It was more of a statement of fact than an insult, wasn't it? I can sense your aura, so I know all about it. The haughtiness is tucked in there between the sun, wind, and forest. Kind of smooshed all over them, I believe."

"If you are not insulting me, you are at least *teasing* me."

"Well, yes. But your hand slipped down to my butt, so I think you don't mind it too much."

"Hm." He squeezed me, smiling, but only briefly before looking toward the Subaru again. "Ask Thorvald about the dark elves. She has battled their kind."

"Here? Or on your world?"

"We have driven them out of our world. Their magic is vile, as are they and what they worship. She fought them in the tunnels under your city, and in your volcano, I believe. I was not there but heard the tale from another."

"Our volcano?" I mouthed, thinking of Mt. Saint Helens, but that had last erupted before I'd been born.

"The one with the glaciers atop it." Sarrlevi nodded toward the south.

"Mt. Rainier?" I *did* remember hearing something about heightened seismic activity there the year before. I would have to ask Val for the story.

"Never mind," came a call from the car that presumably held potential house buyers. With their eyes wide, they backed their vehicle up and drove off.

"I definitely don't have to make up my mind quickly on that house." I had a feeling the goblins weren't bothering to camouflage themselves, or at least not *fully* camouflage themselves. "I can't believe people are more disturbed by goblins and an extremely fine tiny home than the broken glass and branches in the street from your duel earlier. With all the noise that you and Zavryd made, it's a wonder nobody called the police. Are elves allowed to break branches during duels? That is very anti-nature."

"*I* did not break the branches or the conveyance windows. Dueling with a dragon is like dancing with a *drysdaldor*."

"I have no doubt." I mentally replaced the unfamiliar creature with *hippopotamus*. Or even *elephant*.

"Why have they not exited their conveyance?" Sarrlevi continued eyeing the SUV with suspicion.

"Maybe for the same reason the prospective buyers didn't." I pointed at Tinja, who was trotting up to me.

"A dark elf would not be intimidated by a goblin."

"I'm not sure *intimidation* was the problem."

"Matti." Tinja sidled up to me while giving Sarrlevi a wide berth and wary look. She tugged at my sleeve. "This would be a good time to put in an offer on our future home. The enemy agent is vanquished, forlorn with defeat, and will encourage his client to accept even a modest offer."

"That's probably a random buyer's agent, not the one selling the house. And neither of them is an enemy."

"People we must test our mettle against, at least!" Tinja squeezed my arm again, then glanced down, noticed *Sarrlevi's* arm around me, and sprang back. "Oh. You are entwined. Did you seek to engage in coital activities?"

"On the porch?" I asked. "No."

Later and elsewhere, we would enjoy that again. I gave Sarrlevi a sly look.

He returned it, perhaps not *too* disturbed by the nefarious half-dark elf lurking.

Tinja, observing our shared looks, asked, "You are certain?"

Sarrlevi shifted his gaze toward the southern sky. I thought he might mention Mt. Rainier again, but the dyspeptic expression that twisted his face was one he usually reserved for dragons.

"Zavryd'nokquetal returns," he said. "With Thorvald. I do not sense Zondia'qareshi with them, but she may be camouflaged."

"I suggested Zavryd tell his sister to leave you alone, but he said that wouldn't work, that you'll have to convince the dragons through actions that you don't deserve punishment and rehabilitation."

"What *action* would result in their opinion of me changing?" Sarrlevi's face grew a little wistful.

Maybe if we could come up with something that would work, he would do it. He'd achieved his goal with his mother, but as long as the dragons wanted him, he would have to spend his life in hiding.

As if he were thinking of doing exactly that, Sarrlevi released me and stepped away.

I clasped his hand, not wanting him to have to skulk off.

"The ten minutes have long passed," he told me.

"Zavryd isn't going to incinerate you. I think he *likes* having you as a frenemy. Cursing you and dueling gives him something to do when he isn't boinking Val or eating meat."

Sarrlevi's jaw sagged open, but of all the potentially disturbing things in those sentences, *frenemy* was what he mouthed. Without asking for clarification, he shook his head and waved toward the street. "I will wait nearby until you're ready to seek your parents. When you are, I will be far more assistance to you than a half-dark-elf tracker."

"I look forward to looking for them with you." I smiled warmly at him, relieved that I could say that, that I finally knew he wouldn't hurt my mother if he found her first. He was no longer Barothla's pawn, and with his mother recovering, nobody had anything they could use against him.

Sarrlevi nodded and kissed me. He drew back, as if he meant it to be a mere parting brush of the lips, but he returned, cupping my cheek as his lips caressed mine.

I leaned into him and wouldn't have cared about approaching dragons or possible witnesses, but the goblins noticed the kiss and jeered in their own language. Or maybe they were offering encouragement, much like the golden retriever. They elbowed each other and pointed at us, as if they thought they were about to get a show.

"It's true, it's true," one of the goblins said in English in a squeaky voice. "Work Leader Tinja said the city would be more interesting, and it *is*."

Sarrlevi leaned back. "Dark elves are most assuredly not concerned about goblins."

The odious and uptight elf remains in my domicile? Came Zavryd's voice before he was visible in the sky.

"How do they feel about dragons?" I asked as Sarrlevi stepped away, wrapping his camouflage around him.

The same as everyone else, I expect.

That it's good to have one on your side and a bad idea to stab one in the shoulder?

Especially the latter.

His last words came from the street, and I wondered where he would go.

If you need a place to rest that's not on Val's property, the bed in the tiny home may be available, I told him.

Did you enchant it? Sarrlevi shared an image of an elven bed frame hanging from vines attached to—or growing out of—the ceiling. To imply that *his* bed was enchanted? His next image showed us making use of the space. Vigorously.

I don't think so. I rubbed my face, not minding the imagery but not wanting to think about sex when my roommate was tugging at my sleeve and suggesting negotiating strategies. *The countertops and the shower are self-cleaning though. You'd approve.*

Oh? The imagery shifted, and Sarrlevi smirked into my mind as he moved our vigorous bodies from an elven bed to a countertop.

That looks like a good way to get a spigot up your butt.

Zavryd landed on the roof, his eyes flaring violet as he looked down at the busyness in the street adjacent to his house.

"I must help detach it from the wagon and make sure it's level and won't roll downhill into the lake," Tinja announced and scurried down the steps to the street.

Val slid off Zavryd's back, and he levitated her down to the ground. She waved to the SUV occupants, but her lips pursed as she focused on the tiny home, making me positive that she hadn't given her permission for that. Her gaze shifted to the porch and landed on me.

And here I'd thought she might check on her mom first. Sighing, I walked down the steps to join her.

Val pointed at the tiny home. "Matti, why is that large rectangular box being parked where it will block my view of the lake?"

"Foot traffic."

"That explains less than you'd think regarding my view."

I was about to direct her to *Work Leader* Tinja when the two front Subaru doors opened. The tracker and Val's mom must have been waiting for Val to arrive. The golden retriever stood on the back seat and woofed, clearly ready for *his* door to be opened too, but Val's mom told the dog to hold his horses and headed toward Val first. Barefoot.

That made me blink. The seasons hadn't turned cold yet, but with puddles in the street and moisture in the grass, a barefoot meandering didn't sound appealing. Val's mom looked to be about seventy, with a long braid of gray hair, which might have been blonde once, dangling down the front of her flannel shirt.

"That's your mother?" I'd assumed so, but she wasn't quite what I'd expected.

"Yup. Sigrid. And her tracker acquaintance, I believe."

"The dog or the, uh, passenger?" I'd almost said *half-dark elf,* but did Val know? Had Sarrlevi not told me, I wouldn't have. Maybe it didn't matter. If she was like me and had been raised on Earth, she might not know much about her magical heritage.

"Rocket is more than an acquaintance," Val said. "They share a bed. Much to Liam's consternation, I understand. That's the werewolf across the street from Mom that she is still not dating."

"Just sleeping with?"

"So I gather."

As Sigrid came over, she looked up at Zavryd still on the roof with his eyes glowing and his tail twitching. He had to be fuming telepathically to Val about the neighborhood invaders.

With red-blonde hair pulled back in a loose bun held together by chopsticks—or maybe those were just *sticks*—the tracker didn't look like an elf of any kind, no more than Val did. Her ears weren't pointed, and her skin wasn't any paler than normal for a white person living in Seattle. She was on the tall and lanky side and had some of the typical elven beauty but none of the haughtiness, at least not judging by the lack of a chin lift and supercilious sneer as she looked toward the goblins.

Instead, she seemed shy and introverted, letting Val's mom go ahead, as she pulled a bow and quiver of arrows out of the car. The weapon was made from wood and bone held together with sinew. If I hadn't sensed magic emanating from it, I wouldn't have believed it durable. The tracker didn't raise it threateningly as she looked at Zavryd and the goblins, but she did appear prepared to use it if anyone turned hostile.

"There are laws against driving barefoot," Val told her mom.

"It's good to see you too, dear. Your warmth made me eager to come right over to help with your problem."

"Ha ha." Despite the admonition, Val didn't hug her mom, nor did her mother try to hug her. They merely exchanged nods. Val did say, "Thanks for coming. Matti, this is Sigrid. Mom, this is Matti. *She's* the one with a problem."

Sigrid looked at the tiny home, goblins tucking chock blocks behind the wheels. "Are you sure?"

"She's the one with a problem that might be solved by a tracker."

"I brought Arwen," Sigrid said, "the person I mentioned who stayed over on the Olympic Peninsula recently and has done a lot of work out there. She prefers the wilderness to the chaos of the city."

"*Arwen*?" Val asked. "Was her human parent a big Tolkien fan?"

"I believe it's a Welsh name, dear."

"Arwen was a powerful and beautiful half-elven maiden in *The Lord of the Rings*."

We all looked at Arwen, who shrank back under the combined scrutiny, though she managed a tentative smile and a wave with her bow. Never mind that she held it in front of her like a shield while she waved it. I didn't think we had to worry about her sacrificing people to demons. Being startled and having a panic attack in a crowded mall, maybe, but I didn't plan to take her to one of those.

Once more, Arwen glanced uneasily toward Zavryd. Since smoke was wafting from his nostrils, much as it wafted from those of the topiaries, her concern was understandable.

"She's an excellent tracker," Sigrid said. "The authorities, as well as Search and Rescue, make use of her talents often."

"That's good," Val said. "Matti is eager to find her missing parents and take care of the bad guys who've been sending assassins after her. Then she can get back to her normal life."

"And make an offer to buy the house across the street," Tinja, who was under the trailer for some reason and close enough to eavesdrop, called.

"A thought I was more excited about before I realized what might come *with* her if she moved." Val eyed the goblins.

"They're not coming with me," I said. "Well, Tinja might, but not the others."

Admittedly, *Tinja* was the reason for the tiny home's appearance.

"We'll find another place for that," I promised.

The half-dwarf friend of my mate will move into the domicile adjacent to ours? Zavryd asked.

Tinja wasn't the only one eavesdropping.

"She's thinking about the place for sale across the street." Val pointed. "*It* still has a view of the lake."

"There's room in the backyard for the tiny home," I said, though I didn't want it behind the house either. Not if it would bring streams of *foot traffic* to visit.

Would the odious assassin also *live adjacent to our lair?* Zavryd asked, his tone growing menacing.

"No," I said.

Or visit unpleasantly often and challenge me to duels for no reason?

"No," I repeated, though I'd already joked with Sarrlevi about becoming friends with my across-the-street neighbors and going on double dates with Val and Zavryd if I got the house. "Not *unpleasantly* often. He has his own homes."

A rumble floated down from the rooftop. I couldn't tell if it was a sigh or a growl or both.

I was about to walk over and introduce myself to the tracker and thank her for coming—she was, after all, here for my sake—when magic swelled in the intersection. Almost collectively, the goblins squeaked and dove into their steam wagon or the tiny home, doors slamming behind them.

Their reaction told me even before my senses did that the portal forming was made from dragon magic. On the roof, Zavryd sighed again.

"Are you expecting anyone?" I asked Val, anticipating Zondia and glad Sarrlevi had disappeared.

"No."

17

THE BLACK DRAGON THAT FLEW OUT OF THE PORTAL HOVERING ABOVE the intersection was familiar, but it took a moment for me to place him. When I did, I groaned.

"I don't know that dragon." Val looked at me and then up at Zavryd.

One of my cousins has arrived, Zavryd announced from the roof.

"That's the dragon that helped Zondia destroy Sarrlevi's house. You better batten down the hatches on yours," I said, though I was sure the dragon was here for Sarrlevi, not to threaten his cousin's abode.

"Lucky for me, a lot of my hatches are enchanted." Val thumped me on the shoulder.

"Val?" Sigrid asked, her brow furrowed.

I didn't know if she, as a mundane human with no magic, could see the portal or the dragon that flapped his wings to fly in a lazy circle before landing on—

I groaned. The tiny home.

Alarmed goblin cries came from inside, though the dragon didn't do anything except perch on the roof. Fortunately, it was well built—as I knew—and dragons weren't as heavy as they looked. The black-scaled tail *did* flop down against the wall soundly enough to rattle the windows, but the glass held.

Still in the car, Rocket barked out the window a few times until the dragon looked balefully at him. The barks turned into a whine, and he slunk down on the seat, head disappearing from view. Dogs might not have magical blood, but I had little doubt they could sense dragons.

"Mom, why don't you and Arwen head over to the peninsula, and we'll meet you there later?" Val suggested, not offering a ride on a dragon. Maybe Zavryd's back had a maximum-occupancy rating. "Get a hotel in Port Angeles or maybe Forks—that's closest to where Xilneth and Zav detected a dragon's presence—and I'll cover it."

The half-blood tracker, who doubtless *could* see the new arrival, must have had keen enough hearing to catch the suggestion. She ducked back into the car. Eager to leave? I couldn't blame her, but after cowing Rocket, the dragon ignored the Subaru. Instead, he focused on Val and me.

"Uhm," I said.

The mate of Zavryd'nokquetal and the mongrel granddaughter of King Ironhelm will come to the Dragon Council for questioning.

"Questioning?" Val looked up at Zavryd again.

He had been lounging on the roof, but he rose to all fours, his tail sticking straight out behind him. *You come to take my mate and her comrade without asking my permission, cousin?*

The queen sent me. It is a matter of great importance to dragon-kind.

"Please tell me they don't think Sarrlevi is after them again," I muttered, having little doubt what—or *who*—the dragons wanted to question me about. Though I couldn't guess why they needed Val, unless the queen was peeved that Val had allowed Sarrlevi in her home. But why wouldn't she take that up with Zavryd?

She should have spoken to me if that is the case. Zavryd swished his tail like an irritated cat and barely missed knocking the top off the chimney.

You may accompany the mongrels.

Of course *I may. I come and go to the Dragon Council as I wish.*

"I don't think we're going to get to start the tracking tonight." Val glanced toward the SUV.

Sigrid and Arwen were both inside now, but they hadn't yet tried to leave.

"It's probably easier during the day anyway," I said, though I had no wish to leave and be interrogated by dragons. Why couldn't they all take a break from Earth, including the one working with the enemy organization, so I could find my parents in peace?

With a whisper of the dragon's magic, a new portal formed, this one above the sidewalk right outside the wards.

I reached into my pocket, thinking of activating my camouflaging charm and disappearing before he could take me anywhere, but before I touched it, power swept under me and lifted me from my feet. It lifted Val too, and she cursed, reaching for the sword sheathed on her back. I held my hammer, since I almost always kept it close these days, but I didn't know what good Sorka could do against levitation magic. Her barrier wouldn't protect me from this.

You presume to touch my mate, cousin? Zavryd crouched, as if to spring. *That is grounds for a challenge to a duel.*

I am levitating the mongrels to a portal. That is all. The black dragon's eyes closed to slits as he eyed Zavryd warily. *Relax, cousin. They will only be questioned, per your mother's orders. If you object to this, you should speak with her yourself.*

I will do so. Trust me. You overstep your bounds by coming to my lair to steal my mate.

As the dragon levitated us across the yard, his magic having no trouble working through the wards, someone ran up the sidewalk. Sarrlevi.

I stared at him as he headed toward me, one of his swords drawn. What was he doing?

Sarrlevi glowered up at Zavryd's cousin and looked like he wanted to attack, but if he planned that, why had he revealed himself? When he'd been camouflaged, he might have landed a blow before the dragon realized what was happening.

Sarrlevi's magic was wrapped around him in a protective barrier, and it occurred to me that he was coming to my defense.

He hasn't said anything about you, I told him telepathically. *You should stay out of the way. Camouflage yourself again before he notices you.*

I'll not let you be dragged off and mind-scoured by dragons again, not while I hide like a coward.

If you're referring to what happened when the dragons destroyed your home, it made a lot of sense for you to hide. They wanted to tear you to pieces.

This time, I will go with you and face my fate.

The dragon watched Sarrlevi from atop the tiny home but didn't appear concerned as he ran toward me. Sarrlevi sprang and gripped my arm as he landed. No, he *didn't* land. As soon as he touched me, the levitation magic affected him, and he floated toward the portal with Val and me.

Zavryd leaped from the rooftop. I thought—*hoped*—he might land on the other dragon's head and knock him into Fremont. Instead, he swept past us, the breeze of his passing stirring my hair, and flew through the portal before we reached it.

Val sighed. "I guess we're going to see the queen."

Sarrlevi gripped my arm with one hand and his sword with the other as he squinted at the dragon. Contemplating attacking him instead of letting him shove us through the portal? That didn't sound like a good idea. The dragon had an aura as powerful as

Zavryd's and wouldn't likely shift into a lesser form so they could honorably duel.

"Varlesh," I whispered, though I didn't know what to say. As touched as I was that he wanted to protect me—loyally—I hated that he was delivering himself into the dragons' talons. What if, as soon as he arrived, the queen started that dreadful punishment and rehabilitation process? What if, after all we'd been through, I lost him? "Varlesh," was all I could think to say again, my shoulders slumping.

He met my gaze as Val, a little ahead of me, was thrust through the portal first.

"I will not let you face them alone again," he said. "Besides, I have grown weary of running and hiding from them. I am *not* a criminal. I intend to tell the queen myself."

I shook my head, terrified this would go badly.

18

TROPICAL HUMIDITY SMACKED ME IN THE FACE LIKE A WET TOWEL AS we came out of the portal into a lush green canyon. Squawking, hissing, clicking, and chirping came from forests that rose to either side of a wide river, the banks covered in knee-high bluish grass with serrated edges. Right away, I sensed dragons—*numerous* dragons—but I had to look up to see them.

They weren't along or on top of the foliage-covered canyon walls but on ledges atop rock pillars that rose high above the river. One perched at the apex of a rock arch that spanned the waterway and towered higher than any of the pillars. The black-scaled queen.

Eight other dragons were present, not including Zavryd, who'd waited beside the river for us to arrive. Each of the eight had his or her own pillar, the ledges wide enough for them to sit or lie, their tails wrapped around their bodies or dangling down. They all gazed down at us, some of their eyes glowing, and I felt like a rabbit in an open field with hawks circling.

"Not disconcerting at all," I muttered.

"Now I know why Zav loves the steam room." Val wiped her brow.

Yes, I could already feel sweat pricking at my armpits and rising on my forehead. My palms were moist too, and I wiped them one at a time so I could keep my grip on my hammer.

"Is this the dragon home world?" I looked not at Val but at Sarrlevi.

He stood close to and slightly in front of me, both of his swords out as he glared defiantly up at the queen. I hoped he didn't intend to challenge her to a duel. She didn't look happy. Unfortunately, my meat-delivery app wouldn't work here.

Zavryd's cousin flew through the portal before it closed, and unease swept through me. I reminded myself that Sarrlevi could also make portals, so we weren't stranded. Unless the dragons took him from us.

I frowned but took some heart that Zavryd had come along to watch out for us—or at least for Val. I had never gotten the impression, however, that he would defy his mother, so maybe it was foolish to feel even minutely safe because he was around.

Zondia wasn't present. Was this meeting only for the dragons that presided over the Council?

Oddly, the queen wasn't looking at Sarrlevi. Her gaze remained fixed on Val and me, as if she hadn't noticed him at all. Was it possible this wasn't about him?

Don't do anything to rile them up or remind them that they don't like you, please. I reached up to grip Sarrlevi's shoulder.

His muscles were tense under my fingers, and he didn't lower his swords. I might have been relieved that the dragons were well out of his reach, hundreds of feet up on their perches, but remembered that he had levitated us around that volcano without trouble. If he wanted to reach the dragons, he could.

I hadn't intended to, Sarrlevi said.

You're wearing the same defiant and haughty face you have right before you challenge Zavryd to a duel. Okay, I hadn't been there for the start of any of those duels, but I was sure I was right.

My face is as it usually is.

Yeah. You're lucky I think it's handsome. Dragons might not.

I have no doubt.

My queen. Zavryd spread his wings and lowered his head in something akin to a bow. *As requested, I have brought my mate and her comrade.*

As if *he'd* been the one to do it. I eyed his cousin, but the other dragon didn't chime in.

The queen's cold gaze skimmed over him before landing on Sarrlevi. *This assassin was* not *requested.*

The elf intrudes often where he is not desired, Zavryd said.

Sarrlevi's jaw clenched.

Your aura lingers on him. Even though he presumed to injure Zondi-a'qareshi, you have allowed him to be in your proximity often.

Zavryd hesitated. *Not by my desire.*

Her eyelids drooped dangerously, making me wonder if Sarrlevi wasn't the only one present who'd dealt with an abusive parent growing up. Who knew what was typical in dragon culture?

I will have your thoughts, Zavryd'nokquetal. And those of your mate.

Val raised a finger, as if she might protest, but she looked at all the dragons gazing coolly down at us and lowered it again.

And then I'll have those of the dwarf mongrel.

What fun that would be.

I didn't protest out loud or silently since I hoped my thoughts could clear Sarrlevi's name. It wasn't heartening, however, that Zondia had read my mind before and not believed what she'd seen there. Nothing about that experience had been heartening. Being pinned under Zondia's talons while she raked through my memories had been intensely unpleasant, and I couldn't help but imagine the queen doing the same to me.

Dare I hope she would be any better? If anything, she was even frostier than her daughter.

Of course, my queen. Zavryd offered the dragon bow again.

The dwarf mongrel and elf assassin will wait in the Deliberation Chamber while we peer into your minds.

Deliberation Chamber? That sounded like a fancy name for a jail cell.

Val and I exchanged bleak looks.

With a flick of the queen's magic, Sarrlevi and I rose into the air. His own magic swirled around him, and I thought he might fight her power, perhaps springing free to make a portal and escape, but he only wrapped it around me to share a protective barrier. Though I had Sorka for that now, I nodded to let him know I appreciated his effort. I *wanted* to clasp his hand, but under the cold eyes of the dragons, I didn't.

The levitation magic whisked us toward a cave entrance in one side of the canyon. Greenery hung down from the top and dangled around the sides, water dripping from the foliage. The entrance would have been large enough for a dragon with spread wings to fly into, and I felt small as Sarrlevi and I floated through it.

Even in the shady interior, greenery grew, a mossy carpet over the stone walls and the lumpy ground, parting only to flow around a pool in the middle. My senses told me that a barrier rose behind us, blocking the exit, and the walls of the cave emanated magic, glowing softly with yellow light. It provided illumination, beyond what slanted in from outside, but I was sure it did more than that and that a jailbreak wouldn't be easy.

Sarrlevi and I hung a few feet above the ground when the levitation magic released us. I landed in a crouch, and the green carpet of vegetation undulated under my shoes, as if it were alive.

I skittered back, but, unless we wanted to take a swim, there was nowhere to stand that was devoid of the stuff. Fortunately, walking on it didn't appear to disturb it much.

"There is dampening magic in here." Sarrlevi eyed the exit, though neither Val nor the dragons were visible now, only the river and the opposite side of the canyon. "I cannot form a portal."

"I think we—or at least I—need to stay and talk to the queen. Or let her mind scour me."

Sarrlevi scowled, not hiding how he felt about that.

Val, I attempted to project telepathically toward her. *Will you let me know what happens?*

When I didn't receive an answer, I realized the dampening magic might also keep us from communicating.

Sarrlevi rotated in a slow circle, scanning the cave interior with his senses as well as his eyes. "There is no way out."

"I figured."

Sighing, I picked my way gingerly over the green carpet to the wall and sat down with my back against it, the growth damp through my shirt. "I'm sorry you're stuck here, Varlesh."

He removed his sword scabbards and sat next to me, his arm against my shoulder. "I regret that *you* are here. You should never have been brought to the awareness of dragons or endangered by their Council."

I didn't regret standing up for him, but he was probably right, and a wistful sigh escaped my lips. "Do you regret that Val is here too?"

"Thorvald married a dragon."

"So, she's getting what she deserves?"

"She volunteered herself to enter their awareness."

"Hopefully, Zavryd is good enough in the sack to be worth it."

Sarrlevi turned his head toward me. I couldn't tell from his expression if he understood the Earth vernacular or not.

"In bed," I clarified. "Well, for him, the *nest.*"

"Yes, I interpreted your saying," he said dryly.

"You looked puzzled."

"I was debating if you considered *me*, during our admittedly rushed first joining, *worth it*."

Rushed? We'd been together for hours. I decided not to mention that I'd been with guys for whom the phrase *I've been vaccinated slower than that* was perfectly applicable.

"You have to ask?" I looked curiously at him. "I assumed you were extremely confident in that area."

"Confident in my appeal to females and adequacy in satisfying them, yes, but I am uncertain my attention is a fair trade for being in danger from an irritated dragon."

"I see." I clasped his hand. "*You* are worth having to endure irritated dragons, regardless of bedroom satisfaction."

He looked a little skeptical. How could someone be confident of their various abilities in all walks of life but not believe they were a person worthy of another's sacrifice?

No, I decided. That wasn't that weird. I got it. I was confident in my abilities—even if they weren't quite as impressive or far-flung as his—but had always doubted deep down that I could attract someone who valued me for me.

"The satisfaction was very nice, though." I smirked at him. "Thanks for asking."

Sarrlevi squeezed my hand. "Assassins do strive to be *very nice*."

"I also appreciate you wanting to come along to protect me from the dragons." I leaned my head against his shoulder. "Even if I was trying to keep them from finding you."

"As I said, I cannot hide again while you endanger yourself. I would prefer to face them alone while you remain safe and focused on completing your own quest, but, at the least, I will be here at your side."

"At my side is good. We should face things together if we're going to be..." I spread my hand toward the roof of the cave and shrugged. "A thing. A together thing."

I rolled my eyes at my awkward wording. But we hadn't discussed having a future together, and I didn't want to make assumptions. Once, he had brought up the idea of me living in one of his houses, but it had been a joke. I was certain. Another time, he'd said he wouldn't stay on Earth after he finished his mission. Of course, that mission had changed, and he wasn't after my mother anymore. And he was still with me.

Realizing he hadn't responded, I looked at him a little nervously. He was gazing at me. Following my thoughts with his mind reading? Or did the dampening magic mean he couldn't do that in here?

"We don't *have* to be a together thing," I said. "Or make any promises about it or even discuss it. I just feel that we should face dragons together."

"We should." Sarrlevi touched my cheek, then leaned his forehead against my temple. "My people have a saying. *Vyseria hyleeth s'ah.* It is literally when two trees in a forest start their lives growing independently of each other but through time are drawn together, their branches and sometimes even their trunks fusing together and becoming one forevermore. Your people have a word, inosculation, that describes this phenomenon, but I do not believe it also conveys the poetical side. Among elves, there is contentment at seeing different entities bond together in such a way." He looked at me. "Do your people have a saying such as this?"

"Uhm, maybe joined at the hip."

His eyebrows rose skeptically.

"Yeah," I said. "That's not nearly as romantic as fused trees."

Sarrlevi nodded in agreement.

"Are you saying you'd like to be fused to me?"

He threaded his fingers through mine. "Yes."

Longing and love and pleasure welled within me, tightening in my throat. "Me too," I whispered.

"I also wish to reunite you with your family, as you have reunited me with my mother."

When I could find my voice again, I nodded and said, "Thank you. I'm very open to that. If we can escape dragon incarceration."

Sarrlevi opened his mouth but closed it without speaking.

I raised my eyebrows.

"I was going to say that I would do my best to ensure *you* escape," he said, "since they should only want to force *me* to accept their punishment and rehabilitation."

"Then you remembered we're fused now and also realized I'd be beyond distraught if I lost you forever? Before I've even visited your cheese cellar?"

"I did remember. We will escape together." His eyes crinkled. "I know the cheese cellar is important to you."

"*Yes.*" I kissed him, wishing we were there now. Unless the uppity carpet of vegetation was edible, there was no food in the cave. Dragons probably didn't even eat cheese. The savages. "I would also like an opportunity to get to know your mother better. She's nice, and I want to see her healthy again."

"She wishes to get to know *you* better too. She likes you."

"I'm touched, but we've barely spoken. Would she like anyone who rubbed your ears and thought you were amazing?"

"No. She is also drawn to those who are loyal and trustworthy. I told her how you stood by me when I was going mad, how you helped me learn the recipe for her formula, and that you even convinced Broadleaf to *make* the formula."

That warmed my heart, but I couldn't help but grin again and tease him. "Did you tell her how Broadleaf spritzed you with knockout juice, and I carried you up to her lab over my shoulder like a big lumpy sack of potatoes?"

"I did not."

"Can I tell her?"

"No."

"You forbid it?"

"Yes."

"We're going to have to discuss the ground rules for being fused." I expected him to point out that *trees* didn't discuss it before it happened.

But Sarrlevi nodded and said, "Likely so."

"We'll have a lot of time to discuss things after you retire from being an assassin and start working for me." I smiled at him.

"Would I not end up working for your *roommate*? I am certain no elf has ever sought employment under a goblin, but she claims that you work for her. Would it become a chain of command?"

"I do *not* work for her. I suppose if she's ever as wealthy as she wants to be and can hire me to build her urban goblin sanctuary, Abbas and I might take the job, but we'd be independent contractors, not employees."

"Independent contractors who need an elf to carry things and prepare your hot caffeinated beverage." His wry expression promised he was playing along with me but would consider none of this.

"I'm about to have a teenager for that, so I'd have to find another use for you. Head of security perhaps."

"Given your temper and quickness to swing your hammer, you likely *will* need security for the rest of your life."

"There we go," I said, though my budget didn't have room in it to hire security guards. He would have to do the work pro bono. He was independently wealthy after all, right?

More seriously, Sarrlevi asked, "It would disturb you to be mated to an assassin?"

I hesitated, realizing I couldn't ask him to change for me, not unless the idea of retiring actually interested him. But he'd pointed out that with his skill set, there weren't that many ideal jobs for him. He liked to train and test himself against enemies. On a construction site, there wouldn't be much opportunity for that, not unless a bag of cement mix got nettlesome.

"Killing people is... unsettling to me, but I get it if that's your thing and you don't want to quit. I trust you wouldn't come home with blood dripping from your hands and severed heads falling out of your special bag. That might be hard to explain to the children."

"You wish to have children?"

"No. I mean, I don't know. Maybe someday, but it was a joke." That hadn't been the most tactful way to bring up the question of children. "Maybe someday, if things worked out, you would —*we* would—want to explore the idea, but no pressure or anything."

My sister's kids were cute, and I'd thought about having children before, if I ever found someone amenable to the idea, but I'd always known it would have to be a team effort. I didn't want to give up on working full-time and building my business. Hell, I *couldn't*. It wasn't as if *I* was independently wealthy. I hadn't the foggiest idea how single mothers managed.

"It is not something I've considered with my previous female acquaintances." Did he sound slightly thoughtful? "I took great care to ensure none would end up carrying my child. There was one in particular who sought that because she believed my genetic material would be desirable in her offspring."

I snorted with amusement, though I had no trouble envisioning that. If he had ever been hard up for money, he could have made some deposits at the Cosmic Realms sperm bank.

"Your children would probably be a big pain in the ass," I said, intending to tease him.

Sarrlevi, however, nodded in what might have been agreement. "But they would be desirable."

"Oh, I have no doubt," I said, though I knew he referred to

passing along his magical and athletic aptitude rather than his looks.

"It is something we could contemplate once all more pressing issues are resolved. And you have realized that purchasing a domicile across from a dragon would be foolish."

"Clearly, a remote mountain chalet on a frozen, desolate world is the appropriate place to raise children."

"Clearly."

I squeezed his hand, delighted that he was open to the idea, even if it might be a while before we were ready for anything like that. We hadn't even spent a night together yet.

"For your edification, I do not return from assignments with blood dripping from my hands. The blood drips from my swords and only until I clean them, which is always promptly."

"I know. You *do* sometimes have heads in your bag though. I've seen you put them in there."

He hesitated. "Yes. Employers often require proof of a mission accomplished. I can, however, ensure the bag cannot be opened by others."

"It let me in without hesitation when I needed the ingredients for the formula," I pointed out.

"It likes you."

"Your *bag* does?"

"Some enchanted items pick up on the feelings of the owner and mirror them. When you visited my home before its destruction, did you not notice that my hammock cradled you tenderly?"

"I thought that was because it had seen me demolish the soap dispenser and wanted to appease me."

"It could have tossed you over the edge of the ravine when you sat in it." His eyes gleamed with amusement, so I didn't know if that was true or not.

"Are you teasing me, Varlesh?"

"Would I do that?"

"Yes."

He kissed me, and I decided the teasing was okay if it led to that.

Sorka sighed into my mind. *I do not know how much this concerns you, since you are paying attention to other matters, but your half-elf ally is now being questioned and is sharing her memories with the dragons.*

"You can tell what's happening out there?" I asked aloud before realizing Sorka wouldn't have shared the words with Sarrlevi. I held up a finger when he arched his eyebrows. *Is Val volunteering to share her memories or are they forcing a mind scour on her?* I hadn't heard any screams of pain, but our prison might muffle sounds, as it muffled our ability to use magic.

I believe it is a voluntary sharing, with her mate at her side guiding it. She appears to be in no pain.

What memories would Val have that the dragons care about?

Val hadn't interacted that much with Sarrlevi, not like I had. If the queen was questioning her, it had to be about more than him.

I do not know. Their telepathic words are not being shared widely enough that I can hear them, and it is taking much effort for me to pierce the magical veil that insulates this cave in order to see out.

"This might not have anything to do with you, Varlesh." I waved to indicate our prison and the dragons outside on their perches.

"Meaning I need not have revealed myself and sprung through the portal with you?"

"Sorry."

"Hm."

Abruptly, the barrier at the cave entrance disappeared. Without using his hands, Sarrlevi rose, lifting his swords again.

The dwarf mongrel will come out for questioning, the queen's voice boomed in my mind.

After standing, I started for the exit. Sarrlevi walked at my side until a gust of magic swept in and formed a wall of power in front of us. No, in front of *him*. I could continue on, but I didn't *want* to continue, not without him.

What about Sarrlevi, Your Highness? I forced myself to be polite, as seemed wise when dealing with these beings with god-like power, but trepidation filled me at the certainty that Sarrlevi was in trouble, whether he was their priority right now or not.

The urge to swing my hammer and bash the walls crept up in me.

He is not our highest concern at this moment, the queen said, *but now that we have him, we would be foolish to let him go. Once these other matters are resolved, I will return to determine if he is a candidate for punishment and rehabilitation.*

He's not. He's a good ally and helping me find my parents. I need him.

The queen's only answer was to use her magic to forcibly levitate me out of the cave. Frustrated and afraid for Sarrlevi, I looked back at him. Stuck standing immobile, he could only meet my gaze and watch me go.

I'm so sorry, I told him.

Despite our conversation about being fused and facing dragons together, I regretted that he'd leaped from hiding to come along. To protect *me*, or so he'd thought. But he was the one in greater danger from the dragons, of being tortured for two years and having his memories erased and some *new* persona stamped onto his mind.

If that happened, he would turn into someone who didn't know me, someone who didn't love me. Tears formed in my eyes.

Sarrlevi, still holding my gaze, lifted his chin. *I am not. Be careful, and do not irritate the dragons on my behalf.*

Screw the dragons.

I do not recommend that.

I won't ask if you've had sex with one in human form before.

Wise. He smiled.

I didn't. I couldn't set aside the bleakness within me.

Thoughts of using Sorka to bash the cave walls, and maybe destroy the dampening magic, came to mind again. But I was out in the canyon now. I should have tried the bashing earlier, when there'd been time. Maybe Sorka wouldn't have been enough to do anything against the powerful dragon magic, but I hadn't even tried. Now, I was floating away from Sarrlevi against my will, leaving him to a horrible fate.

19

THE LEVITATION MAGIC DROPPED ME ON THE BANK OF THE RIVER beside Val, who stood, leaning against Zavryd's forelimb for support.

Are you okay? I asked numbly, though I struggled to put aside my fear for Sarrlevi to worry about anything else.

Yeah, but mind scouring is unpleasant, even when they're not trying to hurt you.

That was my experience too.

Just let them have what they want, Val said. *They're not mad at us.*

I couldn't help but look back toward the cave. The queen's magic had allowed Sarrlevi to walk to the exit, but the barrier was back up, keeping him inside.

You and I, Val amended. *They want to know everything we saw and heard at Hart's mansion, especially what the dragon Varlat— Varlatastiva—said. They're not explaining anything to me, but I'm guessing that whatever plot is afoot on Earth, they think it might affect dragons.*

I didn't see how, but if the queen wanted my memories of the night at Hart's mansion, she could have them.

The mind scouring of the mongrel will begin, the queen said. *Zavryd'nokquetal, you may monitor again if you wish.*

Since I wasn't anything to Zavryd, beyond being the friend of his mate, I didn't expect his help, but he said, *Yes, my queen.*

His presence wrapped around me a moment before the inside of my skull started itching like mad and I sensed *her* in my head.

Taking a deep breath, I willed myself to remain calm, though I couldn't keep my grip from tightening around my hammer. Val had her sword too. So far, the Council had been indifferent to our weapons. With so many dragons here, they had to believe they had nothing to worry about from us. Sadly, that was true.

The queen's telepathic touch wasn't painful, but it *was* uncomfortable. Fire ants seemed to crawl around under my skull, biting as they went, as memories popped to the forefront of my mind.

The plumbing scheme, driving with Val to the party in my truck, fixing the bathroom toilet, then sneaking upstairs and listening to Varlat speak with Hart. The memories slowed, playing out in real time as the queen tried to dig up everything I'd heard.

Her mental touch grew firmer, shifting from discomfort to pain as the biting ants turned into raking talons. I hissed and gritted my teeth. Beside me, Val stirred, and Zavryd did something, not fighting his mother but soothing her touch—her *scouring* —somehow.

Finally, the queen's presence withdrew from my mind. *He said little that verifies what our other informant told us, but the fact that he's been on that wild world for decades, scheming with those humans, says much.*

More than scheming, I am certain, another female dragon said from a high perch. *As long-lived as our kind are, and as slow to deliberate as we can be, we don't need decades to hatch a plan.*

He may already be enacting his plan, another said. *He may even be close to finalizing it.*

It is difficult to believe a dragon from the Starsinger Clan would truly plot something so ambitious, Zavryd put in.

That one is more like a dragon from the Silverclaw Clan, the queen said. *In his youth, he always caused trouble. This is not the first wild world he's thought to claim for himself.*

I blinked and looked at Val, mouthing, "Claim for himself?"

Earth?

Val shook her head grimly. I couldn't tell if the news surprised her or if she'd heard about this during her questioning. Even if she hadn't, maybe nothing dragons did surprised her. She'd spent far more time around them than I had.

The foolish vermin that live on Earth believe they are using Varlatastiva, one of the dragons said, *and not the other way around. What an ignorant, impudent species. Few will miss them if his plans succeed.*

Miss them? *Humans?*

Those words must have surprised or concerned Val more, because her jaw sagged open. Mine might have too.

Even so, Zavryd said, *it is our duty to protect the intelligent lesser species, including those on wild worlds.*

The queen's eyes closed to slits as she regarded him—and Val leaning against his leg. I expected her to say that Zavryd only cared about protecting Earth because he had a home and a mate there.

Perhaps expecting something similar, Val straightened so that she no longer leaned on Zavryd.

But the queen said, *It is our duty, yes. The denizens of that world may destroy themselves if they continue along their current trajectory, but the Dragon Council cannot let one of our kind commit genocide, even to such an insignificant lesser species. We dragons are powerful, but we are few compared to the other intelligent species, and we must remain aware of that. The elves, trolls, dwarves, and others tolerate our rule but do not love it, and they might identify with the humans more than with us. We would not wish them to have a reason to feel affronted and rise up en masse. Every time in the past that they've risen up, some of our kind have fallen. I've lost offspring.*

Yes, Zavryd said.

I wish to lose no more, not when we can stop this plot before it is enacted. The queen rose to all fours on the high arch, her tail swaying like a pendulum, and she looked toward the other dragons. *Let us fly and discuss this matter further. I have not decided whether to speak with the myriad and confusing number of leaders of that world or not. It may be best to simply take a squadron of our kind there to capture Varlatastiva and destroy the base and artifacts he has gathered.*

"Destroy the base?" I couldn't keep from blurting. "But my parents—Princess Rodarska—may be there." The dragons wouldn't care about my father, but I *hoped* they cared about King Ironhelm's daughter. The Ironhelms were their chosen line of dwarven rulers, and with Barothla gone, my mother had to be considered the heir to the throne. The dragons couldn't crush her in some huge overkill of an attack.

The queen's slitted gaze turned back to me. A *lot* of slitted gazes turned to me.

It is not wise to intrude upon the conversations of dragons, Sorka informed me.

Oh, I know, but can you blame me? You don't want to see them kill my mother by accident, *I'm positive.*

I do not, but tread carefully.

We do not seek to destroy the dwarven princess, the queen said, *but if she has allowed her magic to be used to further this scheme, perhaps it is for the best. She is powerful for one from a lesser species, and that is dangerous. Even if she is not ambitious, if she allows others to use her...*

"How could she have fought a *dragon*? It's not fair to blame her." I lifted my hammer and an imploring hand. "Let me go in before your people do anything. Please. I'll find her and get her out of there, and then you can do whatever you want to the base and the people working with the dragon. There's this elf Caretaker guy that you can *especially* do what you want to." I remembered that most of the numerous trolls, dwarves, orcs, and others I'd seen working on behalf of the organization had worn control bracelets and hadn't been there voluntarily. If I could get in ahead of the dragons, I would do my best to free them too. "Let me go in with Sarrlevi, please. He's a great ally, and we have a tracker now." One I hadn't yet spoken with and that Sarrlevi was suspicious of... "We can find my mother. I'm positive."

Sarrlevi. The queen's maw opened, revealing her long fangs, and her tongue flicked in distaste. *The assassin cannot be trusted. He might set traps for us.*

"No, he won't," I said. "He's never plotted against dragons. I promise. Look in my mind. Look in *his*."

The queen's tail swished in irritation. *This is not important. Stopping Varlatastiva is, as well as destroying whatever he's made—or had the dwarven princess make—to facilitate his scheme. We do not wish another to be able to take up where he left off.*

"What exactly *are* his plans?" Val asked.

Zavryd'nokquetal, the queen said, ignoring her. *Take your mate and her comrade back to Earth. Leave the assassin. He will be dealt with once the larger concern has been resolved.*

Yes, my queen.

Come, my colleagues. Let us discuss our plans further. Then we will take action. The queen sprang into the air. All the other dragons perched on the pillars did the same, flapping their wings and flying off down the canyon.

"Zav." Val turned to face him. "What's going on?"

Dragons like to fly while they think. Much as your people pace.

"No." Val glanced at me. "I mean, what's going on with Varlat? What do they think he's up to? Is this another plan to destroy humans and take over Earth?"

Another plan? I stared at her. How often did this happen?

"And if so, why?" Val added. "I thought your kind—all the intelligent magical beings—thought Earth was super lame. Not enough inherent magic to draw upon."

Its lack of natural magic does make it unappealing. I do not know what this long-lost Starsinger dragon is thinking. Zavryd summoned his magic and formed a portal. We will return. If your comrade wishes to ensure her parents live, it would behoove her to take the tracker and find them now. Before the Council finalizes their course of action. Once they decide what to do, they may act swiftly.

"I'm ready, but I need Sarrlevi." I pointed my hammer toward the cave.

Aside from Zavryd, all the jail keepers had left. There was no way I wouldn't find a way to break him out and take him with us.

The queen ordered him to remain where he is.

"He can help us. I need him."

Val gave me a sympathetic look. "Can't you let him out, Zav?"

Deactivate the queen's magic and defy her? Certainly not. Besides, she would know immediately if the barrier were lowered so he could escape.

"Isn't she too busy deliberating to care?" I jogged over to the cave, hoping to spot the equivalent of a light switch for the barrier. If its magic came from an artifact instead of power that one of the dragons was currently maintaining, there *ought* to be a switch. If not, maybe there was something I could bash to pieces...

"Mataalii?" Sarrlevi stood in front of the barrier, peering beyond me, though he wouldn't be able to see from inside that the dragons had left. Could he sense it?

My magic had been hard to call upon inside the cave, but out here, it bubbled up within me, infused with power from the ground and the world around, wanting to be unleashed. I also wanted to unleash it. And would.

"Stand back, Varlesh. I'm planning a jailbreak."

Easier said than done. I couldn't sense the source of the barrier, nor could I tell what all the strands of dragon magic did. My experience with their artifacts, if that was indeed what imprisoned Sarrlevi, was limited, and everything about the cave felt alien. And powerful.

Friend of my mate. Zavryd, still in his dragon form, strode over, his wings spread. *We must depart and leave the assassin behind.*

"I'm not going without him. We're *fused* now."

Zavryd looked at Val. *Of what does she speak?*

"She's into him. And he's into her."

I hefted my hammer, tempted to slam it against the translucent barrier across the cave entrance. Breaking that was the most obvious way to get Sarrlevi out, and Sorka had punctured barriers before. Maybe she could pierce this one.

But Sorka issued a grunt of warning in my mind, followed by, *Unwise.*

"What about going in from underneath again?" I thought of how I'd sent my magic through the pipes and under the barrier around Hart's mansion to manipulate the bathroom plumbing. Since the barrier hadn't extended deep into the ground, it had been doable. Would it be the same here?

There were no pipes leading into the dragon cave, but I willed my power into the earth, envisioning creating a tunnel that Sarrlevi could crawl out through. There was more rock than dirt, but with the magic of this world practically leaping from the soil and into me, I found myself capable of using my power to dig. The power inherent in the cave's defenses resisted me, but Sorka lent her strength, and I was able to push through it. The ground *was* less strongly defended than the entrance and walls.

That didn't mean the digging was easy. The excavated earth had to *go* somewhere. I willed the dislodged chunks to fly up in the cave, landing on the uptight carpet of foliage.

Sarrlevi's eyebrows drifted upward as he looked over his shoulder, but he didn't appear surprised by the flying clods of dirt. He smiled at me and nodded.

Before I'd made nearly enough progress for him to crawl out, great power wrapped around me from behind. It hefted me from the ground and blocked my stubborn attempts to continue. *Friend of my mate, I cannot allow this destruction. You are in the canyon of the Dragon Council, and you are doing damage to the land. This is blasphemous.*

Zavryd floated me toward the portal. I tried to swing the hammer, to break his grip, but the same power that made my magic stronger made his stronger too. I didn't have a shot at dislodging the bonds around me.

"Val," I blurted. "Please help me."

Even though I dangled in the air and was floating away from the cave, I attempted to funnel my magic toward the ground, to continue excavating. Sarrlevi had disappeared from my view—hopefully, he was in the cave, digging. He couldn't be resigned to this fate. We were finally together. He couldn't let *dragons* steal his memories and everything he was from him.

"Why don't you go through the portal ahead of us, Zav?" Val suggested as chunks of dirt and rocks from my efforts flew up, this time from the ground outside the cave. "I'll grab Matti and follow right behind."

Right behind with that odious elf? How is she breaking through dragon magic to reach him? That is not enchanting. She is using her power to tunnel like an overzealous vole.

"You know what they say," Val said. "You can't keep true love apart."

The queen will be furious.

"Your mom is so busy she won't even notice," Val said.

That is not true. I cannot be a witness to this.

"Perfect!" Val pointed to the portal. "You leave before anyone escapes, and then she can't be mad at you. It won't be *your* fault that an assassin escaped. Assassins are *good* at that."

It is a mongrel dwarf plumber that is excavating him.

"Yes, and dwarves are good at *that*."

More dirt flew away from my tunnel-in-progress, a clod sailing past Zavryd's horned head.

He harrumphed into our minds. The magic binding me released, and I dropped to the ground. As I ran back to the cave, the tip of a vine thrust out of the hole on this side of the barrier. I grinned. Sarrlevi's magic was helping mine.

More vines thrust from the ground, widening the tunnel and flicking more dirt outside. Though scarcely aware of how I was digging out the earth with my power, I kept going.

Make sure you do not permit her to cause the foliage in the Sacred Canyon to burst into flame, Zavryd said with another harrumph. *It took your half-sister much time to heal my scorched topiaries.*

With that, Zavryd leaped through the portal, deliberately not looking back at us before he did.

"I hope he doesn't get in too much trouble," Val said.

Now digging with my hands as well as my magic, I hardly cared. I had to free Sarrlevi. And then get back to find my parents before the dragons did whatever they were planning. After we accomplished that, we could worry about the queen—and figuring out how to convince her to leave Sarrlevi alone forever. I wanted a happily ever after with him, damn it.

I'm coming, Mataalii.

Abruptly, I sensed Sarrlevi. He was crawling through the tunnel and must have crossed under the barrier and the magic that muffled everything in the cave. I reached down, wanting to grab his hands and help him out. Even though I'd excavated an impressive amount with nothing but magic, it wasn't a wide and spacious escape tunnel.

Something flat and cool landed in my hand. A sword scabbard. He thrust the other one ahead of him as well.

"Getting the most important things out first, huh?" I pulled the weapons free and laid them beside us.

"The items that can easily be caught when you are climbing through a tunnel like a ferret," Sarrlevi said, his voice muffled.

"A vole."

"You're the vole. According to Zav." Val reached down to help clear dirt, but one of the vines flicked her, and she drew back. "I see your assassin's magic is as abrasive as he is."

"His magic likes me." At least, the vines weren't trying to keep me away.

"I have no doubt," Val said.

Blond hair full of dirt, Sarrlevi finally came into view. He gripped the edges of the hole and pulled himself out.

After a quick hug, I handed him his weapons, well aware that the dragons might finish their flying and deliberating at any moment and return.

We turned toward where Zavryd had left the portal hanging, but we'd taken too long, and it had extinguished.

"Uh." For a panicked moment, I could only stare at the green walls of the dragon canyon around us, afraid we were trapped.

Then Sarrlevi waved his hand, and a new portal formed.

"The muffling magic is only in the cave," he said.

I laughed in relief. Of course.

"Maybe you should hide the evidence of the jailbreak before we go." Val was eyeing the piles of dirt inside and outside of the cave.

Somehow, I doubted the dragons would be fooled if we kicked the dirt back into place, but Sarrlevi's vines did precisely that, grabbing the dislodged earth and pulling it back into the tunnel. I willed my magic into the cave, attempting to do the same in there, though I could sense so little inside that I probably failed.

"Good enough," I said. "We need to get back before they do." And not only because the queen would be irked that Sarrlevi was gone.

"Sounds like," Val said grimly.

I wished I knew more about what that Starsinger dragon was planning—and what the other dragons intended to do about it. All I could do was hope dragons took a *long* time to deliberate.

20

Full darkness had fallen over Green Lake by the time we returned, Sarrlevi's portal dropping us on the street in front of Val's house. I checked my phone to make sure I hadn't missed any news related to my family, but it didn't look like anything had happened while we'd been gone. That was one small relief.

Zavryd, who waited perched on the roof, said nothing beyond giving Sarrlevi a long baleful look. He *should* have given the long baleful look to Tinja. She stood by the steps to her tiny home, handing out flyers to more than a dozen people, most of whom had magical blood. They were wandering in and out of the home to examine it. Or they *had* been wandering. Now, those with magical blood were casting worried glances at the roof and its large scaled occupant. Maybe Zavryd had been baleful with Tinja and her customers before we'd arrived.

Sarrlevi brushed dirt off his shirt and ignored Zavryd. "I will check on my mother and then be ready to depart."

He nodded toward the living room where I sensed Meyleera's presence. Not that many hours had passed since I'd last seen her, but her aura was already stronger. Hopefully, her move from the guest room to the living room meant she also felt perkier. Maybe she and Dimitri, who I could also sense, were playing video games together. Meyleera might never leave if he got her addicted to *Elden Ring*.

"I'll be ready to go as soon as I pack a bag and grab the grenades you requested," Val told me.

"Oh, Nin made them already?"

"She had some tucked away under her rice cooker."

"The natural storage place for explosives."

"You never know when you'll have to deal with uppity customers." Val smirked. "She actually had them ready for *me*. She's been my supplier for a few years and knows my needs well. I've got some fresh magical ammo for Fezzik too." Val patted the magical gun in her thigh holster. "Not enough to take down a dragon, or even give one a hang-talon, sadly, but I can perforate lots of lesser bad guys."

"Always handy."

Val's phone rang. "What's up, Mom?"

I couldn't hear the answer, but it prompted Val to lift her eyes toward the night sky.

"I was planning to head right over and meet you there," Val said. "Sorry. There was a dragon intervention... No, not that kind of intervention, and we don't have sex *all* the time." Her next look went toward the roof.

In his dragon form, Zavryd never appeared that emotive to my half-dwarven eye, but maybe he looked the faintest bit smug now.

"Dragons came here and took us to their home world. I'll explain when we get out there. Which hotel are you at?" After a pause to listen, Val said, "Okay, we'll be there soon. Yes, I said I'll pay... I'll pay you *back* then... Yes, your food too... No, not Rocket's food. *He's* not dining out, I'm sure." Val gave me a sour expression after she hung up. "I hope you find your mom soon so that you, too, can enjoy being lectured."

"I look forward to it."

Maybe it was strange, but an ache of longing filled me as I imagined my mother tartly informing me that intelligent hammers shouldn't be used for home renovations. After all, Sorka had to have gotten that opinion from someone, right?

Maybe my mother would also have acerbic things to say about how often I lost my temper. And how I ate too much cheese and not enough greens. No, wait. If my grandfather's charcuterie tray was indicative of dwarven preferences, she might lecture me on not eating *enough* cheese. I grinned at the thought.

Val, not privy to my thoughts, only shook her head. "I predict you'll enjoy it for the first two weeks and then wish you could stuff her back in her cage."

"I vow to enjoy it for at least *four weeks*."

"Uh huh. We'll see." Val smiled, then jogged for the front door. "I'll be right back."

Left alone in the yard, I wished there were time to go home and pack a few things—at least grab some food, because my stomach was reminding me it hadn't eaten in a long time—but we couldn't delay. We needed to find my parents tonight. *Maybe* the dragons would deliberate for days, but I couldn't count on that.

Xilnethgarish is not answering my call, came Zavryd's telepathic words from the roof. A few mundane humans remained around the tiny home, not able to sense him, but those with magical blood had scattered. Tinja had gone inside, perhaps to count her money from the sale of house plans.

I didn't know if Zavryd was speaking to me, or simply including everyone in the area, but I felt compelled to answer. "I haven't heard from Hennehok and Artie for a while either."

It is possible they are not on this world.

"The last I spoke to them, they were still looking for the entrance to the base."

It is possible they are on this world and unable to respond.

"Another reason to head out there as soon as possible. Are you able to... Uhm, are you *willing* to carry three people over there? If not, two of us can ride." I waved to where I'd parked my motorcycle earlier and hoped it wouldn't be too late to catch a ferry.

I am unsettled that you have freed the elf.

"I know, but I need him, and I care about him. The way you do Val. You'd defy dragons to break her out of a prison, wouldn't you?"

Yes. Val is my Tlavar'vareous sha. *I do understand, but I cannot carry the assassin or assist him. Should the queen arrive now, she would find it egregious that he is within my lair.*

"Okay. We'll get over there on our own. Thanks for helping to look for these guys."

The front door opened, and Sarrlevi walked out, guiding his mother, who wore slippers and a bathrobe. Presumably Val's slippers and bathrobe. They were an improvement over the rumpled gown from before, but I wondered where he was taking her in that outfit until he formed a portal. Then I remembered that Meyleera had wanted to go back to the elven capital.

After he helped her down the stairs, he stopped, and they murmured to each other in Elven. He hugged her, then gestured toward the portal, though fresh sadness had entered his eyes. Maybe he'd hoped she would stay longer.

If I succeeded in freeing my mother, would *she* stay on Earth? At least for a time? Or be compelled to return home and take a full-time role as King Ironhelm's heir?

And what of my father? It saddened me to realize he and my mother probably wouldn't be able to have a future together. I hadn't glimpsed him in that smoky prison, but as a mundane human, he would have aged far more than she over the years. My long-lived mother might not look much older than I, and Dad would be in his sixties now.

After their hug, I thought Meyleera would head through the portal, but she walked to me and gripped my arms.

Be careful on your quest, please, Meyleera said telepathically. *It would pain me to lose you before I get the opportunity to know you better. And now that my son has found love, who knows what he would revert to if he lost it?*

Really, Mother, Sarrlevi said. *Though I shall strive not to let her be lost, I led a respectable life before I met Mataalii.*

Meyleera gave him a tart look. *Respectably inserting daggers into people while bedding different females every night?*

It wasn't every night, and I don't remember you being this outspoken in my youth.

I've reached the age where one says what one wishes, for repercussions are not likely to be long-lasting.

You will now live many more centuries.

Perhaps so, but I believe I shall still say what I wish.

I patted her hand. *You do that, Mrs. Sarrlevi.*

"Meyleera," she said aloud.

Meyleera.

She bent and rested her forehead against mine. *Be well.*

You too.

Meyleera hugged her son once more before stepping through the portal. Concern hooded Sarrlevi's eyes as he watched her disappear, but I trusted King Eireth and the elves would treat her well.

Val jogged out with a backpack slung over her shoulder, her sword in its scabbard across her back, and her ammo pouches jammed with magazines. Nerves fluttered in my belly. Would we finally find someone high up in the organization to battle? Varlat? The Caretaker? Someone who could lead us to my parents?

Val handed a spare pack to me, the magical grenades nestled inside, then called, "I'm ready, Zav," up to the roof.

He levitated her up to his back. I fished in my pocket for my keychain.

"Zav," Val's voice floated down. "You *have* to take him."

I do not, and I have already informed her that I will not.

"Well, she's not going without him, and we need to get over to the peninsula. Mom and Arwen are waiting. While ordering expensive room service to irk me with the bill."

"It's okay." I raised my keychain. "We can take the Harley."

"We can take a portal," Sarrlevi said dryly.

Yes. The elf will make a portal and meet us there. Not waiting for confirmation, Zavryd sprang from the roof, the leaves on nearby trees shivering as he flapped his wings and flew off. Maybe he also worried about the dragon deliberation finishing soon and us running out of time.

"You haven't been over there before, have you?" I asked Sarrlevi.

"No, but haven't you?"

"Only to the towns, and I don't think they're anywhere near where Xilneth sensed his dragon relative. When we were searching earlier, we only landed for a minute. The rest of the time, we were in the air on Zavryd's back, and I don't think we want your portal to appear two hundred feet above the trees." I supposed Sarrlevi could levitate us if it did, but could I accurately imagine an area I'd only flown over? "I suppose if you remember Artie's axe-throwing place in Port Townsend, and we rode my motorcycle through a portal to there, that might work. It would get us closer than starting from here."

Sarrlevi eyed my Harley dubiously, as if it might leave skid marks on his portal. "Where did you land before? Were you not hunting close to the area where the dragon presence was detected?"

Assuming we'd been in the right vicinity, it *would* be better to go directly there.

"Yes, but there wasn't a road." I remembered Zavryd perched on the edge of the cliff, the water churning far below, and shuddered. "It was an emergency pit stop."

"Pit stop?" Sarrlevi tilted his head.

"A place to stop to pee. In the elven way."

He opened his mouth but hesitated before finding a reply. "The *elven* way is akin to the human way. There are few biological differences in that area."

"I understand the elven way involves more trees."

"Show me the destination." Sarrlevi touched his fingers to my temple.

I shrugged and envisioned what I remembered of that tree-filled cliff overlooking the Strait of Juan de Fuca, trying to emphasize the land rather than how I'd hung over the edge on Zavryd's back.

"We will go there," Sarrlevi said.

"You're the driver."

He glanced at my motorcycle.

"The creator of the portals," I corrected. "There's no way I'm letting you drive my baby."

"I am certain such a simple device would be within my means to direct."

"Uh huh. Even if that's true, you're too tall for it. It's made for someone short. At least it is *now*. I did some modifications."

"I do recall that when I rode behind you, my knees were almost in my armpits."

"That's what you get for being tall."

"Hm." Sarrlevi waved a hand to form another portal.

"Thanks for helping tonight," I told him, impulsively gripping his free hand. Zavryd, Val, Sigrid, Arwen, and Sarrlevi were all helping me when there was nothing in it for them, no reason for them to be bothered. I appreciated that. Of course, if there truly was some horrific human-dragon scheme that could affect all the citizens of Earth, most of them *did* have another reason to join the hunt. They all lived here too.

All but Sarrlevi. He was only doing this because of me.

"You are welcome." He squeezed my hand before turning toward the portal.

I was about to step through with him when Tinja ran up.

"Wait, Matti. Did Dimitri tell you?"

"Tell me what?" I asked.

"I am not certain Dimitri noticed, but earlier, before Lord Zavryd and the Ruin Bringer returned, someone else arrived in the area. Through a portal."

"Who?" Thinking of the Caretaker, I winced.

"I don't know. He did not say his name. He looked like an elf, but he had a very powerful aura. It reminded me strongly of dragons. If I didn't know it was impossible, I would have thought he *was* part dragon."

Hell.

The look I exchanged with Sarrlevi was grave. When I'd inadvertently, or at least unwisely, unleashed the ancient half-dragon war criminal, it had sounded like he might be a problem for the dwarves. As much as I'd regretted that, I hadn't thought he would become a problem for *me*.

"I was in the tiny home when his portal formed, and he landed in the intersection there. He looked around and then right at me through the window. My head itched inside. I think he was reading my mind!" Tinja shuddered. "He wore armor and was chilling and deadly, like, uhm." Tinja glanced at Sarrlevi. "Like an assassin. But really powerful. I got—what do humans say?—a very *bad vibe* from him, so much so that I did not come out and attempt to sell him plans to build a tiny home."

"That *is* a bad vibe," I said.

"Yes. He did not say anything, and, fortunately, he did not come to the tiny home. He stood and looked at Val's house for a long time, though, and I was concerned. The topiaries' eyes glowed, and smoke wafted from their nostrils, but he was unperturbed."

"It is unlikely that the wards of even a dragon would deter someone with that much power," Sarrlevi said.

"He did not step onto the property," Tinja said. "Eventually, he swept a hood over his head and disappeared from my senses. I did not see him again, but I wanted to warn you, in case... Well, I do not know who he is or what he wants, but I feared he's another assassin."

I doubted the half-dragon had been unfrozen from that stasis chamber long enough to hear about the reward out for me, but that didn't mean he couldn't cause trouble for another reason.

"How would he have known to come here?" I asked Sarrlevi. "If he's been frozen since that war centuries ago, this house wouldn't have been here then. *Seattle* wouldn't have been here then."

Eyes grim, Sarrlevi said, "When I left Dun Kroth, I came here." He waved toward Zoltan's basement laboratory. "So the vampire could help my mother. Starblade may have the power to track people through portals, as some dragons do."

"But why would he care where you went? Wouldn't he be an ally to elves? You spoke to him, right?" I frowned. "You weren't haughty or rude, were you?"

"To someone with some of the power of a dragon? No." His eyes remained concerned, but he managed a smile when he added, "I save my haughtiness for mongrels who appreciate it."

"I'm not sure *appreciate* is the right word, dude."

His smile widened.

"Maybe you should head home, Tinja," I suggested. "That guy shouldn't know or care where our house is."

"You wish me to leave my tiny home unguarded?"

"It's guarded now?"

Tinja touched her chest. "I brought the Goblinator with me."

"A weapon that will strongly deter a super soldier with the powers of a dragon," Sarrlevi said.

"Does anyone like being sliced by flying blender blades?" I asked.

Sarrlevi shook his head, not bothering to point out that someone powerful could keep those blades away with a barrier, if not by outright incinerating them. "Let us go." He waved toward his portal. "We will worry about Starblade and what his appearance means after we free your parents."

"Good idea. Then my mother can enchant the pants off all my enemies."

"Enchanting magic is rarely violent or meant to harm enemies." Sarrlevi looked toward the drainpipes on Val's house, though it wasn't raining, so no leaves, pine needles, or chipmunks were shooting out tonight. "I suppose there are exceptions."

"Mom makes killer magical helicopters with weapons that vex even dragons. I'm sure she can figure something out."

"Yes. She will be a good ally for you. A good teacher."

I nodded as we stepped through the portal. It was more than time to find her.

21

An owl hooted as we landed in the dark forest overlooking the Strait, the rumble of the nearby Pacific Ocean audible, the briny air of the sea mingling with the earthy scents of the temperate rainforest. The portal had brought us out within five feet of the cliff, and I took a large step away from it. The heel of my shoe squished on the soggy ground. It hadn't been raining in Green Lake, but a steady drizzle fell here, with rivulets running from the leaves, needles, and beards of moss that dangled from the branches.

Sarrlevi rested a hand on my shoulder. I thought he was going to point out the moss and recommend we *forest bathe* later. Instead, he said, "I sense dragon magic."

"Really? When we were here earlier..." I trailed off, realizing I also sensed something. It wasn't a dragon, and I detected only the faintest of signatures, but it reminded me of the prison cave in the Dragon Council's canyon, as if something in the area might have been *built* by a dragon. "I didn't sense that earlier. None of us did. Zavryd and Xilneth were with us, and dragon senses are superior to—" I stopped short of saying Sarrlevi's, not wanting to offend my still-occasionally-haughty elf, "—mine."

It was too dark for me to tell if his eyebrows rose, but with his mind-reading capabilities, he probably knew what I'd almost voiced.

"Nonetheless," he said, "I sense dragon magic. It's too distant for me to tell if it's from an artifact—their kind are not known for making them—or residue from magic that was used earlier in the area."

"How long can *residue* last?"

Maybe Varlat had come by since we'd looked earlier and done something. Opened the entrance to his lair, perhaps?

"Not long. It's some distance that way." Sarrlevi pointed through the trees, in a direction paralleling the coastline, with the ground covered in ferns and other undergrowth. There wasn't so much as a hint of a path. "I will lead."

"While using one of your swords as a machete?"

Magic wrapped around me, gently lifting me from my feet as Sarrlevi also rose beside me. As we had at the volcano on Dun Kroth, we levitated over the ground, moving more quickly than we could have walked.

"Have I mentioned lately how handy you are?" I asked, happy to avoid climbing over logs and bushes and stepping in mud.

Sarrlevi looked over at me with what I didn't need light to know was a smug smile. Though we weren't touching, he sent a warm trickle of magic through me, teasing my nerves and making me wish we had time to enjoy each other's company once more. One of his tendrils of power stroked me tenderly—and a little erotically—to promise we would be together again soon before he withdrew everything but the levitation magic.

"I said *handy* not *handsy*."

"Oh? In your language, those words are easy to confuse." Sarrlevi waved, and we continued along the coastline.

The dragon magic grew a little stronger as we traveled farther but not a lot. If it was *residue*, as Sarrlevi had suggested, that might make sense. Even when we found the spot it emanated from, the signature might not be that strong.

My phone rang once but stopped before I could get it out of my pocket. Val's name popped up, but the call had already ended. At first, I thought she might be in trouble, but there wasn't much reception, and I remembered she'd had difficulty making a call earlier.

Did you find a way to the peninsula? a text from her came in.

Yes. And the residue of dragon magic. I tapped in the reply, trusting Sarrlevi would keep us from crashing into a tree, but it felt a bit like texting and driving—and that I shouldn't do it. *We're trying to find the source now.*

Wow, already? Where are you?

Near where you whizzed earlier.

There wasn't any magic there.

There is now.

Huh. After a pause, Val added, *Arwen said she saw some strange activity off and on earlier in the summer in the hills a few miles southeast of there, so we're flying over with Zav to check it out. Arwen said she saw a dragon once too.*

Like Varlat?

He didn't introduce himself to her, but that's what I'm thinking. She's sure it wasn't Zav. Mom and Rocket are going to get as close as they can in their car. Strangely, Zav objected to having Rocket on his back as much as Rocket objected to being on his back. I think we should check out this lead. Do you want us to come get you, or do you want to investigate the dragon residue first? And are you sure it's not something Xilneth did?

I'm not sure, no, I replied, *but we're looking for him too, right? Since nobody has heard from him lately?*

If he's in danger, I suppose we should help him. Who else will sing to Zondia?

Nobody. Sarrlevi and I will check this out and then join you if nothing comes of it.

Same here. Just because a dragon was here months ago doesn't mean he is now, but I'm hoping *to find something like that cave full of artifacts from before.*

Keep me posted. I caught Sarrlevi wiping his brow as I tucked my phone back into my pocket.

Sweat? The misty night wasn't warm, though a fir might also have dumped water on his head.

"How much work is it levitating us over the ferns?" I glanced back, but the spot where we'd arrived had long since disappeared from view, great cedars and spruces rising up behind us.

"It uses a not-insignificant amount of magic."

"We can walk for a while if you want. I'll clear a path through the undergrowth." I patted Sorka, though she would have something snarky to say about being used for such purposes.

On cue, a miffed *harrumph* came from the weapon.

"Maybe I could borrow one of your swords," I added.

My stomach growled, making me wish I'd popped into Val's house to look for a snack when we'd been there.

"I can carry us the last couple of miles without withering from weariness. As I've informed you before, elven stamina is vast."

"I believe you."

Sarrlevi looked over at me, perhaps expecting teasing. Since I'd enjoyed being with him that afternoon, I decided *not* to tease him, thus to encourage such a performance again later.

As we continued to float over ferns and salmonberry brambles, weariness crept over me. It wasn't surprising, given how little I'd slept lately, but the sudden heaviness to my eyelids didn't seem natural. Was the Caretaker trying to influence me again? I blinked, willing my eyes to stay open, but they drooped closed, and a dream came to me.

I stood on a roof in a familiar neighborhood, but from the high perch, it took me a moment to realize where I was. Penina's house. Josh and Jessie were clambering about on the elaborate swing-set-and-slide play fortress in the backyard.

Someone stepped into view beside me. The Caretaker.

"You have not heeded my warning."

I spun, looking for my hammer, but it wasn't on the roof with me. Balling my fingers into fists, I faced him, ready to club him with my bare hands. "Leave my family alone, or I'll pound you to pieces."

"A hollow threat."

"I'll hollow your head." Furious and afraid for my niece and nephew, I punched him in the face.

But my hand encountered nothing but air, and I lurched off balance. He was an illusion. Frustrated, I punched at his face several more times, in case I could somehow get through.

His image didn't waver as he reached behind his shoulder and pulled out his rifle. He pointed it at Josh and Jessie. "If you do not cease your hunt, they will not survive the night."

Even though an illusion shouldn't be able to hurt them, that didn't keep my heart from hammering with fear.

I shouted, "Vishgronik!" and willed Sorka to fly into my hand from wherever she was. Maybe a magical weapon could find a way to hurt him, the real *him, wherever he was.*

Unperturbed, the Caretaker gazed coolly at me. "For thirty years, we let you be, let you live your life. If that was a mistake, so be it. We will not now have you ruin everything. We will terminate you and everyone you care about."

He lifted the rifle to fire, but he paused and looked past my shoulder.

Sarrlevi had appeared on the roof behind me, his swords in hand. "Stay out of her mind, elf. And leave her family alone."

The Caretaker curled a lip at him. "If you get in my way, assassin, I'll make you one of our minions."

"I will slay you before you can do that."

"Do not underestimate our power."

22

A JOSTLING OF MY SHOULDER WOKE ME FROM THE DREAM—THE *nightmare*. I gasped and flailed, almost dropping Sorka. Thankfully, she was in my hands, where she belonged, and Sarrlevi hovered next to me. We still floated over the foliage, but we'd stopped, his hand on my shoulder and a concerned furrow to his brow.

"Are you all right?"

A tremor took me, but I made myself nod. It hadn't been real. Josh and Jessie were in bed and fine.

"I severed his connection to you," Sarrlevi said, "but I don't have the power to stop him from trying again. Dream magic isn't like physical magic or even exactly like a mind attack. It's intangible and elusive. I couldn't trace it to its source, but I do believe that he's not that far away from us."

"Comforting." I said it sarcastically but afterward realized that maybe it *was* comforting. If he was here on the Olympic Peninsula, he wasn't at my sister's or grandparents' houses, threatening them.

"I'm sorry I can't do more, but if we come face to face with him, I *will* protect you."

"I know, and you're doing plenty." I hugged Sarrlevi, our dangling feet making it awkward, but I didn't care. I wanted him to know that I appreciated him. "Thank you." Releasing him, I took a deep breath and nodded toward the route ahead. "Let's keep going, please."

"Of course." Sarrlevi touched my shoulder gently before his magic swept us onward.

We floated over a few more logs and around a tree growing out of a stump, then slowed down above a bare, rocky slab of land overlooking the Strait. After setting us down, Sarrlevi walked to the edge.

The dragon magic no longer came from farther along the cliff but from beside it and below us. From the rock face itself? Was there a cave down there?

Though my healthy respect for heights made me want to stay back, I crept forward, needing to see. It would be hard to pick out a cave from above, but maybe Sarrlevi could float us down. Or maybe *he* could float down while I waited on solid ground.

He touched my hand and pointed at something, not below but on the cliff with us. Two ancient moss-covered trees rose a few yards away, branches outstretched over the edge to take advantage of the sun when it shone.

I couldn't tell what he was directing me to. Something *on* the trees? In the dark, I couldn't see much and was about to admit that half-dwarven night vision wasn't as good as elven night vision. Then I realized what he saw and smiled. About ten feet up, the two trunks connected, and the trees had grown together in that spot.

"That's us, huh?" I asked.

"It happens because the trees rub together in the wind and abrade each other's bark. That causes them to form callus tissue—

like our scar tissue—as a protection mechanism. The calluses grow outward, and the sap or pitch that is emitted for healing has an adhesive quality. Eventually, the two trees become one and are strong in that spot so they don't rub and cause more damage. As the trees grow together, the vascular tissues connect, and they can exchange nutrients and water."

"Are you saying this fusing happens because the trees initially irritate the crap out of each other? Like with their haughtiness?"

"With their bark," Sarrlevi said dryly.

"It's probably haughty bark."

He snorted and wrapped an arm around my shoulders for a squeeze before turning his consideration back to the cliff below. After a thoughtful moment, he said, "The magical residue seems to come from the water."

"Are you sure? I thought a cave in the cliff face would make more sense." We stood above a narrow inlet, the rock walls towering a hundred feet or more above the water. Thanks to the clouds, there wasn't any moonlight to illuminate them, so there could have been dozens of caves, and I wouldn't have known it.

"A cave would be visible to all who passed through the waterway." Sarrlevi pointed toward the Strait, though no ships were meandering through tonight. "Unless it was camouflaged by magic, which is possible. Still, I sense the signature we've been following coming from there." He pointed at the water below, its churn making it frothy and white. "Though it grows faint, I believe it may be, as we discussed, residue from the dragon passing through and activating some magic."

"An underwater cave?" I wondered how deep the inlet was.

Sarrlevi conjured a silver globe of light and sent it floating below. It played over the cliff, the lower portion dark with dampness from the spray of the waves striking. Though the Strait was calmer than the ocean, the inlet created more churn than out in the open water.

His illumination gleamed off the cliff walls like moonlight. It showed no caves, but it did reveal a rocky beach on one side of the inlet, with logs pushed up to the top by the tides.

"Perhaps if we go down there, more will be discernible," Sarrlevi said.

"Perhaps if we go down there, the tide will come in and drown us."

"I can levitate us back up."

"Assuming a dragon doesn't come out and nosh you to pieces, leaving me stranded down there."

Sarrlevi considered the beach again. "It is likely that a dragon that chose to nosh me would also nosh you."

"Oh, good." I waved to let him know I was grousing because I didn't like the scenario, not because I wouldn't go with him. "It's fine. I'm ready."

Before levitating us down, Sarrlevi looked thoughtfully toward the connected trees again. He walked over, cut a large clump of moss from one of the branches, and returned.

"Souvenir?" I asked.

"Perhaps."

His power swept under me, lifting me into the air. As he levitated us down, my stomach churned with anxiety as soon as we weren't over solid ground. I told myself that a lot of the beach was visible below the logs, meaning it had to be close to low tide rather than high, but it was hard not to see the inlet, with its frothy water and rock walls towering up on three sides, as a potential trap.

"The tides," I mused as we landed on the pebbly beach. "Is it possible they have something to do with when the dragon magic can be sensed?" I pulled out my phone to look up the tide table before remembering the poor reception. "What if instead of residue, this is indicating a magical doorway, but we can only detect it when the water recedes?" The phone merely thought about the search I typed in, not receiving enough reception to load a page from the internet.

"A few feet of water would not diminish the aura of something magical."

"I suppose."

Sarrlevi watched in bemusement as I paced around the beach, pointing my phone in different directions, trying to find enough of a signal to load the day's tide table. Maybe I didn't need it, but, if nothing else, it would be nice to know how long we had before the inlet started filling again.

Once more, Sarrlevi floated his light around the area, but standing on the beach and looking at the cliff wasn't more illuminating than gazing down from above had been.

Another text came in from Val. *We've found something.*

Glad my one bar of reception let text messages through, I replied, *Oh? I thought* we *had.*

There's a cave entrance back here. It was covered with moss and further camouflaged by magic, but it's huge. Huge enough for dragons to fly through. Easily.

And some moss covered that?

The moss over here grows like curtains.

True.

And I'm sure it was cultivated with magic. Arwen has some magic of her own and detected it before Zav did.

I bit my lip. Had they found the front door of the base? If so, I might have made a mistake in not asking to go with them.

In a fit of bandwidth exuberance, the tide table finally loaded. I checked the date and time.

"Low tide, the third lowest of the month, is due in... thirty minutes," I murmured.

"The dragon magic is fading further," Sarrlevi said.

He was right. Soon, we would be in an empty inlet with no hint of anything magical about it.

Maybe the dragon had stopped here earlier to catch a fish, and that was all we were sensing. No, there wouldn't have been a lingering magical residue from that. Zavryd wandering through an area didn't leave magic behind, at least not that I could detect.

"I do sense..." Sarrlevi considered the water. "No, I should say that I do *not* sense much underneath this inlet. No sea vegetation, which makes sense if the tide goes out and leaves that area bare, but I have no sense for the ground below the water either. Do you? Your magic would be more attuned to the earth."

I swept out, trying to send my senses down into the ground, but he was right. There was nothing there. Even though my magic was more muted here than on the dragon home world, I could usually sense the dirt under my feet. But I couldn't tell anything about the ground under the inlet.

"Nothing." I turned back to Sarrlevi, wishing I had an answer, wanting my burgeoning magic to be useful.

He'd fished out his recently collected clumps of moss and was calmly... braiding them? Well, at least he wasn't agitated by my failure.

He gazed contemplatively around as he wove the clumps into whatever, so maybe it was something he did to help him think. Moss, the elven equivalent of a fidget spinner.

"We could wade out and poke around." My stomach growled loudly enough to be heard over the churning water.

Sarrlevi regarded me. "We could also eat while waiting to see if the tide going completely out reveals anything."

I eyed his moss, hoping he wouldn't suggest *that* as a snack. "Do you have food in your pack of bounteous things?"

"Some." Sarrlevi slipped his project into his pocket, removed his swords and pack, and sat on a log where he could watch the water. "My supplies were running low, as I've not been to any of my homes for a time, so I asked Thorvald if she had any ration bars. She said I could *raid her fridge*. I believe that was the term, but I found more shelf-stable foods in the cupboard next to it." He fished in his pack and drew out a box of grape Pop-Tarts, conjuring light to make the label readable. "She did not remain for consultation, so I am unsure if these are equivalent to my ration bars."

"Uh, I think not. Unless you have a sweet tooth you haven't told me about, you're probably not going to like those."

"Though I do prefer palatable food, flavor matters little as long as they provide nourishment."

"They don't do that. Trust me."

"Then what is their purpose?"

"Do elves have the term *empty calories*?"

"No. Is that not an oxymoron?" Sarrlevi looked at the back of the box. "The primary ingredient is enriched with niacin, reduced iron, and thiamin mononitrate."

"Yeah, they have to enrich the flour because they denude it of all the healthy bits in the manufacturing process."

"Denude?"

"Trust me, dude." I put the box aside. It had to be Dimitri's. I couldn't imagine the sugar-hating Zavryd allowing Val to kiss him with Pop-Tart breath. "Did you get anything else?"

He gave me a sly smirk. "I did find a box of what I believe is cheese."

"A *box* of cheese?" I tried to think of any cheese I'd purchased in a box.

He withdrew a long yellow rectangle. Velveeta.

I issued something between a groan and a laugh as I slumped down on the log next to him. "I think that might be Dimitri's too. Maybe Val has gone straight carnivore to please her mate."

"This is not cheese?" Sarrlevi opened the lid and sniffed the contents, then wrinkled his nose.

"It's cheese-*like*. I don't think your palate will be impressed by it." Even *I* was too much of a cheese snob to consider such an offering ideal. Though I was hungry enough to think the Pop-Tarts sounded good enough to eat and opened the box.

Sarrlevi must have also been hungry after making all those portals and levitating us for miles. Despite my warning, he unwrapped the Velveeta and drew a knife to carve off a piece. After another nose-wrinkle-inspiring sniff, he took a small bite.

"The flavor is strange," he said.

"Yup."

"The texture is also strange."

"Yup." I chewed on a Pop-Tart but also eyed his pack, hoping he might have pulled something more appealing from Val's shelves. Maybe some salami? Or leftover barbecue? Hoping for *leftover* meat in a house where a dragon lived was probably vain, but Val's smoker seemed to run around the clock.

Reminded of the bag of grenades she'd given me, I slung it off my back. She hadn't mentioned throwing anything else inside, but I rooted around in hope.

"I do not care for it." Sarrlevi returned the cover to the Velveeta box and seemed to debate whether to return it to his pack or chuck it in the ocean. His gaze drifted to my half-eaten Pop-Tart.

Still poking hopefully in the bag, I offered it to him.

He sniffed liberally at both the plain and frosted sides. "It is... a dessert?"

"Yes. Do elves like desserts?"

"Occasionally. We make them out of berries and cream. Sometimes, we make pastries out of acorn flour."

"You probably don't denude your acorn flour so that it's shelf-stable for decades." My fingers brushed against something rectangular in a wrapper.

"We do not. We use magic to give our travel rations a long life." Sarrlevi touched his tongue to the grape filling, as if not willing to commit to a full bite.

Had his nose not still been wrinkled, I might have found watching him tongue something erotic. Mostly, I wanted to laugh.

"It's dreadful," he said without taking a bite.

"Yup," I said, though I would eat the other one from the package. I was hungry enough not to mind empty calories. Curious, I pulled out the rectangle. Ah, a granola bar. That was more promising.

Sarrlevi flicked the piece of Pop-Tart I'd given him onto the log for a less discerning seagull to find in the morning. "I would not inflict such food upon my most-loathed enemies."

"Really? You wouldn't pelt Zavryd with Pop-Tarts?"

Given Zavryd's feelings on sugar—or anything that wasn't meat or fish—he might find a Pop-Tart attack more egregious than having swords drawn upon him.

"Here." I opened the granola bar, broke it in half, and gave Sarrlevi a piece. "It'll probably be sweet to you, but it's not connected with grape jelly."

I chomped it down and dug into the Pop-Tart wrapper for the other pastry.

Sarrlevi ate the granola bar more slowly as he watched the water in the inlet swirl. His eyes grew a touch thoughtful as his gaze shifted to me. I waited for a comment—or was he reading my thoughts?—but he said nothing as he continued to gaze.

"Are you admiring my hotness?" I asked.

That prompted a slight smile. "Often. But at this moment, I'm wondering if you ever figured out the significance of the mark on top of your hammer that glows when you call *eravekt* and bash it against a magical wall. And that was replicated on a valuable trinket added to a chest of gold and given to the Assassins' Guild as payment for whoever succeeded in bringing in your head."

"I haven't thought about it for a while, I admit. I folded up the rubbing and put it in my nightstand drawer."

"Can your hammer tell you about it?"

"I can ask."

Sarrlevi had made the rubbing of the trinket for me before I'd known Sorka could speak.

Sorka? Did you hear his question?

I did not. I rarely listen to the utterings of he who once sought to slay my maker.

He's over that now and here helping me find her. We were wondering if you know of the significance of all your runes? Specifically the one on the top here between your double heads. It looks like a sun shining from the entrance of a cave mouth. I rubbed the spot with my thumb. Nothing appeared there now, nor could I feel an engraving or anything else in the flat metal, not like with the runes along the heads and haft.

I whispered the Dwarven power word for illumination, and the whole weapon glowed silver-blue. The rune on top did as well, revealed as if it were painted on with invisible ink and had been triggered.

It is Rodarska's sigil, Sorka said. *She used it—uses it—in many of her creations. You would have to ask the meaning from her, but it may simply be the equivalent of a maker's mark. Among dwarves, many craftsmen and craftswomen have such.*

Here too. I thought it might mean more, especially since it's hidden on you until you glow.

I glowed often when your mother wielded me.

Because she liked light, or because you were filled with an inner happiness and contentment that made you naturally sparkle in her hands?

I wasn't discontent, Sorka said, *but she employed my power words often, and many of them prompt illumination.* She hesitated before adding, *I actually thought—she often told me—that I belonged in the hands of a warrior, not a crafter, but she found it difficult to part with me.*

Did you want *to be parted from her?* I asked in surprise.

I was in no hurry to belong to another wielder, but I do enjoy going into battle. Rodarska does not. She enjoys crafting items for others from the protection of a forge within a city, worrying about little but her art.

Well, I'm planning to whack some bad guys with you tonight if we can find them.

Good.

Sarrlevi was still watching me, as if he expected me to spit out new useful information. If only.

"It's Mom's maker's mark, Sorka says. What prompted you to ask right now?"

Sarrlevi lifted a hand and pointed as he looked toward the water. "That."

I blinked. A large image glowed up through the five or six inches of water that remained with the tide out, an image that precisely matched that which emanated from my hammer.

23

"IT MUST BE A DOORWAY, THE ENTRANCE TO THEIR LAIR, TO *something*," I reasoned, staring at the sun-in-cave rune glowing up through the water. But if this was the front door, what were Val and the others investigating?

"Perhaps your weapon is the key to gaining entrance." Sarrlevi pointed to the still-glowing rune—the still-glowing and *matching* rune—beaming from the top of my hammer.

In the dark, I couldn't tell if anything besides sand and pebbles lay under the water, and when I poked around with my senses, I still couldn't detect anything underground. But if that dragon had passed this way, it *had* to be a doorway. Maybe he'd made it for his own use, and that was why his signature lingered in the area. Though why would he have made a door marked by a dwarven rune?

After checking the time to see if the tide would recede further —it wouldn't—I walked into the cold water, wincing as it soaked through my shoes and jeans. Maybe I should have taken them off, but I didn't want to burst barefoot into an enemy stronghold and have bad guys trample on my toes.

The image didn't stir as I walked on it. Only the water swirled about in the inlet.

My apologies for getting you wet, Sorka, but I need to try something. I prodded the top of the hammer—and the glowing rune—into the pebbles.

Sorka sighed into my mind. *I suppose it is no worse than being bathed in the blood of our enemies.*

Slightly better, I'd think. More hygienic anyway.

Saltwater is corrosive.

You can't tell me Mom's enchantments don't protect you from rust. The first magic I learned was to make nails resist that.

That only earned me an indignant *harrumph*, which I took to mean Sorka wouldn't be damaged, and dripping ocean water was merely undignified.

Too bad. I kept poking. When I stirred the pebbles, the image didn't move. Rather than being painted on with some magical substance, it appeared superimposed. And was that the faintest hint of magic I detected? Not dragon magic but *dwarven* magic?

A boom sounded in the distance, somewhere inland.

I paused my poking to look in that direction, though I couldn't see anything with the cliff rising up on three sides. Had the explosion come from where Val and the others had gone? She had a stash of magical grenades too.

I checked my phone, but there weren't any new messages. If they'd gone into battle—or been ambushed—Val wouldn't have had time to text me.

"I believe your mother made this," Sarrlevi said, drawing my attention back to the water and the rune. "The enchantment is subtle—maybe even hidden—for I did not sense dwarven magic among the dragon magic until we were right on top of it."

He'd joined me, levitating instead of wading out. Maybe I should have requested he float me in the air too, but I had a feeling we were going to get wet going through this door—once we figured out how to open it.

"Would this rune have shown up if I hadn't come with the hammer and said *eravekt*?"

"It appeared before you did that, which is why I asked about the rune, but it is possible the hammer is the key to unlocking it."

I rocked back. "That's what Hart and the others were talking about when I was spying on them."

Damn, I'd forgotten about that. When that night had erupted in chaos, what I'd heard eavesdropping had dropped out of my head. The dragon queen's mind-scouring had stirred up some memories, but she hadn't lingered on the parts about me and my hammer.

"Sorka is the key to something," I said, "but if the dragon can go through the door any time without the hammer, I doubt this is what they were talking about."

"It could be key to many things that your mother crafted." Sarrlevi gave me a significant look. "Perhaps she knew you had it and *wanted* you to be able to gain access. She might have designed this so her captors wouldn't see it but you would. It was glowing before you said a power word, but it was *not* glowing before you arrived on the beach."

If Mom had designed this to let me in, if she'd been trying to give me clues all along, I felt like an idiot for not figuring things out earlier. Except that I *hadn't* figured things out. Not yet. I kept prodding the pebbles, hoping to find the equivalent of a keyhole.

Sarrlevi lowered the tip of one of his swords, also poking it into the water-covered beach. I wondered if it shared indignant *harrumphs* with him.

"Your mother may have arranged to have that particular trinket sent along with the reward of gold coins for your assassination," Sarrlevi said, "hoping you would see it and believe it was a clue."

"Maybe, but how could she have known *I* would ever see something given to the Cosmic Realms Assassins' Guild? Unless she knows I'm working with you." I was skeptical of that. Mom would remember Sarrlevi as the assassin who'd been sent to hunt her down. It was doubtful that her captors were letting her out to learn about current events, such as that Sarrlevi and I were on the same side now. "Like I said, Sorka implied it's a maker's mark, so she may put it on everything she crafts, at least what she wants to claim." I wondered if her rune was somewhere on those attack helicopters she'd enchanted.

"Hm," Sarrlevi said noncommittally.

Another text came in while we were poking through the water —I was sure I'd prodded every inch under the symbol. An update from Val.

We haven't been able to get inside yet. Whoever runs the defenses of this place realized we're here and sent out minions to fight us. Minions with glazed eyes, magical bracelets on their wrists, and powerful weapons, including grenades. There are some flying metal drones attacking us with magical laser beams too. They're enchanted and resist dragon fire.

As I read, another boom sounded in the distance.

Zav is able to block the beams, Val's message continued, *but the grenades are powerful enough that they can break through a dragon's barrier. He's having to make sure he detonates them before they get close. I'm getting Mom and Arwen out of the area, then going back to help him. If the defenders have much more to throw at us, we might need your help too. At least if we're going to get in.*

Sarrlevi and I have found what we think is a back door. Maybe you should come over here. After I sent the text, I realized it might be ideal if the others kept the defenders occupied while we snuck in. *Or we can get in and try to come at them from behind and meet you,* I offered, though I had no idea if that was realistic. Val and Zavryd were miles inland, and the two entrances might not connect.

Okay, we'll try that. These guys might have glazed eyes and not think anything of us leaving, but someone *is controlling them and could find it suspicious.*

Yeah. I hoped that *someone* wasn't my mother, that, even if she'd been forced to make those control bracelets, she had nothing to do with ordering the minions around.

There's something else. The dragons have arrived.

The ones from the Council? I glanced up, but I couldn't yet sense any dragons.

Yes. They're not here on the peninsula yet. They came out of a portal over my house in Seattle. They probably don't know this area or exactly where things were going down, but it won't take them long to fly over here.

Will they help or be a problem? After hearing the queen talk, I feared the latter.

Sarrlevi sank his sword almost to the hilt into the beach, but it did not clunk against wood or do anything to suggest a door.

Zav thinks they're going to utterly destroy this area without bothering to go in and look for prisoners. All they care about is making sure Varlat can't enact his scheme.

Once more, fear clutched my heart as I imagined my parents being killed because they were captives inside as the dragons did the equivalent of bombing the base.

Thanks for the warning. We're going in. I scowled at the beach as I stuffed my phone into my pocket. We *were* going in. One way or another.

As if to mock my determination, the glowing symbol started to fade.

Sarrlevi summoned his elven magic, and I sensed him trying to thrust downward with his power. He probably didn't want to unleash everything he had at the door, especially if he was also thinking of sneaking in, so it wasn't surprising when nothing happened.

I rested Sorka's head in the middle of the fading image and willed the passageway to open. When that didn't work, I also tried to thrust downward with my magic, to excavate an entrance the way I'd dug a hole under the dragon cave. Nothing.

The fact that the ground resisted my efforts seemed to *prove* magic was obstructing us. With the tide creeping back in and the water rising, I groped for something else to try.

Sarrlevi wiped his blade clean with his kerchief and sheathed it. "What's the Dwarven word for *open*?"

"I don't know." *Sorka?*

Bondar, she replied.

Hammer pressed to the beach, I lifted an arm and commanded, "*Bondar!*" in my best open-sesame voice.

The ground beneath me disappeared. I cried out in alarm as I not only fell but was sucked downward.

Water swirled and gushed down with me, like a toilet flushing. Panic blasted me as I went under. Flailing, I almost lost Sorka, but I tightened my grip with both hands before she could be ripped away by the current. Completely submerged in cold dark water and being sucked farther and farther downward, I was helpless to do anything to avert my fate.

A trap. It had to have been a trap, not a door, and I was going to drown. With so much water pulling me downward, there was no way I could swim back up.

At least Sarrlevi wouldn't die. He'd been levitating.

Before my lungs could start begging for air, the water sloughed away from me, and I tumbled through open air into darkness. Again, I flailed, now more afraid of the fall than drowning.

I splashed down in water, landing on my back and hitting hard enough to knock the air out of my lungs and jar my entire body. It was as if I'd belly-flopped off a high-dive—*back*-flopped. I squirmed about, getting my feet under me so I could tread water. At least I could breathe and suck air back into my lungs.

Unable to see anything in the dark, I dashed water out of my eyes and rasped, "*Eravekt.*"

Sorka glowed silver-blue, illuminating a pool of water all around me, the surface rippling from my landing. As I tried to tread water with one arm and lift her higher to extend her glow, movement above made me flinch. My foot hit the ground, startling me further.

More water rained down from above, and Sarrlevi, arms pointed downward in a dive, came out of a rocky hole in the ceiling. I scrambled sideways so he wouldn't land on me, my feet again brushing the bottom.

"It's not deep!" I warned since Sarrlevi was plummeting toward the pool like a diver.

With water gushing down around him, as it had with me, I couldn't tell if he heard. But when he landed, he must have curled quickly upward in the water, because he came up on his feet not far away.

"*Tardokon, tardokon,*" a voice emanated from the depths around us.

"Uh?" Before I could say anything else, red beams shot out from the dark air above the water.

Magic swelled around Sarrlevi as he formed a barrier around us. Sorka did the same, acting before I blurted, "*Hygorotho,*" and melded her power with his.

With unnerving accuracy, the beams struck us from several directions. Our invisible barriers deflected them, but I could tell they were powerful, both from the way Sarrlevi winced and stepped back, as if to brace himself, and because Sorka growled into my mind as she sent even more power into our defenses.

"Stay there," Sarrlevi said, "and add your power to that of your hammer."

"Okay."

He and his barrier departed from mine but slowly—he made

sure Sorka and I could keep the beams from getting through before he fully left. When he did, he strode toward one of the beams, the water not rising as high on him. Though he was careful to keep his barrier up, he also summoned light and sent it ahead.

"*Tardokon, tardokon,*" the voice—it sounded like a male dwarf —kept repeating.

Why did I have a feeling we'd set off an alarm as *well* as the defenses?

At first, all the beams remained focused on me, but the one Sarrlevi was wading toward shifted toward him. Some intelligence guided it, telling it he was coming for it.

He reached a ledge around the pool, climbed out, and sprinted for a foot-wide black volcano-shaped device mounted to the rock wall. The beam was coming out of its center.

Drawing his swords, Sarrlevi darted to the side of the beam. He cried out something in Elven and struck the device with both blades. Though they didn't slice it in half, he succeeded in knocking it from its mount and battering it enough that the beam stopped. He smashed it several more times until only smoke wafted from it, then ran along the ledge toward another one.

Five more continued to shoot at me. I sensed Sorka's magic waning and didn't know how long she could maintain the barrier.

Intending to emulate Sarrlevi's action, I pushed through the water toward the source of one of the other beams. But the pool grew deeper before I reached a ledge. I had to tread water and paddle one-handed with Sorka in my free hand. Her protection kept some of the water out, but other water had been caught inside with me and sloshed around, making my swim even more awkward. At least the barrier shifted and flexed so I could maneuver through the water, and I didn't bob about like a ball.

Sarrlevi destroyed another beam, but the others weren't accessible from his ledge. He ran back toward the water, leaped into the air, and levitated himself across the pool toward another mounted device.

"I need to learn how to do that," I grumbled as saltwater splashed into my mouth.

As he destroyed the devices, the words, "*Tardokon, tardokon,*" continued, echoing from the rock walls.

Finally, I made it to a ledge and clambered out. Only one device remained, the beam aimed at my chest. With only one assailant left, Sorka didn't have trouble keeping the barrier up. Hammer raised, I stalked toward the wall, looking forward to bashing the crap out of the device.

Mr. Levitation swept by me, heading toward it.

"Don't you dare," I told him, determined to destroy something. To be *useful*.

Sarrlevi stopped and landed a few feet from the device, his eyebrows raised. Since he was closer, the beam shifted toward him, but his barrier deflected it.

I ran up and smashed Sorka into the device, not only knocking it from the wall but causing it to split in half. Not satisfied, I smashed both pieces again and again until nothing but dented and battered black material remained. In pieces.

Maybe it was my imagination, but satisfaction seemed to emanate from Sorka too.

Sarrlevi, dripping water the same as I, watched in mild amusement, but he didn't comment on my rage. He only smiled, managing to look handsome even with his blond hair plastered to his head and a piece of seaweed draped over one pointed ear.

Feeling much calmer now, I reached up and plucked it free for him. "There." I showed it to him. "It was affecting your sexy elf allure."

"Truly?"

"No, you were still hot."

He gave me his typical smug smile and inclined his head

toward me before considering the rock walls. We'd taken care of the beams, but the alarm was still going off.

Sarrlevi drew a dagger, then sent his conjured globe of light across the water toward the source of the *tardokon, tardokon.* It revealed a little box mounted to another rock wall. He hurled his dagger across the pool, and it slammed point first into the device. The words halted with a spit of static. He levitated the dagger back into his grip, then drew his kerchief—it was as wet as the rest of him—to wipe down all his blades before sheathing them.

What does tardokon *mean, Sorka?* I suspected it was a Dwarven word.

Intruder.

I'd been afraid of that. An alarm going off. If Varlat or the Caretaker were around, they would know someone had come through the back door.

"It's unfortunate that we can't delay." Sarrlevi wrapped an arm around my shoulders and looked down. "The water molding your shirt to your body is *enhancing* your half-dwarf allure."

"Like a Wet T-shirt Contest, huh?"

I was positive he didn't know what that was, but he smiled agreeably before lowering his arm and pointing toward the darkness at one end of the pool.

"There is a tunnel over there."

Though I couldn't see it, I took his word for it. The dragon wasn't in here with us, so he must have flown off somewhere. To deal with Val and Zavryd?

Sarrlevi summoned his levitation magic and swept us into the air and over the pool toward the tunnel. I looked up at the hole we'd dropped through and had the surreal experience of seeing water hanging in the air above us. Against gravity, the hole had filled in.

If Mom had meant for me to find this place, she must have had a lot of faith that Sorka and I could handle those beams on our own. I didn't know if that would have been true.

"Let's hope the defenses don't get worse," I murmured as Sarrlevi navigated us into a tunnel wide enough for a dragon to fly through.

"Given that it is likely known that we have entered the lair, I believe they will."

"I was afraid of that."

24

As the wide tunnel continued, we switched from levitation to walking so Sarrlevi didn't have to draw upon his magic. Though he always promised his elven stamina was great, I'd seen the sweat on his face when he'd floated us through the rainforest. Such magic couldn't be easy to maintain.

Weariness was creeping into me too. It had been a long day, and lending my power to Sorka's to deflect those beams had been draining. With luck, we could connect with Val and Zavryd before we were out of juice.

Hoping an update from her had come in, I pulled my phone out of my soggy pocket. A piece of seaweed came with it.

Scowling, I did my best to dry the phone and wished I'd thought to do that right away. Not surprisingly, the screen didn't come on. I hoped it would work again once it dried out. Not that there would have been reception down here anyway.

I also checked the grenades, glad I hadn't lost the bag in the fall. A lot of water had gotten in.

Sarrlevi used his magic to dry the grenades, but he didn't know if they would still work. I hoped so. Other than my hammer, I didn't have any other secret weapons to unleash on our enemies.

"This was carved out by dwarven magic." Sarrlevi nodded at the even sides of the tunnel as we continued on.

Not surprised, I nodded. My mother had been these people's prisoner for thirty years, and she wasn't the only dwarf they had. "I got disoriented during that fall, *majorly* disoriented, but I'm assuming we're heading inland and we're under the Olympic Peninsula now rather than walking out under the water."

"Neither idea is appealing." Sarrlevi considered the arched ceiling.

To my eyes, it appeared sturdy, with no hint of crumbled rock on the ground, but he'd admitted that tunnels of all sorts made elves uneasy. Since their swaying vine bridges hundreds of feet above ground made *me* uneasy, I wouldn't tease him for that.

Not for the first time, I rubbed the camouflage charm in my pocket. Sarrlevi also had his camouflaging magic wrapped about him. So far, nobody had come running—or flying—back to check on us, but it seemed inevitable that someone would eventually.

A couple of times, Sarrlevi held up a hand to stop me, pointed at a faint magical signature on the ground, and levitated us over what might have been a booby trap. Once, we spotted a couple of the beam-shooting devices mounted on the walls, but we dismantled them before they could attack us.

A faint shudder coursed through the earth, and we paused. No rocks rained down, but Sarrlevi eyed the ceiling with even more wariness. I thought of earthquakes until I remembered the earlier booms and Val talking of magical grenades.

Were they still going off? Or had the dragons arrived and started an attack? If so, we might not have much time.

I couldn't detect any dragons above us, but I suspected magic in the walls and ceiling prevented people from sensing this place from outside—and that would work both ways. Would Sarrlevi be able to form a portal to get us out of here if needed? Or might we be trapped?

The tunnel grew wider and taller as we continued, and we came to a great vault door set in a steel wall that blocked the way. In a large alcove to one side, a number of six-wheeled amphibious vehicles were parked. They emanated magic and gleamed as if they were new, but they looked like the armored versions from World War II.

"The escape vehicles, I'm guessing." I grew more and more convinced that we'd found the back door to this place.

"Clunky," Sarrlevi said.

"It probably wasn't practical to keep a stable of elven riding birds down here." I wondered how the vehicles navigated the hole in the top of that cavern. Maybe there was another way out of there, a passageway under the pool that led to the Strait.

"*Evinya.* They would not care to be stabled in tunnels."

"Just like elves, huh?" I walked to the door, not seeing a way to open it.

"Quite."

I pressed the top of my hammer against the metal, sensing magic within it. Sarrlevi drew his swords and crouched. Bracing himself for a trap?

"*Bondar,*" I said more tentatively than last time.

The top of my hammer glowed, and the door also glowed, the same symbol emanating from it. A *click-clunk* came from within the door. With a hiss of air escaping, it opened outward.

I scurried back to Sarrlevi's side, also expecting an attack or a booby trap to spring.

Beyond the now-open door, lights came on. They revealed rounded cement walls instead of more carved rock. Twenty or thirty feet down the passageway, another vault door stood closed. *Sealed,* I thought, thinking of the released air.

"Like an airlock," I murmured.

Sarrlevi looked back. "I am uncertain why they would wish to flood the area out here with water."

"Maybe that happens automatically when the tide comes in." Did that make sense? We were well under the surface, so if the place was prone to flooding, it would *always* be flooded, wouldn't it?

"Neither the walls back there nor conveyances look like they're inundated regularly with water."

He was right. There weren't any barnacles growing on the hulls of the vehicles, no seaweed dangling from the tires.

"Let's see if I can open the second door." I headed in, but Sarrlevi hesitated, eyeing the walls inside now.

Maybe what I'd deemed the airlock was what flooded. I could envision both doors shutting, trapping us inside, and water pouring in to drown me.

"A cheery thought," I murmured, then reminded myself that Mom had likely built the doors, or at least enchanted them, and they'd opened for me. For Sorka. I couldn't believe she would have wanted me to die. She wanted me to get in and *save* her. I was sure of it.

When I touched the hammer to the second door, the first started to swing shut. Sarrlevi cursed and ran inside to join me.

"Did you decide it would be romantic to die by my side?" I asked.

"I decided it would be wise to stick with the person who carries the hammer that opens doors."

"Practical."

"Romantically so?" Sarrlevi raised his eyebrows.

"It might be if you ogle my chest again and tell me about all the exotic cheese you're going to feed me after this."

"I will do those things."

Behind us, the door sealed. The lights didn't go off, and I didn't *see* any spigots through which water could flow in, but that didn't keep my nerves from making themselves known. There *were* little divots in the walls. Damn, I hadn't noticed those before.

"*Bondar*," I whispered, not wanting to loiter.

Something clicked in the wall, and nozzles protruded from the divots.

"Shit."

The light shifted from white to reddish-purple, and water sprayed from the walls. Sarrlevi whirled toward the nozzles, raising his swords, but there were a *lot* of nozzles.

"Wait." I gripped his arm, realizing this was more like a shower than a flooding of the chamber. "I think we're being decontaminated."

"What?"

"Like in science-fiction movies."

Sarrlevi looked blankly at me. Once we had time for recreational activities, I would introduce him to the classics.

After a couple of minutes, the shower went off, and the lights returned to normal. I breathed a sigh of relief.

"Why would we need to be *decontaminated*? We were submerged in sea water, nothing inimical." Sarrlevi pushed a hand through his damp hair, making it stick out in spicules.

"I don't know, dude. Maybe we're entering some kind of clean lab. You don't think they'd be making viruses or bacteria or something, do you?"

"Like in science-fiction movies?"

"Yeah, but all that stuff actually happens these days." I frowned and tried the open-door command again.

This time, the same glowing symbol appeared, and, with another *click-clunk*, the great metal door swung inward. When we'd opened the first door, the lights in here had come on. This time, the lights beyond were already on.

"Activate your charm again," Sarrlevi said.

"Good idea," I murmured, feeling we were getting close.

To *what* exactly, I didn't know.

Though I was inclined to pad slowly and stealthily through the tunnel, another earthquake—another explosion?—convinced me to jog. Not so much as a light had gone out from the ground shakes, but that didn't mean I wanted to linger to find out what the dragons would do when they arrived. If they hadn't arrived already.

I did my best to keep anything from jangling. Sarrlevi, of course, didn't make a sound, and any time he moved more than two feet away from me, he disappeared from my senses.

Ahead, the tunnel widened, and the light brightened. We slowed as we passed vast rooms filled with garden beds growing lettuces, tomatoes, beans, and other vegetables. The Earth equivalent of the dwarven rock beds growing edible algae.

No root vegetables? Sarrlevi asked, switching to telepathy as he pointed at cameras on the walls.

My mother must not have been the one to plant them.

Past the grow rooms, we found huge tanks rising so high that they had ladder rungs up the outside to climb. One read *potable water,* and pipes ran from it into the cement walls.

I'm beginning to get what this place is, I told Sarrlevi, remembering the dragons' discussion of genocide and *missing humans.*

A protected self-sustainable bunker in which a number of people could survive for a time?

I think so. I'm half-expecting the next chamber to be a silo full of nuclear warheads. I shuddered at the thought and *hoped* we wouldn't find that, but who knew. Maybe this organization was all about destroying a huge chunk of humanity and then hiding out until it was safe to roam about on the surface again. Rebuilding the world and the civilization to be more in line with their vision. But why would they have needed my mother and her magical powers for that?

Can not the dwarven energy reactors be turned into weapons? Sarrlevi asked.

I winced. *Yeah, Willard said something about that.*

We passed a room full of ducts and what I wanted to call HVAC equipment, but it was all much larger than anything that went into my housing projects.

This would be for filtering the air down here. I thought of the airlock and the decontamination chamber and grimaced again. *The radioactive air. Hell, Varlesh, we have to stop these people, not only rescue my parents.*

These chambers are all defended with magic. Strong magic. I would not advise running in and bashing everything with your hammer. Sarrlevi shared a vision of magical booby traps going off and killing us.

No promises if we get to a place holding nuclear warheads.

I am not that familiar with your Earth technology, but I believe you would especially not want to bash those.

Probably not, but maybe I could enchant them in some way to render them inoperable. Pleased by the thought, I almost *wanted* to find that room, but we passed hallways heading off toward private quarters, not missile silos—at least according to the signs. *Maybe they're not planning to pull the trigger themselves,* I mused as we passed storerooms and freezers. *The world has been getting tense lately. Maybe these people are instigating things, prodding the dragon, so to speak, and trusting humanity will escalate to war with enough provocation.*

A grim thought.

Should your world devolve into war and become uninhabitable, I will take you to one of mine.

Thanks, but I'd much rather stop *that from happening. I—* I shook my head, fighting down emotion as images of Penina and Josh and Jessie came to mind. Of my grandparents. Of my parents. Of Abbas and Zadie and Tinja.

This wasn't the time for me to dwell on everyone I knew and cared about and all the work I'd put into various homes for people over the years, but the thought of everything being destroyed...

I drew a shaky breath. We would stop this scheme. We would find Mom and Dad, and we would stop it.

Sarrlevi rested a hand on my shoulder. This wasn't his world, and he couldn't care the way I did, but he cared about me, and I appreciated that.

We hadn't stopped walking, but I picked up the pace. If we could find my mother, she would, after thirty years, know much of what these guys were up to. And maybe she would know how to stop their plans and put them out of business.

Another tremor coursed through the ground. The dragons might be out there, trying to put them out of business *now*.

"Let me find my parents first," I whispered, hoping we hadn't made a mistake by passing the areas labeled as private quarters without searching them. What if all the minions slept back there when they weren't out flying helicopters and attacking people with their glassy eyes?

One wonders what a dragon would gain from a war on a wild world that his kind rarely visits, Sarrlevi said.

I know. Why would Varlat be wrapped up in this?

We passed a room with three cement walls and one wall of glass that faced us. I stared. Not at one but *four* dwarven reactors resting on pedestals inside. Unlike in the home video we'd watched, they were all dark, and I didn't sense power emanating from them.

Why aren't they plugged in and powering this place? I waved to indicate the whole underground lair. We'd already traveled a mile, if not *miles*. Who knew how much the organization had excavated down here and how much power everything took? *Unless it's because they don't have the key.* I raised my eyebrows as I held up the hammer.

If that's the key, Sarrlevi said, *I am surprised they didn't try sooner to acquire it. Or force your mother to make another.*

Another? Sorka chimed in with indignation. *I am not a simple gewgaw that can be mass-produced in a factory.*

Do dwarves have factories? I envisioned a Model-T assembly line.

Of course. Hand-crafted items are more valued and desirable, but dwarves make unimportant cogs in factories.

They'd had electricity in the capital, I reminded myself. They weren't *Lord of the Rings* dwarves, despite their fondness for plate armor and large axes.

Maybe the metals that go into a weapon like Sorka aren't available on Earth, I suggested.

These people traveled to the Assassins' Guild on Zokthoran to deliver their reward, Sarrlevi said. *They have access to resources beyond what's available on your world.*

I guess so. Maybe they asked, but Mom refused to make another key. I wanted that to be true, for her to have realized what the organization was up to and to have drawn a line, but would she have been able to deny them? *Or maybe she tricked them and convinced them that she couldn't make another key. Dwarf minds are supposed to be hard to read, right? You've said that.*

Yes, but a dragon ought to be able to get the gist. At least to detect a lie. Sarrlevi twitched a shoulder. *The princess is powerful, so perhaps not.*

Maybe the reactors haven't been that big of a deal yet for them. Right now, everything on Earth is still working, but if there's a war that knocks out the power grids and supply chains, then they'll need the reactors if they want power. These aren't the kinds of people who would happily live like cavemen going forward. They've clearly been setting things up for comfort. I waved to indicate the underground installation. For all I knew, they had more places like this around the world. *Everything they've done so far over these past decades could have been nothing but preparations for executing their plan.*

What does the dragon plan?

We might not figure that out until we can sit him down for a chat. Or until the other dragons capture him and torture him for what he knows.

That latter seems a more likely possibility, Sarrlevi said.

When another tremor coursed through the cement floor, we resumed walking. I was tempted to try to get into that room and ask Sarrlevi to stuff the reactors in his magical backpack, but they were too large for that.

We can get them on the way out, I told myself, not willing to put aside my priority.

A familiar magic emanated from somewhere up ahead. Not my mother's signature, at least I didn't think so, but something I'd encountered recently. With so much magic coming from all over this place, I struggled to identify it.

Gnomish magic, Sarrlevi said. *Interesting.*

We hadn't seen many gnomes among the minions that had attacked us these past months, but they were a short and slight people, not much larger than goblins, so they wouldn't have been chosen by anyone to be attackers or defenders.

Were we about to run into a brick wall enchanted by gnomish magic? Such as had kept the furnace guardian under the Bridle Trails house? Or—

I halted so quickly that Sarrlevi bumped into my shoulder. *The stasis chambers on Dun Kroth. That's where I sensed magic like this before.*

Sarrlevi nodded. Maybe he'd already figured that out.

We're not going to find more ancient badass war prisoners trapped here, are we? I wondered.

I do not know.

We entered another vast cement-walled area, with the ceiling arching high above us. One could have put a city block inside.

There were indeed stasis chambers, like those from the volcano lab, built into alcoves along the left wall ahead of us. There were dozens of them, some dark but some with green glows emanating from them with barriers blocking access.

Pipes, conduits, and computers, along with gnomish artifacts, rested on pedestals or were mounted on the walls around us. Just past the alcoves, the base of a metal tower rose up from the cement floor and disappeared into the ceiling. The place looked like a giant mad scientist's laboratory, though surprisingly ordinary flat-screen TVs were mounted on a wall across from the alcoves.

Though I wanted to head straight for the stasis chambers to see if any were occupied, Sarrlevi veered off toward a glass window overlooking a sunken room. Or a silo? I hoped we weren't about to find the nuclear missiles I'd imagined.

Sarrlevi gripped his chin as he contemplated what lay inside. A great capped pipe with the girth of a house ran vertically down into the earth, disappearing through the cement floor. Mundane computers and what might have been magical monitors were mounted to the walls around the pipe. Great magic emanated from a number of huge bins in the back. They held what looked like piles of crystals.

Gnomish and dragon magic built this pipe, Sarrlevi mused. *And I believe those crystals are vythorium.*

I looked blankly at him.

It's a material found deep in the ground on many worlds in the Cosmic Realms. It's believed by some to be the origin of magic on those worlds, a natural substance that emanates its power underground, which trickles upward and is accessible to the beings who live on the surface and evolved to use it. Sarrlevi touched his chest.

Are these people... dropping them into the ground? To try to get more magic to exist on Earth?

Possibly. I have not heard anything to suggest that such would work, but I am not a scientist.

With so much magic in the area that I was developing a headache, it was hard for me to single out artifacts or get a strong idea of what anything did, but I tried to send my senses through the pipe. All I could tell was that there was a lot of magic down there.

Someone might be trying to turn your Earth into a more appealing world to colonize, Sarrlevi suggested.

Earth is already colonized.

Not by life forms a haughty dragon would consider significant or important.

I thought of the dragons calling humans *vermin* and winced. *So, that's Varlat's plan? Cull or completely destroy the existing population and take over Earth for himself? The humans who help the dragon get to stay down here while the plan is being enacted so they can live? And then what? They get to serve Varlat afterward? Why would they sign up for that?* I couldn't imagine anyone wanting to wreck the world and spend the next however many decades underground until it was livable again. What kind of life would that be if they came out of their bunker and all the good things that humanity had done over the centuries were gone? No comforts of life to be purchased at the store. No Pop-Tarts factory still in production.

It is possible the humans and the dragon have different plans and both believe they are using the other to achieve their goals, Sarrlevi said.

Then they're all idiots.

Delusional perhaps. Probably not stupid.

I disagree.

Sarrlevi turned his attention from the pipe toward the strange metal structure rising up beyond the stasis chambers. It reminded me of the base of a high-voltage-power-line tower. Only the bottom half was visible, with the rest disappearing through a large hole in the ceiling. Was the top peeking out of some hill above us? If so, this place wouldn't be airtight. Maybe it just needed to be *close* to the surface to operate.

"And do what?" I wondered.

Beyond the tower, giant roll-up garage doors lined the cement walls on either side of the vast chamber. Ten of them. Since magic emanated from behind them—magic emanated from *everything*—I doubted we wanted to see what was back there. Not the organization's weekend camping vehicles, I was sure.

Matti, can you hear me? That was Val.

Yeah. Are you in the lair? My phone died.

Right inside the entrance I told you about. The queen and other dragons are here now, but some heavy-hitting enchanted stuff showed up to defend the place. A bunch of those helicopters are flying and shooting magic missiles, and weapons platforms are unfurling from the walls. I'm not sure even dragons are going to be able to destroy all this. The queen is ranting about how the Dragon Council forbids this, and they're throwing around magic like crazy, but Zav is concerned.

We've felt a few quakes. A fresh one punctuated my words, and I rested a hand on the wall for support. That had been stronger than the others. Or maybe we were closer to the source now.

Trust me, this is more than earthquakes. You might get buried alive if you don't find your parents and get out of there soon. The dragons are getting pissed.

I'm trying. Thanks for the warning. I turned to speak to Sarrlevi, but he'd moved off and now stood in front of the stasis chambers.

I believe I know how they kept your mother from escaping, he said without looking at me.

With foreboding filling me, I ran to join him.

Not all of the stasis chambers had occupants. Some were turned on, and some weren't. Maybe the empty ones were for the humans involved in this plot, and they planned to sleep in suspended animation until Earth recovered from their war. I shook my head, hoping the dragons destroyed every last one of them.

I stumbled when I passed a chamber with two dwarves inside, two *familiar* dwarves. Artie and Hennehok. Hell. Was Xilneth frozen somewhere in this complex too?

When I stopped beside Sarrlevi, the person he was looking at came into view, someone else frozen, just as the half-dragon prisoner had been frozen.

"Mother," I whispered.

25

INSIDE THE STASIS CHAMBER, MOM'S EYES WERE CLOSED, BUT SHE looked almost exactly as I remembered her, with frizzy red hair, a stout build, broad face, and a vintage UW sweatshirt over heavy canvas work pants. Maybe it hadn't been *vintage* when she'd been taken. How much of the last thirty years had she spent out here working on projects for these people and how much in this stasis chamber? Did they keep her in it when the dragon wasn't around to prevent her from escaping?

What's the deal with these stasis chambers? I asked Sarrlevi telepathically as I stared through the invisible barrier at my mother. I could barely sense her aura, which explained why nobody from Barothla to Sorka to the dwarven priest had been able to track her down. *Is there a Cosmic Realms Kwik-E-Mart where you can pick them up?*

I am unaware of a vendor that sells them, and I had not heard of them until recently. The clan of dragons that opposes the Stormforges had imprisoned a number of them in large stasis chambers, also of gnomish make, I believe. Thorvald was instrumental in their release.

I wish she was with us to be instrumental here.

Maybe that wasn't true. The fact that Val and Zavryd and the dragons were at the main entrance had to be the only reason nobody had come to investigate our intrusion.

As I gazed at Mom's face, her skin tinted green by the light, tears threatened. Emotion I'd kept tamped down bubbled to the surface. Before realizing what I was doing, I reached out, filled with longing to touch my mother for the first time in thirty years.

The barrier buzzed and zapped my finger with a strong shock. I jerked back.

A slight buzz of static sounded elsewhere. At first, I thought it came from the metal tower, but two TVs on the wall behind us came on. They showed camera feeds. One was of a suburban neighborhood from above, streetlights the only thing very noticeable since it was nighttime. The other showed the inside of a building full of cells. The view was familiar, but it took me a moment to place it.

Is that the prison building that held my father?

The camera pointed toward an empty cell. The cell where he'd been a prisoner for so many years? The feed had to come from one of the security cameras inside the facility. Maybe someone from the organization had hacked into it. Or maybe they'd bribed a soldier to set this up?

The hole that had been blown in the outer wall of my father's cell the night I'd been there had been repaired, but of course he was not back inside. I wondered where *he* was in this compound and prayed his kidnappers hadn't killed him after they'd gotten him.

Yes, Sarrlevi replied, *and that is your home.*

I rocked back, my gaze whipping to the screen I'd only glanced at. Numerous dark roofs were visible, but... Hell. That *was* my house in the center of them, the front yard and driveway in shadow but faintly distinguishable thanks to the corner streetlight. An opossum started into the yard before encountering the wards and scurrying away, and one of my motion-detecting lights came on. That made the front door visible, including the vines and leaves adorning it. No mistaking that house.

Well, that's not at all creepy. I wondered where the camera was placed. It had to be high up in one of the pine trees around the neighborhood. How long had it been there? Since I'd moved in? *Very creepy.*

Sarrlevi looked from the television to Mom's stasis chamber. *Maybe they showed her images of you and your father to motivate her.*

Though chilled by all of this, I nodded. Barothla had once implied something similar, that I might be the lever the organization was using on my mother to ensure her good behavior. But she must not have been *completely* compliant. Or they wouldn't have had to keep her in the stasis chamber.

We must break her out. Sorka's haft warmed in my hand.

I agree.

Turning my back on the televisions, I reached toward the panel next to the stasis chamber, but my senses told me right away that it was different from the one on Dun Kroth. Though gnomish magic once again flowed from the panel to the device that kept the stasis chamber working, I didn't see anything like the conduit I'd used my power to snip last time.

Use me to strike that panel, Sorka said. *I will bash it to pieces so we can get her out.*

As tempting as that is, I'm afraid she'll be hurt if we wantonly destroy things.

After wantonly destroying the interiors of so many old homes, you will balk at swinging me at this?

Old homes aren't as important as my mother.

Sorka subsided at that.

I need a minute to figure this out, I told her and Sarrlevi. *Unless a furnace guardian wants to come crash into it and break it in such a way that the prisoner inside isn't harmed and escapes.* An act that had probably only worked back on Dun Kroth because I'd gotten the barrier down first. It had surely been luck that the half-dragon criminal hadn't been hurt and had walked away from that.

Someone may be coming. Sarrlevi looked through the tower supports and past the roll-up doors toward a bend we couldn't see around. *Not a furnace guardian.*

I made sure my camouflage charm was active, and Sarrlevi almost disappeared from my awareness as he also refreshed his magic.

Six people walked around the bend and into view, all with strong auras. Only one did I recognize. In the center and in the lead, a blond elf in a three-piece suit carried a magical rifle in one hand. The Caretaker, exactly as he'd appeared in my mind.

A short gnome male in overalls walked at his side, wispy white hair growing only above his ears. Instead of a weapon, he carried a toolbox, almost as much magic radiating from the contents as from anything else in this place.

With my recently lost toolbox coming to mind, I might have looked at it with wishful longing, but the four armed and armored warriors walking to either side of the gnome and elf drew my attention. They were from a mix of ancestries but all full-blooded magical beings, and they carried swords or axes instead of firearms. In addition, they had the powerful auras of mages and looked like badasses. Their eyes were glazed, and they wore magical bracelets, but that wouldn't diminish their fighting prowess.

Those four are members of the Assassins' Guild, Sarrlevi said telepathically.

Are they as deadly as you? I hoped not since they outnumbered us.

They would be challenging opponents one-on-one.

What about four-on-one? I asked, though I knew the answer. *Or two-on-one,* I added, though I didn't want to spring into battle with anyone who might be Sarrlevi's equal.

Challenging, he repeated. *Perhaps more concerning, I sense dragons now, the dragons from the Council. They are hurling tremendous amounts of power around.*

They've been distracting these guys, but we can't think of them as allies. As I watched the Caretaker, in particular, approach, I wished we could.

I certainly do not.

"I need you to quit dithering around, and turn it on." The Caretaker pointed the gnome toward the tower.

"*Now?*" the gnome asked in accented English.

As far as I could tell, none of them knew we were in the area. Thanks to the alarm we'd triggered, they had to know we were in the base, but, hopefully, they believed we were taking the scenic route and hadn't gotten this far.

Careful not to make a sound, I eased the flap of the grenade bag open.

"*Before* all the cursed dragons showed up at our door would have been better." The Caretaker shoved the gnome.

He acted more like a human—an asshole human—than an elf. Maybe he'd been on Earth a while, and humans had rubbed off on him.

"Hurry up, Yeenok. And you four." The Caretaker pointed at the assassins and then toward the open area where Sarrlevi and I stood. "That intruder alarm hasn't been going off as part of a test. Find whoever got in, and kill them."

The assassins didn't reply but fanned out and headed in our direction. We might be able to avoid them, staying far enough away that they couldn't see through our camouflaging magic, but we might not.

The ground shuddered in response to another explosion in the distance.

Even if we could have hidden, we dared not. We had to free Mom and find Dad before we ran out of time.

One of the assassins pointed a sword that emanated as much power as my hammer or Sarrlevi's blade and started swinging it back and forth in front of him like a metal detector. But it didn't start beeping and looking for coins. A ten-foot-long stream of flames shot from it, and I jumped, glad we hadn't been close.

Sarrlevi squeezed my shoulder before moving away. Yeah, we had better split up and try to get to the Caretaker. Or maybe the gnome? Whatever he was doing to the tower, we probably wanted to stop him.

Though I was reluctant to leave my mother, one of the assassins would walk right past her chamber in his search, so I crept toward the tower.

The gnome had gone to what looked like a junction box on one of the legs. Like everything else, it radiated magic, so I knew it was something much more significant. Choosing another leg to crouch behind, I pulled out a grenade. Water that must have been caught inside dribbled out into my hand. I winced. What were the odds that these would still work?

Afraid I would have to throw three to get one to work, I decided to pull out *all* of the grenades. I lined them up behind the tower leg, using it to hide them from the Caretaker and the gnome. The assassins were intent on looking for *us*.

I didn't know where Sarrlevi had gone, but I hoped he was creeping up on the Caretaker. The guy radiated magic, however, and not only from his aura. He might have armor under that suit or a device that created a barrier around him. I couldn't tell for certain, but a hunch told me he wasn't wandering around unprotected.

If you are here, girl, the Caretaker spoke telepathically, *and you didn't heed my warning, I'll deliver every punishment I promised and more.*

I wanted to snap back something defiant, but I could tell he didn't know where I was. He'd broadcasted those words far and wide, not directly to me.

Forcing myself to ignore him, I finished laying out the grenades. As I did so, I watched the gnome. It occurred to me that he probably knew how to operate the stasis chambers. How to turn *off* the stasis chambers and free those locked inside.

"They might be camouflaged." The Caretaker lifted the rifle, holding it in both hands with his index finger caressing the trigger. "Look slowly and carefully."

The elf's sleeves had shifted enough that I could tell he wore a clunky watch but not one of the control bracelets. Unlike everyone else we'd encountered, he was here voluntarily. Was he Varlat's right-hand man? Or in charge of maintaining the base until the organization needed it?

As I set down the last grenade, the roar of a dragon sounded in the distance, from somewhere beyond the bend. I grew aware of more noise emanating from that direction as well, the rumble of machinery accompanied by a constant *thwumping*.

Do you have a plan, Varlesh? I did my best to make my telepathic question pinpoint by envisioning his face and whispering the words, but the Caretaker's eyes narrowed, and he swung his rifle toward the tower. Not straight at me, but I worried he'd caught my words. Or caught *something*, anyway.

The elf is protected by a barrier, came Sarrlevi's soft reply. *I'm attempting to determine if I can break through it. I may only get one chance at him before the assassins spring at me.*

"Did you say camouflage?" The gnome opened his toolbox. "I have a device that deactivates camouflage."

Uh oh. I looked around for somewhere to hide—the leg of the tower wouldn't cover my whole body. But everything else was built into the walls of the vast open chamber, leaving few things to duck behind.

"Here it is." The gnome held up what reminded me of a large magical version of the Pop-It firecrackers that kids had thrown around when I'd been young. I was positive his doodad did more than snap when it hit the ground.

If you can't get the leader, I suggested telepathically to Sarrlevi when the Caretaker looked away, *maybe the gnome? He'll know how to work the stasis chambers.*

Not that we could do anything with them until we dealt with the assassins.

Squinting toward the tower again, the Caretaker pushed up his sleeve and pressed a button on the watch surface. A *thwump* of power pinged at my senses, flowing outward from the elf.

I was far enough away that I didn't feel its effects and couldn't tell what it did, but Sarrlevi sighed into my mind. *He used that device to amplify the power to his barrier. It also created a pulse that knocked me back. I think he knows I'm close.*

The Caretaker spun in what might have been Sarrlevi's direction and fired the rifle. As the shots rang out, I hefted my hammer, hoping Sorka could get through the elf's barrier, amplified or not.

When the magical bullets landed, striking the cement walls, they blew holes. *Large* holes.

The second I hurled Sorka, the gnome twisted the top of the large Pop-It and threw it at the ground. It flashed as a wave of power swept outward. Energy sizzled over me, and I knew my camouflaging magic had been knocked out even before the assassins looked toward the tower and pointed at me. And Sarrlevi. He was running from the Caretaker, diving and rolling to avoid shots being fired, and toward the gnome.

My hammer struck the Caretaker's barrier but didn't pierce it, bouncing off instead. I called for Sorka to return to me.

The gnome squawked, dropped his tools, and scurried back, but Sarrlevi reached him, sweeping him off his feet and pressing the gnome's back to his chest as he spun toward the Caretaker and the assassins. With one of his swords in hand, he held it to the gnome's throat, his meaning clear.

The Caretaker stopped firing but didn't lower his rifle as he gazed calmly at Sarrlevi.

Irritation emanated from Sorka, and she spat lightning unbidden as she flew back toward me. The vibrant branches of electricity wrapped around the Caretaker's barrier, trying to get through, and also shot toward the rock ceiling, the tower, and one of the assassins. But they were capable of creating barriers too, and they did so as they charged toward Sarrlevi and me.

Sorka landed back in my palm. Her lightning hadn't gotten through anyone's barrier.

With a growl, I grabbed two grenades and backed toward the wall so the assassins wouldn't be able to reach me from behind. Not that it mattered. With two running toward me and two toward Sarrlevi, I doubted I would have a chance against them.

Hoping to keep the assassins from reaching us, I threw one of the grenades at them. The Caretaker glanced at it, sneered, and flicked at it with a whip of power.

The grenade exploded in the air. Though the ground rocked, and the tower rattled, it didn't detonate close enough to the assassins to hurt them or even slow them down.

"Call off your men," Sarrlevi told the Caretaker, the gnome's feet dangling a foot above the ground as he struggled to escape, "or I'll kill your engineer."

I wasn't sure if it was a bluff or not, but the assassins kept coming.

The Caretaker shrugged. "Kill him, then."

I wanted to throw Sorka at him again, but I had to worry about the assassins. The one with the fire-spouting blade was heading toward Sarrlevi with a buddy, but the two angling toward me also had magical weapons. Of course they did. These were Sarrlevi's peers, not random thugs.

The two assassins ready to kill me stopped a few feet away from me and used their weapons to prod my barrier, assessing it, assessing *me*.

Sarrlevi, his own barrier around himself and the gnome, watched the Caretaker instead of the closer threats. "Are you certain his life means nothing to you? Was he not supposed to activate this tower for you? Do you have so many gnomish engineers that you can throw one away?"

"No," the gnome cried, reminding me of a goblin.

I almost felt bad about picking on him, but those were probably *his* stasis chambers. He'd imprisoned my mother, and he was helping these people try to start a war. There wasn't a control bracelet on his wrist either.

"He's been trying to activate the global scrambler for months," the Caretaker said as the assassins stabbed at my barrier.

Reflexively, I whipped Sorka up, in case they got through. The barrier held, but I sensed the power of their weapons and how hard Sorka had to work to keep them from piercing her defenses.

"If the gnome was a *useful* engineer," the Caretaker continued, "he would have gotten it working by now, and Earth wouldn't be infested with dragons."

Another roar came from beyond the bend. Irritation flashed in the Caretaker's eyes.

Sarrlevi tightened his grip, his blade cutting enough to produce a trickle of blood on the gnome's pale throat.

"Kill him, assassin," the Caretaker said, proving he knew who Sarrlevi was. Of course. Sarrlevi had intervened in the last dream vision he'd inflicted me with. "He means little to me, but I'll offer you another option."

One of my attacker's swords surged with power and slipped through my barrier. Cursing, I barely raised Sorka in time to deflect the stab. No triumph entered the assassin's glazed eyes. He merely adjusted his grip to try again.

I willed my own power into the barrier, and his next attack didn't get through. Nor did the slashes from the assassin on my other side, a muscular orc with an axe that looked like the blade was made from bone instead of metal. The energy required to help Sorka, however, drained me quickly. We couldn't keep this up for long.

If the Caretaker could detonate the grenades with a glance, I couldn't use them on him. What if I tried to blow up the tower? Or something else in here?

"What other option?" Sarrlevi glanced over at me, his eyes tense.

His two attackers were slashing and hacking at his barrier too, not caring that he gripped the gnome and they were as likely to strike him. But if the Caretaker was bartering with Sarrlevi at all, that had to mean the gnome mattered to him, didn't it? That he'd been bluffing and didn't want to see his engineer die?

The Caretaker pointed his rifle toward Sarrlevi's head but lowered one hand into a pocket and withdrew one of the magical bracelets. "Work for us. We pay well. These other assassins are being handsomely rewarded for their assistance."

"Sure they are," I said. "That's why you need the bracelets. Who *are* you, anyway? What do you care about this Earth plot?"

"I am the Caretaker. But we've spoken, so you already know this. Though you've demonstrated that you're obtuse and slow, so perhaps you forgot."

"That's not the name your parents gave you, dumbass."

The elf eyed me with irritation before turning his gaze back to Sarrlevi. "I am authorized to make deals."

More roars came from around the bend, along with a screech of pain. It sounded human. Or elven or dwarven, maybe. Hopefully not *half-elven*. Not Val.

Thanks to all the magic around us, I still couldn't sense much about what was going on in that direction.

The Caretaker smiled smugly, as if he knew exactly what was happening and that his side was gaining the upper hand. I hoped not.

"You have been assisting the half-dwarf female because she's entertaining in bed, I assume, but that's no reason to throw away your life," the Caretaker told Sarrlevi. "And trust that you are doing precisely that. If these assassins can't best you—and I doubt even you can keep away four—then our machines will take care of you once they drive off the dragons. And that *will* happen. The many defenses of this place ensure that we have the advantage."

Gunfire rang out, punctuating the sounds of the dragon battle, and a *boom* followed.

Val? I asked, trying to project my words to her, wherever she was. *Is that you firing? Are you in here?*

"Why do you want the half-dwarf dead?" Sarrlevi clenched his jaw as one of his attacker's blades almost got through his barrier. Like me, he wouldn't be able to hold them back indefinitely. "Isn't she what's keeping your kidnapped dwarf enchanter working?"

"She has been, yes. For many years, but now that she's *hunting* us—" the Caretaker shot me a sour look, "—she's too dangerous to keep alive. She kindly brought the hammer we've been looking for, so we have no more need for her."

"Screw you too," I muttered, then had to focus on parrying the axe. With a crushing blow, the orc forced it through Sorka's barrier.

Though I swept my hammer up in time, it struck the haft with joint-jarring force. My knees, weakened from all the energy I was using to keep the barrier intact, almost gave out.

Snarling, I gave up on the barrier and swung my hammer at his groin. His axe swept down with blazing speed, parrying my attack, the weapons clanging loudly.

"Join us, or my assassins will kill you." The Caretaker glanced at me as I parried another sword that poked through Sorka's quickly shredding barrier. It came in so quickly, I almost missed it. "She's as good as dead, so it hardly matters if you fight us or not."

The Caretaker tapped another button on his watch. The giant garage doors started opening.

Oh, wonderful. I'd been dying to see what was behind them.

26

As the roll-up doors opened, rumbles started up inside the dark bays, mingling with the continuing roars, clangs, and gunshots in the distance.

Try the rest of the explosives, Sarrlevi spoke into my mind. *We need to even the odds.*

Tell me about it.

Throw them at objects or the assassins instead of the elf.

I can't get to them. I grunted, forced to deflect an axe once again as it crushed through my barrier. *We need to do more, Sorka. What else have you got?*

She blazed silver-blue, funneling more of her power into the barrier, repairing the holes, but her haft heated in my hands, growing warm from her efforts. The glazed-eyed but tireless assassins kept swinging. I glanced at the grenades lined up by the tower leg, but the fight had moved me away from them. Even if I'd had a free hand, I couldn't grab one.

"You must make your decision soon, assassin." The Caretaker gestured toward the open garage doors, though, other than the rumbling noise, nothing had come out yet. That didn't keep me from sensing the magic inside. It reminded me of the enchanted helicopters.

A clang came from Sarrlevi's battle as he also had to deflect a blade that had made it through his barrier. Since he held the gnome, that put him at a disadvantage. "I'm listening."

He spoke calmly, but I could hear the strain in his voice. He glanced over at me again; his face was unreadable.

I trusted he wasn't contemplating the elf's offer but only trying to buy time. Had I not been there and in danger, he might have simply dropped the gnome and battled the two assassins. Maybe. With the Caretaker holding a rifle on him, a rifle loaded with magical bullets, he might have deemed the odds against him too great.

In the forest, he had trees for cover, but in here, he was out in the open. We both were.

"Put down the gnome, and come put this on." The Caretaker held up one of his odious control bracelets. "I don't quite trust you to turn sides."

"I don't quite trust *you* not to make me a permanent minion with that thing," Sarrlevi said. "What are you offering as payment? I don't need money, but if you could convince the dragons to leave me be, perhaps I would be interested."

"I could ensure the *dragons*, at least the Dragon Council dragons, would never be a problem for you again. Of course, you would have to stay here on Earth once it's removed from the portal network."

Sarrlevi squinted at him. "Removed? How are you going to manage that?"

The Caretaker jerked his chin toward the tower.

"Alter the magnetic field around the planet to keep magical travelers from getting through it. The gnome engineer has already done the hard work and is merely refining the activation system."

"You still need me to finish it," the gnome blurted, his fingers tight around Sarrlevi's arm as his feet continued to dangle. "Get this elf off me."

More gunfire and roars sounded in the distance. The Caretaker peered in that direction, head tilted as if he were listening. Or maybe someone was speaking telepathically to him? Varlat?

He nodded to himself and tapped another button on his watch. Sarrlevi looked at me, our gazes meeting briefly. He didn't widen his eyes or nod or do anything the Caretaker might pick up on, only whispering, *Be ready,* into my mind.

The bone axe pierced Sorka's barrier and would have cleaved my skull in half if I hadn't been ready. I whipped up my hammer, crying, "*Hyrek!*" and caught the head on my haft. As our weapons met and stuck, the assassin tried to force me to my knees.

Snarling, I fought back. Lightning crackled around me, and a branch streaked along the assassin's axe and toward his face. Though he blinked in surprise, his magic protected him. Maybe it was in vain, but I kicked him in the gut while his arms were overhead. This time, he was distracted and didn't evade my attack, but his armor took the brunt of the blow. I only succeeded in knocking him back a step, our weapons unlocking.

Trust me, I'm ready, I told Sarrlevi, though my focus had to remain on my assailants.

The rumbling grew louder, and movement stirred in the open bays. Huge armored tanks on treads rolled into view.

The sword-wielding assassin swung at my face, my barrier again faltering. I parried while giving ground. If I let the assassins back me toward the tower leg, toward the grenades, maybe I could find an opportunity to grab them.

But out of the corner of my eye, I glimpsed the grenades lifting from the ground. Sarrlevi's doing? Or the Caretaker's? Either way, they floated over my head and toward their confrontation. Then they disappeared, as if shifted into another dimension.

Hell. I had nothing else left except Sorka.

We must free Rodarska, she told me. *She can help. She has the power to deal with the enchanted artifacts.*

I'm sure she does, but— I broke off as I had to defend against a flurry of sword strikes that shredded our barrier completely. *Sorka. I need more help against these guys.*

"You *will* change sides, assassin." The Caretaker waved toward the tanks. Most had turned and were heading toward the other battle, but one rumbled toward Sarrlevi, pointing its huge gun at his back. "Or you will die."

I had no doubt the enchanted tanks fired magical ammunition and worried Sarrlevi's barrier couldn't withstand it. These machines had been designed to give even dragons trouble.

"You're going to fire tanks in your own base, you idiot?" I yelled.

The Caretaker tapped his watch again. Before the tank could fire, or whatever he was commanding it to do, a grenade appeared and clanked down on top of it. Another hit the ground between Sarrlevi and the Caretaker. They hadn't disappeared into another dimension, merely been camouflaged.

As the explosives blew, Sarrlevi thrust the gnome toward one of his attackers, then dove to the side and rolled away. Thunderous booms rocked the ground under me, hurling me away from my attackers.

A tremendous *thwump* sounded. The tank firing?

My back struck one of the metal legs, knocking the air out of me. Another boom rocked the entire place, and the tower rattled ominously above me.

Smoke filled the air around Sarrlevi, the other assassins, and the Caretaker. I lost sight of them but not the two closer assassins. Unfazed by the explosives, they charged at me.

"*Hyrek,*" I called again as I scrambled to my feet, the ground still shuddering.

Lightning sprang from Sorka, splitting to form two branches

to strike each assassin in the chest. Their barriers still protected them, but fury about the situation filled me, and I summoned every last bit of energy in my body. I willed it into Sorka, needing her lightning to get through their defenses and stop them.

Gunshots rang out—the Caretaker firing his magical rifle.

Weapons clanged. That had to be Sarrlevi battling the assassins. But the clangs stopped abruptly, and he grunted in pain. I couldn't see their confrontation through the smoke, and fear clenched me.

Fueled by my fury and power, Sorka's lightning knocked my two attackers back. One *flew* back, as if a battering ram had struck him.

"Good girl," I crooned to my hammer.

I glanced toward the tower leg in case any grenades remained, but they'd all floated away.

The tank fired again. Who or what its shell hit, I couldn't see, but it flashed as it exploded, half-blinding me. Pieces of shrapnel —or was that cement from the floor?—flew and pelted the walls and the tower. One cracked off a metal leg beside me, ricocheted, and struck one of the assassins.

His defenses were down, and it gouged a bloody hole in his cheek. Good.

Since I had a moment with nobody attacking me, I ran back toward the stasis chambers. Sorka was right. We had to get my mother out. Maybe she could control those tanks—and destroy the Caretaker's button-filled watch.

With smoke filling my nostrils and making my eyes water, I flattened my hand to the panel beside her alcove, though I didn't know what to do to it any more now than I had earlier. And I didn't have much time.

Though another explosion rocked the base—that had been a magical grenade, not the tank's ammunition—the assassins who'd been attacking me knew where I'd gone. Any second, they would run over. I was surprised they hadn't already.

I sensed the gnome crawling away from Sarrlevi's battle and reached out to him. Trying to fill my telepathic voice with magical coercion, I said, *Come free Princess Rodarska if you want to survive this mess and get out of here.*

Nobody had taught me how to magically coerce people, but he crawled a few feet in my direction before halting.

The gunshots stopped, at least the ones in our area. The other battle continued to rage. The dragon roars paused, and the *thwumps* of tanks firing came from around the bend.

Use me to bash the panel, Sorka said. *It will not kill her. She is strong.*

Are you sure?

Sorka hesitated. *No. If the chamber is broken, it may leave her in that frozen state. Or she may die because she's not properly regenerated.*

Damn it. I doubted Sorka knew how the stasis-chamber technology—the *magic*—worked any more than I did.

One of the assassins that had been attacking me asked a question in Orcish. The smoke was clearing, but I still couldn't see much. My senses told me that Sarrlevi wasn't moving, and unease crept into me. The two assassins he'd been battling weren't moving either. When I squinted through the haze, I could make out their bodies on the ground.

The tank loomed out of the smoke behind them, its gun glowing red and shifting left and right. Was it tracking body heat? Or magic? Like those missiles the helicopter had blasted at us?

As the smoke cleared further, I could verify with my eyes that Sarrlevi wasn't moving.

The fear I'd felt before tripled, for the Caretaker stepped into view to stand above Sarrlevi, his rifle still in hand.

"*No!*" I threw Sorka reflexively, without thinking.

The Caretaker looked toward me but didn't duck or even

flinch, convinced his barrier would protect him. And it did. Sorka halted two feet away and bounced off.

I swore. The Caretaker barked an order in another language, and the two remaining assassins charged toward me. Snarling in frustration, I stepped away from the panel and lifted my hand, calling Sorka back to me.

Surprisingly, the Caretaker didn't shoot Sarrlevi. Instead, he bent over him.

Now on his feet, the gnome tottered toward the stasis chambers on unsteady legs.

Free her, I tried to order him as Sorka sailed over the assassins' heads and landed in my hand. Not a second too soon, because I had to defend myself.

Fury radiated from Sorka, and she didn't raise our barrier. Was she too depleted to do so?

Just as I had the thought, tremendous energy poured from her. Silver-blue light flared from the hammer as white lightning shot forth, attacking the assassins. I swung the hammer, almost feeling compelled to, and realized she was choosing offense over defense this time. We had to get rid of these guys.

And we did. They'd been injured, I soon saw, and weren't fighting as well as before. Blood ran from both their faces, and also from the neck of one, a piece of shrapnel embedded there.

Sorka's powerful lightning struck that assassin, piercing his defenses. He jerked, dropping his sword, and I kicked him in the chest to knock him away. He dropped to his knees, eyes more *dazed* than glazed now, and grabbed his neck.

The gnome wobbled closer, but he also gave our battle a wide berth. Thinking he wanted to reach the panel, I made room as I fought the remaining assassin. But he continued past. He was trying to *escape,* not help.

My temper flared again, and I knocked the axeman's weapon aside and slammed Sorka into his chest. His armor couldn't block her fury, which was equal to mine, and she again flared with power, sending him backward. His axe flew from his hands, skidding toward Sarrlevi and the Caretaker.

Sarrlevi wasn't flat on the ground anymore, and that gave me hope, but he wasn't attacking either. Strangely, he stood with his chin down, his swords drooping at his sides, the Caretaker at ease in front of him. What the—

Sarrlevi's wrist glowed. No, the glow came from a new *bracelet* on his wrist. I gaped in horror.

The Caretaker stepped back and pointed at me. "Kill her, assassin, and bring me the hammer. It's the last thing we need, the key to the power generators."

Sarrlevi's chin lifted, and through the smoke and over the rubble-strewn ground, his eyes met mine. His *glazed* eyes.

I shook my head in denial as he stalked toward me, his swords raising for battle.

Sorka rested in my grip, still furious and spitting lightning, but I couldn't lift the hammer to attack Sarrlevi.

As the Caretaker watched smugly, I realized I would have to. I had no choice.

27

THE GOOD NEWS WAS THAT THE REMAINING TWO ASSASSINS BACKED off. The Caretaker called for them to go help with the other battle, where booms continued to thunder as tanks fired and dragons roared.

The bad news was that Sarrlevi was now under the spell of his new control bracelet, the same as all the other minions here. And the Caretaker remained to watch the battle, a triumphant smile on his lips.

I wanted to throw my hammer at his smug face, but Sarrlevi was almost upon me, and I dared not give up my weapon.

Defense or offense? Sorka asked.

Meaning did I want a barrier or did I want more power funneled into attacking *Sarrlevi's* barrier. His powerful magical aura crackled about him, promising that his defenses were up. Even if I could somehow get past his two deadly and experienced blades, I couldn't pierce his barrier.

Defense. I raised the hammer. *We can't kill him.*

If you don't kill him, he will kill you.

No, he won't. I wanted that to be true and searched Sarrlevi's eyes, hoping for a wink, for some indication that he was on my side. *Varlesh? Fight that thing. The Caretaker is alone now. You can go kick his ass.*

Granted, the elf still had his magical rifle, and it was pointed as much at Sarrlevi as me, but I'd seen Sarrlevi use his power to parry bullets. Without the other assassins there to distract him, he ought to be able to deal with the Caretaker.

Unfortunately, Sarrlevi didn't respond or slow his approach. His eyes still glazed, he sprang for me, both blades coming toward my head.

Knowing I could only swing my hammer fast enough to parry one sword, I ducked and skittered back. Fortunately, Sorka's power wrapped around me, keeping Sarrlevi's weapons from reaching me. But *his* power surged and tore at hers. I thought she might be a match for him—it didn't seem like his sentient sword was helping him—but Sarrlevi ripped Sorka's barrier to pieces.

All I could do was back farther, willing Sorka to help me deflect his blows.

Guide my hands, please, I told her and tried to focus on the bracelet on his wrist.

Somehow, I had to break the enchantment, but I well remembered from Sorka's vision that forcibly removing the bracelet might kill the wearer. I'd have to alter it, not simply destroy it.

Focusing on enchanting was hard with swords whizzing toward my chest and clangs ringing out next to my ears. To make matters worse, the Caretaker came over and shadowed us, watching eagerly, like he had money on the fight and couldn't *wait* to see me slain.

Nothing like an audience for one's death.

With what concentration I could spare, I tried to use my power on Sarrlevi's bracelet, groping for a way to alter it. But its magic was too strong, the enchantments too sophisticated. In Sorka's visions, only my mother had possessed the power, once she was free from her prison, to remove the bracelets.

But Sarrlevi wasn't giving me the opportunity to further study her prison. And the gnome had disappeared, running back the way we'd come.

Sweat dripped into my eyes. Worse, it moistened my palms, threatening my grip on the hammer. Sarrlevi's powerful blows rattled my joints even when I parried them. And he was unrelenting. His swords slashed toward me so quickly that I never could have blocked them on my own. Only Sorka was keeping me alive now, her magical power guiding my hands and feet. Even with her assistance, I couldn't last long. Tired from the first battle, I was already panting, my lungs and muscles burning.

The cursed Caretaker cheered, egging Sarrlevi on. Didn't the bastard have another battle to worry about?

One of Sarrlevi's blades slipped past my hammer, clipping the top of my ear. Hot blood ran down the side of my face.

"Damn it, Sarrlevi," I snarled, taking a swing even though he hadn't paused in his attacks, and I risked opening myself to more wounds. "Why can't you keep bad guys from taking control of you?"

Barothla hadn't been in *control* of him, but it had been just as bad. No, I decided, as he swung for my neck. This was worse. This was a cold and calculating—and deadly—Sarrlevi. Not a crazy Sarrlevi.

Either way, I hated having him as an enemy instead of an ally, and frustration made me swing far harder than was wise toward his chest. He used a sword to deflect my blow, batting it aside as if it were weaker than a mosquito.

A gust of his power knocked into me, and I tottered off balance. Though I was quick to recover, he darted in and swept his leg toward mine. I jumped and avoided the sweep, but more power crashed into me.

Though I could sense Sorka trying to remake my barrier, to protect me, there wasn't enough time. Sarrlevi's power flattened me to the ground, and he followed me down. I kicked upward to delay him and tried to roll free, but he was too quick. He pinned me, one of his swords coming to my throat as he grabbed the haft of my hammer.

Let go, he whispered into my mind as I tightened my grip to resist, tried to summon the power to thrust him away from me.

The Caretaker, his legs scant feet away, barked, "Yes! Kill her, and give it to me."

Trust me, Sarrlevi added. *Let go.*

The bracelet on Sarrlevi's wrist flared, but his eyes weren't glazed. I let go of my hammer.

He jerked his sword, as if to cut my throat, but the blade didn't touch my skin. When he lifted the hammer, the Caretaker stepped in to grab it. But Sarrlevi lunged up, his sentient sword, the one that hadn't used any magic when he battled me, flaring with intense power. When he thrust it at the Caretaker, it channeled great energy into piercing his barrier, and it succeeded. Sarrlevi drove the blade straight through and into his heart.

Though it was a mortal blow, Sarrlevi wasn't finished. He pulled his sword out and, as the Caretaker toppled, swept it horizontally and decapitated the elf.

I slumped back with relief, not caring when I cracked my head on the hard cement. Sarrlevi wasn't an enemy. He was on my side.

"I apologize for the cut," he whispered, dropping to one knee and handing the hammer back to me.

Though exhausted, I sat up. Letting the hammer fall into my lap, I wrapped my arms around Sarrlevi. His face was as sweaty as mine as our cheeks pressed together.

"Did I manage to deactivate the bracelet," I asked, "or were you acting the whole time?"

"The spell never fully took hold. I was acting, as you say, in the hope that the elf would send some of his men away, or at least that armored conveyance, if he believed he had me." Sarrlevi leaned back, though I didn't release him fully, and touched his hip.

Before, I hadn't seen it, but his trousers were shredded there, his skin bloody and charred. From one of the rounds exploding?

Not dwelling on the wound, Sarrlevi removed the bracelet. It was loose, more like a chain than a metal cuff, and it slid over his hand and clunked onto the ground. Smiling slightly, he pushed up his sleeves and showed bands of braided green moss around his wrists.

"Are those made from the moss you pulled off the tree out there?" I realized they emanated faint magic. They hadn't come off the tree that way. "Did you make them?"

"Yes. Moss is a known insulator against all types of magic except elven, and the bracelets are dwarven magic."

"Known to elves maybe."

"Yes. I was concerned because the Caretaker *was* an elf, but the smoke and my other magical items must have kept him from noticing anything significant about these." Sarrlevi lowered his sleeves. "I believed he might try to make minions of both of us and thought about making cuffs for you as well, but I did not know if you would wear them." His brows rose. "You haven't been that interested in moss."

"That was when I thought you wanted to wash your armpits with it. If I'd known it could repel artifacts bad guys try to stick on you, I would have thought it was amazing."

"I wasn't sure if my magic would be sufficient to repel those bracelets, given who made them."

My gaze shifted to my mother, still frozen in her stasis chamber, and I pushed myself to my feet. "We have to get her out of there." The battle continued to rage beyond our view. "And help Val and the others. I assume she's in that mess."

"I am not certain if she is there, but I sense numerous dragons from the Council. Battling minions but mostly the magical mechanical constructs."

"Did the gnome get away entirely?" I peered back into the tunnel we'd come from. "Or can you sense him?"

"Not any longer. You'll have to figure out how to release your mother."

"Right," I muttered, though I doubted I would be less flummoxed about how to do that now than before.

As I stepped up and placed my hand on the panel again, Sarrlevi spun toward movement beyond the roll-up doors. Two male figures ran into view, and I tensed, my senses noting the significant aura of the one on the right. It was the half-dragon guy. Starblade. How had he found this place? And why did he keep showing up?

Distracted by him, I almost didn't notice the second man running beside him, a mundane human with no detectable aura. A mundane human that I knew.

I stared in shock. My father.

I hadn't seen him in thirty years, having only briefly heard his voice in the military prison, and his hair had turned gray, but I recognized his face. He remained surprisingly fit and muscular, appearing much as the soldier he'd once been.

"Dad?" I whispered.

Sarrlevi, who crouched with his swords raised and his focus on Starblade, glanced at me. "That is your father?"

Nodding, I called louder, "Dad?"

Maybe I shouldn't have shouted, but it wasn't as if we hadn't already made a ton of noise back here. So far, those in the dragon battle had been far too busy to come check on the goings-on. Hopefully, that would continue to be true.

"Mataalii?" my father called, his dark eyes filling with relief as he kept running. He must have escaped from whatever prison the Caretaker had kept him in. Maybe one of the explosions had knocked down a wall, this time in his favor. Somewhere along the way, he'd found weapons and carried a dagger and pistol.

The half-dragon, clad in the same clothes and armor he'd worn when we'd freed him on Dun Kroth, had acquired an axe. A familiar axe with a magical blade made from bone. I assumed that meant the orc assassin hadn't made it to join the other battle.

"Yes, it's me." My voice cracked with emotion as he came closer, and I struggled to hold myself together. "Mom is in here." I pointed to the alcove, though he probably already knew. He had been a prisoner here for weeks. Of course, the bad guys might have rudely refused to give him a tour and let him see her.

My father nodded and glanced at the stasis chamber but rushed forward and crushed me in a hug. I returned it gratefully, relieved we'd finally found each other. Back in the prison, we'd been so close, only to be cheated of even seeing each other. A part of me wanted to cry, to give my emotions a release, but we weren't done yet. Knowing that didn't keep a few tears from leaking down my cheeks.

"Mataalii," Dad whispered, holding me tight.

Starblade slowed to a stop, calmly asking Sarrlevi something in Elven.

Sarrlevi responded, then lowered his swords and gestured toward the panel.

"Step back," he told my father and me. "Starblade is here to free your mother."

Dad nodded, as if he already knew, and released me so we could step aside. He wiped tears from his own cheeks.

"He's what?" Why was I the only one here confused?

Maybe I shouldn't have been, since he'd freed Sarrlevi's mother back on Dun Kroth, but he couldn't have come all the way to Earth to free my parents. How could he have even known about all this?

Starblade lifted his chin, holding my gaze for a long moment before stepping up to the panel. Then I remembered the crawling under my skull back on Dun Kroth. He had read my mind in that laboratory, and I *had* been thinking about all the people I needed saved from enemy clutches.

I still didn't understand why he would have bothered and, even as magic flowed from the half-dragon's fingers and into the panel, I looked to Sarrlevi, as if he might know more.

"He said he was indebted to you for freeing him on Dun Kroth," Sarrlevi said, "and that he is not someone who likes to owe anyone favors."

"So he came all the way to *Earth* to help me?" I looked at my father.

"He blew open the metal cell door that was keeping me a prisoner. I wasn't important enough—or dangerous enough—to warrant the magical treatment." Dad's mouth twisted as he watched Mom in the stasis chamber, her eyes still closed.

The green light faded, and a warm red light beamed from the walls inside. A soft beeping that reminded me of a heartbeat started up.

The barrier keeping Mom trapped faded, and, as the red light continued to bathe her—to *thaw* her?—Starblade stepped back. He nodded to my father and me, as if to say he was done.

"Wait, can you free her friends too?" I pointed at the chamber that Artie and Hennehok shared, then realized he wouldn't understand and asked the question telepathically.

His eyes narrowed, as if I'd presumed too much, and I remembered that King Ironhelm and the dwarves were afraid of Starblade. Just because he felt indebted to me for freeing him didn't mean he was a good person or on our side. Still, he stepped past me to the panel of their stasis chamber and rested his palm on it.

My father didn't notice. His eyes remained locked on Mom. After three decades apart, three decades that he'd spent in jail, he still cared for her. I could tell. I hoped she wouldn't see him as an old man and her love for him wouldn't have faded over the years. I didn't even know how many of those years she'd been awake. Enough to make numerous enchanted items, but it was possible she had also missed decades.

In the other stasis chamber, the light turned from green to red, and the barrier disappeared. Starblade stepped back, said something to Sarrlevi, and formed a portal.

That surprised me, since I would have expected the magic embedded in this place to squelch the possibility of doing that, just as it had in the Dun Kroth laboratory. Maybe, thanks to the ongoing battle, the facility had taken enough damage that there were cracks in its magical defenses.

Thank you for your help, I told Starblade, though he'd yet to speak to me, telepathically or otherwise, and he didn't acknowledge me now.

"Before he goes, can you tell him that the elves and dwarves aren't at war anymore?" I asked Sarrlevi, "and that it would be great if he *didn't* harass anyone on Dun Kroth?"

Before Sarrlevi could say a word, Starblade leaped through the portal. I grimaced, afraid we hadn't seen the last of him. As grateful as I was for the help, I worried he might be a problem in the future.

Oh, well. So be it. I had my father back, thanks to him, and I was about to have my mother too.

No sooner had I had the thought than her eyelids fluttered open. Dad lifted an arm and stepped toward her.

Mom started to smile, wonder in her green eyes, but she saw past his shoulder to Sarrlevi and cried out in alarm.

Shit. I'd forgotten that she would know exactly who he was— and fear him.

Or maybe *hate* him. There was no fear in her eyes as she lifted her arms and sent a powerful blast of magic straight at Sarrlevi.

28

Mom's blast of magic caught me by surprise, but Sarrlevi must have expected her to recognize him, because he was ready. His barrier took the brunt of it, but it wavered and wilted under her great power. He stepped back, reflexively bringing his swords up.

"No," I blurted and lunged to put myself between them. I didn't *think* Sarrlevi would hurt her, but if his defenses faltered, he might feel forced to attack.

Even as I sprang, I realized how stupid my action was and commanded Sorka to wrap her barrier around me once more. She did, but it also wavered under Mom's power.

Fortunately, when Mom saw me in the way, she stopped the attack.

"*Nika?*" she whispered, a word—a nickname—I hadn't heard in thirty years. Dwarven for *little girl* or *my girl.*

She recognized me. I hadn't been sure she would. *She* looked nearly the same, but I had changed a lot.

Then I remembered the televisions and that her captors had

been showing me to her, using me to gain her compliance. And promising her I would only live as long as she cooperated?

"Hi, Mom. Good to see you." What an inane thing to say, but she was still tense and poised to attack, her gaze shifting from Sarrlevi to me and back. Though I longed to hug her, I waved the hammer, fresh booms and gunfire from the battle reminding me that the reunion would have to wait. "We need to get out of here."

Mom shook her head. "Not with that one." She pointed past me to Sarrlevi, who'd lowered his swords again, but he hadn't sheathed them. He watched her warily. "Do not stand with your back to him. My sister—"

"Is dead." I almost added that Sarrlevi had done it, thinking to prove that he was on our side now, but learning that he'd killed her sister might not do anything to warm Mom's feelings toward him. "It's a long story, but Sarrlevi is working with us now. He's not a danger to me or you."

"Not if she can rip down my defenses like a hurricane tearing into a coastal forest," Sarrlevi murmured.

"You should have gotten more moss to make a shield," I murmured back.

"Undoubtedly."

"Roxy," Dad whispered, stirring and stepping forward. He said something in Dwarven, a language that he, the former Army linguist, knew much better than I.

"Malosi." Mom swallowed and gripped his hand, though she couldn't take her gaze from Sarrlevi.

I'd done my best to block her view of him, but that was hard when he was a foot taller.

A groan came from the other stasis chamber—Hennehok and Artie waking up. Would they help convince Mom that Sarrlevi wasn't a threat? Or back up her beliefs about him? They hadn't been there when he'd killed Barothla, nor did they know the full story of his mother and the extortion.

Sarrlevi rested a hand on my shoulder. "I will go help with the battle."

I started to object, but wouldn't it be easier to get Mom and Dad moving in the right direction if she wasn't plotting ways to get at Sarrlevi? "All right."

"You may wish to take your parents and allies out the back way," he added as he released me and wrapped his camouflaging magic around himself.

"I need to check on Val." I hesitated. "*You* could go out the back way." As much as I appreciated Sarrlevi's assistance, this wasn't his battle. He'd helped me find my parents. I couldn't ask for more from him. What did he care about Earth?

You have forgotten about the trees?

The fused trees? I smiled. *No.*

Excellent. Sarrlevi's telepathic tone turned dry when he added, *I apparently also need to show the dragons that I am an ally, or at least not a threat to them.*

That sounds like a good way to get yourself killed.

I'll endeavor to stay alive.

You'd better. My cheese supply is running low. I would be distraught if you didn't survive and couldn't bring me more.

And here I thought you would miss me warming your bed more than me delivering cheese.

Losing those things would be equally distressing.

Mom finished her exchange with Dad, then hesitantly stepped toward me, though she glanced about at the same time. Reassuring herself that Sarrlevi hadn't remained nearby after camouflaging himself?

"He's going to help with the battle." I waved toward the continuing noise, but by then, Mom was reaching for me, and I stepped into her hug.

"*Nika,* you are so tall." She laughed and smashed her face against my shoulder.

"Oh, yeah. I tower over the world." I returned the hug fiercely, her frizzy hair brushing my cheek. Tears crept into my eyes again, and I wiped them with the back of my hand, almost clunking myself on the head with Sorka.

"You might tower over the *dwarf* world." Dad stepped close enough to rest a hand on my shoulder, though he was careful not to interrupt Mom's embrace.

"I'm only slightly above average there too."

"You've been?" Did he sound *wistful*? It was hard to imagine someone with fully human blood craving tunnels that never saw sunlight. Maybe he was curious about the world and the people of the language he'd learned.

"Yeah," I said. "It's okay. King Ironhelm is decent. He misses you, Mom."

"I'm glad he's still alive and that my sister didn't..." She pulled back enough to look in my eyes. "You said Barothla is dead?"

"Yes. I'll tell you all about it later. And Penina and Grandma and Grandpa all miss *you*, Dad. Penina has two kids now, Josh and Jessie. I'll tell you about that too. We'd better—"

Another explosion rocked the base, and the ground shook, the tower rattling again. Even if the underground facility had been built to withstand a war, I was amazed the whole place hadn't caved in yet.

"Where is that cursed dragon?" came Hennehok's voice from the other stasis chamber. He limped out, a dazed-looking Artie coming after him. Neither had weapons and, with abrasions and bruises, they both looked like they'd lost a battle before being captured. "He was supposed to nobly lead our enemies off so we could get away."

Matti? Val spoke into my mind. *The dragons are doing their best to bring this place down. We haven't been able to gain the upper hand against all these magical machines, and destroying the facility around them is their new plan. If you're still back there, you might want to get out.*

We're coming. Thanks.

"We need to go now." I wiped my eyes again and stepped out of the hug to point toward the battle noise. "Once we handle that and get out of here, we can meet at my place and get all caught up."

"Are you sure we want to go that way?" Dad asked dubiously as Artie and Hennehok, realizing they'd been imprisoned next to their princess, hurried to Mom and bowed and then hugged her.

I almost said that Sarrlevi had gone toward the battle and I needed to help him—and Val as well—but the others didn't need to go. Maybe it would be better to send everyone else out the back. But if Mom could do something to stop the creations she'd enchanted, the dragons might not *have* to destroy the base. Not that I had fond feelings about it, but there were other people yet in the stasis chambers, and I doubted the minions under the spells of the control bracelets had volunteered for this hell.

"My friends are out there and need help," I replied to Dad. "And we need to make sure this scheme can't be enacted." I waved toward the tower and also that pipe funneling magical crystals into the depths of the Earth. "Our world is in danger."

Mom was the one to nod. "Yes. And I am partially responsible." She noticed the beheaded Caretaker on the floor and curled her lip. "I will help. Come."

She strode past me, taking the lead.

I hurried to match her pace and lifted Sorka. "Do you want your hammer back?"

Silver-blue light flared from Sorka as she emanated contentment. I tried not to feel a twinge of sadness and maybe even envy that the hammer preferred my mother to me, but it was a silly emotion. I'd always known it was her hammer and that I would have to return it when I found her. One day, maybe Mom would teach me how to make another one.

"You keep it for now," Mom said. "I have my magic."

"But you're an enchanter, right? Not a warrior?" I glanced back at Hennehok and Artie, who'd both suggested that, though Mom had almost flattened Sarrlevi with her power.

"She does all right," Dad said fondly. He'd caught up and was walking on Mom's other side.

"An enchanter may be what's needed." Mom smiled tightly, though sadness shadowed her eyes. And regret? For helping to make the creations now being used on people?

I promised myself I would be there for her if she wanted to talk about it later.

A sustained crash came from the battle—a rockfall?—and someone screamed in pain.

Mom broke into a jog. Hammer in hand, I hurried to stick with her. I wouldn't let her out of my sight again.

29

Even at a run, it took longer than I expected to reach the battle. I huffed and panted as we pounded over the shaking ground, and I was glad I had longer legs than the dwarves, or, after all the earlier fighting, I would have struggled to keep up. Dad ran beside Mom, offering support if she needed it, and he watched out for me as well, though I had to be a stranger to him after so many years.

It didn't matter, his eyes said. He would still watch out for me. The feeling of warmth and success of having brought my family back together gave me the energy to keep going. I couldn't wait for this all to be over so we could do something normal, like sitting down for barbecue in the backyard.

The vast cement-walled passageway went on and on, curving around bends more than once. The thrumming of machinery and chopping of helicopter blades grew more noticeable, underlying the roars. The floor slanted downward, with the ceiling soaring even higher before the great underground battlefield came into view.

Even though I'd known what to expect, I stumbled and gaped

at the sight of dragons and helicopters flying through smoky air that smelled of warped metal and burning hair—or scales? Wind generated by the chopper blades whipped at my hair and clothes, and, now that we were close, their noise was thunderous.

As the combatants twisted and dove, they threw magic and magical weapons at each other. Several helicopters had crashed before we arrived and lay as twisted wreckage on the cement floor, but more than one dragon was down too. One was slumped and groaning against a nearby wall, his wing crooked in a manner that had to mean it was broken. Xilneth?

I'd expected to find him in a stasis chamber. A magical collar around his neck suggested he'd been a prisoner of some sort though. Armored dwarves, elves, orcs, trolls, and other minions bound by bracelets were out on the floor, some shooting bows or rifles, but their weapons didn't appear to bother the dragons.

A flash of silver drew my eye. Sindari. Val's tiger companion bowled over a troll that had been aiming at one of the dragons.

I wanted to yell at the minions that their masters were dead, that they were free. I didn't know if that was entirely true. The *Caretaker* was dead, but we'd seen no sign of the founders of the organization. Not that I'd expected billionaires to be hanging out here.

Great *thwumps* sounded over the noise of the helicopter blades as guns fired. In addition to the aircraft, all the tanks had arrived and rolled about amid the carnage. A few had been destroyed, but many resisted the fire and magic the dragons cast at them.

Even as we watched, a black-scaled dragon—was that the queen?—dove for one of the tanks with her talons outstretched, her maw open wide. She looked like she would tear the thing to pieces, but the tank glowed with power, *dwarven* power, and Mom winced beside me. Yes, those were her creations. At the least, the enchantments on them were her doing.

A round fired at the queen, exploding as it hit a barrier

protecting her. Fire and smoke filled the air, but she flew through it, landing on the tank and trying to tear it to pieces with her talons. Even with her tremendous power, she struggled to do more than scratch it.

"The tanks are even tougher than the helicopters," I whispered in amazement.

"Do we attack them?" Hennehok called over the noise, raising his bare fists with uncertainty. He and Artie had no weapons, certainly nothing that could damage the tanks or the helicopters. "Do we want the dragons to win?"

They both looked at me.

"I think so?" I couldn't make it a statement instead of a question. The dragons, the queen included, had told me so little, but they'd mentioned wanting to stop this plan, and *I* sure as hell wanted to stop it. When I spotted Zavryd flying near the cavern entrance, Val on his back as they attacked a helicopter, I nodded with more certainty. "Yes. We want them to win and put an end to this place."

"Damn straight, we do." Dad strode forward, his purloined dagger and pistol in hand.

But Mom reached out and stopped him. "This is for me to do. Now that my family is with me and they can no longer hurt you." She lifted a hand toward me. "Lend me Sorka, please, *Nika*. I may need her strength for this."

As I held the hammer out, I was about to offer *my* strength too, as meager as it might be compared to hers, when one of the dragons that had been on the ground sprang to its feet. *His* feet. It was Varlat, the one behind so much of this.

He appeared injured but enraged and leaped at the queen. She had managed to tear a piece off the tank and had her jaws around the gun, crushing it and preventing it from firing again. She must have dismissed Varlat as dead or too injured to worry about for she didn't see him coming.

Something dropped from a helicopter flying overhead. No, not something—*someone*. Sarrlevi.

The helicopter, its pilot disabled, careened toward one of the cement walls as Sarrlevi dropped onto Varlat's neck. He slashed with his blades, sinking them between scales and drawing blood.

Instead of snapping at the queen, Varlat crashed into the side of the tank. Sarrlevi ran up his neck to the top of his head and drove his swords downward, puncturing flesh and skull.

The queen screeched in alarm and sprang into the air, flapping away before she realized what had happened. Sarrlevi was helping her. I sure hoped she understood that.

Eyes closed, Mom lifted her arms, Sorka now in her grip. The hammer flared silver-blue, and *Mom* even glowed, almost like an angel as she radiated power. It flowed from her and out into the chamber, branching dozens of times and heading toward the tanks and helicopters that hadn't yet been destroyed.

When we'd first entered the subterranean battleground, nobody had noticed us in the back. Now, the dragons, the minions, and even some of the tanks rotated toward us. I didn't think there was anyone in the tanks, and only magic controlled them, but who knew?

Sweat dripped down the side of Mom's face as she continued to employ her power. I could sense the great magic flowing from her, but it was too complicated for me to parse it, too many tendrils woven together that were like nothing I'd yet seen. I could only assume she was trying to reverse all of her enchantments. Or maybe that would be too great a task, and she merely hoped to turn them off.

With the Caretaker dead, I didn't know who was controlling the minions, or if the bracelets stamped them with a mindless order to defend the compound. Whatever it was, the orcs, trolls, elves, and dwarves started shambling toward us—no, toward *Mom* —with their weapons raised.

Sarrlevi yanked his swords from Varlat's skull and leaped down, landing in a crouch as the dragon collapsed, either dead or dying. He ran toward our group, and Mom's eyes widened in recognition.

"Keep going," I told her. "Sarrlevi will help us. I promise."

Maybe not wanting to worry her, Sarrlevi stopped ten feet away, putting his back to us and raising his weapons, as if he meant to keep all the minions from reaching us. Dozens of them were coming out of the wreckage. Stopping so many would have been a tall order, even for Sarrlevi, but then Zavryd flew over the battlefield toward us, with Val urging him on.

They landed near Sarrlevi and also turned to face the minions. Sindari sprang over a downed tank to join Val and Zavryd.

Zavryd erected a barrier that extended not only around him and Val but included Sarrlevi and Sindari. It flowed back to protect our group as well. The queen also flew over to land protectively, to give Mom the time she needed.

Taking a deep breath, Mom closed her eyes and went back to work. I wiped my sweaty brow and tried not to feel useless, but I didn't even have a weapon at the moment.

It didn't matter. The weapons weren't needed. With Sarrlevi and the dragons using their power to keep the minions back, Mom was able to finish. All at once, the tanks halted, and the remaining helicopters crashed to the ground.

The battle that had been raging since we arrived fell silent. The minions, who'd been eager to reach us, halted and peered blankly around, seeming surprised to find themselves here. Off to the side, Xilneth groaned, shook his horned head, and sat up. The collar around his neck unfastened and clanked to the ground.

The queen flexed her wings and spoke to the dragons who'd come with her. *Varlatastiva has fallen.*

She didn't so much as glance at Sarrlevi, though he'd been responsible. Someone else might have injured Varlat, so that his defenses hadn't been up, but he'd been the one to land the killing blow.

Sarrlevi didn't say anything or look like he wanted credit. Maybe he didn't want the queen contemplating his ability to be a threat to dragons.

The plot to cut this wild world off from the Cosmic Realms and annihilate the native population has been thwarted, the queen continued.

I wasn't positive we'd put an end to everything, but I didn't say so. The dragons had already helped more than I'd ever expected.

We will return to our home. Destroying the rest of this lair can be dealt with by the lesser species who carry out justice on this world. The queen flicked a dismissive wing, then formed a portal.

"I guess that means I need to call Willard," Val said from Zavryd's back.

"She'll need something bigger than her corpse-mobile to take care of this place," I said.

"She can figure it out. That's why she's a colonel and gets the big-girl pay."

"Did your mom and the tracker—Arwen—make it to safety before the battle broke out?"

Val nodded. "Arwen was willing to stay and shoot helicopters with her arrows, but I doubted that would have done anything. I asked her to escort my mother and Rocket back to the hotel. She seemed a little disappointed to miss out on the action, but I promised her that she could shoot anything inimical in the rainforest that threatened them."

"Like coyotes? Cougars?"

"Maybe coyotes *and* cougars." Val slid off Zavryd's back. "Rocket's bark doesn't do as much to scare away wildlife as you'd think."

"The goblins were unconcerned by it."

"The goblins are unconcerned by *most* things."

The queen and the other dragons, all save Zavryd and Xilneth, flew through the portal, and the cavern felt much less crowded.

As the smoke cleared, the entrance at the far end grew more noticeable. Sunlight slanted in. Had we been in here all night?

I checked my phone before remembering it had gotten wet. But it must have dried sufficiently to work again, because the screen came on, the time verifying that it was indeed the next morning.

"You okay, Matti?" Val left Zavryd's side and came over, giving Mom, who still gripped the hammer and radiated a lot of power, a wide berth. That hadn't kept Dad from stepping close and wrapping an arm around her. "Looks like you found your parents."

"Yes." I smiled at them, relieved anew to see them—and see them together. "Thanks for the help, Val. We never would have gotten through to them if you hadn't been out here, beating on the door and distracting everyone."

"Well, that's why we're here. To distract people so you can be a hero." She smirked at me.

"You and your scaled mate make adequate assistants, Thorvald." Sarrlevi also gave Mom a wide berth as he came to stand by me. "Perhaps Mataalii can employ you on her job site."

"That's not necessary," Val said calmly as Zavryd asked, *Assistants?* with great indignation. "Matti is going to be too busy employing my daughter to take on more new workers," she added.

"You think Amber will be a handful?" I asked.

"I have no doubt." Val pointed back the way we'd come. "Anything interesting back there? More baddies to fight?"

"I don't know. The Caretaker is dead, and his gnome scientist got away." Overcome with weariness, I longed to go outside and escape this place. "You'll need to get Willard out here to look at everything and make a report. It's an extensive setup. She might be daunted." More at what the organization had intended to do than at the work, I judged.

"Don't worry about it," Val said. "Willard enjoys tallying things and writing up reports."

"She's kind of a weird person, huh?"

"Not everybody gets their satisfaction in life from thumping things with a hammer."

"Huh."

"It is uncommon for my kind to say this," Mom said quietly, "but I long to see daylight."

"Me too. *Immensely.*" Dad lifted a hand toward me. "Mataalii?"

"I long to see daylight too." I nodded at them, then took Sarrlevi's hand, not wanting him to feel he had to stay away from my family. "The dragon queen didn't mention if she forgave you for being an elf assassin and stabbing her daughter with a sword."

"I'm pleased she didn't comment on my presence here instead of in the jail cell where she left me." Sarrlevi walked with me, and we followed my parents, picking a path through the wreckage.

Thank you for your help, I told him silently and clasped his hand. *For everything.*

He squeezed my hand. *You are welcome.*

For future reference, you can make me magical moss bracers anytime.

I will keep that in mind.

I threaded my fingers between his. *I like being fused to you.*

He gave me his smug I-know-this smile. *And I you.*

When we reached the moss-draped entrance, my mother looked back, and Sarrlevi released my hand. I wanted to protest but decided there was no need to rush things. Later, I would convince her how wonderful he was.

Outside, there wasn't a road or even a path down the slope, so I stopped after a few steps and flopped down, exhaustion setting in. The ground was damp, but sunlight streamed through the branches to dapple the ferns all around, and I didn't care that my butt got wet.

Dad walked over to plant himself in a sunbeam, his face tilted toward it. He probably hadn't seen the sky or felt the warmth of the sun on his face that often in the last thirty years. Mom took his hand.

Val and Zavryd also came out, he shifting into his human form. Though they hadn't yet stepped outside, I sensed Xilneth, Artie, and Hennehok arguing near the cave entrance. Deciding who was to blame for them all being captured? I shook my head. They hadn't exactly been the dream team.

My phone buzzed three times, as if indignant that I'd been out of reach for hours. All three text messages that popped up were from Zadie.

The seller lowered the price again!

I heard from another agent that a half-orc with ties to clans of orcs might be interested.

Don't you want to save your friends across the street from having to live with orcs in the neighborhood? They might eat goblins and tear up their tiny homes and use them for kindling!

A part of me was tempted to ignore the texts, at least until I'd showered, slept, and eaten more than Pop-Tarts and granola bars. But as I looked at Sarrlevi and my parents, all of them gazing around the rainforest and inhaling the fresh air—Sarrlevi looked like he might grab a clump of moss for some forest bathing at any moment—I realized that I'd accomplished my goals. Maybe I *could* think about moving now. Maybe it would even be nice to be close to others with magical blood. Val and I could spar, I could teach her kid how to make enchanted shower-curtain hooks, and if my parents stuck around, there would be room for them to stay over.

Would they stick around? I didn't know. Mom might have to go be King Ironhelm's heir and do all that entailed, and Dad... he was still wanted by the Army and probably the police too. He and Sarrlevi *both* were. It might be problematic if I gave them rooms at my house.

Still, I was learning how to enchant, right? I wagered I could find a way to hide my father or obscure his features to others. And Sarrlevi, with his camouflaging magic, was supremely unworried about the Earth authorities.

And I *would* prefer to keep goblin-eating orcs from moving into Val's neighborhood. It was what friends did for each other, right?

Perhaps curious about what I was contemplating, Val squatted beside me. When I showed her the messages, her eyes widened, and she whispered, "Orcs? A lot of them want me dead. I would have to hope the wards are sufficient to stop sniper fire from across the street."

"I'm sure Zavryd would flambé anyone who tried to shoot through your turret while you're making love."

A true statement, but why put Val through that? I tapped in a reply to Zadie: *Type up an offer for me. I'll sign it, and you can submit it today.*

Val gave me a thumbs-up.

"Do you think Zavryd will find Sarrlevi a more appealing neighbor if he knows orcs were the alternative?" I asked as I typed a text to my sister.

My phone didn't have much of a charge left, and now that I'd resolved some of my problems, I wanted to let her know that I would be there for my nephew's tennis tournament—and that Dad might come too. I grinned, delighted to tell her about that news. Tears threatened again as I imagined reuniting them and Dad seeing his grandchildren for the first time.

"Is Sarrlevi moving in with you?" Val asked. "I thought he would only visit from time to time."

"I don't know, but I want him to spend the night whenever he wishes. Days too." I smirked at her. "Weekends. Holidays."

Val looked toward Sarrlevi, who was walking over with a clump of damp moss pressed to his temple. It dribbled water down the side of his face, and he smiled contentedly. Whether it was because he was using it as a compress to soothe an injury or he felt the need to caress himself with nature after spending harrowing hours underground, I didn't know. Either way, it did nothing to detract from his elven beauty. Or the zing of desire that went through me when our eyes met.

"I see," Val said.

"Yeah."

"I suppose if Sarrlevi is busy indoors, Zav won't have much reason to complain."

I didn't mention Sarrlevi's interest in showing me the wonders of having sex while pressed up against a tree. Presumably, we would engage in such activities in the backyard if not some remote forest campground.

Zadie sent back a congratulations text with balloons flying up on the screen and a promise to get the paperwork over to me soon.

I pushed myself to my feet. "Mom? Dad?"

They'd wandered farther away for a private discussion, their shoulders—well, Dad's arm and Mom's shoulder—brushing, but they turned toward me, both asking, "Yes?"

"Nothing." I grinned. "I just wanted to say that."

EPILOGUE

THE GUARDS ON THE STEPS IN FRONT OF THE CITY GATE NEARLY FELL over when Mom and I arrived on Dun Kroth. Their hands had been on their weapons at the formation of a portal, but they must have recognized her right away for they jerked them away.

After they gaped at Mom for twenty or thirty seconds, the guards registered that I existed, but I earned little more than a glance. That was fine. As long as nobody tried to shoot me.

I didn't *think* that would happen, but one could never be sure. The last time I'd visited—been imprisoned here—I'd left the city without shackles on and with my pocket full of King Ironhelm's cheese and salami, but that had all been his doing. The guards, the high priest, and General Grantik might still be miffed with me. I didn't know if I should update them on their escaped half-dragon or not. Whether he would be a threat to Dun Kroth in the future remained a question mark.

I rubbed my translation charm in time to hear the guards blurt, "Princess Rodarska!" with equal parts surprise and delight as they hurried to open the gate for her. One lifted a hand toward

me, as if to suggest a search or to demand my weapons, but I held
up my open palms, and he noticed that Mom carried Sorka.

Without the hammer in hand, I felt naked, but I would find
another weapon. Mom had already spoken of smithing and
enchanting lessons for me, so my hope that I might one day make
a new hammer held promise. Nothing as fine as Sorka, I knew, but
maybe a normal, non-sentient weapon wouldn't be as fussy about
occasionally assisting with home renovations.

*You have a fixation about using hammers to engage in such activi-
ties,* Sorka said, apparently keeping an eye on me—and my
thoughts—despite being in someone else's hands.

*On Earth, it's a perfectly normal thing to use a sledgehammer for.
Even brawny people have trouble ripping down drywall with their bare
hands.*

*A sledgehammer, yes. Not an exquisitely crafted magical and sapient
dwarven weapon.*

"Your hammer is being snarky with me," I told my mother as a
new set of guards showed up to escort us into the city.

"Me as well. I believe she's making up for lost time."

"Did you also once use her to demolish cabinets? Or is she
complaining to you about *my* activities?"

"I used to make and enchant pottery when I needed a break
from the forge. Quite often, I spattered her with wet clay."

"Egregious."

"She believed so and often pointed out that I could store her in
a locker or vault or some such when I was crafting. But I always
felt the need to keep her close." Mom gave me a significant look.

"Because of Barothla?" I guessed. "And her ambitions?"

"Yes."

"I wondered how much you knew about that back in the day.
Someone pointed out that you made charms for you and your
father that protect against poisons."

Mom nodded. "Little did I know she would hire an assassin in the end. I wasn't that surprised though. She wasn't the type to confront a person directly."

"Does it bother you that..." I hesitated to bring up Sarrlevi. Despite being paramount in her rescue, he had kept his distance since we'd freed her, and she'd watched him warily whenever he'd been in sight.

"You're spending time with the assassin she hired?"

"The assassin she extorted into working for her." I'd already told her the story of Sarrlevi's mother. A part of me hoped Mom and Meyleera would get to meet each other one day and might even get along, but I didn't want to rush anything. Right now, it was enough that his mother and my mother were both alive.

"Not originally," Mom pointed out.

"I know. I'm working on him."

"*Working on?*" She arched her bushy red brows.

"Trying to convince him to give up his assassinly ways and come work for me in my business. He's great with windows, and when it comes to elven repair vines... the results are functional and, uhm, aesthetically interesting."

"For those for whom *vines* are a desirable aesthetic?"

"Precisely. That's more people on Earth than you'd think. The Green movement has taken off." Never mind that such usually referred to green energy and not green vines sprouting from one's walls.

"Well, if the enthusiastic sounds coming from your room last night were an indicator, you may have some sway over him."

Heat flushed my cheeks. Sarrlevi had promised he'd magically muffled the walls so that my parents, who'd stayed in Tinja's room while she slept in the tiny home, wouldn't hear us. Admittedly, he had grown rather distracted a couple of times. Maybe I'd challenged his focus when I'd been thanking him once again for all of his help. I smiled a little smugly at the thought before, aware of Mom watching, clearing my throat to answer her.

"I hope you weren't disturbed."

"Not at all. We were busy ourselves." She winked.

I was glad I hadn't heard that. When we'd gotten back to my side of Puget Sound and shared dinner, Mom and Dad had been surprisingly amorous with each other. I had expected Mom to be disturbed by how much my father had aged, but he'd kept himself fit over the years. Apparently, she still considered him her *noble soldier.*

"Sarrlevi has promised me," I said, turning the conversation back in a less disturbing direction, "that he'll take more care in researching his future targets before accepting assignments. If it helps, he wasn't that delighted to hunt you down."

"Because assassinating princesses can irritate a lot of people?"

"Because you're a crafter, and he likes to go after warriors. He likes to challenge those he's been hired to kill to honorable battle and take them out directly rather than through more skulkery methods."

"Skulkery?"

"I don't think that's a real word," I admitted, "but it encompasses assassins, I believe."

"Yes."

Shouts came from the city all around us as we approached the open-air trolley system that would take us to the royal quarters. The air was full of announcements that Princess Rodarska had been found. Dwarves flowed out from every street and doorway to look and cheer.

"Are you happy to be home?" I asked as we climbed aboard a car, the guards sternly telling people to stay back and not mob the princess. "I can't imagine hiding out in a little apartment on Earth was that appealing."

"Some of the people were appealing." She smiled and tousled my hair. "The last time I did that, you only came up to my hip."

"My towering five-foot-one-inches must be startling." I was only a few inches taller than she, so not exactly a giant.

"I'm glad your human half didn't make you too tall. Some of the forges here are a little tight." Mom waved her palm over her head. "And I look forward to teaching you a few things."

Emotion welled in my chest. I'd longed for that for so many years. "I look forward to that too."

"After Malosi and I get settled in, we can start whenever you have time."

"Settled in? You're both going to live here?"

"Yes, as long as my father doesn't object, and I doubt he will. He'll be happy to have me home. I understand Malosi is still wanted by the Army, if not *all* of the Earth authorities."

"I'm afraid so."

"He wants to visit his parents and you and Penina—and his grandchildren—often, but he expressed a desire to stay with me if I wish it. Since he was putting his tongue to the most amazing use at the time, I eagerly agreed."

"I—what?" I reached for a handrail for support but almost missed it and might have fallen out of the moving trolley car if she hadn't caught me.

"You didn't think it was only his skill in mastering my language that made me fall in love with him, did you?" Her eyes gleamed with wicked humor.

"I... no. I just didn't think we would discuss such things right away." Or at all.

"You didn't? I want to hear about your elf lover. He's arrogant and, I thought, the type to assume all females exist only to pleasure him. To be honest, I was relieved to hear your enthusiastic cries last night."

"*Mother*." I looked at the guards in the car with us. They were politely looking toward the city instead of at us, and we were speaking in English, so I *hoped* they didn't understand, but they were scant feet away, close enough to see my flaming cheeks.

"I trust he was putting his tongue to good use," Mom continued, not disturbed in the least. She seemed to be *enjoying* watching me squirm.

"Yes, it's fine. I mean, it's really good. *He's* really good." I rubbed my face, flustered.

Val had warned me that I needed to brace myself for the possibility of maternal lectures from my mother. This was worse.

Mom put away the gleam in her eyes to pat my hand. "I'm glad. When you were a little girl, I wondered if you would want to live in the human world or the dwarven one. Back then, I always thought I would eventually find a way to elude the assassin and deal with my sister, and that I would be able to return home and introduce you to my father. I wanted you to be welcome in both places. I never would have guessed that you might end up spending time on the *elven* world."

Given that Sarrlevi wasn't welcome there, I wouldn't likely visit Veleshna Var anytime soon, but I asked, "Do you mind? Sarrlevi said it's rare but it happens sometimes that elves and dwarves hook up. And compromise by living on the ground instead of in trees or tunnels."

"Yes, it occasionally happens. True love isn't swayed by the curve—or point—of one's ear. I certainly do not mind, as long as he treats you well."

"He does. Better than any human guy ever has. That's for sure."

"Are you certain you don't want to try some dwarven males before committing to the elf? Your height might attract them."

"Words nobody has ever said to me before."

"And yet, it's true here." Mom extended a hand toward the guards, all of whom were shorter than I. "And the stoutness of a good dwarven warrior can be quite satisfying." The gleam returned to her eyes.

"I had no idea you were this smutty, Mom."

"I tried to keep it to a minimum when you were toddling around the apartment and coloring on the walls with crayons."

"Sorka should have warned me."

"She finds all discussions of sexuality puzzling and uninteresting."

Our car came to a stop in front of the royal quarters.

"Well, FYI, I'm very satisfied with Sarrlevi and don't need you to set me up with any dwarves."

"As you wish." Eyes still gleaming, she stepped out of the car and waved toward the entrance.

King Ironhelm had come outside to greet us, and he rushed down the steps to meet her at the bottom, wrapping her in a fierce embrace. His bodyguards flowed down after him, but they gave them room. I stopped a few steps away and stuck my hands into my pockets to wait, but Ironhelm soon looked at me and waved for me to come over.

He gripped my hand and, with tears in his eyes, whispered, "Thank you for bringing my daughter home."

"You're welcome. I'm sorry it took so long."

"She's here now. That's what's important." He turned the grip into a hug, and I found myself smashed together with both of them and returned the embrace. I'd found more family than I'd expected when my search for my parents had begun, but it felt right.

"I want her to be able to come whenever she wishes, Father," Mom said when we stepped apart—semi-apart, for he didn't release either of us fully. "I want to teach her. I understand she has great potential as an enchanter and crafter." An odd expression crossed Mom's face as she glanced at me before looking back to him. "The assassin once hired to kill me told me this."

Ironhelm harrumphed. "One can tell that simply from her aura. And because she's *your* daughter."

"And your granddaughter?"

"Well, everyone knows the Ironhelm blood breeds wonderful crafters." He thumped himself on the chest. "And that assassin—" He shuddered. "Did you hear about how Barothla passed?"

"Yes. It sounds like she brought that upon herself. I wouldn't have wished her death—I wouldn't wish anyone's death—but I'm not sure you and I don't owe the assassin a favor."

"A *favor*," Ironhelm sputtered.

"He would be delighted if he were simply allowed to travel the Cosmic Realms without being hunted down by vengeful dwarves," I was quick to point out. While *I* would enjoy being allowed to visit my mother in the capital city here, I doubted Sarrlevi craved permission to wander about, uneasily eyeing the tons and tons of rock overhead.

"That was not going to happen under any circumstances," Ironhelm said. "I won't say that dwarves aren't ever vindictive, but... unfortunately, Barothla was not the kind of person that bestirred men to want to avenge her passing."

Mom and Ironhelm held each other's gazes, neither saying it was a relief that Barothla was gone, but I thought they both might admit it to themselves. Mom had said as much.

"Then he asks nothing," I said with a shrug.

"But you wish to come here and visit, yes?" Ironhelm patted my arm. "Often? There is so much to learn to become a master crafter."

"I would like to visit often, yes."

"Good, good." Ironhelm turned toward one of his bodyguards. "The artifact, please, Dendoran."

A dwarf armed not only with weapons but a box carved from the same salt as the cavern walls around the royal quarters stepped forward. He presented it not to the king but to me. My senses told me the box was enchanted and that something inside was too, something powerful.

"Do you recognize it?" Ironhelm asked Mom.

"I believe I *made* it," she said.

"You did. As an assignment for your master when you sought to be awarded that title yourself. Though I did not personally need it, I have kept it all these years."

"Because you're sentimental? I'd intended it to go to someone who had a use for it."

"And now it shall." Ironhelm extended his hand toward me.

Mom smiled and nodded.

I reached for the lid, wondering what I would find inside. It sounded like the Earth equivalent of a project for school, and I envisioned a lumpy ashtray made for a pottery class or perhaps a picture frame crafted for a woodworking grade.

When Mom snorted, I wondered if she was reading my thoughts.

What lay nestled within the box reminded me of a Magic 8 Ball made out of marble, with a circular display on the top. A Dwarven rune glowed in green in it.

"That says Dun Kroth, doesn't it?" I asked.

"Yes." Mom lifted the sphere from the box and tilted it sideways and then back up. "And that says Veleshna Var." Another tilt brought up another unfamiliar rune. "The orc home. Eleven of the twelve worlds that comprise the core of the Cosmic Realms are in there. I left out the dragon home world. I didn't think any sane person would want to visit them."

"Definitely not." Nor did I think the dragons wanted *me* to visit their world after I'd tunneled into their cell to break out Sarrlevi.

"I'll add Earth when I have a few quiet minutes." As Mom tilted through the options and showed them to me, it dawned on me what this had to be. *Visit,* she'd said.

"Is this a portal generator?"

"It is. So you can visit here anytime."

More than once, I'd fantasized about crafting such a thing, but, given how much power it took and how few people could make portals, I hadn't thought it would be possible. Unless one was an extremely powerful dwarven enchanter who'd built one for a school project.

"This is *so* much better than an ashtray," I whispered.

"I'll have a room in the royal quarters prepared for you and will make sure the guards know to let you in." Ironhelm pursed his lips. "No matter *who* you show up with."

My jaw dropped. Did that mean I could bring Sarrlevi?

"It's not *necessary* or even *desirable* that you bring him," Ironhelm was quick to point out, "but if you wanted him to witness you crafting a final project for an exam or some such, I would allow this."

"He does seem supportive and interested in her enchanting," Mom said. "I understand he arranged a teacher for her."

"He wanted me to learn everything I could so I'd be able to take care of myself."

"Perhaps it is *your* tongue that's impressive," she said.

I gaped at her, more because she would suggest sexual acts with her father present than because I was surprised by smutty comments by this point.

Ironhelm only smiled and nodded agreeably, like someone who didn't get the joke. I *hoped* he didn't.

"It's the enchanting magic, I think," I muttered.

"Ah, yes. I should have known." Mom winked.

Nobody had mentioned this side of my mother when they'd talked about her being a sweet and gentle soul. She returned the sphere to the box and handed it to me.

"Thank you," I said.

Then she surprised me by handing Sorka to me. "She wants to be in the hands of a warrior."

"I..." My first instinct was to be self-effacing and say I wasn't a warrior, not really. But I'd been training to fight my whole life, and these past few months, I'd been doing little but defending myself. I could kick an orc into the next county, and even though I'd finished my quest and achieved my goal of finding my parents, I was still working for Colonel Willard. She might be busy helping to mop up—or cover up—the mess on the Olympic Peninsula, but I had little doubt she would remember that I was on the payroll and find jobs for me again. "I would be honored to carry her until you want her back."

I would be honored, Sorka said, *if nobody uses me to bash down doors, drawers, or walls.*

Only skulls?

Skulls, rib cages, and tusks. I enjoy shattering the tusk of a belligerent orc.

Are doors okay if they lead to the enemy stronghold? I asked.

Yes, I'll allow that use.

"Is there a problem?" Mom asked.

"No, we've reached an understanding."

"Good." She gripped my shoulder. "You aren't planning to take up pottery, are you?"

"Nope."

Excellent, Sorka said.

～

"Val?" I shifted the box in my arms as we walked from the moving van toward the front door of my new house.

"Yes?" Val carried a lamp that could be dimmed and also had a flash mode, all controlled by the fishing-pole reel and handle integrated into the side by my roommate.

"I appreciate you helping me move, but does *he* have to watch from the roof of your house? While in *dragon* form? It's a little unnerving."

Val looked across the street. "I don't think Zav is watching so much as fuming about Sarrlevi while his snout is pointed in this direction."

"Shouldn't his snout be pointed toward the smoker in your backyard? I can smell the ribs cooking from here."

"Well, of course you can. We're having a party to welcome you to the neighborhood. That's another reason he's fuming."

"I thought he only objected to Sarrlevi, not me."

"He objects to sharing the ribs."

"Ah."

"He's also not tickled by the goblins."

"There's only *one* goblin, and she moved her tiny home over to this side of the street." I waved toward it, though I wasn't sure the *side* mattered when it took up so much room.

Neighbors had been honking and glaring as they drove around it. I had reluctantly suggested taking down a section of the fence so we could park it in the backyard, but Tinja had pointed out that we might not want her potential customers wandering back there day and night. Night? I'd asked. She had a couple of vampires interested in building tiny homes, as long as the plans could be altered to remove the windows.

"She has a lot of visitors beyond her potential customers," Val said.

"Well, she's grown popular of late. Goblins like successful entrepreneurs with wrenches. They call her Work Leader Tinja. I think that means a clan might be forming with her in charge."

"They're not all going to live in the tiny home, are they?"

"I don't think so," I said. "Don't most of them spend the majority of their time at your coffee shop?"

"I don't mind them over there, where I only visit. This is our home."

"Are you worried about your small appliances?"

"No. The wards should keep them from disassembling and stealing anything on our property, but we have neighbors."

"Whom you've been terribly concerned about up until now."

Val flicked her fingers in acknowledgment and continued inside with her load. I was about to follow, but three heavy boxes floated past me, Sarrlevi's levitation magic carrying them into the house while making me wonder why I was doing this the old-fashioned way.

He stepped out onto the stoop, looking dashing in a forest-green shirt and brown trousers. Very *Lord of the Rings*. Perhaps disconcerted by the dragon observer, he wore his swords, but he had rolled up his sleeves and almost appeared relaxed—or maybe content—as he helped me with moving day. Sorka leaned against the wall inside the door, occasionally making comments to me about how boring this was and how my mother had promised her great battles if she stayed with me.

"Thanks for coming by to help," I told Sarrlevi.

He'd been gone for a few days, visiting his mother at one of his homes. King Eireth still wouldn't allow him on Veleshna Var, but Meyleera had recovered enough to travel.

"When you invited me to visit you in your new home," Sarrlevi said, "I did not realize it would be in a state of disarray and that labor would be required."

"You can't possibly object to a little work. You train for hours a day with your swords and get all sweaty and... sweaty." I blushed, remembering *my* visit to one of his homes, the remote mountain chalet, and getting to witness such a workout. One in which he'd been shirtless outside in front of the window. Even though he hadn't commented on my observation, I was positive he'd chosen the spot because he'd *wanted* an audience. When he'd come in, he had proven that his stamina was as legendary as he'd been telling me all along. I smiled at the memory.

"I do not object to work, but I'd assumed the bed would already be assembled." His eyelashes lowered as he gazed at me.

Ah, my elf had arrived horny.

"So we could visit it horizontally while Val and Dimitri were downstairs unloading my moving van?" Admittedly, Dimitri's contribution had only been to bring in and set up my TV. When he'd found out I didn't have a gaming system or games to borrow, he'd wandered off.

"Their activities interest me little, and the *van* will be unloaded soon." Indeed, Sarrlevi drew me to the side as my couch floated toward the door.

"But there's unpacking to do once everything is inside. We should probably wait until tonight to visit my furniture horizontally."

I watched as the couch got stuck and Sarrlevi had to pour his magic into backing it out, tilting it, and finding an angle at which it could fit. He grimaced from the effort, proving that magic could be as draining as physical activity, if not more so. I knew that myself. My enchanting lessons had recently resumed, some with Santiago and some with my mother, who always made time for me when I popped through the portal to Dun Kroth. It was strange to be able to visit another world in less time than it took to drive downtown. Well, maybe that wasn't strange. Seattle traffic could be egregious.

"It is odd that your people do not magically grow their furniture out of the nearby trees or the materials that comprise their homes," Sarrlevi said as the couch finally made it through and came to rest in front of the fireplace. He rested a hand on the doorframe, hopefully not contemplating growing vines out of it. Though I hadn't yet done any of the remodeling I planned, I did *not* need elven foliage wrapped around anything.

"We humans hear that all the time."

"You are only *half* human."

"Yeah, but my other half doesn't contemplate growing furniture out of trees either."

"I am surprised it does not call to you to mold chairs and tables out of boulders."

"This house didn't come with any boulders." I scratched my jaw, wondering if I *could* do that. I'd only ever carved wood, not chiseled marble—who could afford marble?—but I'd seen sinks and bathtubs made out of granite. That might be an interesting challenge. Though I would have to add support to the old floors in this house to make sure they could handle something like a granite bathtub.

A smile spread across Sarrlevi's face. "You are contemplating it."

"Well, you made me."

"Does this mean the next gift I bring you from the Cosmic Realms should be a large exotic boulder?"

"That's not necessary. I appreciate your gifts—" my mouth started salivating at the thought of the latest cheese he'd brought, the remains of the block sitting in the kitchen and waiting for lunchtime, "—but you don't have to keep bringing me things."

"No?" Sarrlevi shared an image of what looked like a giant blue and green agate with the most fascinatingly beautiful striations.

"Oh, wow." That would make an *amazing* bathtub.

His smile widened. "I will arrange its delivery."

I stepped closer and slid my arms around him. "You spoil me."

"And you like it." He wrapped his arms around me and bent for a kiss. Lips pressed against mine, he switched to telepathy. *You will soon send away your helpers and assemble the bed.*

That does seem like a good idea.

Yes. I could do it while you finish down here, but it would be assembled in the elven way.

Hanging from vines? I wouldn't admit it to him, but the sway of his elven bed in his chalet had added some intriguing sensations to our lovemaking.

Of course. His hand slid down my back to rest on my butt as he shared thoughts of what we would do once my bed was assembled.

Since we were in front of the house, where anyone wandering by—and the overly observant dragon across the street—could see us, I should have put a stop to the embrace—all right, it was *more* than an embrace—but my hand crept under his shirt of its own accord, my fingers sliding over the hard muscles of his abdomen. The memory of his shirtless training session returned, and he smiled against my mouth and shared what memories of *me* were in his mind, including one where I'd been soaked with water in the enemy stronghold. Still pleased that I could inspire randy thoughts in him, I pressed my chest against his.

Maybe it wasn't necessary to wait for tonight. Maybe we could slip upstairs and—

"No, no," Val said, as she walked out and past us for another trip to the van, "enjoy yourselves. I'll do all the work."

"Sorry," I mumbled, pulling my lips from Sarrlevi's.

He wasn't quick to release me, despite a couple of goblins ogling us through the window of the tiny home, and I had to pat his chest and tell him, "Tonight. We'll go upstairs, and I'll show you how excited I am about the boulder you promised me."

"Only one with dwarven blood would say such things."

"Well, obviously." I grinned and kissed him, not letting my lips linger too long before squirming out of his grip.

Sighing, Sarrlevi released me, though his gaze was molten as he watched me walk away. At that moment, Willard drove up in her SUV, parking it in front of the tiny home. That made me glad we hadn't been kissing when she arrived. She would have had even more acerbic words for our overly active lips—and hands.

"Hey, Willard," Val called as she carried a couple more lamps out of the van. "I didn't know you were coming to help Matti unpack. That's thoughtful of you."

"I didn't." Willard had stepped out of her SUV and was pulling something out of the back. "I brought housewarming gifts and an assignment for you two, if you're interested."

"I think Matti's interested in spending time with her elf lover." Val smirked at me.

I blushed, afraid she would share the details of our embrace with our boss.

"Who wouldn't be?" Willard turned, two potted plants in her hands, though one looked like little more than a clump of grass. Decorative grass? "He's almost as sexy as your dragon."

Sarrlevi's eyebrows flew up. "*Almost?*"

When Zavryd was in his dragon form, his face didn't have a lot of expression, at least not discernible to me, but I was positive I caught the equivalent of a smug smile stretching his scales.

"Willard isn't as moved to ardor by blonds," Val told us.

Sarrlevi watched Willard through slitted eyes as she approached with the plants, either annoyed that her arrival had helped end our make-out session or disapproving of her inferior taste in men.

"In more important news," Willard said as she walked up, "I've reported the Olympic Peninsula base and all its contents to my superiors. A team went over to investigate, but they haven't updated me on what they found, what they're doing with everything, or if they're going to look for the people—the *humans*—who were ultimately responsible for it all."

"Wasn't Varlat ultimately responsible?" I asked, though it had sounded like the humans and the dragon had been enacting their own versions of the plan.

"Since he's dead, we have no way to know," Willard said. "Nobody found the gnome engineer you mentioned, and, from what I saw, there was a dearth of humans in the base to question, none of the people from our earlier list."

"Because they hang out in their mansions and private yachts, not underground bunkers," Val said.

"The Caretaker—the elf guy—was in charge of the base, I think," I said.

"And he's *also* dead." Willard slanted Val a look that suggested prisoners to question might have been nice.

Val lifted her hands—and my lamps—in a gesture of innocence. Willard turned her look on me. I made a similar gesture, even if Sarrlevi and I had been responsible. He gazed blandly back at her without making any gestures whatsoever.

"I'm hoping," Willard said, "that taking away their enchanter, their overpowered weapons and tools, and their dragon ally will put the plan on pause—or halt it altogether—but you might want to watch your back, Puletasi."

"Trust me, I'm installing a permanent set of eyeballs back there."

"I'm serious." Willard squinted at me. "Those people are powerful and might now be feeling vengeful."

"Yes, it was terribly rude of Matti to kidnap back her kidnapped parents," Val said. "They have every right to be mad about that."

Willard snorted.

Sarrlevi lifted his chin. "*I* will watch Mataalii's back."

"Is that hard to do while you're groping her ass?" Val asked.

"It is not." No hint of embarrassment turned Sarrlevi's cheeks pink.

My cheeks were another story.

"With that image unpleasantly stuck in my head, I'll change the topic." Willard held out the pots. "I brought you some house-warming presents, Puletasi."

"Thank you, ma'am," I said, relieved to move on—why were Val's eyes twinkling with such pleasure? "The new place is big, so it'll be no problem finding a spot for them."

"Try the kitchen. They're herbs. Basil and chives."

Ah, chives, not grass. That made sense. I leaned forward to sniff the herbs.

"Mataalii rarely consumes greens," Sarrlevi said. "She prefers root vegetables."

Now, Willard adopted a disapproving expression.

"Not *exclusively* root vegetables," I hurried to say. "I like herbs. And these are tasty ones. Have you had basil or chive cheese? I think there's even a basil-*and*-chive variety." I wondered how hard it would be to *make* such a cheese. Maybe, now that I had a larger kitchen, I could give it a try. Zadie had pointed out the spacious basement, now free of its sex swing and mirrors, and mentioned that she'd always wanted to try making wine but that it took up too much room for her condo. We could start all sorts of projects here.

"Do all foods make you think of cheese?" Willard asked.

"Not *all*. Just the good ones."

"Maybe someone who has more money to spend on house-warming gifts can give you a cheese-making kit and a dairy cow." Willard looked pointedly at Sarrlevi.

"He's going to get me a big boulder." I smiled warmly at him.

Willard's brow furrowed.

"She has dwarven blood," Sarrlevi said, as if that perfectly explained a desire for a boulder.

"And dwarven strength," Willard said. "And the ability to move earth with magic, I understand. That's why I've got her in mind for a new mission up at Snoqualmie Pass, one in which some yetis need to be convinced to make their home elsewhere and stop eating hikers. Maybe Puletasi can hollow them out some nice caves miles away from the highway and the lodge."

"If the yetis have a good home and a plentiful supply of food —" Val grimaced at the implication that the *hikers* were the food, "—they may not want to move."

"I'm sure they won't. You can go along to poke them in the butts with your sword while Puletasi digs caves."

"Did you realize working for the military would be so glamorous?" Val asked me.

"I did not."

Val pointed at the chives. "How come you got her *normal* herbs, Willard, and you got me special anti-inflammatory ones?"

"Because you have asthma and need that, and yours were perfectly normal herbs."

"You also planted a medicinal tree in my backyard."

"A maritime pine tree, yes, and I hope you're making tea out of the bark and drinking it regularly."

"Oh, of course I am."

Willard squinted at her. "You didn't let it *die*, did you? You have to water plants, Thorvald. And give them sunlight."

"It's alive. Every plant, shrub, or tree that comes onto my property is alive. Whenever Freysha visits, she wiggles her fingers and uses her elven magic to ensure they stay that way. In fact, I believe the pine tree has grown at twice the predicted rate."

"Well, good. You can make *plenty* of tea then."

Val made a face. "Matti gets cheese-making supplies, and I get bitter tea."

"Maybe the bark can be used in a cheese," I offered, though it didn't sound appealing. "Thank you, Val, in case I forgot to mention it, for *your* housewarming gift."

"What did you get her?" Willard asked.

"A cool cheese storage kit." I showed Willard the photo I'd taken on my phone. "With windows."

"It's a cheese *grotto* that sits on the counter," Val said.

"Grotto?" Willard peered at the picture. "It looks like a box to me."

I nodded to her. It was a *nice* box though. I had already tucked Sarrlevi's gifts into it.

"You didn't pay a lot for it, did you, Thorvald?" Willard asked.

"It's temperature-controlled and preserves the cheeses' freshness, aroma, and taste," Val said. "There's a clay brick that you soak in water and put in the bottom, and it's supposed to control the moisture inside and keep the cheese from getting moldy."

"So... you paid how much for a box and a *brick*?" Willard smirked.

Val folded her arms over her chest. "Less than Sarrlevi is going to have to pay for a dairy cow."

"I like it." I nodded to Val. "It's a great gift."

"Uh huh. I'll send the details for the mission later." Willard deposited the potted herbs in my hands and frowned toward the street. Two goblins had slipped out of the tiny home with wrenches in their hands and were examining the bicycle rack attached to the back of her vehicle. "Get away from that, you two." Willard ran toward them, waving her fists.

"It's possible she won't be willing to come over for weekend barbecues," I said.

"She might if you get some fancy coffee and brew it fresh for her." Val headed inside with the lamps.

"Is a milk-producing cow something you desire for your new domicile?" Sarrlevi asked.

"No." I shook my head. "Willard was joking."

Sarrlevi gazed thoughtfully at the lawn—debating if the grass could support a cow? It most certainly could not.

"No cows," I said firmly. "It's against the codes to have large livestock in the city. I'm not even sure if you can have chickens in this neighborhood."

"Hm."

"Besides, my neighbor would be tempted to eat it." I waved toward Zavryd, though his eyes were closed now, and he appeared to be basking in the sun. Like a cat on a windowsill.

"Yes, I am certain he would. The cow would have to be warded.

Or perhaps I could bring a milk-producing herbivore from one of the other wild worlds." A smile curved Sarrlevi's lips. "The *yugrothnor* is naturally resistant to magic and has venomous prongs on its hooves *and* its tail. They're capable of piercing even dragon scales."

"Just the kind of animal I want to escape my yard and maul the neighborhood children."

"Given the denizens now making this street their home, it is unlikely you will have mundane neighbors for long. And the offspring of magical beings tend to be hardy."

I was about to head inside, but Tinja, who'd shooed her comrades away from the SUV so Willard could leave, walked up. She was carrying her goblinator or maybe a newer version of the original. Previously, the cannon-sized barrel had been made from scrap metal welded together. More homogeneous, the new barrel appeared sturdy enough to launch cannonballs as well as the sharp blades and other scavenged pointy things she integrated into her ammunition.

"Matti, I have good news and bad news for you," Tinja said.

"Oh?"

"The good news is that I've made this fine home-defense weapon for you. It is far, *far* more useful than leaves and grass." Tinja sniffed disdainfully at the potted herbs.

"I have no doubt. Thank you for the useful present, but you're moving in with me too, aren't you? It's not that typical for room-mates to give each other housewarming gifts." I wasn't sure it was *atypical*, but I would be fine with her keeping the weapon for her own use. I had Sorka to defend my home with.

"Well, that leads me to the bad news, at which you will be deeply chagrined."

"Oh?" I asked again.

"My tiny home is so wondrous that I've decided to live in it instead of in your new home."

"That *is* distressing news. Will you live in it in the street in front of my house?"

"Or in the backyard if we decide to remove the fence, as discussed, so we can maneuver it back there."

"So, you won't be far."

"No." Tinja smiled brightly. "I will continue to use your tools and scavenge your shed for detritus, and I will also sample food from your refrigerator. You won't be entirely bereft of my presence."

"That's a relief."

"Yes. And thanks to the excellent insulation we incorporated into the tiny home, I should not hear the nocturnal *and* diurnal cries coming from your bedroom."

I glanced at Sarrlevi, but he only looked smug. He *liked* it when I got... enthusiastic. Of course, I enjoyed it when I could prompt *him* to audibly demonstrate his pleasure as well. Maybe it was for the best that my roommate was moving out.

"Worry not," Tinja said. "As I stated, I will not be far, and, should the need arise, I will join you in defending the property from intruders."

"That's kind of you."

"Yes." Her nose twitched, and she peered through the open door into the house. "Have you acquired new exotic cheeses from other worlds?"

"Yes. Sarrlevi has been keeping me well-supplied. Help yourself. They're in the cheese, uhm, grotto."

"Grotto?"

"The box on the counter."

"Excellent."

Tinja skipped inside, and I set the pots on a box, so I could go out for another load from the van. But Sarrlevi caught me and pulled me into a hug again.

"Are you still thinking of the woefully disassembled bed?" I asked.

"It is not far from my mind, and perhaps I will go *assemble* it while you unload the remaining furnishings, but that is not what I was thinking about."

"No?"

"Your new domicile has many rooms, but you will now not have a roommate, only a frequent elven visitor who is *much* sexier than a dragon."

"I don't disagree." I leaned against him.

"Wise." He kissed the top of my head. "Perhaps, one day, you will wish to fill the extra rooms with young."

"Young? Like children?"

"As we contemplated."

As I recalled, he hadn't said he was dying to have some. Maybe he'd been thinking about it since our conversation?

"Are you... offering to help me fill my house with young?" There were six bedrooms. Maybe *fill* wasn't the right word. I didn't aspire to have that many, but two might be nice, the same as my sister had. But with elves being so long-lived and not known for their fertility, would Sarrlevi be able to lend his seed to such an endeavor? Or would we have to go to a fertility clinic? I snorted as I imagined him, swords and all, being handed an erotic magazine and a cup.

Sarrlevi must have been monitoring my thoughts, for he said, "It is not the *seed* of male elves that causes the birthrate of our people to be low. Elven females only go into heat once every ten years."

Go into heat put dogs in my mind, but it was the ten years part that made me gape. I didn't know whether to be horrified or envious of PMS that only came around once a decade. Probably envious.

"Does that mean that most of the half-elf mercenaries and

assassins we've encountered were the result of randy male elves being frustrated that their females were only interested in them once a decade?"

"Elves enjoy recreational sex that has nothing to do with fertility," Sarrlevi said, "as humans do, but it *is* likely most half-elves have been born to non-elven females."

"I see. Just to be clear—and no pressure or hurry or anything here—would you be offering to help *raise* offspring? Not only assist in their procreation?" I watched his face, not sure I'd read his words correctly. Even though we'd discussed being *fused* now, we hadn't talked about marriage or even made long-term plans.

His eyebrows rose. "Do you believe I would be an adequate father?"

"Sure. You're amazing, and you have a ton of skills. You could teach them all about—" my gaze drifted to the sword hilts poking up over his shoulder, reminding me that most of his *skills* revolved around a profession I would hope no children of mine would want to enter, "—being haughty."

"It *is* important for elves to develop that skill."

"Oh, I know." I smiled and wrapped my arms around his shoulders.

He responded promptly, returning to what we'd been doing before the interruptions.

Maybe we should put the unpacking aside and go set up that bed, I suggested.

As I have been suggesting.

You're a wise elf.

Obviously.

THE END

Made in United States
Orlando, FL
30 June 2023

34664741R00214